Praise for

Money, Honey

"Fast, hot, fresh, and outright fun. You'll love it!"
—Susan Kay Law, author of *The Paper Marriage*

"Fast-moving with humor, some tense moments of danger, and a satisfying ending. Sey's debut is entertaining."
—*Romantic Times*

"The dialogue is witty, the main characters sexy, and the sexual tension hot enough to steam." —*Book Binge*

"I enjoyed this debut novel and will definitely read the next Sey story." —*Dear Author*

"I loved this book . . . Not only did I enjoy the characters and the fast-paced dialogue, but I thought she did a great job with the changing points of view throughout."
—*Fiction Vixen Book Reviews*

"A book filled with hot sexy banter, an even sexier hero, and many moments that will have you smiling. I definitely recommend this one." —*Smexy Books*

"Sparkles with energy and heart . . . A delightful debut."
—Jane Porter, bestselling author of *Flirting with Forty*

"Laugh-out-loud funny and fantastically hot."
—Victoria Dahl, author of *Lead Me On*

Money Shot

SUSAN SEY

BERKLEY SENSATION, NEW YORK

THE BERKLEY PUBLISHING GROUP
Published by the Penguin Group
Penguin Group (USA) Inc.
375 Hudson Street, New York, New York 10014, USA

Penguin Group (Canada), 90 Eglinton Avenue East, Suite 700, Toronto, Ontario M4P 2Y3, Canada
(a division of Pearson Penguin Canada Inc.)
Penguin Books Ltd., 80 Strand, London WC2R 0RL, England
Penguin Group Ireland, 25 St. Stephen's Green, Dublin 2, Ireland (a division of Penguin Books Ltd.)
Penguin Group (Australia), 250 Camberwell Road, Camberwell, Victoria 3124, Australia
(a division of Pearson Australia Group Pty. Ltd.)
Penguin Books India Pvt. Ltd., 11 Community Centre, Panchsheel Park, New Delhi—110 017, India
Penguin Group (NZ), 67 Apollo Drive, Rosedale, North Shore 0632, New Zealand
(a division of Pearson New Zealand Ltd.)
Penguin Books (South Africa) (Pty.) Ltd., 24 Sturdee Avenue, Rosebank, Johannesburg 2196,
South Africa

Penguin Books Ltd., Registered Offices: 80 Strand, London WC2R 0RL, England

This is a work of fiction. Names, characters, places, and incidents either are the product of the author's imagination or are used fictitiously, and any resemblance to actual persons, living or dead, business establishments, events, or locales is entirely coincidental. The publisher does not have any control over and does not assume any responsibility for author or third-party websites or their content.

MONEY SHOT

A Berkley Sensation Book / published by arrangement with the author

PRINTING HISTORY
Berkley Sensation mass-market paperback edition / June 2011

Copyright © 2011 by Susan Seyfarth.
Cover design by Lesley Worrell.
Cover illustration by Alan Ayers.
Interior text design by Laura K. Corless.

ISBN: 978-0-425-24184-4

BERKLEY® SENSATION
Berkley Sensation Books are published by The Berkley Publishing Group,
a division of Penguin Group (USA) Inc.,
375 Hudson Street, New York, New York 10014.
BERKLEY® SENSATION and the "B" design are trademarks of Penguin Group (USA) Inc.

PRINTED IN THE UNITED STATES OF AMERICA

10 9 8 7 6 5 4 3 2 1

This one's for my sisters, Maureen, Kelly and Cheryl. They are the smartest, funniest women I know, and if not for their loving, gentle intervention, I would still be wearing jeans from 1994. Love you, girlies.

And to Claudia and Greta, who like to see their names in my books.

Chapter

I

BELLS JINGLED merrily as Mishkwa Island park ranger Rush Guthrie pushed through the jaunty red door of Mother Lila's Tea Shop.

"Coming!" Lila sang out in that wavering soprano of hers.

Rush slid into the room, his back to the wall, his fingers hooked casually into the custom-sewn pocket in his jacket that concealed his SIG Sauer. He scanned the cozy, doily-splattered sitting space of his aunt's tea shop with the calm, flat eyes of the professional killer he used to be. He'd come a long way since he'd landed on this island nearly two years ago, but not so far that he could walk into a room—any room—without performing at least a basic threat assessment. He wondered if he ever would.

The room was empty save for his two cousins, Yarrow and Einar. Yarrow—Lila's step-granddaughter if Rush felt like splitting genealogical hairs, which he usually didn't—sat behind the register. She had her chin propped on the flat of her hand, one black-painted fingernail flicking with desperate nonchalance at the little silver ring in her eyebrow. Between that ring, the little stud in her nose and the hardware dangling from her ears, the kid had half a dozen extra holes in her head, easy. Rush had never understood why a kid with a perfectly serviceable face would want to perforate it, but now, watching her try like hell to look like she wasn't thrilled to little girlie bits by the attention of the man across the counter, he sort of understood why she might feel like she needed a little extra help looking hard.

Kid had a crush. A bad one.

Couldn't really blame her, though. For all that Einar was Rush's first cousin, for all that they'd been raised more or less as brothers, they couldn't look less alike. *Be* less alike. Where Rush was stoic, Einar was charming. Where Rush was useful, Einar was flat-out beautiful. Weird word to use on a dude but what could you do? Classic example right here in front of him.

There Einar was, all golden curls and chiseled cheekbones, lounged up against the counter like it was a grand piano, hitting Yarrow with a smile of such dazzling intensity that the poor kid was hunched over like a puppy, practically squirming with unwilling delight. He caught Rush's automatic scan of the room and his smile downshifted to a smirk. He poked lazy hands toward the ceiling.

"Dude," he said, his blue eyes twinkling with wicked laughter. "I surrender. Don't shoot."

Yarrow yelled, "Grandma! Rush is here!" She glanced at Einar's smirk and quickly copied it. Poor kid. "So. Any terrorists lurking in the tea shop today, Ranger Rush?"

"Nope."

She lifted the lid off the teapot at her elbow and peered gravely inside. "All clear here, too."

The urge to smile took him by surprise. The kid was flipping him crap. How about that? It wasn't so long ago that she wouldn't have dared. Nobody would have. Nobody but Einar, anyway.

"Too bad." He put on a frown. "I haven't shot anybody all day."

Her eyes went round as lollipops, and she and Einar shared a moment of shocked silence. "Did he just make a joke?" she whispered.

"I don't know," Einar whispered back. "It's not like him. And it wasn't really funny, so . . ."

This was the part where Rush should have smiled, or even laughed. But normal conversation had a rhythm, a beat pattern. It went fast and if you missed your mark, the moment was lost. Rush's timing was terrible. Had been for the last, oh, ten years. Give or take.

He pulled off his knit cap and stuffed it into his pocket. The one that didn't have a gun in it. "So, Lila called me?"

His aunt glided into the room, tall and handsome as a ship in full sail with scarves and skirts swirling, her long gray braid swinging. Yarrow said, "Grandma, Rush made a joke."

Lila clasped pretty ringed hands together and beamed. "He did?"

"It was about shooting people, but it was definitely a joke," Einar said. "We think." He quirked a brow Rush's way. "Wasn't it?"

"I don't talk about shooting when I'm serious," he said. "It spoils the surprise."

Lila's mouth fell open and Yarrow said, "See? He did it again."

They all gazed at him in wonder, then Yarrow leaned toward Lila and dropped her voice to a stage whisper. "I'm scared, Grammy," she said. "Is this the Apocalypse?"

"No, dear. Of course not." Lila patted Yarrow's shoulder absently while she continued to study him. "It'll rain frogs first."

A tiny trickle of unfamiliar warmth bubbled up in Rush's chest as he stood in front of these laughing people. Together they constituted all the family he had in this world, and for just a moment the gift of them pierced his soul, sweet and sharp. The urge to laugh with them kicked in, but as usual the moment had already passed.

Yarrow broke the circle first, deliberately shifting out from under Lila's hand, as if she'd just noticed it resting on her shoulder. The rejection sent a wisp of grief over Lila's face, but by the time she turned to Rush, it was gone. "So," she said brightly. "What are you doing here besides being unusually amusing?"

"I have no idea. You called me, remember?"

"Oh, yes." Lila came around the counter, slid a confidential hand into Rush's elbow. He tensed automatically, then forced himself to relax. *Jesus, Rush*, he thought. *She's your beloved aunt. She's not going to stick a knife between your ribs.*

Then the bells at the door jangled and years of training so rigorous it had replaced instinct took over. Lila leaned in to kiss him hello, and Rush lifted her clean off her feet. In the space of half a heartbeat, he'd moved her three long strides to the counter, where he could put her, Yarrow and most of Einar behind him. By the time the door flew open with a sweep of wind and the frantic tinkle of sleigh bells, Rush had the women covered and his hand wrapped around the butt of the gun in his pocket. He'd domesticated himself enough not to actually draw the gun, but not so much that he wasn't prepared to blow a hole clean through his new jacket and whoever came through the door.

Then the door opened, and in walked in that rarest of all commodities on Mishkwa in December—a stranger.

And not just any stranger, either. Lord, no. This stranger was about six feet of long-legged, dark-eyed woman, all smooth hair and golden skin, with a let's-be-friends smile lighting up an extraordinary face.

Not a pretty face, exactly, but certainly one that deserved a second look. The discerning man might go back for a third. It was all those sharp edges and uncompromising slants against the lush oasis of that mouth, he thought.

The contrast or something. It made a guy want to do stupid things. Rash things. Hot, wet, sweaty things, for sure.

"Hoo, boy," Einar murmured. "Dibs."

Fuck, Rush thought. For a guy who never stood when he could sit—or hell, lie down—Einar could move when it counted.

Chapter

2

SECRET SERVICE Agent Maria "Goose" di Guzman had hardly cleared the door of the little tea shop when Rush Guthrie himself—because who else could it be?—strode forward and engulfed her hand in a hearty grip.

"Welcome to Mishkwa," he boomed, his voice radio-announcer cheerful, his eyes Caribbean blue. Goose blinked. Good Lord. His file hadn't included a recent photo—a convention designed to protect behind-enemy-lines types against intel leaks—but it had included a basic physical description: six three, blue/blond, approximately 190. Based on that, she'd been ready for the Captain American type, but this guy was a recruiting poster come to life. She wondered if the military was still kicking itself over losing him.

"Can I help you?" he asked.

"Well now, that depends." She gave him a smile with just a hint of flirt around the edges. Based on the smug interest in those clear blue eyes, Ranger Guthrie sort of dug the glamazon type. Maybe not as much as he dug himself, but enough. A surprising number of men did. But yard-wide shoulders, thick hair the color of fresh butter and a jaw that could make Superman himself feel weak-chinned did not necessarily translate into the confidence to deal well with the double whammy of a tall girl and her badge. Thus the little bit of flirt-insurance. Flattery worked on everybody.

"On?"

"I'm looking for somebody," she said.

He stepped just close enough to edge into her personal space, and grinned down at her with very white teeth. "Dare I hope you've found him?"

Goose kept her smile on high beam. "Depends." She freed her hand from his and produced the badge she'd stashed in the Prada purse she'd treated herself to last Christmas. "Special Agent Maria di Guzman," she said. "Secret Service. Ranger Rush Guthrie?"

Captain America shook his head and stepped closer yet. Close enough that she could smell his breath mint and the chewing tobacco it was trying to cover. "Now, what would you want with my cousin when all the man you need is right here?"

She tipped her head and gave him a curious look. "You're one of those guys who likes getting arrested by girl cops, aren't you?"

He gave her a lingering once-over. "I'd try anything once."

She patted his arm. "I bet you would." She tried hard to make it sound like a compliment. "You could start by directing me to Ranger Guthrie."

"I'm Ranger Guthrie."

She looked past Captain America for the first time and met a pair of eyes so pale she couldn't tell if they were blue or gray. The color hardly mattered. Not compared with the intense attention in them, and the wary spark it sent dancing all the way down her body to her half-frozen toes. If she hadn't been purposely holding her ground against his cousin's hokey moves, the impact might have knocked her back a step. Possibly two.

She glanced between the men. Ranger Guthrie was maybe two or three inches taller than Captain America, but a good twenty pounds lighter. Not that he was skinny. Hardly. He just had the lean, wiry build of a distance runner rather than his cousin's gym-toned muscle mass. He lacked his cousin's classic looks, too, with hair clipped so brutally short she could only speculate about its color. It was a fashion choice that did nothing to soften the bones pressing harsh and sharp against wind-touched skin.

But where his pretty cousin had sailed forward with supreme confidence toward the stranger at the door, this guy had put his body in front of the only other occupants of the shop—women, Goose suspected. And unless she was dreadfully mistaken—which she almost never was—his fingers were hooked casually into a pocket that held a weapon.

Sound and fury, she thought looking back at Captain America. No mistaking which cousin was which.

"Good afternoon, Ranger Guthrie," she said. She sent him a friendly smile but didn't move in for the handshake. She wasn't about to crowd a guy with his particular skill set.

"Agent di Guzman."

"May I speak with you?"

"Regarding?"

God, that voice. It was low, slow and a little rusty, like he'd just woken up, or maybe hadn't used it in a while. She'd bet on the second scenario, though it was the first that caught her imagination. An image of him waking up hijacked her mind's eye—all those efficient muscles and long limbs tangled up in some plain white sheets, the sleep in his gray eyes giving way to that powerful focus.

Another spark shot through her body, but this one wasn't wary. It was all heat, and it didn't make it to her toes. It detoured to places best left unmentioned and set up a nice little glow there. A bolt of fear, pure and reflexive, chased it down. Snuffed it out before it did anything stupid, like bloom into actual desire.

Because desire, Goose knew, was not her friend. It ran

through her character like a fault line—thin, deep and potentially catastrophic. It could lie dormant for years, but then, out of nowhere, she would simply *want*. Want with a passion that drove her beyond reason, limits or perspective. A passion that left her heedless. Unpredictable. Uncontrolled.

Dangerous.

She'd indulged that passion exactly once, and though she'd survived, others had not. The experience had marked her. Defined her. At this point, resisting desire was no harder than putting on her badge, firing up her laptop or straightening her hair. Just one more thing she did every day that made her who she was.

Which was not a woman who indulged her weaknesses. Not here, not now, not with this man. Not ever.

She put a hand to the smooth sweep of her hair. The calm, orderly fall of it reassured her.

"I'd rather speak with you in private," she finally said.

Guthrie jumped as if pinched, then stepped aside to reveal a tall woman in her midsixties. She favored vibrant jewel tones, a choice Goose approved given the dramatic silver of her hair. A startlingly sweet smile transformed the patrician sternness of her face as she stepped forward.

"Agent di Guzman, is it?"

"Yes, ma'am," Goose said.

"I'm Lila."

"As in Mother Lila's Tea Shop?"

"The very one." Lila threaded her arm through Ranger Guthrie's and beamed at Goose. "You'll have to forgive my nephew here. His job keeps him from civilization most of the winter. He's lost the habit of polite conversation." She took Goose's elbow in her other hand and turned them both toward a little wire-legged table in the bay window that framed a heartbreaking sweep of Lake Superior's jagged beauty. "You just have a seat right here. Yarrow will bring you a nice hot cup of tea and Rush"—she nudged the silent ranger into the chair opposite her—"will remember his manners shortly, I'm sure."

Lila bustled toward the counter, snapping her ringed fingers at the teenage Goth queen Goose was startled to find sitting at the register. Good Lord, she thought. How many people had Guthrie been hiding behind those broad shoulders?

"Yarrow!" Lila sang out. "Two cups of Lady Grey at table five, please!"

Captain America stopped at the table's edge on his way to the door. "See you around, Maria."

She sincerely hoped not, but sent him a smile anyway. "Nice meeting you."

He turned to his cousin. "I'm out of pocket for a few days starting tomorrow morning," he said. "Some fat cats from Winnipeg are having a conference down on Mackinac and can't be bothered to drive. Keep an eye on the girls, will you?"

"Feed still in the kitchen?"

"Yep."

"Will do."

Goose watched him saunter out the door, jacket unzipped, curls dancing in the bitter wind. "Your cousin, was it?"

"Einar."

"Guy's going to freeze to death going out like that." She sent Guthrie an amused half smile. "Look pretty doing it, though."

He shot a dubious glance at her cranberry wool beret. "Guess you'd know."

Okay, so no common ground poking fun at the ridiculous cousin. She touched her hat—her *adorable* hat—and gave a self-deprecating chuckle. "I would, actually. It if gets much colder than this, I might have to consider earflaps." She shuddered dramatically.

"It does."

She paused, backtracked. "Does what?"

"Get colder."

"Oh." She looked into those pale eyes, saw not a hint of humor. She tried again. "Surely that's not possible. It's already ridiculous out there. I think I freezer-burned my lungs just walking here from the ferry dock. How much colder could it get?"

He gave her a long, steady look. "Much."

Irritation pressed in on her. What, was there some kind of word rationing in effect on Mishkwa she hadn't been informed of? A law against small talk? Or had Guthrie simply ceded his lifetime supply of words to his chatty cousin? She swallowed a few acidic words of her own—sure to give her heartburn later—and summoned up her best look of laughing chagrin.

"So. Earflaps? Really?"

Pause. "Depends."

"On?" She smiled around gritted teeth.

"You."

She sighed. "Not one for small talk, are you, Ranger Guthrie?"

"I suck at it."

She shook her head solemnly. "Surely not."

A corner of his mouth flickered, like maybe he wanted to smile but didn't quite remember how. "So how about we skip it and you just tell me what you're doing here?"

"Fair enough." She swung her legs to the side—there wasn't much room for them under the teeny table—and crossed them. She took a moment to admire the supple leather boots that encased her calves like a butter-soft second skin until they disappeared into the dark wool of her plaid wrap skirt. So, she noted with a sharp satisfaction, did Ranger Guthrie. Maybe he hated her hat but he didn't mind her boots so much. Or the legs inside them.

"How about you tell me why a guy with a gun in his pocket would want to stab the governor with a flaming pitchfork?"

Chapter

3

A SINGLE eyebrow crept up the barest fraction of an inch, the first sign she'd surprised him. "This is about *that*?"

"If by *that* you mean the fact that you're the founding member of a registered political party whose platform includes a stated intention to stab the sitting governor with a flaming pitchfork, then yes." She gave him a friendly smile. "This is about that."

"Huh."

"You can't be surprised that the Secret Service has a few questions." Goose let a beat of silence pass, then felt compelled to point out the obvious. "Questions you haven't actually answered yet."

More silence. She suppressed a sigh. "Ranger Guthrie? Why would a man with a gun in his pocket want to stab somebody with a flaming pitchfork?"

"I don't," Guthrie said finally.

Goose refrained from an eye roll, but it was a near thing. Two words? Really? That was the best he could do? "Don't what? Have a gun in your pocket?" she asked. "Or want to stab the governor with a flaming pitchfork?"

"The pitchfork thing."

"Then you won't mind explaining to me how you came to be the founder and only member of a political party whose platform consists solely of a promise to do so."

Goth Girl—Yarrow, Goose reminded herself—appeared at the table in the speculative silence that followed. She was all pale skin, gorgeous bones and angry black eyeliner, with enough need-fueled revolt hanging overhead to make Goose wonder if Marilyn Manson and Winona Ryder had had a drunken fling one night and accidentally reproduced. She plunked two steaming teacups down in front of them with a much-maligned sigh.

Goose smiled at her. "Thanks, Yarrow."

Yarrow blinked at being name-checked by a stranger. Maybe at being name-checked at all. An unexpected twinge of compassion for the kid rolled over her. She remembered only too well being old enough to recognize what a burden you were but too young to do anything about it. She herself had never gone in for piercings/tattoos/heavy makeup, but she understood why kids did. Making your outside ugly was a hell of a lot easier than making your inside pretty, and teenagers did like things to match.

Yarrow opted for an eye roll over the more traditional "you're welcome," prompting Goose to wonder if she'd been taking lessons in verbal economy from Ranger Guthrie. The girl stomped off to her stool behind the register and Goose turned back to her erstwhile companion.

"So. Ranger Guthrie. You were saying?"

Another flicker of almost-smile. Damn, she was on a roll.

"Rush."

"Excuse me?"

"Rush." He paused, then clarified. "It's my name."

"I know," she said, at sea. "You want me to use it?"

"Yes."

"Why?"

"Because that was nice."

She waited for an explanation. None arrived. She sighed. "What was nice?"

"What you did for my cousin just now."

"Einar?"

"Yarrow."

"She's your cousin, too?" Goose blinked. "Goodness. Are you related to everybody on this island?"

"No."

She touched the headache brewing at her nape. "Are you always this literal, Ranger Guthrie?"

"Rush."

"Are you always this literal, *Rush*?"

"Yes. I'm taciturn, irritating and pessimistic, too."

She gave him wide, disbelieving eyes. "No."

His gaze warmed abruptly, and kindled a corresponding—and alarming—warmth in her stomach. "I don't count kindness among my particular gifts, but I know it—and respect it—when I see it in others. Particularly in situations when there's nothing to be gained by it."

She gaped at him with perfect sincerity this time.

"Most people ignore kids who look like that," he said, pointing his chin toward the girl behind the register. "Or worse, they don't see them at all. But you? You called her by name."

"Well, sure," Goose said stupidly. "What else was I supposed to call her?"

"It was enough that you thought to call her anything."

"Enough for what?"

"For me to decide you might be deeper than your lip gloss, Agent di Guzman."

"Goose." She frowned at him, stung. "If we're going to insult each other, we ought to be on a first-name basis."

One pale brow headed for the ridge of stubble that served as a hairline. "I thought your name was Maria."

"People call me Goose." She shrugged. "From di Guzman. Or maybe from the fact that I was an incredibly tall, awkward teenager." She gave him a smile that invited him to share the joke, but he didn't return it.

"I'm not insulting you, you know."

"You just called me shallow."

"I said I suspected you were shallow." His eyes drifted north, to her perfectly acceptable—if, okay, impractical—beret.

"Oh, for heaven's sake."

"I also said I was wrong."

She gave up trying to work up an appropriate hauteur. The guy did brutal honesty better than most. She suspected it wasn't a choice so much as a case of his simply being wired that way. "So, Rush." She took a moment to appreciate the irony of calling this fiercely deliberate man Rush. "Tell me about the Radical Agrarian Party."

"Not much to tell."

She treated him to a stern dose of his own silence, which he acknowledged with a smile so faint she felt more than saw it. She couldn't have enjoyed a victory more if she'd battled a chess master to checkmate.

"My aunt—" He tipped his head toward the counter and lifted a brow.

"Lila?"

"Yeah. She thinks I spend too much time alone."

Goose put on an expression of polite disbelief. "You?"

His lips twitched. "She likes to arrange outings for me."

She indulged in an expectant silence until he cleared his throat and said, "Volunteer opportunities, mostly."

She maintained her silence with an almost vindictive glee.

"With kids," he said. He shifted. Cleared his throat again. "She thinks they're a good warm-up."

She took pity on him. She was, as he'd noted, a basically kind person. "For?"

"I think she's working me up to something more age appropriate. Interaction with my peers, maybe."

He said it with a heartfelt resignation that had a reluctant smile curving her lips. "Poor baby."

"Thank you."

They shared a moment of companionable silence. Then she said, "So how does this tie you to the Radical Agrarians?"

"It's a long story."

She let her smile grow. "I've got all day, Rush."

GOOSE. HOW could a woman who looked like this let people call her *Goose*? And she wanted to know about the Radical Agrarians. Crap.

"I'm a party of one, which you already know," Rush said as she settled in across from him with every appearance of comfort. She crossed those long, slender legs again, one booted foot tick-tocking casually in the air as if her chair weren't as miserably uncomfortable as his. Why the hell Lila had chosen to furnish her shop with furniture two-thirds normal size, Rush would never know. The woman was nearly as tall as he was. "None of the others are old enough to vote."

"I see." She tapped glossy lips with pretty pink nails. "And the point of launching a party with supporters who can't actually go to the polls is what now?"

He tore his eyes from those pursed, candy-colored lips. *Jesus, Rush, focus.* He wasn't what you'd call articulate on a good day. How was he going to explain exactly why he'd signed his name to those stupid papers if he was wondering what her lip gloss tasted like?

"Don't you remember being sixteen?" he asked, a little desperately.

Something flared in her eyes, and recognition caught in his chest like a clenched fist. Rush had seen it before, that sharp intensity of sorrow and grief. Over and over, he'd watched battle-hardened soldiers collapse under the weight of it like a house of cards. But this woman—this shiny woman with her silly hat and her dark sad eyes—she just smiled around it.

"Well enough to know that there's a pretty good reason we don't let teenagers vote," she said.

"Point taken. And yet you can't deny that a sixteen-year-old is fully capable of adult thoughts and ideas and emotions."

"I wouldn't deny it. But I would argue that he's entirely without an adult's capacity for patience, reason or delayed gratification."

"But should we keep him locked into the *child* box just because he isn't quite ready for the *adult* box?"

She studied him. "You think not."

"I don't think anything." He spread his hands, at a loss to explain himself much further. "I just—for one afternoon—challenged some kids to go beyond complaining and into problem solving. They're going to inherit a complicated world in a few years. Better for us all if they hit the ground running."

"So the Radical Agrarian Party was an experiment," she said slowly. "A forum for teenagers to act and think on an adult level. A way for them to participate in the democratic process, to float their ideas about how to make our nation a better place and get actual, real-time feedback?"

"Exactly." He took a moment to envy the verbal dexterity that allowed her to sum up another person's jumbled thoughts into a few perfect sentences. "All it took was a couple hours and signing my name to a few pieces of paper."

"Whose idea was it to put offing the governor with a flaming pitchfork into the bylaws?"

"I believe that one was unanimous." He scratched the back of his neck. "Guy's kind of an ass."

Her lips twitched with what he suspected was the first genuine amusement she'd shown all day. "And how will the kids feel about their little experiment putting you under investigation by the Secret Service?"

"Sobered, I hope." He dropped his hands to his lap. "Only the young and foolish bait the government on purpose."

"And you?" she asked. "How do you feel about it?"

"Being under investigation?" He met those dizzying, grief-drenched eyes. "I'm starting to see the upside."

"ARE YOU?" Goose's stomach clenched with an uneasy mix of nerves and heat, but she sent him her standard look of speculative assessment. The one she generally followed up with regretful dismissal. "That's . . . flattering, really, but—"

"Why do you do that?" he asked.

She frowned. "Do what?"

"Flirt when you aren't interested. Smile when nothing's funny." He watched her with eyes the color and texture of flint.

"I—"

"I'm not coming on to you, Goose."

She snapped her mouth shut. "Then what was all that about seeing the upside of being the target of a federal investigation?"

"Just being honest. You're attractive, sharp and clearly good at what you do. You're messed up as all hell, but I seem to like that."

"Excuse me?"

"You're excused." He leaned in, put his palms flat on the table. The crazy urge to lean in to meet him seized her, and suddenly she *wanted*. Wanted to touch the hard plane of that cheek, the unforgiving slice of that mouth. Wanted to put her lips on the long line of his throat and pull the scent and the vital warmth of him into her lungs. Absorb the sharp sting of his honesty and the hot slap of his interest.

She reared back from it, from the punishing heat of her own want. Oh God. Not this. Not now.

"The sad fact is," Rush went on relentlessly, "I like you. You want to investigate me, fine. I've got nothing better to do. Lila'll be thrilled to see me interacting with somebody my own age. Go ahead. Follow me around, ask me questions, interview my neighbors. My life's an open book. Start reading. But don't expect me to pretend I don't see what you are."

She stared at him, the air driven from her lungs. Her blood beat madly in her temples, pooled hot and dangerous between clenched thighs. She barely recognized her own voice when she said, "And what I am?"

His hand opened on the table between them, his fingers long and tanned. Every cell of her body yearned toward him like a flower leaned into the sun. "You're a lot of things," he said softly. "Complicated. Beautiful. Harsh." He closed his fingers into a fist—a somehow regretful gesture—and disappointment came down on her, crushing and shameful. "But mostly? Mostly you're just sad."

"Sad?" She summoned up a light laugh. "How positively gothic of me."

"There you go again," he said. "Laughing when nothing's funny. That can't be good for you."

Her chuckle died on the vine. He rose and glanced at a silver watch Goose suspected could launch the space shuttle if necessary. "Last ferry's at four," he said. "Nice meeting you."

She jumped to her feet on a breathless spurt of panic. She could wonder later why this curt dismissal hurt her. For now, she simply had to stop it. "Rush."

He turned back, nothing but polite interest in his stony face. She hesitated, took her time arranging the camel-colored wool of her coat over her arm. He waited.

Finally she said, "I've got a job to do here. I'll get it done faster with your cooperation."

"You've heard my conditions."

She swallowed even as her body burned with a treacherous heat. "Honesty. Nothing less."

He studied her while her stupid heart galloped around in her chest, then nodded once. "Best get started, then."

Relief buzzed through her, hot and startling. What the hell? She'd known the guy half an hour. When exactly had his approval come to mean something to her? She cleared her throat and stepped forward, near enough to shake hands if she wanted to. A good, friendly distance. Professional.

"So. Any chance you can point me to the Ranger Station?"

"The Ranger Station?"

"Yeah. Apparently it includes quarters for summer staff that are vacant for the season. My boss arranged for me to room there while I'm on Mishkwa."

"I live at the Ranger Station, Goose."

"Oh."

"Alone."

"Well." She had a near-hysterical urge to laugh. "I won't be a bother. I'll stay out of your hair, promise." Oh God. He didn't *have* hair. And what little he had, she wanted to be in so badly she could taste it. What was *wrong* with her?

"What if I want you to bother me?" His eyes were hot and silvery, and her knees went weak. Ridiculously, shockingly, girlishly weak.

"Well." She patted his arm. It was like tempered steel under her hand, and her palm tingled with a completely inappropriate appreciation. She withdrew it hastily and dredged up a friendly smile. "I'm sure we'll manage to keep things professional."

"Honesty, Goose." He shook his head. "This won't work without it."

"I'm doing the best I can," she snapped. "There's a fucking lot of pheromones flying around here, though. Give me a break."

She broke off, aghast at her language. Her tone. Her *honesty*. Oh God. She was falling apart. She was. She was sixteen again and racing heedlessly into a firestorm of raging desire. Again. And Rush was going to watch it happen. How could he miss it when he was staring at her with flat, unreadable eyes, likely as startled by her outburst as she was?

Then he smiled. Slowly. It moved over the stern, unforgiving bones of his face like the rising sun moved over a cliff, transforming rocky harshness into breathtaking beauty.

"Let's go."

She blinked, still stunned by the smile. "Go?"

"Next door." He shook his head at her beret. "You're staying on Mishkwa, you'll need decent gear. Ben'll figure you out. Come on."

He seized her hand in his, and a heady sizzle shot up her arm straight to the base of her skull. He marched toward the door, and she stumbled along behind him.

"Oh, and Goose?"

"Hmm?"

"For the record? When I do come on to you, you won't have to wonder." He sent her a look over his shoulder, his eyes molten silver. "You'll know."

She smiled brightly—perhaps moronically—at him. "Oh. Right. Um, thanks."

He grinned at her. Actually grinned.

"Just being honest."

Chapter

4

RUSH WAS enjoying the feel of Goose's hand in his—damn, how long had it been since he'd held a woman's hand?—when Lila pushed through the swinging door from the kitchen. Goose yanked free of his touch like he was on fire.

"Rush? Before you go?"

Right. Lila had wanted to talk to him about something. Which was why he was here in the first place.

"Sure." He turned to Goose. "Mishkwa Island Outfitters is right next door," he said. "Ben Barnes is the owner. Tell him I said you needed gearing out. I'll be over in a few."

"It was lovely meeting you, Lila," Goose said with a bright smile. "And you, Yarrow."

"You, too, dear," Lila said, returning the smile with a beatific one of her own. Yarrow grunted. Then Goose shot out the door with a haste that bordered on insulting, all expensive fabric and exotic perfume. Lila turned speculative eyes on Rush. "So . . . she seems nice."

"For a woman who thinks I may be gearing up to assassinate the governor."

Lila gave this an airy pass. "You walk around all day armed to the teeth," she said. "What did you expect?"

Rush didn't really feel like getting into the Radical Agrarian thing, so he just said, "You needed something?"

Lila sighed. "Oh, it's nothing, but I thought you should hear it from me. It seems my dear neighbor Mr. Barnes has his shorts in a knot over the compost again."

Rush glanced automatically toward Ben's place next door. Midsixties with the build and endurance of a guy thirty years younger, Ben ran an outfitter in the summers and built birch-bark canoes by hand in the winters. A pretty straightforward guy for the most part, but not overly patient with Lila's kookier endeavors. Probably didn't help neighborly relations at all that Lila had the *kooky* market pretty well cornered.

"Ben doesn't like your compost?"

"Evidently not."

"He thinks it's attracting Sir Humpalot," Yarrow said from the register.

"Sir Humpalot?"

She arched the brow without the ring. "Sure. Seven, maybe eight feet tall? Long brown beard, big rack?" She put her free hand to her head, thumb against her scalp, fingers fanned out, miming antlers. "Unsuccessfully humping the Dumpsters since September?"

Rush blinked at her. The kid had nicknamed a rogue bull moose with sexual identity issues Sir Humpalot.

He frowned down at Lila. "This kid needs to go back to normal school."

"Normal school. Pah." Lila fluttered her fingers in the air. "She joined your little ski team, didn't she? That's plenty of interaction with her peers."

"More than," Yarrow muttered. Rush felt for her. Yarrow, like Rush, had fallen prey to Lila's belief that good health required regular human interaction. The end result was poor Yarrow sweating it out with the high school cross-country ski team that Rush—Jesus help him—was now coaching.

"If you want to talk about people who ought to reengage with their peer group, however—" Lila began.

"I don't."

"Hey, that's true." Yarrow sat up, her eyes dancing with wicked glee. "Sir Humpalot gets more action than you."

Rush experienced a pang of nostalgia for the good old days when nobody dared screw with him. "I don't date Dumpsters."

"You don't date anybody," Lila said.

"Nobody to date. It's December, in case you hadn't noticed. Single women aren't exactly thick on the ground this time of year." He held up a hand before Lila could mention Goose. "Single women who aren't trying to arrest me, anyway."

"You didn't date when it was July and the pretty hikers were all faking sunstroke and sprained ankles to get your attention," Yarrow pointed out helpfully.

"You didn't get here till September, cuz," Rush said.

"Doesn't mean I don't hear things." Yarrow lifted her thin shoulders. "People talk."

"About stuff that's none of their damn business." Rush turned to Lila, who was peering at him with a disconcerting intensity in those bird-bright eyes. He snapped his mouth shut. His misanthropy was showing, damn it. And he'd been doing such a good job today. Now he was in for it.

"Rush. People aren't talking about you out of malice. They're talking about you out of love." She rubbed her palm briskly up and down his arm. "They want you to be happy. We all do."

"I *am* happy." His aunt gazed at him skeptically. "Happy enough, anyway." She didn't blink, only arched one pale brow. "Okay, maybe not 'tra-la-la, baby-ducks-and-chicks' happy, but I'm doing okay. Honest."

And he was. Compared with the condition he'd been in when he'd arrived on Mishkwa spring before last, he was doing fucking great. At least his brain wasn't buzzing anymore. At least he didn't wake up angry and leashed and whipcord tight anymore, his trigger finger ready for a quick day's work. Something about putting a couple miles of cold, clean space between him and the next beating heart had dulled his sharper edges. Quieted the static that had lived inside his head so long he'd forgotten how blessed silence could be.

Now, if only he could find the inner voice that used to speak into that silence, he'd be set.

Lila's face clearly indicated her skepticism on this point, but it was an old argument. One they weren't going to resolve today.

He drew a battered notebook from his jacket pocket and gave Lila his professional face. "So. Moose been around lately?"

She sighed and let it go. For the moment, anyway. "Not here more than any other place in town." Lila examined the end of her long white braid. "Ben objects to me more than to my garbage and we all know it, so let's not get all legal about it."

"Fine by me." He stuffed the notebook back into his pocket and headed for the door.

"Rush, wait." She caught his elbow and he stopped.

"Are you going to spit it out, then? Because I don't have all day to wait around while you figure out how to ask me for whatever it is you want."

She gave him a lofty look down the length of her nose. "What, you have a more pressing engagement?"

He ducked his head to look out the window at the fat, gray clouds tumbling down from Canada. Clouds that looked likely to steam straight across Mishkwa on their way to Wisconsin. "Weather's coming," he said. "Thought I'd turn that deadfall up on the ridge trail into firewood before it gets here."

Lila curled her lip. "Another lovely afternoon of battling nature into submission?"

"Well, sure." Rush liked his job for a lot of reasons, but

foremost among them was the number of days he spent working up a good, honest sweat with nobody for company but his chain saw. Plus, he got firewood. It was always nice when a huge amount of effort yielded a tangible reward. Unlike this endless interview with his aunt.

"Rush." Lila pinned him with eyes entirely too sharp for the soft curve of her smile. "First of all, you can't fight nature. But second? You spend too much time alone."

"Oh. Oh, no." He held up his hands and backed toward the door. "Whatever it is, I'm not doing it."

Lila followed him. "You haven't even heard what I want yet," she said, her voice dangerously reasonable.

"The last time we had this conversation, I ended up coaching a high school ski team." And the time before that it was supervising the little anarchists who'd talked him into signing those damn Radical Agrarian papers. He groped behind him for the doorknob, unwilling to take his eyes off his aunt when she was in this particular mood.

"Which is a problem how? They're children, Rush. Harmless."

Yarrow snorted and Rush wholeheartedly agreed. Lila ignored them both.

"The point is, you have a duty to take up your place in this community. The place that's been waiting for you."

"What place might that be?"

"There's a full moon next week," she said. "The coven is gathering here for esbat, cakes and ale to follow. I think you should come."

He frowned at her. Stripping away all the traditional language of his childhood religion, this was essentially a request for him to come to church. "That's it?"

"That's it." She treated him to her warmest smile. "Think it over, Rush. Surely you can squeeze some pondering into your busy schedule of hiking and chopping things up."

Yarrow swallowed a chuckle, though when he looked her way she was inspecting her nails with studied innocence.

"Okay," he said. "Sure." His hand finally landed on the

knob, thank you, Jesus. He yanked open the door and the fresh, cold smell of freedom filled the little shop. "I'll think about it."

"Thank you, dear."

GOOSE TRAMPED behind Rush along a path that zig-zagged up the face of a steep incline. The little Kevlar sled holding her suitcase, computer bag and purse glided along behind her, clipped to a body harness Lila's neighbor Ben had fitted her with. He'd also thrown in a Marmot shell in a gorgeous eggplant color, complete with a down liner that—in terms of warmth rather than fashion anyway—beat the snot out of her own winter coat. He'd provided her with a pair of muscular boots that looked a lot like the ones Rush was sporting, too. Oh, and snowshoes. Of course.

The wind pushed at her back like an impatient com-muter and she leaned into her stride. Her leg muscles sang pleasantly as she drew in a lungful of icy air that seemed to rush straight to her heart like pure oxygen. Her head buzzed with the hyperclarity it provided and it surprised a little chuckle out of her.

"What?"

She glanced up the trail to find Rush standing on the spine of the ridge they'd been climbing toward this past thirty minutes.

"What what?" she asked, startled. They'd been snow-shoeing in complete silence since they left Ben's little shop.

"You were laughing."

"I was?"

"Yes. Something funny?"

"Besides the fact that I have to schlep my gear a couple miles to the Ranger Station via sled because of an arcane law banning motor vehicles from the entire island?"

If she didn't know what to look for, she'd have com-pletely missed the amusement warming those pale eyes. She bet a lot of people missed Rush entirely.

"We do allow emergency vehicles on-island," he said. "The Urgent Care has a snowmobile. But yeah. Besides that. What's so funny?"

"Nothing." She slogged to the top of the ridge and pulled up beside him. "It's pretty, that's all." She glanced behind her and found the little village of South Harbor curled up next to the slate-gray boil of Lake Superior like a hibernating hedgehog. "Aw," she said. "Cute."

Rush followed her gaze then looked back at her, questions about her good taste clear in his eyes. Then he stepped to the side and Goose got her first look at the rest of Mishkwa.

"Oh my," she said as she took it in. The island stretched out into Lake Superior like a bony, arthritic finger, all knobs and lumps and twists. She'd thought they were heading for a ridgeline, but in fact found herself now standing atop a hill that constituted the first knuckle of the finger. The peak was rounded and rocky, sporting a shallow bowl in its center, like somebody had reached out and left a careless fingerprint in a loaf of rising bread. A sturdy little log cabin nestled down in the base of the bowl, surrounded on all sides by a crowd of snow-splattered fir trees standing skirt to skirt like dancers at an ice queen's ball. The quiet was profound, a presence rather than an absence, and it clicked into Goose's soul like she'd been waiting her whole life to hear it.

"Did I step into a snow globe?" she asked.

He considered that with his usual serious attention. "I never thought of it like that, but maybe, yeah." Rush started down the path that led into the trees. "Wait till Mother Nature shakes it up. Happens about twice a week come January. You think this is funny, you'll think that's hilarious."

"I don't think it's funny," she said, falling into step behind him. The PVC-like stoppers on the leads of her harness kept the sled from running over her snowshoes on the downhill.

"And yet you're laughing."

"Haven't you ever laughed because something really beautiful took you by surprise?"

He threw her a look over his shoulder. "No."

She snorted. "And you think *I'm* sad."

"You are."

She frowned. Why not? He wasn't looking at her. Not that it would have mattered if he was, as he'd already banned smiling unless she was actually happy. Which was pretty much . . . never.

Never? Really? She scowled. It felt wonderful. Wrinkly. Snarly. She tried to remember the last time—aside from two minutes ago—that she'd laughed out of pure delight. Nothing came to mind. Was he right? Was she really so unhappy?

No, of course not. She simply wasn't happy. There was a lot of neutral ground between the two extremes. She'd guess most normal people occupied that in-between zone right along with her.

"Speaking of sad," she said, "do you know what Ben told me when I tried to pay him for the gear?"

"That he was powerless in the face of a pair of giant doe eyes and that megawatt smile you like to blast people with?"

"I don't do doe eyes."

"Not going to argue about the smile?"

"Nope," she said, and purposely beamed a fat smile at his back. It didn't feel nearly as good as the scowl. "Do you want to know why Ben wouldn't take the money, though?"

"Why?"

"He said it was because he missed his wife."

"His wife?"

"Yeah. Apparently, back when they ran an outfitter up on Sawbill, she used to test-drive all the women's gear so she could tell customers if it was really designed for women or just men's gear cut out of pink material. Ben said he's pretty used to being widowed—she's been gone five years now—but he still misses her like crazy whenever he gets something new in the women's department. He said as long as I swing by his place before I leave the island to give him a thumbs-up or -down on the gear, we're square. Isn't that the saddest story you ever heard?"

She felt his gaze touch her, then a queer sense of loss when it moved away.

"Not quite," he said.

Chapter

5

RUSH TRAMPED up to the Ranger Station door, popped the clasps on his snowshoes and shoved them into the nearest snowbank. He grabbed the suitcase off Goose's sled and led her inside.

An eerie and somehow pleasant sense of familiarity washed over him as he ushered her into his home, but it wasn't déjà vu. If anything, it was the opposite—a wide-awake awareness that he might be creating rather than fulfilling a destiny. Something whispered inside him, familiar as a lover, elusive as a dream. It slipped away like smoke when he reached for it, leaving both hope and regret in its wake.

"Kitchen," he said, passing through the tiny galley that sported a two-burner stove, a minifridge and a microwave on a peeling laminate counter. "Living room," he said two steps later, in reference to the battered plaid sofa and wood-burning stove. "Bathroom." He jerked his chin at the harvest-gold sink/toilet/shower combo jammed into a shoe-box-size bump-out on the back of the cabin, then turned left. "Guest quarters." He hefted her suitcase onto the creaky twin-size metal cot perched on a braided rag rug that hadn't seen a vacuum in many a moon. Between himself, Goose and the cot, there was maybe a square foot or two of floor space left over, and Rush felt a little light-headed, as if there weren't enough oxygen for them both to share.

"I'm back there," he said, tipping his head toward an identical room on the other side of the bathroom.

"Good to know," she said, hitting him with a one-sided version of the usual stunner smile. "Do we have electricity, or are we full-on *Little House on the Prairie*?"

"There's power," he said, and pointed toward the outlet on the same fixture as a single bulb dangling from the ceiling.

"Internet?"

"Dial-up."

"Yikes."

"People don't come to Mishkwa to stay connected, Goose."

She looked up at him, her lips parted and laughing, ready to deliver one of those smoothly amused replies he was coming to think of as her trademark. But tilting her head up to meet his eyes put her mouth scant inches from his and the air between them went suddenly thick and electric.

The amusement on her face didn't budge, but a quick spark of panic leaped in the dark pools of her eyes. Normally he'd have stepped back immediately. Some guys got off on scaring women, but Rush wasn't one of them. When the panic instantly melted into something more calculating, though, he stopped.

Maybe he was a fool, and maybe he was letting a sexual dry spell—a really, really *long* sexual dry spell—cloud his judgment, but damn, this woman was fascinating. That had been fear in her eyes, genuine and spontaneous. But she'd mastered it in the space of a single heartbeat, then turned it into a plan with astonishing efficiency. He'd known war-tested soldiers who didn't operate with that kind of automatic self-control, and he was dying to see what she'd do next.

"Rush," she said. He felt it on his skin, the warm wash of her exhale, the invitation of his name on her lips. He went instantly, painfully hard.

"Yeah?"

She stepped forward, leaving a bare, aching inch between their bodies, but her eyes when they met his were clear and frank. "You wanted honesty, right?"

"Yeah." God, listen to him. He'd never been much of a talker, but she'd reduced him to single-word responses. She was close enough for him to smell, and all the blood in his body instantly headed for his dick, leaving the areas in charge of speech and thought entirely unmanned. Wonderful.

"Well, listen up, then, because you're about to get a great big shot of it."

"Should I brace myself?"

She laughed and Rush actually felt dizzy. "Maybe." She reached up with long, cool fingers, slid them into the stubble at the nape of his neck. Her eyes dropped to his mouth and she said, "I'm thinking about kissing you."

"Are you?" If they were giving out trophies for the stupidest questions ever asked, Rush felt certain he would have at least made the finals. He wanted to close his eyes so he could berate himself in private, but he couldn't look away from that mouth so close to his.

"I am." She swayed in until her lips, moist and lush and *right there*, nearly brushed his chin. Rush fought a brief but fierce internal battle and came up with control of his higher-level cognitive functions. For the moment.

"Why?" Not eloquent but to the point. Plus he really would like to know where on earth she was going with this before he decided he didn't give a good goddamn and just kissed the hell out of her.

"Because for some reason I want to." Her mouth curved in a smile that had the blood pounding in his temples. And in other, more interesting places. "And since I'm clearly not going to get any work done until I satisfy my curiosity"— she took that last step and fitted herself against him, curve to angle, soft to hard—"I figure I might as well scratch that itch."

She slid her other hand over his shoulder while Rush struggled for words, for thought, for coherence. She linked her hands together behind his neck and snuggled her stomach right into the aching evidence of his desire. She smiled like a cat, all sleek and self-satisfied.

"So why don't we just get this out of the way?" she asked, and kissed him.

GOOSE HAD braced herself for impact, but the sheer scale of Rush's kiss shoved her into territory she'd never charted before. His mouth was hot on hers, hard and hungry. His fingers speared into the spill of her hair, and he yanked her to her toes while he plundered—no other word for it—her mouth. Desire surged up in her, fierce and hot, and she groped desperately for the reins she'd held so confidently two seconds before.

This wasn't how it was supposed to go, she thought wildly. Even as she kissed him back, even as she opened her mouth under his and offered up everything she had, everything he demanded, the panicked drumbeat of her fear shook her. This wasn't what she'd planned.

She'd planned to ignore the crackling sexual tension between them. When that hadn't worked, she'd given herself a stern mental lecture on professionalism. The guy was a *suspect*, for God's sake. But that was crap and she knew it. Maybe she didn't have any concrete proof one way or the other, but her gut scoffed at the very idea of a guy this fundamentally straightforward as a criminal. So she'd moved on to good old suppression.

But then she'd found herself bare inches from Rush's hard, beautiful mouth, and the raw churn of desire inside her shot straight to a rolling boil that terrified her. So she'd retreated to her last line of defense. The big guns. She was going to sleep with this man. She was going to jump him, tear off his clothes and do him.

Sex with a stranger was dangerous, of course. But what was more dangerous was allowing this lust inside her to grow unchecked. To sink its sneaky little roots deep into the vulnerable soil of her heart and whisper its evil lies about romance. About hot sex and warm promises and happily ever after. About love.

Once the mystery was gone, once the unknown was known, she'd be fine. The curtain would be pulled back and she'd see that this man was exactly like every other man. No more, no less. He'd be made blissfully happy by the kind of fuck that normally only happened in adult movies—ding dong, delivery! Wanna do me?—and she would deposit this dangerously hopeful lust in the trash can along with the used condom.

Then she found her back against the door frame, pinned there by the unexpected solidity of Rush's body. He rocked into her, his want hot and demanding and aligned exactly with hers. A shower of stars burst behind her eyes, sending her plans and her thoughts and her self-control into the wind. His mouth commanded hers, and his hands were big and absolutely confident as they slid down to the curve of her bottom and lifted her more fully into his erection.

Desire exploded low in her belly, and her nipples tightened, shameless and needy. He jerked aside her jacket and tunneled one of those big, warm hands under her sweater as if he'd read her mind. She arched into his touch, filling his hand with the aching heaviness of her breast. He made some kind of noise—masculine, satisfied, infinitely gratifying—and flicked his thumb over her nipple. The first shimmer of orgasm fluttered through her, slapping her into a shocked self-awareness.

Jesus Christ, had she really come to *this*? Was she truly so far gone that a virtual stranger could dry-hump her into coming against a rickety door frame of a bedroom that hadn't seen a vacuum since 1973?

The plan, she reminded herself bitterly, was to give in to her lust in a controlled, orderly fashion. The so-so if not outright disappointing sex that traditionally resulted would force her to acknowledge that fabulous, brain-melting, consciousness-altering sex simply didn't exist.

But okay, maybe she was wrong. Maybe wild, screaming jungle sex *did* exist, and maybe Rush was its king. Good for him. And hey, good for her. This could be a much better afternoon than she'd anticipated, but she needed to keep her head in the game here. She was trying to bleed off the tension in a civilized manner, not wreck herself on the rocks of unbridled desire.

She grabbed at her self-control with both hands, and the promise of a return to sanity cooled her blood. Not much, just a degree or two. But enough that she could take a conscious, controlled part in the action instead of simply feeling and reacting. Instead of letting her desire—and his—buffet her about like a ship on a storm-tossed sea.

She gave him a breathy moan, curled one hand around the taut column of his nape and did the two things she knew that would put her firmly back in the driver's seat: she shoved her tongue into his mouth and her hand down his pants.

The taste of him sent a dizzying surge of need through her, but the feel of him in her hand—smooth, hard and disconcertingly large—nearly drove her to her knees. A shower of sparks danced through her blood even as a wave of embarrassment pinked her cheeks. Oh God, she had her hand in his *pants*. She'd met him two hours ago and now she had her hand wrapped around his dick. She was such a fucking mess.

He drew back, his forearm braced against the door frame over her head, his other hand still under her shirt, but the question in his eyes was unmistakable.

"Goose?"

She forced her lips into a knowing smile and stroked the length of him. "Do you really want to talk right now?" she asked. "Or would you like to see what else I can do with my mouth?"

And cue the porno music, she thought, but she'd never

met a guy who'd turn down an offer like that. And she needed to finish this before she lost her nerve.

Rush dropped his forehead to hers and for a moment she thought she'd won. She reached up for his mouth but he turned away. He slipped his hand out of her shirt and gingerly backed away from her touch while she gaped at him in utter astonishment.

"That's an extremely generous offer," he said. "You have no idea what it's costing me to say no."

She flicked a glance at the impressive erection tenting the front of his jeans. "I have some idea."

He followed her gaze. "Oh. Yeah."

She threaded her fingers through her hair until it lay neat and smooth against her shoulders again. If only it were so easy to restore order to her thoughts. To her body. Both of which still buzzed and stumbled like drunks on a weeklong bender. "Do you mind if I ask why you're saying no? I thought we were both on the same page."

"We were. Right up until you disappeared on me."

"Disappeared?" She stared at him. "I had my hand in your *pants*, Rush. How is that disappearing?"

He shrugged. "It's hard to explain. One minute you were kissing me and I was going to die if I didn't have you naked and under me in the next two minutes."

Lust slapped at her, left its glittery fingerprints all over her nervous system. She crossed her arms under breasts that still ached and tingled. "And then?"

"And then the kiss became an agenda."

"What does that mean?"

"It means one minute we were in it together, and the next I was all by myself." He touched his lips, as if savoring the taste of her. "I don't know what you were doing, but whatever it was, you were doing it *to* me, not *with* me."

"And that's a bad thing?"

He shook his head. "I won't lie to you, Goose. I want you. A lot."

She glanced at his pants again. "Yes, I can see that."

"You're missing the point," he said grimly. "That?" He waved a hand at his crotch. "That's biology. If scratching that itch were my only goal, I could do it by myself. It wouldn't be as much fun as what you're offering, but in the end I'd be just as alone. And I've been alone a really long time now. I'm tired of it. What I want from you is more than sex. I want to make love to you. With you."

She stared at him, the breath driven from her lungs. "You don't even know me."

"Yeah." He shrugged. "Go figure. But I don't argue with my gut anymore."

"And your gut wants to make love to me?"

He smiled. "With you."

"Even though I stand here ready to blow you, fuck you, and otherwise fulfill whatever adolescent fantasy you can come up with?"

He closed his eyes, pained. "Yes. I'll forgo that in the hopes that, once you get to know me, you'll be willing to make love with me as yourself and not some porn-star wannabe."

She chewed the inside of her cheek and tried to work up some anger. Anything was better than the shame and guilt chasing each other through the emptiness inside her. "Did you just call me a porn-star wannabe?"

He winced. "No. I said you were *acting* like a porn-star wannabe. I don't know why either, because believe me, you were doing fine on your own."

She sighed. "You don't have any other mode, do you? It's just all honesty, all the time."

He lifted those surprisingly solid shoulders. "Yeah. Sorry. I'm hoping to grow on you." He stepped forward, put a knuckle under her chin and lifted her gaze to his. "For what it's worth, I'm sorry if I hurt your feelings. I guess I want more from you—more *of* you—than you're ready to give me right now. But I'm a patient man, Goose. I'm not afraid to wait—or work—for what I want."

She gazed at him, half horrified, half entranced. She

cleared her throat, slid her mouth into a familiar, wry smile. "Is that a threat, Ranger Guthrie?"

He leaned forward and pressed a kiss to her mouth that was so solemn and sweet it made her throat ache. "It's a promise."

"I don't want your promises, Rush." She curled her hands into his lapels. "I just want your—"

"Coat hooks are by the front door," he said, breaking gently free of her grip. "Snowshoes stay outside."

"Rush?" She blinked at him. Was he really walking away? "Where are you going?"

"Out."

"When will you be back?"

"Later."

He let the door slap shut behind him and she watched through the window in baffled astonishment as he snagged his snowshoes from the snowbank, grabbed his chain saw from the shed and took off for the trailhead at a near run.

Chapter

6

IT TOOK her a great deal of experimentation, but Goose eventually discovered that if she stood in the very center of the tiny kitchen and leaned toward the window, she got an adequate cell-phone signal. She dragged out one of the rickety bar stools crouching under the overhang and made herself comfortable. Because she was getting off this damn island. Right now.

Resident Agent in Charge Peter Harris answered his phone with a terse, "Harris."

"Peter. It's Goose."

"Goose." The tone didn't exactly warm up. Damn. "How's Mishkwa?"

"Not the witch-infested hotbed of assassins one might think."

"I believe the politically correct term is *pagans*," he said mildly. "And if they're still dancing naked and speaking in tongues up there, I'd be surprised."

"Me, too," Goose said. "Because, damn, Peter, it's *cold*

up here. Way too cold for naked dancing, though apparently it used to happen quite a lot. I guess there's this pile of stones somewhere on the island that catches the moonlight just so a few times a century. It's been closed for decades, but people used to—" She caught herself mid-ramble and cleared her throat. "I read about it on the ferry on the way over."

More skeptical silence.

"My point is," Goose said, "Rush Guthrie is clean. I can chase down the paper trail if you want, but this guy's a real American hero. If he's gunning for the governor, I'm Wonder Woman."

Harris barked out a laugh. "Do you really not know how many of your coworkers are sitting in their cubicles at this very minute having Wonder Woman fantasies about you?"

"First, eww. Second, not my business or my fault." Here in the privacy of a tiny cabin on an island in the middle of Lake Superior, she felt free to grimace. She took care to keep her voice smooth and amused, though. "Listen, Peter. You've made your point, okay? Can I come home now? Or am I still being punished?"

"For heaven's sake, Goose, I'm not punishing you."

"No?" Sourness crept into her tone.

"No. First of all, Snow had it coming."

"Amen."

"But even if he didn't, even if you took him down out of pure meanness, I'd still back you based on your record alone. Three languages, expert marksmanship, a few dozen counterfeiters behind bars? I don't like playing favorites, but you're by far a bigger asset to the department."

"So how is that a day after defending myself against the inappropriate and unwanted sexual advances of a colleague I'm the one interviewing homicidal park rangers with dubious political ambitions at the frozen ends of the earth?"

"Think of it as a time-out."

"A *time-out*?"

"You lost your temper, kid."

"The guy waved his boner at me, Peter. What was I supposed to do?"

"You could've brought it to me. I'd have fired the kid posthaste and you'd still be sitting in your cozy little cube playing with that computer you love so much. But no, you had to snap a quick picture with your cell phone and e-mail it to your entire contact list. Which included me." He paused. "And my boss."

Goose winced. "Okay. I lost my temper."

"Hey, I don't have any objection to your ripping Snow's guts out. Kid deserved it, no question. But, damn, Goose. There are ways to do stuff like that. And you're the last person I'd have thought I'd need to point that out to."

"I know," she said miserably.

"So you should also know that I have absolutely no use for an angry, impulsive agent making emotional decisions."

She took a moment to master the panic bubbling up inside her. Sweet Jesus, was she about to get *sacked*?

"Okay, fine." She forced a smile. "You caught me. I lost my temper. It won't happen again."

"Bet your ass it won't. Because you're not coming home yet."

Goose closed her eyes. "Come on, Peter. Have you read this guy's file? He's an ex–Navy SEAL sniper. I'm pretty sure he's one of the good guys."

"SEALs don't generally just resign," Harris said. "Particularly not to become park rangers. They get that far into the game and they play until their knees give out or their luck does."

Goose frowned. The man she'd met today was alive and well—more than Goose would have liked, actually—so his luck had clearly held out. "Did I miss the part of his dossier that mentioned a medical discharge?"

"Nope. Our boy went the less conventional third route."

"Which is?"

"Resigning in disgust over his superiors' actions, orders and opinions."

"Ah. I can see that, actually."

"Now put that together with the fact that a handful of supernotes have turned up at the Federal Reserve bank here in Minneapolis over the summer. Supernotes that were traced to a half-dozen casinos scattered along the North Shore of Superior."

"Interesting," Goose said, and it was. Since the advent of cheap, good-quality color printers and scanners, Goose—along with nearly every other agent specializing in anti-counterfeiting—had spent a lot of time busting enterprising teenagers trying to Photoshop fives and tens into fifties and hundreds. Supernotes, however, were a whole different beast. Supernotes were virtually indistinguishable from genuine currency, and producing them was no joke. It usually required the resources of an entire government—most recently that of North Korea—and the services of a virtuoso counterfeiter. The kind of counterfeiter an agent with any ambition would give her eyeteeth to bust.

"Churning out supernotes takes lot of infrastructure," she observed carefully. "Offset intaglio printing presses, reverse-engineered starch-free paper, constant upgrades to the security strips, the color-shifting ink, the microprinting. Nobody up here could keep that kind of operation a secret. This place is ridiculously tiny."

"We're not looking at Mishkwa as the point of origin. We're looking at it more as a point of entry. You have to admit it's ideal. A remote, largely uncontrolled international border."

Goose didn't like where this was going, but she didn't hesitate to connect the dots. "So we have Ranger Guthrie, a guy with an established history of thinking and acting outside normal civilian parameters who might have good reason to want to screw his government." She closed her eyes as she rolled into the inevitable conclusion. "Who also happens to live in a prime location to do so."

"Have I mentioned today that I value you as an employee?"

"Why haven't we moved on this before?" She opened her eyes to glare out the window at the fat white flakes dancing on the frigid wind. "Why couldn't I have checked this out in, say, July?"

"Because in July you weren't going off on wet-behind-the-ears rookies with more testosterone than brains."

"I'm—" *Fine.* She'd planned to say "fine," but she wasn't. The leftover fury at Snow still choked her and the desire Rush had refused to help her slake this afternoon still burned with an inconvenient persistence. Her boss might have a point there. She cleared her throat in lieu of finishing her sentence.

"Plus, in July this guy was a highly decorated military vet with a chestful of medals and the glowing praise of his ex–commanding officers. Now, however, he's a crackpot who wants to stab the sitting governor with a flaming pitchfork."

"I don't know if I can play the pitchfork angle as a credible threat," Goose said carefully. "The guy strikes me as more of a double-tap-to-the-forehead man."

"The Secret Service doesn't make assumptions about which threats are credible. We find out for sure." Harris indulged in a significant pause. "You'll want to be very thorough in your investigation, I imagine. Take your time. People with pitchforks are nothing to sneeze at. Remember what a truckload of fertilizer did in Oklahoma City."

"Right," Goose said, resigned. As if she needed a reminder about how explosive her situation was. "I'll keep it in mind."

THE NEXT morning found Goose up with the sun. Which wasn't so surprising, considering she hadn't slept worth a damn. Her stupid, analytical brain wouldn't let go of a number of things—supernotes, a wildly arousing kiss, the shocking rejection that had followed it.

She'd finally given up on sleep around sunrise. She'd dressed as quietly as possible, thinking to sneak out before Rush woke. But upon tiptoeing into the tiny kitchenette, she'd found a note on the counter. *Clearing deadfall from the ridge trail. Go back to sleep.*

She snorted out a laugh in spite of herself. Apparently her version of quiet and Rush's version of quiet were several decibels apart. That was what she got for trying to sneak around an ex-SEAL. She took a moment to wonder if there was actually any such thing as ex when a guy had had the kind of training Rush had. Probably not. When she considered all the years he had to have spent perfecting his craft—

She caught herself up short and pulled the thought out of her head with deliberate firmness. When Rush was in her head, she couldn't think. She could only feel. Want. Crave.

Damn it. She knuckled tired eyes. She wasn't going there. She'd offered him a nice, civilized liaison, and he'd rejected it. Rejected her. End of story.

Or it should have been. But while he *had* passed on her offer, he'd also made her a counteroffer. A surprising but very tempting counteroffer that she'd spent half the night considering, though she knew damn well she wouldn't accept it. Couldn't, even if she wanted to.

First off, he was a suspect. Not that she believed for a minute that a guy as inherently honest as Rush was running supernotes. But with lust still sliding warm and sneaky into her blood at the memory of his wicked, no-holds-barred kiss, it was nice to have an official reason to say no. But even if she didn't, her answer would still be the same. It had to be. Because he'd made it clear that he wasn't after her body. Not only her body, anyway.

He wanted her soul, too.

But Goose's soul was in no condition for sale or barter, so it didn't matter what or how much she wanted. What he wanted she didn't have. What she wanted, he wouldn't give. And that *was* the end of the story, at least until she escaped this damn island.

And the only way to do that was to finish her job here.

Do it well, do it quickly and get back to reality before she did something irretrievably stupid. Like kiss him again.

Coffee, she thought hastily when her brain veered into a high-def replay of yesterday's kiss. A big, hot slap of caffeinated good-morning, that was what she needed. She rummaged around the tiny kitchen until the air went warm and promising with the smell of brewing coffee. Then she strapped on her snowshoes and headed for Lila's to start doing her damn job.

It occurred to her after about thirty minutes of hard hiking that the sun was barely up. She had no idea what she could do in South Harbor to kill the sizable gap between now and polite visiting hours, so she was relieved to see the "Open" sign aglow in the tea-shop window as she approached.

Sleigh bells jangled as she entered the little shop. It was like walking face-first into a cloud of Christmas, she thought, all warm cinnamon, ground cloves and fresh nutmeg.

She snorted. Like she had any idea what nutmeg smelled like, fresh or otherwise. She doubted she'd recognize a nutmeg if it skipped up and French-kissed her. Her own family had stopped celebrating anything the year she'd turned sixteen. Even before that, Goose hadn't been at the heart of any tradition her mother deemed important. So even if genuine nutmeg *had* come into play somehow, Goose wouldn't have known about it.

"Agent di Guzman!" Lila came around the counter, wiping her hands on a crisp white apron. "How lovely to see you! Are you in the market for a cup of tea?"

"Whatever you've got brewing would be great." Goose's stomach grumbled something about how coffee didn't actually count as breakfast, and she glanced toward Yarrow. The girl was filling the glass case near the register with an assortment of baked goods that likely accounted for the Christmas-scented air. "I wouldn't say no to one of those Danish-looking things, either."

Lila beamed. "Smart girl. I recommend the cherry cheese."

"I'll take it. Can I get a minute of your time to go with it?"

Lila gave her a sharp look but she nodded. "Have a seat at the counter. Yarrow will get you that Danish while I see to the tea. It'll be just a minute while it steeps."

"Thanks." Goose seated herself on a stool near the register while Lila disappeared into the kitchen. She watched Yarrow plop pastries onto big trays and knock them into the display case like she was racking pool balls.

"So," she said. "You're Rush's cousin?"

"Yeah."

"You two close?"

"Sure." Yarrow rolled a bunch of glazed doughnut holes willy-nilly onto a tray. "We have sleepovers every other Saturday. We talk about boys, paint each other's toenails, make prank calls. It's a riot."

Goose gave herself a mental slap. *Cripes, pay attention*, she thought. She was usually better at this part of her job. Reading people, figuring out how they saw themselves and how they wanted her to see them. It was the key to a successful interview, and it was a particular strength of hers. Not that an impartial observer of the last, oh, say, twenty-four hours would know it.

"It sucks that bad, huh?"

Yarrow didn't glance up, just shifted her less-than-tender mercies to some hapless bagels. "Yes."

Goose lifted a brow. "You don't want to narrow it down at all? Specify what exactly I'm referring to before you agree that it sucks?"

"Not unless you're completely disoriented. Are you?"

"Disoriented?"

"Yes. As in unaware of your location in space and time?"

"We're on Mishkwa Island in Lake Superior," Goose offered. "Maybe five miles from the Minnesota-Canada border? It's December."

"Very good." Yarrow shoved the bagels into the case with a thud. "Now add in the fact that I'm sentenced to at least two more years here, then ask yourself if there's any portion of my life you think might *not* suck." She gave Goose a scathing glance. "Or, I'm sorry, were you trying to open a discussion as to the *level* of suckage I've achieved in various arenas? Because I could talk for a while about that, if you want."

Goose suppressed a smile. This kid might grow on her. "Two years, huh? What happens in two years?"

"I turn eighteen."

"And then?"

"And then I'm officially an adult and can get the hell out of Dodge."

"But until then?"

"Until then, I'm Grandma Lila's hired help."

"And the only teenage girl on-island?"

"You're a sharp one, Agent Smiley Face. Is that why they pay you the big bucks?"

She wants to be a victim, Goose thought. *Has been, probably.* Kids didn't grow this kind of hard, cynical shell without help. But there was something else, too. A bleak echo of something more than mere anger tucked under that tough veneer. Something that tugged at her in spite of the smart mouth and the unrelenting snark.

"Well, you know what they say." Goose smiled easily. "If you want to get rich, work for the government."

Yarrow snorted but she reached behind her for a pretty china dish and plated up a doughnut. She dropped it on the counter in front of Goose.

Goose arched a brow. "I thought I was getting the Danish."

"Cops like doughnuts."

"Do I look like a cop to you?"

Yarrow gave her a narrow once-over, from her perfectly straightened hair to the Italian leather flats she'd carried along in her backpack for indoor use. "You have

decent shoes, but otherwise? Yeah. You do. No Danish for
you, po-po."

Goose was still debating whether to be offended or
amused when the bells at the door jingled. A gust of icy
wind sliced through the pie-scented air, and she turned to
see Einar saunter into the shop, all wind-tossed curls and
behold-me-ladies smirk.

Chapter

7

"WELL, IF this isn't a vision of loveliness," he said as he helped himself to the stool beside Goose's. "Good morning, girls."

"Hey, Einar." Yarrow went back to filling the display case with a studied offhandedness that had Goose looking sharply in her direction. The kid's eyes might be elsewhere, but Goose felt her attention lock in on Einar like a lightning strike. She half expected to smell burned ozone. "You flying out this morning?"

"Yep. Any chance I can get one of those Danishes before I go?"

Yarrow plated up one of the beautifully gooey cheese Danishes Goose was starting to desire with an intensity second only to her craving for Rush. What *was* it about this place and her appetites? she wondered as Yarrow slid the pastry under Einar's nose.

"You," he announced as he closed his eyes and inhaled buttery Danish fumes, "are an angel."

Yarrow's mouth sneered but her eyes melted. "Boys." She shook her head at Goose. "They're such simple creatures."

Einar took a huge bite of Danish. Goose treated herself to a nibble of her perfectly adequate doughnut. "There's something to be said for simplicity," he mumbled happily while he chewed. Goose thought of Rush and envied Einar a desire so easily and safely sated.

He flicked his amused gaze to Goose as he touched a napkin to his lips. "So, Agent di Guzman. I imagine it's pretty clear what I'm doing here. But what brings you to the tea shop at this hour?"

Goose looked at Yarrow, who looked back with lifted brows. "Nothing much. Just, you know, grilling your entire family about your cousin's more criminal inclinations."

Einar shot a quick look at Yarrow. "I thought your parents got all the charges against you dropped."

"They did." Yarrow held his gaze, steadfastly refusing to look at Goose, though her cheeks pinked and her lips flattened. "I think Agent Smiley Face here is talking about your other cousin."

Einar turned back to Goose while she made a mental note to have a look at little Yarrow's record later. Underaged mules were a staple of the illegal import business, and just because Rush wasn't playing reindeer games on Mishkwa didn't mean nobody was.

"You're investigating *Rush*?" he asked, his eyes big and shocked.

"That's the one." She gave him a confiding smile, the kind guys like Einar ate up. She made solid eye contact, really leaned into it. "Do you have any insight you'd like to share with the Secret Service regarding the likelihood that Ranger Guthrie might be planning to stab the sitting governor with a flaming pitchfork?"

Einar was still lapping up the eye contact when Lila bustled back through the swinging door from the kitchen with a fat teapot in one hand and a cup-and-saucer combo in the other. She set the pot and the cup down on the counter and said, "Oh, for heaven's sake, Rush is *not* going to stab anybody."

"I don't know, Lila," Einar said slowly, a wicked gleam dancing in his pretty blue eyes. "He *is* trained for that kind of thing."

"And all his jokes *are* about shooting people." Yarrow tipped her head. "To be fair, though, when I say 'all his jokes,' I mean the one joke he's told since I've been on-island." She paused. "And I'm not sure he was entirely aware he was being funny, either."

"Plus, it wasn't about pitchforks." Lila swatted Yarrow's shoulder and shifted her glare to encompass Einar, too. "This is nothing to laugh about, you two. Your cousin has made tremendous progress these past eighteen months or so." She turned back to Goose. "Rush is no more dangerous than you or I."

"Except for the fact that he is." Einar shrugged at Lila's exasperated stare. "What? The guy walks around with a loaded handgun in his jacket pocket, Lila. He's constitutionally incapable of sitting with his back to the door, and he draws down on anybody who happens to catch him off guard."

"Which you delight in doing."

"Well. It's a long winter. Everybody needs a hobby." A smirk crawled across Einar's handsome face that Goose understood was meant to be charming and mischievous. The strength of her urge to slap it all the way to the mainland was a sharp reminder that her self-control wasn't what it used to be. Indulging her impulse to deliver impromptu etiquette lessons to handsome pricks was what had landed her in this pretty mess to begin with.

"You're just like your mother sometimes," Lila told him. The laughter died out of Einar's eyes with an abruptness that had Goose wondering about the accessibility of the Glock in her backpack. "A little empathy wouldn't go amiss here, Einar."

Lila turned to Goose. "Rush is a soldier, Agent di Guzman, and as such has a certain facility with the uglier aspects of this world. If we're safe enough to judge him for it, it's only because he—and men like him—have battled back the darkness to the point that the rest of us can question its existence."

"He's not a soldier anymore, though, is he?" Goose asked.

"Not by profession, no. He left the military almost two years ago."

"Why?"

"I don't know what happened exactly, but there was an incident of some sort. He wasn't physically hurt, but it damaged him all the same. He lost his way, and he came here to find it again. To heal."

Einar rolled his eyes. "Lila, please. Not the prodigal son thing again."

Lila shot him a speaking look. "He came *home*. And he's getting better." She turned to Goose. "He *is* better. Whatever you're concerned he might have done, he didn't."

"Home." Einar gave a dismissive snort. "If Mishkwa meant crap to him, he wouldn't have walked away from it when he was eighteen. He definitely wouldn't have stayed away for the next twelve years without so much as the occasional postcard. He's been back on-island for nearly two years, Lila, and you haven't gotten him to one single service." Einar shook his head. "Rush would be the first one to tell you you're giving him too much credit here."

"I give credit where it's due," Lila said softly.

An angry flush stained Einar's cheekbones. "And withhold it where it's not, is that it?"

"This isn't about you, Einar."

"I've earned your trust, Lila. I've earned my place here."

"You have," she said as Goose wondered what the hell was going on. "I don't dispute that. But I deserve your trust as well, for my experience if nothing else. And while I'm still the head of this family, you'll respect my authority."

"Even if your authority threatens the future of the family?"

She shook her head slowly. "Our financials aren't our future."

"Of course they are. This place is a gold mine, Lila, and I don't understand why you won't at least consider tapping into it."

"I'm not going to have this argument again. If you want to turn this island into a theme park, you'll have to wait until I'm dead and gone."

"I hope you're planning to kick the bucket sometime before 2024, then."

Lila drew back sharply.

"What? That's years away."

She continued to stare at him in offended silence until he held up hands. "Okay, okay. I'm sorry. It was a joke."

"And not a very good one."

"Granted. But come on, Lila. Money's important. Maybe it isn't everything, but it matters. Sooner or later, you're going to have to admit that."

She relented enough to give him a crooked smile so like Rush's that Goose stared. "Probably later rather than sooner, then."

Einar leaned over the counter to press a kiss to Lila's cheek. "Probably." He zipped up his jacket and threw a cocky grin at Goose and Yarrow. "But hey, it wouldn't be a week without our usual go-round. I'll check it off my to-do list."

"Fly safely," Lila said.

"Will do." He scooped up the half Danish still on his plate and sauntered out with the same cocky assurance he'd sauntered in with. Goose watched Lila and Yarrow as their eyes followed him out the door with patient love.

The door jingled shut and Lila turned to Goose.

"Any more questions, Agent di Guzman?"

Yeah, Goose thought. *What the hell was* that? *Also, do you know your granddaughter has a raging crush on your nephew? And, hey, did you know that nephew is harboring a raging resentment toward the other nephew? And nursing a healthy resentment toward you as well?*

And that was just off the top of her head.

But all she said was, "That'll do for now, I think. Thanks for the doughnut."

Lila blinked at her, then at Yarrow. "I thought you were going to have the cherry cheese Danish?"

Goose gave Yarrow her biggest, shiniest smile, which the girl met with a flat, brittle indifference. "I was. The doughnut went better with my shoes, though."

TWO DAYS later, Goose had chatted with every last soul on Mishkwa. She'd lost count of how many doors she'd knocked on, how many cups of tea she'd sipped and how many cookies she'd choked down under the guise of common courtesy.

Aside from that first conversation with Rush's family, the visits had fallen into a predictable pattern. Hello, badge flash, refreshments, chitchat. Nobody claimed close friendship with Rush, or even the friendship of proximity a small, isolated community normally forced, but everybody seemed fond of him.

As well they should, Goose thought as she sipped yet another cup of tea, this time with Bernie and Veronica Samuelsson. The Samuelssons ran what they claimed was the island's most popular fudge shop. Goose didn't doubt it. Both short and round, Bernie and Veronica looked like people who knew quality fudge when they saw it.

"So," Goose said as she nibbled at the half-pound slab they'd pressed on her with the requisite cup of tea, "how long has Ranger Guthrie been killing rabbits for you?"

Bernie scratched his ample stomach and squinted into the middle distance, perhaps at some mental calendar. "Started last summer, yeah, Ronnie?"

Veronica shook her head. "Spring."

Bernie turned the squint on his wife. "This or last?"

"This." She wagged her head at Goose. "Rabbits around here are just heck on gardens. And you know we do a decent mail-order fudge business in the winter, but it's our herbals that keep us afloat."

"Herbals?"

"Natural remedies. Tinctures. Dietary supplements. Teas."
She pointed her chin at the teacup on Goose's knee. Goose
lifted it for an obliging—and vaguely weedy—sip. "We
depend on those gardens. But the rabbits." Veronica pursed
her lips and her jowls waggled sorrowfully. "Merciful
heavens. Greedy little things ate a good half of everything
we put out."

"We tried everything," Bernie said. "Fences, chicken
wire, Tabasco, egg whites, little bundles of hair. Even put
out cups of beer one time."

"That was for the slugs."

"Slugs," Bernie echoed sagely. Veronica gave him a
fond smile.

"Finally we decided to trap 'em."

"The rabbits?"

Bernie laughed. "Who else? The slugs?"

Veronica chuckled, too. "Not those drunkards."

Goose forced a smile. Why not? Rush wasn't here to
judge her. "It didn't go well? The rabbit trapping?"

The Samuelssons sobered abruptly.

"No," Veronica said.

"What happened?"

"We ordered a bunch of traps—off the Internet, see?"
Bernie said. "They were supposed to be no-kill."

Veronica pressed her lips together. "You should've seen
the letter I wrote to that company. Gave them a piece of *my*
mind, I don't mind telling you."

Bernie nodded. "Ronnie does a real good poison-pen
letter. Used to do it for money in college."

"And when you discovered the traps were harming the
rabbits?"

Veronica paled and looked away. Bernie drew a breath
so deep it rattled in his lungs. "Middle of the night," he
said finally. "Sounds so awful I can't describe them. Coming from the gardens. Thought maybe some raccoons were
fighting, and I went out back to turn the hose on 'em."

"It wasn't raccoons?" Goose prompted when Bernie paused.

"No. Half-killed rabbit." Tears started in his eyes but he blinked them back. "Full moon," he said. "Plenty of light to see how the trap had broken the thing's leg near in half." He swallowed hard. "Rabbit was finishing the job with its teeth when I found it." His voice wobbled and he cleared his throat. "Should've just hit it with a shovel. Tried to, tell you the truth. Couldn't do it. Didn't have it in me to kill something that small and defenseless."

"Of course you didn't. You don't need that kind of ugliness in you." Veronica touched her husband's knee then turned her gaze on Goose. "Not when Rush has enough for everybody."

Chapter

8

"YOU THINK of Ranger Guthrie as a killer?" Goose asked carefully.

"Of course." Veronica drew back her chin until it disappeared into her ample neck. "He killed about anything that moved when he was in the army, you know."

"Navy," Goose said. She was startled to find herself talking through gritted teeth.

"Excuse me?" Veronica blinked big, bovine eyes.

"Ranger Guthrie spent twelve years in the navy, not the army," Goose said. "He was a SEAL."

"A seal?"

"Special Operations." She had an idea her face might be a little scary, so she forced it into a smile that would've had Rush in spasms. The Samuelssons seemed to appreciate the effort because they relaxed into their flowery couch again.

"Think of enlisting in the military as going to college," Goose told them. "Getting onto a Special Operations team is like going to Harvard or Yale."

"Oh." Bernie frowned as he puzzled that one over.

"And being a SEAL is like graduating from Harvard or Yale. With a Ph.D." Or two. Possibly three.

"I see." Veronica gave her a dubious look. "Be that as it may, the boy's not sentimental."

"He is, however, useful?" Goose treated her to an ice-pick smile.

"We've certainly found him so," Veronica said calmly.

"Mishkwa can't afford year-round police," Bernie told her. "We have Chief May and a couple part-time deputies for the tourist season, but Rush is the nearest thing to law enforcement we have November through April."

Veronica fixed Goose with those huge eyes again. "Taking care of us is his job," she said simply.

Goose sincerely doubted Rush's official duties included de-pesting local gardens but refrained from saying so. "And you're satisfied with his work?"

Veronica opened her mouth but Bernie laid a hand on her arm. He leaned forward, belly drooping between spread knees, his face open and sincere. "We may be a small town, Agent di Guzman, but we're not slow. We know Rush isn't obliged to trot down here with his .22 every time we call him. But he does it. He knows we can't, and he knows he can. It's a favor and we're grateful."

The burning anger inside Goose fizzled into an indignant puff. "I see." She cleared her throat. "Are you aware of his affiliation with the Radical Agrarians?"

Bernie frowned. "Is that a rock band?"

"No, a political party."

"Oh. No."

"Do you have any reason to believe Ranger Guthrie intends to harm Minnesota's sitting governor?"

Husband and wife shared a baffled look. "No."

"Have you noticed anything different about him in the last twelve months? Change in daily habits? An increase in standard of living?"

They gazed at her, nonplussed.

"Has he come into money, bought anything extravagant,

taken any vacations? Spent time gambling at any of the local casinos?"

Bernie scratched the back of his neck. "Seen him with a nice Husqvarna last week."

"Husqvarna?"

"Chain saw," Veronica supplied.

Bernie rolled his jaw side to side. "Think it belonged to the Park Service, though."

"Right. Okay." Goose flipped to a fresh sheet of paper, tapped it with her pen. "Is there anything else you'd like to tell me?"

The Samuelssons exchanged another look, one of troubled concern this time. "Um, yes," Bernie said slowly. "Maybe."

Goose looked up in polite expectation.

"You'll pass this on to Rush?"

"Not if you don't want me to." Goose had offered confidentiality to a handful of people over the past few days and had received for her trouble some bitter complaints about Rush's strict enforcement of the no-motorized-vehicle law. He was not a popular man with the snowmobile crowd.

"No, we'd like you to speak to him about this. If you would."

"Of course." Goose put her pen to her paper. "Go ahead."

"Ronnie and I hiked down to the old copper mines last weekend," Bernie said. "There's this tincture-of-pyeweed recipe we've been working on that we think might benefit from an infusion of copper—"

"The girl doesn't need our recipe, Bernie," Ronnie said. "Tell her about the—"

Bernie shot his wife a look that closed her mouth. Goose quietly revised her initial assumption regarding who did the pants wearing in the Samuelssons' house. "Let's just say that we saw evidence of activity while we were there."

"What sort of activity?"

"Been a warm fall. Ferry's running late this year, which means it's likely just mainlanders. High school kids doing what high school kids have always done." Veronica shrugged.

"But somebody official needs to check it out. Post some signs or something."

"We'd just hate for somebody to get hurt," Bernie said. "Kids are so impulsive, and they get into stuff they have no idea how to control. If you could just, I don't know." He spread his hands. "Have Rush look into it?"

"I'll tell him."

THE NEXT morning, before the sun was even a wish on the eastern horizon, Rush knocked on Goose's door.

"Rise and shine, di Guzman. Time to get hiking."

A noise emanated from behind the closed door, the creak of rusty metal mingled with the groans of a person jerked rudely from a sound sleep. Rush buried his grin in a cup of coffee and knocked again. Louder this time.

"Come on, sunshine. Time to make hay."

The door under his knuckles opened a bare inch, and Goose squinted through the crack with one eye. "What time is it?"

"Early."

"Too early for hiking, for sure."

"Never too early for hiking."

"Says who?"

"Me. And I'm the authority on such things in these parts."

"Fine. Have a nice one."

The door clicked shut and Rush heard rusty metal shriek as she presumably crawled back into her cot.

He knocked again. "Do I need to come in there?"

Say yes. She didn't.

There was another chorus of cot springs and the door cracked open again. The eye returned, less squinty this time, more irritated. "Forgive me," she said, her voice overly calm. "I had the impression you preferred to work alone."

"Normally I do." He took a leisurely sip of his coffee. "But I find myself strangely desirous of company this morning."

That one dark eye narrowed sharply, sending a stab of warm interest through his gut. It utterly charmed him, the way her native crankiness defeated that sleek exterior sometimes.

"Is that so?"

"It is." He stared her down. "I also prefer not to waste my time taking reports on, then chasing down, frivolous if not completely fabricated incidents that people dream up in lieu of anything better to do." He gave her a pointed look. "It appears that we may not always get what we want."

"Tell me about it," she muttered.

Rush wondered abruptly what had really brought her all the way to Mishkwa. Because if an agent with Goose's polished smile and fierce intelligence was really chasing down flaming pitchforks near the Canadian border, Rush would eat his proverbial hat.

"Come on," he said. "Mishkwa at dawn isn't something you want to miss."

"Oh, but I do." She fixed him with that baleful eye. "I really, really do."

He sighed. "Are you going to make me pull rank?"

"What, it's against the law to refuse a predawn hike on this island?"

"It is when you're the reason I have to take the hike in the first place."

She treated him to an icy silence. He had to hide another smile in his coffee cup.

"You have to admit, you collected quite a list of random chores for me while chatting up my friends and neighbors."

"I don't know, Rush. I think the moose with the Dumpster fixation is pretty obviously a public safety concern."

"Yeah? And what about Lila's compost? Is outlining the correct manner in which to rot your food scraps compelling police work? And the Whitfords' dreadful habit of keeping their trash barrel out front instead of around back? Mary Beth Swinton's refusal to invest in shades? Or, good Lord, Hal Donavan's tardy sidewalk shoveling? Heaven protect us from the peril of these lawbreakers."

She sighed. "Don't forget the Samuelssons' high school partiers."

"That, Agent Make Work, is where we're starting."

The tiny slice of mouth he could see curled into what he suspected was a terrible scowl. The urge to kiss it was almost unbearable. His first taste of her lips the other day had been brief but viciously potent. Addiction, he realized, wasn't out of the question.

"Get dressed," he said. "We leave in five minutes."

Her eye drifted south to his coffee cup. "Is there more of that in the kitchen?"

He smiled and treated himself to a sip. "Nope."

"Aw."

SAY WHAT you would about rustic accommodations, Goose thought ten deliciously steamy minutes later. Rush's hot-water heater was a champ. A thing of beauty. A joy forever. A stern rebuke to the pansy-assed appliance posing as a water heater back in her Minneapolis condo.

She pulled the towel from her head, wiped a clear space into the foggy bathroom mirror and gave her reflection a critical once-over. Same face as always. Long and angular. Strong cheekbones. Pointed chin. Quizzical, slanting eyebrows.

Decent raw materials, she supposed. Decent enough to produce—with the application of time, effort and a lot of good cosmetics—the illusion of beauty.

Her mouth, though. She allowed herself a frown in the privacy of the bathroom. Her mouth was an off-note in an otherwise mannerly symphony. Full rather than fine, inclined to bray out great barks of laughter rather than silver bell chuckles, it was a Botticelli mouth in a Picasso face. Slicking it the deep red of ripe cherries helped, though. Civilized it a little while owning—maybe even playing up—the basic sexuality of it. Not ideal but she made it work.

Her hair was a different story. It sprang directly—stubbornly—from that same dangerous wellspring of unruly desire that ran through her character. That wild propensity to want that Rush spoke to so unexpectedly and mercilessly.

It tumbled dark and tangled to her collarbones, where, if left to its own devices, it would dry into a riot of fat, touch-me curls that didn't suggest innocent exuberance so much as recent hot sex. The rest of her features could be interpreted through a civilized lens, but her hair was her scarlet letter. Keeping it under control required daily, intensive intervention. Especially with temptation so near at hand and Rush's stubborn unwillingness to help her defuse it.

She picked up a thermal flat brush, plugged in a professional-grade blow-dryer and prayed that Rush's wiring was as accommodating as his hot-water heater.

RUSH PUT his cooling coffee into the microwave, clicked the door shut and punched the quick-minute button. The cottage plunged into darkness, and all the friendly morning sounds—the burble of the coffeemaker, the hum of the microwave, the blast of Goose's blow-dryer behind the bathroom door—dwindled into a sudden, electricity-free silence.

"Rush!" The bathroom door slapped open and he cursed the predawn darkness. If this had happened an hour from now—even half an hour—he might have caught a glimpse of Goose in nothing but a towel. A sight well worth seeing if that brief, blessed moment he'd spent with his hand up her shirt a few days back was anything to go on. But sons of Norwegian fisher folk did not sleep in, so here he was, faced with nothing but a vague shadow.

"What happened?" she asked, her voice tight. Anxious. Was this laughing, polished woman afraid of the dark?

"Blew a fuse, probably." Rush reached for the flashlight he kept in the cupboard for just such emergencies. Norwegian fisher folk did not believe in unpreparedness any more than they believed in sleeping in. He flicked it on and beamed it toward the bathroom.

She stood there, hair dark and clinging to her neck like

tangled vines, fists twisted between her breasts into the
towel that swathed her from shoulders to knees. His towel,
he realized. Desire was a swift clench in his stomach as
he took in the long, clean lines of her limbs, the way her
collarbones spread like delicate wings from the vulnerable
hollow at the base of her throat.

"Can you fix it?" she asked.

"Fix what?" He had the insane urge to lick that shallow
dent. Just put his tongue right there against all the warm
silk of her skin. Would it taste as sweet as her mouth had?
he wondered. Could anything possibly taste that good?
Even her skin?

There was really only one way to find out.

"The fuse."

The fuse? Oh, the fuse.

He took a step toward her. "You in a hurry all of a
sudden?"

She edged behind the door. "I'm cold."

"Heat's from the woodstove." He swung the flashlight to
the ancient iron stove squatting in the corner of the living
room. She followed the beam and he moved closer while
she was distracted. She smelled like cloves and rosemary
and warm water. Spicy and clean and somehow . . . green.
Fresh. He wondered if it was her shampoo, her soap or just
the scent God had given her.

Need opened inside him, raw and urgent, flaying him
with sharp imperatives. Without the armor of her perfect
hair and makeup, she didn't just appeal to him. She *sang* to
him. He wanted to snatch her up, lay her down, mark her as
his. He wanted to dip his fingers, his tongue, himself, into
all her secret fragrant places until he wore her scent as easily as she did. Until she wore his. Until even the greediest
of interlopers would concede that this territory was taken.
Held. Cherished.

"I need to dry my hair," she said.

Rush smiled. "Come on and sit by the stove, then. It'll
be dry before you—"

"I need to blow it dry."

"Why? Come on, Goose, this is Mishkwa. Nobody's looking at your hair. And even if they were, it looks fine. *You* look fine." God, *fine*? She had him half insane with lust and the best he could come up with was *fine*? He cleared his throat. "Better than fine, okay? You look—"

Delicious, he was going to say. That was a good word, and perfect for the primitive churn of hunger she'd touched off inside him with that kiss of hers the other day. She *was* delicious. Edible. Snackable. Any word that involved his mouth and her person would do.

"Rush." The thin anxiety in her voice, a near desperation, pierced the haze of desire and Rush stopped. "Will you please fix the fuse?"

He studied her, from her huge eyes to her bare feet. "This isn't about a hair dryer," he said. "You wouldn't panic over a stupid thing like that. You're afraid."

"Afraid?" She huffed out a little laugh.

"Yeah. Terrified."

"Rush, please. What would I be afraid of?" But she shivered as she said it, a fine trembling that started in her center and moved outward until it claimed her all the way out to her fingers. Rush put a savage rein on the desire riding him, on the curiosity biting at him with sharp little teeth, and turned away.

"Two minutes," he said between his teeth.

Chapter

9

GOOSE EMERGED from the bathroom fifteen minutes later to find Rush pacing the cabin like a mountain lion flying coach.

"Feeling better?" he asked, his pale gaze touching everything from her newly smoothed hair to her ugly wool socks.

She touched her head furtively, but her native ringlets remained utterly straight, perfectly obedient. "You have no idea," she said.

"I really don't, no."

She ignored the implied invitation to explain herself. Hair dryers and blown fuses didn't begin to cover the kind of danger those curls represented.

"So," she said. "How far to the old mine?"

He studied her for a long moment. Deliberating, she'd guess, whether or not to let her off the hook. How far did that honesty thing go, anyway? Did omission count? Or did it apply only to actual statements?

"Five miles," he said finally.

Relief loosened her stiff shoulders. "Nice day for it. I'll be ready after breakfast."

"Breakfast?"

"Sure. You know, food in the A.M.?"

He glanced pointedly at his coffee cup. "Breakfast of champions," he said. "You can have a travel mug. Now let's—"

She gave him a pity-filled look. "I sincerely don't know how you expect to intimidate a grizzly bear or whatever it is you have out here—"

"Moose."

"—moose then, on an empty stomach." She squatted in front of the lopsided cabinets under the little counter and found an ancient container of Quaker Oats. A quick rummage in the freezer produced a packet of frozen blueberries.

"Skipping breakfast isn't healthy," she said, throwing a couple handfuls of oats into two bowls, adding water and tossing them into the microwave.

"I don't think a moose takes my eating habits into account when he decides whether or not to charge."

She lifted her shoulders and retrieved the bowls from the microwave. "We aren't all naturally terrifying, Rush," she told him, sprinkling both bowls with the frozen blueberries. She dug out a couple spoons, pushed one bowl across the counter to him and sat down with hers. "Some of us need fortification before a five-mile hike in the frigid, moose-strewn wilderness."

"You think I'm terrifying." He peeled off his navy fleece pullover and hung it up, apparently having given up on shoving her out the door without sustenance. The long-sleeved thermal he wore underneath gave Goose her first good look at his body, and the breath left her with an audible *whoosh*.

Her first impression back at Lila's had been dead-on. The guy was built like one of those Kenyan marathoners— all bone and sinew and long, efficient muscle. Put that kind of physical purity together with the brutal edges and planes of his face, and a girl would have to be dead or blind not to appreciate the view. And Goose, sadly, was neither.

She touched her ruler-straight hair one more time. A reminder. A promise. A warning.

He yanked out the stool opposite hers and started eating with that methodical, food-is-fuel efficiency.

"Yes," she said. "I find you utterly terrifying." She took a perverse satisfaction in knowing she spoke the complete, vile, unpalatable truth, though she'd be damned if she'd tell him why. "I'm not scared to admit it, either. No need to fish for compliments."

He paused, his spoon halfway to his mouth. "I do *not* fish for compliments."

"Of course not," she said serenely. He glared at her and she concentrated on looking innocent. "If a moose does charge, however, I expect you to behave heroically."

"Oh, indubitably," he said, his tone acid. But that twitch at the corner of his mouth gave him away. He wanted to smile, she knew it. And that didn't surprise her so much as how badly she wanted to make him do it.

"So long as we're on the same page."

"Eat, Goose."

"Eating."

TWO AND half hours of hard hiking later, Rush was hoarse from unaccustomed conversation. Not that he was doing all that much talking, comparatively. A lot for him, yeah. But Goose? Damn. She was some kind of one-woman word factory—full of nonstop questions, comments, thoughts, wonderings.

Normally, Rush didn't care for talkers. Air this pristine? This unequivocal? All words did was junk it up until there wasn't a moment of peace or silence anywhere.

But somehow, Goose didn't. Maybe it was her voice—a wonder, now that he considered it, of amused musicality—or the fact that her questions were good ones, her observations razor sharp. But she'd been talking nonstop for the better part of two hours, and while Rush was a little hoarse from the effort to keep up, he wasn't bored. Or irritated.

Interesting.

They crested the last rise and started down a steep incline toward the section of the island known as Copper Beach.

"So," Goose said. "At the risk of stating the obvious, can I assume they were mining copper here?"

"Yeah." Rush pointed at a handful of shallow basins dotting the landscape between the peak of the hill and the rocky beach. "See those small depressions? Look like frozen lakes?"

Goose squinted against the glare of the morning sun bouncing off the snow. "Sure. Four—no, five of them?"

"Right. Indians found copper here originally and mined the basins by hand. Then the white man came and sank actual mine shafts. Never got anything worth mentioning out of them, but there are five or six scattered around the island. Only one of them is really attractive to teenage daredevils with illegal alcohol, though."

"That's the one where we're headed?"

"A-plus for detective work."

The trail steepened abruptly and conversation stopped while they gave it their complete attention for a few minutes. Eventually they stopped in front of the yawning black eye of an abandoned shaft. There was no sign of human activity that Rush could see, but they'd gotten a good couple feet of fresh snow since the Samuelssons had reported being here.

"We'll have to go inside," Rush said.

Goose eyed the frozen tunnel drilled into the hillside with distrust. "We will?"

"If we want to find out if there's been a recent party here, we will."

She frowned at the sagging beam capping the entrance, the rusty "No Trespassing" signs, the newer signs warning of certain death and/or dismemberment, along with the fact that the Park Service was in no way liable for any injury sustained by those boneheaded enough to proceed beyond this point.

Rush dug a headlamp out of his backpack, slipped it on and said, "Stick close."

"Yeah, don't worry about that." Her voice was immediately no more than two inches from his shoulder. He smiled into his coat collar and led her into the main shaft, her breath a warm puff he only imagined he could feel against his sleeve. A thick darkness engulfed them as they made their way into the shaft. It extended maybe fifteen, twenty yards into the side of the hill then opened into a low, round room. Rush swung his beam across the dirt floors and found them empty. Completely empty. No beer bottles, no bottle caps, no gum wrappers, no trash. No footprints. Not of the two-legged *or* the four-legged variety, which was strange, considering what opportunists wild animals were when it came to decent housing.

But there *was* something. Something that sent a shot of dismay straight into his gut. A flat rock sat in the dead center of the little round room, maybe two feet high, two wide, six or seven long. That wasn't the problem, though. No telling how a rock that size had gotten there, but it had been sitting in that exact same spot for generations as far as Rush knew. No, what bugged him was the bowl sitting neatly on top of the stone table. Now that *was* new. Shit.

"What the heck?" Curiosity overcame her nerves and Goose stepped away from his elbow toward the rock. "Is that a bowl? There on the coffee table?"

Rush had to admit, the rock did look sort of like a coffee table. It was low and oblong, with a carved stone bowl sitting on it as if Fred Flintstone had abandoned his salsa a couple thousand years ago. She moved toward it and Rush stepped forward.

"Don't touch it."

She sidestepped him and peered into the bowl. Then she reached up, grabbed his headlamp and aimed it the same way. "There's something in here," she said.

I'll bet, Rush thought.

"Looks like blood. Dried, I guess. Or frozen. Ick."

"It's nothing," Rush said. But it was a lie. It was definitely something, but not a something he was planning to discuss with Goose. "Animal blood probably."

Goose stared at him, and even half blinded by his own headlamp, he could see her arch a skeptical eyebrow. "What, some raccoon cut himself shaving and happened to bleed into this handy bowl?"

"Listen, I told you, it's nothing—"

She reached into her own pack—damn Ben Barnes—and pulled out what Rush assumed was a field kit of some sort. She unearthed a razor blade, a cotton swab and a Ziploc and proceeded to take a sample of whatever the hell was in the bowl. Then she tucked her kit back into her pack, hefted it onto her shoulders and squinted up at him, cheerful in victory.

"Okay," she said. "What's next on that honey-do list of yours?"

Rush scowled at her and adjusted his headlamp until they could both see again. "Einar's chickens."

"Excuse me?"

"The chickens," he said. "Einar's."

"Einar keeps chickens?"

"Yes."

"And you need to see them?"

"Feed them."

"Why doesn't he feed his own chickens?"

"He's out of town, remember?"

"Oh. Right."

He headed for the rectangle of blue sky and leaden waters that marked the mouth of the mine. Goose hovered at his elbow, so close he could practically hear her thinking. Close enough to feel the warmth from her breath, for sure, which screwed—in an increasingly predictable way—with his thinking.

Which was a problem. Because given what he and Goose had just stumbled across, he had some serious thinking to do.

And somebody on the island had some serious explaining to do.

She blinked as they emerged into the brilliant light of midmorning, those straight, dark brows drawn together while that quick brain of hers churned. She opened her mouth, and he braced himself. He really, really didn't want to get into what they'd just discovered.

"Einar keeps *chickens*?" she asked, nose wrinkled in puzzlement. "Really?"

He laughed, though whether from amusement or relief he didn't know. "Really."

EINAR'S CABIN crouched low and gray in a rocky wrinkle on the opposite side of the island from the mines. It clung to the earth with a crooked, white-knuckled grip produced by decades of wind-whipped water. It wouldn't win any beauty contests, but it wasn't going anywhere, either. Not now, not ever.

Goose squinted at it, tried to square the shabby utility of the building with the flash and dazzle of Einar himself.

"How far are we from South Harbor?" she asked, lifting her voice above the rhythmic shush of their snowshoes.

"It's just around the point there," Rush said, jerking his chin at a sharp jut of rock fighting with the swirling water straight ahead of them. "Five minutes by boat, fifteen by foot."

"Nice," Goose said.

"Grandpa was no fool. He built close enough for convenience but far enough that he didn't have to greet—or unload—every boat that docked."

Goose blinked. "This was your grandfather's house?"

"Sure." He kicked free of his snowshoes as they approached the cabin. She could see tarpaper between the drooping shingles as Rush propped his snowshoes against the wall. "Einar could keep it up a little better, but when Grandpa built something it didn't come down." He frowned out at the lake. "Not accidentally, anyway."

Goose kicked out of her snowshoes, too. She followed Rush as he rounded the corner of the cabin. The tiny

backyard sported an equally dilapidated shed of some sort
that Goose assumed had to be the chicken coop. There was
also a plastic-covered arch maybe ten yards long, six feet
wide. It was a bit taller than Rush, and insulated on either
side by a long row of stacked hay bales. Chicken wire and
vinyl sheeting capped both ends.

"Now I know your grandpa didn't build that," she said,
nodding toward the hay-bale structure. It looked like it
would come down in a stiff wind. "Is it a greenhouse?"

"Nope. That's the chicken coop."

"The chicken coop?" Goose looked back at the shed.
"Then what's that?"

"That's the slaughterhouse."

"Oh."

"It's not pretty but it's up to code."

"Don't tell me you're the island's health inspector, too?"

"No," he said as he shouldered open the cabin's back
door. "I helped Einar convert it when he decided to raise
chickens, that's all."

She considered that as she followed him into a minis-
cule galley kitchen. "You helped him? Or you turned his
nasty old shed into a legitimate slaughterhouse while he
walked around with his shirt off in case any ladies happened by?"

He chuckled as he wrestled the lid off an old-fashioned
metal trash can inside the pantry. "Some of both, I guess."
He dipped a plastic bucket into the can and came up with
a scoop of chicken feed. He filled a second bucket and
headed for the chicken coop. Goose followed.

The plastic arch was maybe six feet wide, and just high
enough for a tall man to walk under without stooping. A
complicated arrangement of chicken wire, plastic sheeting and two-by-fours spanned the butt end of the arch, and
Rush untwisted a series of wires that allowed him to swing
it open like a gate. He held it open and waved for her to
precede him.

"You're kidding, right?"

"Come on, di Guzman. You're letting the cold air in."

Goose gave him a look that promised retribution should this be some kind of elaborate practical joke, then stepped under the PVC arch supporting the plastic sheeting.

The air was close and surprisingly warm, thick with the distinct but not unpleasant odor of living things. Light filtered in through the sheeting, watery and gray, and Goose realized that rows of hay bales lined the interior walls of the coop as well as the exterior. Chickens of all sizes, shapes and colors roosted by the dozens on long poles suspended horizontally above each row of hay bales, facing each other across the narrow walkway that bisected the space. Not, Goose thought, that anybody could actually walk on the eight inches of wood shavings littering the floor.

The birds all swung blank chickeny eyes toward the source of the draft—toward her—and Goose tensed. In terms of decent ways to die, getting pecked to death by angry fowl wasn't exactly taking a bullet for the president. But the chickens only whirred and chucked and snicked to each other, supremely unconcerned by her unannounced arrival.

Then they saw Rush.

Chapter

10

MORE ACCURATELY, Goose supposed, they saw the feed buckets dangling from his hands.

Chickens exploded off their roosts as if catapulted and screeched through the air toward her like fat, feathery hand grenades. Goose squealed—a shameful, girlie noise—and threw her hands over her head. She dropped into a crouch on the wood shavings and braced for impact.

It took two hard thuds of her heart to realize that she wasn't dead yet, her eyes pecked out by savage poultry. She risked a peek through her arms in time to see that Rush—good, strong, *wise* Rush—had heaved the feed buckets over her head to the far end of the coop.

The chickens, in an unexpected feat of aerial dexterity, reversed direction en masse to land in a squawking, scrabbling pile in and around the buckets. Within seconds, the coop was once again filled with the soothing chirr of fluffed feathers and placid birds.

"What," Goose managed, "was *that*?"

"Feeding time," Rush said, climbing up to sit on a hay

bale. He shrugged out of his backpack, unzipped it and offered Goose a bottle of water. "Better hydrate," he said. "We've been hiking all day."

Goose accepted the bottle and climbed up on the hay to sit beside him. Her knees were a little wobbly still. "Is it always like that?"

"You get used to it."

They drank in silence for a minute or two while Goose turned a fascinated eye on her surroundings. Finally she said, "There must be four dozen chickens in here."

"Easy. More like five or six."

"So between the hay and the body heat, it stays pretty warm. I get that part. But how is it that this place doesn't stink to the high heavens? I mean, I'm no farm girl, but even I know chicken shit stinks."

"Einar's a deep litter man."

"Yeah. I got that." Goose eyed the thick blanket of wood shavings on the floor. "But deep litter usually equals deep odor."

"No, deep litter is a method of coop maintenance. It means you just throw down another few inches of pine shavings every time it starts to stink, sprinkle it with a chemical that dries the shit faster, and basically let the coop compost itself. Which, in one of those neat little synergistic things farmers are so good at, generates yet more heat."

"Huh." Goose was impressed despite herself. "Einar's a good farmer?"

"Einar's a lazy farmer." He smiled without malice. "In this instance, it happens to work."

They drank in companionable silence for a minute or two more.

"So," Rush said eventually. "How's the investigation going?"

She cast him a sidelong look. "You mean have I decided whether or not you're a stone-cold assassin yet?"

He didn't smile. "You've read my file, Goose," he said quietly. "You know what I am."

Something bleak and terrible moved through his eyes,

a profound aloneness that tore at her heart. Warning bells sounded in her head—do *not* touch this man!—but she slipped her gloved hand into his anyway. Screw danger. When a man this strong hurt, decent women comforted.

"I do know what you are," she said. "But more importantly, I know what you're not."

"What am I not?"

"You're not an attention whore, and you're not a coward. Men who make threats—particularly big, grandiose threats like stabbing people with flaming pitchforks—are inevitably both."

He dropped his eyes to their linked fingers, then looked back at her. What she saw now in those silver eyes stopped the breath in her lungs. "So I'm in the clear?"

She didn't pull her hand away. "Looks like."

"On the pitchfork thing, anyway. What about the other?"

She did pull her hand back this time, and stared. "The other?"

"You don't expect me to believe the Secret Service wastes personnel like you on flaming pitchforks, do you? I know you're looking at me for something else."

"Am I?"

He lifted his hand, traced a finger down the line of her cheek. He came up with a piece of straw from the ends of her hair and flicked it away. Goose didn't breathe the entire time.

"A girl doesn't kiss a stranger like you kissed me unless she's looking for something."

"Ah. And what was I looking for?"

"Hell if I know." He cocked a brow, leaned in. "You want to have another go at kissing it out of me?"

Because *yes* churned in her gut, she forced a smile. "Ah, no," she said. "Thanks, though."

He shrugged, lifted his water bottle to his lips. "Your call. But if you're not going to interrogate me the fun way, maybe you should just ask."

"Ask what?"

"Whatever it is you want to know."

But she didn't need to ask. Not really. Rush was no counterfeiter, and he was no smuggler. She knew that. He was too real, too good. Too absolutely, brutally *honest*. He said he was a killer, but he wasn't. He was a soldier. Goose knew the difference even if he didn't. Laws, rules, order—they meant something to Rush. Meant everything.

"You in a hurry, Rush?"

His eyes dropped to her mouth. "Yes."

Heat bloomed, rich and sultry, inside her. She breathed through the first, overpowering wave of it, then forced it into the deepest corner of her consciousness.

"Easy, slugger. We're just going to talk."

"Talk, then," he said with a focused intensity that had Goose pausing to gather herself. Sheesh. This guy went to her head like hard liquor. She had to think. Tread carefully. Everybody on this island had some connection to Rush, and if there was one thing Goose knew without question, it was that Rush honored his connections. One way or another every single one of these people—his neighbors, his employers, his family—fell under the considerable umbrella of his responsibility and authority.

Most of them returned the regard. Or seemed to. But appearances, as Goose knew only too well, were malleable. The exterior had no responsibility to reflect the interior, and somebody on Mishkwa had perfected the art of smiling betrayal. Because that would be how Rush saw it. It wouldn't be about the money to him, but about the deception. About dirtying his home with greed. About breaking the law when it was Rush's responsibility to uphold it.

She cast around for a neutral topic to start with. "This is your ancestral home, huh? Handed down from your grandfather?"

"Yeah. It's the only privately held property within the park borders."

"Were you born here? On Mishkwa?"

"Yep."

"What kind of name is Rush, anyway? The predominant ethnicity up here seems to be Swedish and Norwegian.

Shouldn't you be a Sven or an Ole or a Soren or something? How'd you end up named after an eighties hair band?"

"Your mom delivers you in a fishing boat six weeks early, you get named Rush."

"Whoa." Goose blinked. "Your mom sounds like some woman."

"She was."

"Where are your folks now?"

"Dead."

"I'm sorry."

"It was a long time ago."

"Still."

He accepted the sympathy of a genuine smile, squeezed her fingers in reply. Warmth crawled into her chest, knelt down alongside the dangerous throb of banked desire. She cleared her throat.

"Were they commercial fishers, your folks?"

"Yeah. It was a family business. My grandfather held one of the original fishing claims on Mishkwa. My mom was his middle daughter; she and her husband—my dad—fished with Grandpa every summer. His oldest daughter—that would be Lila—ran the house. His youngest daughter—Gerte—ran wild. I don't know much about her, other than that she came back to the island only once after she left. Pregnant, alone. She delivered Einar here. He's two months younger than I am, in case you were wondering."

"And the father?"

"She never said anything about him. To hear Lila tell it, one day she was here, the next she was gone."

"She abandoned her baby?"

"She left him with her family. My folks took him in and raised him like he was my brother. Is that abandonment?"

She conceded the point with an inclination of her head and he went on. "My folks had built a cabin on a claim down the shore from Grandpa's when they married. Earliest thing I can remember is untangling fishing nets in the boat shed. By the time we were eight, Einar and I were fishing alongside Grandpa and Dad every summer."

"And in the winter?"

"Grandpa and Lila stayed here on the island. We—my folks and Einar and I—wintered over in Hornby Harbor on the mainland. Went to school."

Goose smiled at the way he said "school." Like somebody else might say "prison" or "hell." "Must've been tough on a kid like you to spend six, seven hours a day cooped up in the classroom."

He twitched a shoulder. "I survived. Well enough to graduate."

"And then you came back here?"

"No. By that time the fishing had gone to crap and the Park Service had taken over the island. Decided to lure in the tourists by returning it to a pristine wilderness condition."

"That sounds ominous."

"Anybody who squatted on the island, didn't own their property, was booted off outright, their cabins burned to the ground."

"Hurrying up nature's triumphant return?"

"Exactly."

"But your parents owned their land?"

"No."

Goose closed her eyes. "They burned your house down?"

"Yep."

"God. I'm sorry."

"Einar and I watched from Grandpa's dock."

"He owned his land?"

"Yeah. Landowners got a slightly better deal. They were allowed to keep their property and their fishing rights, but only if somebody kept their primary residence on the island year-round and fished commercially at least three months a year."

"Which would be, what, approximately nobody?"

"Nobody but Einar. Grandpa died that summer, and Einar moved into this cabin. Summers, he fishes just enough to satisfy the letter of the law. Keeps the restaurant down in South Harbor in lake trout a couple times a month."

"Why Einar and not you?"

Rush shrugged. "I didn't want to fish. Not when I was eighteen and ready to take on the world."

"And Einar did?"

"Want to fish? No."

"Then why wouldn't he just sell the land to the Park Service?"

He rolled a single shoulder. "It's his home."

"It's your home, too. You left."

"Eighteen's not quite old enough to be sentimental about the ancestral home, I guess."

"And yet Einar was?"

He locked his eyes on hers, and she felt it all the way to her toes. "What are you asking, Goose?"

"Not asking anything," she said. "Just thinking."

"About?"

"About what happens to a child when his mother abandons him. Seems like a kid's self-esteem might take a hit. Might have some trouble belonging."

"He was taken in by family."

"But by necessity, not by choice. And in a tiny community where everybody knew it, too." She shook her head. "Tough on a kid's self-worth, I'll bet."

Rush regarded her steadily over their joined hands, and she stepped carefully because she knew this was dangerous ground.

"And if that wasn't enough to shake a kid's foundation," she continued, "then the government comes along and tosses his *family*"—she purposely emphasized the word— "off its land and burns down what little claim to a home he has. Call me crazy but I think it's enough to turn a normal person into an antigovernment gun nut with revenge fantasies."

"Nice analysis." Rush lifted his water bottle, took a long pull. "Psych degree, I assume?"

She stiffened. "Criminal psychology, yeah. Minor in family counseling."

"It shows. Only one little fly in the ointment."

"Yeah? What's that?"

"Einar doesn't want to stab anybody with a flaming pitchfork, either. He's too lazy."

"I'm not talking about pitchforks anymore, Rush."

"I know. You're talking about something else. Something you haven't trusted me with yet but are comfortable accusing my cousin of."

"I'm not accusing anybody of anything. I'm just . . . it's complicated, okay? I'm thinking out loud."

"So let me help." He took her other hand, turned her to face him, to face those brutal, honest eyes. "Tell me what we're fighting here, and I'll put my back against yours and we'll figure it out. Or tell me to back off and get lost if you don't want me or my help. I'm a big boy; I can take no for an answer. But I'm interested, Goose. In you. All of you. The yes or no is up to you, but do me a favor and make an honest decision. Don't leave this hanging between us like an excuse."

His words thudded into the vulnerable center of her, drove themselves into her like splinters or maybe roots. Anchored themselves there and made her want to rock or howl or rage or sing. They made her want, period. She closed her eyes for a long moment, struggled to get what was in her under control.

"Rush," she said on a shaky exhale. "You're so honest and you're so brave, it shames me. I'm not good like that. Like you. But I'm doing my best here."

"It's enough," he said, twining his fingers into hers, dragging her closer. "Whatever you are, it's enough for me."

She let him hold her for a moment then gently pulled free. "It's not," she said. "I'm not. Trust me on that. But what I will be is honest. As honest as I can be."

"Then tell me you feel this, too," he said. He didn't try to touch her again, but pinned her with his eyes. "Tell me you feel what I feel. In your gut. In your bones."

She loosed a hoarse chuckle. "That doesn't begin to cover where I feel you, Rush."

He nodded once, hard. "Okay. Okay, then. That much'll

do. For now. Because I *will* push for the rest." The smile that grew on his mouth was sleek, predatory, beautiful. "Fair warning."

She pressed a hand to her stomach, where she could, indeed, feel him. "Great. Thanks."

"Now," he said. He handed her a water bottle. "Tell me the rest."

Chapter

11

BY MIDMORNING the next day, the weather had done one of those capricious early-winter one-eighties. The sun hung low and golden in a lazy blue sky, snow melted from the fir branches with wet, cheerful plops and Goose, snow-shoeing behind Rush in winter wear rated to sixty below, was sweating like a fat guy at a disco.

"Hey, hold up a minute, will you?" she called to Rush. He stopped reluctantly on the soggy trail ahead of her. Goose stripped off her outer shell and looped it through the straps of her backpack. The cool breeze cut through her fleece underjacket and felt like heaven.

"Ha," she said. "*So* much better." She jogged forward until she was level with Rush's stiff shoulders and poked his elbow through his shell. "Dude. Aren't you hot?" She squinted into the unexpectedly strong sun. "It's got to be in the forties."

"Fifties."

"Nice," she said. "Does it warm up like this a lot in December? Some weird lake-effect thing?"

"Not usually." He jerked his chin at her jacket. "You ready?"

She sighed and fell in behind him, trotting in the prints of his snowshoes. "You're angry."

"Yeah. I am."

"With me?"

"With the situation."

She sighed again. She'd known he would take this hard and had hoped forcing him to take a night to think on the situation would cool him off. And it had. Boy, had it. The heat of his anger had cooled all the way down to the icy, purposeful drive now propelling him along the trail toward South Harbor at a near sprint.

"Rush, I know this is your home and you feel betrayed, but it's nothing personal. To this person—whoever it is—I guarantee you, it's just about the money."

"It's more than that."

"No, Rush, it isn't. It's—"

"I'm going to show you something," he said. "Something most mainlanders don't know about. Something that'll make you understand. This is about way more than money."

"What?" She jogged to catch up, grabbed his sleeve. "What are you going to show me?"

He gave her a flat, silver glance. "You'll see."

Ten minutes later, they were pushing through the shiny red door of Mother Lila's Tea Shop.

"The sign said closed," Goose pointed out as sleigh bells announced their arrival. "Shouldn't we at least knock?"

"Doesn't smell closed," Rush said, and Goose had to admit he was right. Gingerbread and cinnamon hung in the moist, warm air as usual and bold sunshine spilled across the wooden floors.

"Upstairs!" Lila's voice drifted through the door behind the counter leading to the private spaces of the house.

Goose followed Rush through the door and into the kitchen. It had obviously been retrofitted to meet commercial standards—stainless-steel countertops gleamed, a tiny industrial-strength dishwasher squatted in one corner and

refrigerators and freezers with temperature gauges built
into the doors sidled side by side like a pair of muscle-
bound bouncers near the door.

In spite of the high-tech makeover, though, it still felt
like a kitchen Lila might live and work in. Potted plants
marched across the sill, while a filmy set of honey-colored
curtains made the most out of whatever sun found its way
into north-facing windows. Terra-cotta tiles the color of
freshly baked bread marched across the floor at a diagonal,
the center taken up by a geometric mosaic. The jagged,
inlaid pieces didn't render a picture so much as suggest
one. Goose had to squint hard before she decided it was a
stag in front of a full moon.

"Lila?" Rush called.

"Up here."

Goose turned to find a pretty circular staircase in black
wrought iron tucked into the corner. Rush waved at it.
"After you," he said.

"What are we doing here?" she whispered, threading
her way carefully up the tiny, wedge-shaped steps.

"You'll see."

They emerged a moment later into a sitting room that
made Goose want to toe off her shoes and have a cup of tea.
And she didn't even like tea.

The wooden floors shone like spilled maple syrup, the
gleam broken up by the warm expanse of a blue-and-gold
woolen rug. A fire snapped in the pretty hearth that took up
most of the far wall, while two dormered windows fram-
ing breathtaking views of the lake occupied the adjoining
wall. Built-in bookshelves ran above, beside and between
the windows, while a thickly cushioned bench ran beneath.
Plants hung from the ceiling in front of the glass, bushy
with the kind of good health that Goose had only ever seen
in magazines.

"Hello, dear," Lila said, rising from the window seat.
She padded across the floor on bare feet and took Rush's
hands in hers. "Blessed be."

She turned to Goose and held out her hands. Goose took

them automatically and received kisses on both cheeks with surprised pleasure. "Blessed be, dear."

"Ah . . . same to you," Goose said.

Lila indicated a little love seat facing the bench and curled into her sunny window seat again, feet tucked neatly under her like a cat. Goose and Rush sat. It was a tight squeeze for two tall people, and the hard press of Rush's thigh against hers sent a hot spark of awareness dancing in her stomach.

"Something's happened," Lila said, reaching for a delicate china teapot on the low table between them.

"Are you asking me or telling me?" Rush asked.

She handed him a steaming cup of tea. Goose wondered if she had cups and pots at the ready all over the house, or if she'd been expecting them. "Asking." She handed Goose a cup, which she took and balanced on her knee.

"Agent di Guzman and I went down to the old mines yesterday," Rush said.

"Really?" Lila turned cool eyes on Goose. "Looking for pitchforks?"

Goose glanced at Rush. "Ah . . ."

"We've moved somewhat beyond pitchforks at this point, Lila," he said. "But it's nice to know you've got my back. Thanks."

Lila blinked at him. "You're most welcome, Rush." She leaned forward, her eyes direct and intense. "You always have been."

He patted her hand, and she stared at him like he'd conjured a bouquet of tulips out of thin air. She turned to Goose again with considerably more warmth. "Whatever you're doing, Agent di Guzman, you have my permission to continue."

"Um, thanks."

"So, the old mines," Rush said. "We'd heard kids were partying down there and went to check it out."

Lila raised her steaming cup to her lips. "And?"

"And there was nothing there."

"Nothing?"

"No beer cans, no cigarette butts, no used condoms."

"So that's the good news out of the way." She tipped her head. "What's the bad news?"

"There was nothing else, either. No footprints, no tracks, no nests, no burrows."

She set her cup onto the coffee table with a soft chink. "Well, now. That *is* unusual. Nature abhors a vacuum."

"Exactly. But this was no vacuum."

"Oh, dear."

Goose listened as Rush described what they'd found in the old mine. The rough-hewn bowl on the low, flat rock. The traces of blood inside.

"Somebody's using the Stone Altar," Lila said, a tiny V creasing her brow.

"The Stone Altar?" Goose asked. "That was an altar we found?"

"Before it was a mine, it was an ancient structure our people used to honor the lunar standstill."

Goose blinked at her, startled. "The lunar what now?"

"The lunar standstill," Rush told her. "It's an astrological phenomenon that occurs once every eighteen-point-six years. It's a two-week period when the moon takes both its lowest possible route and its highest possible route through the night sky."

"It's also the time at which the moon rises at the northernmost point on the horizon of which it's capable," Lila said. "And when that happens—" She paused, gave Rush a significant look. He gave her a go-ahead shrug.

"And when that happens?" Goose prompted.

"It sends a beam of light directly down the mine shaft that illuminates the Stone Altar." Lila sipped her tea. "The last one was in 2006."

"Oh my God," Goose said, wide-eyed. "I've heard about this. I thought it was destroyed or ruined or something."

"No, just closed." Lila wrinkled her nose. "I find the whole thing a little too Indiana Jones, to be frank. It panders to thrill seekers rather than true believers, and that's not an element I'm interested in attracting to Mishkwa."

Goose frowned as the argument she'd heard between Lila and Einar the other day started to make a great deal more sense. "Einar disagrees, though, doesn't he? He thinks the Stone Altar is a potential moneymaker for the family, doesn't he?"

"Unfortunately, yes." Lila sighed. "My father owned the piece of land on which the Stone Altar sits. It was part of his original claim, and thanks to Einar's willingness to meet the government's requirements for retaining that claim, it's still in the family."

"But you don't want to open it to the public."

"You've been there," Lila said, shaking her head. "That place is dangerous. Plus I don't care for the Stone Altar. I never have. It doesn't feel sacred to me. We hold our rituals outdoors. Why would we suddenly go underground for the sake of something that happens once every twenty years?"

"Rituals?" Goose asked. She had a bad feeling about this conversational turn. "We?"

"Our coven, dear."

Well, shit. RAC Harris was going to have to update his file on Mishkwa. She made a mental note to send him an e-mail, ASAP. In the meantime, Goose turned to Rush. "Her *coven*?"

"Oh. Sorry." He extended a polite hand toward his aunt. "May I present Lila Olsen, Mishkwa Coven's pagan high priestess?"

Goose pinched the bridge of her nose. "I was given to understand Mishkwa didn't have witches anymore."

Lila shook her head and smiled. "We keep a low profile but we're here."

"Do you call yourself witches?" Goose asked. "Or am I supposed to say 'pagans'?"

"I prefer 'pagan' myself, but I'm not a stickler for vocabulary."

"And you?" Goose turned to Rush. "What do you prefer?"

He lifted his shoulders. "I lost religion when I lost my folks." He shifted his attention to Lila. "But if we can get back to the subject at hand? Who's using the Stone Altar, Lila?"

"I have no idea," Lila said, frowning. "Our worship is moon-based. Why would we put ourselves underground when Our Lady's face is in the sky? When Our Lady's light could fall on our skin?"

"Maybe because somebody's calling on magic Our Lady wouldn't approve of. Magic that prefers the dark. Magic that requires blood."

Goose poked her hand into the air like a slow student. "I'm sorry, why aren't we looking at Einar here? I know he's your relative, but he's also the one with a long-standing—and financial—interest at stake. All logic dictates taking a hard look at him first."

Lila waved that off. "Oh, heavens. Einar doesn't *believe* in the Stone Altar. He just wants to turn a profit from it. What Rush is talking about is something else entirely. Something far more disturbing." She frowned. "Far more disturbed."

"She's right," Rush said. "Einar believes in money, not magic. Black or otherwise. But somebody on this island is taking the dark arts seriously. Seriously enough to try their hand at bloodletting, anyway."

"Our ceremonies don't involve any sort of ritual bloodletting," Lila told Goose as she sent Rush a disapproving look. "As my nephew very well knows."

"I do know that. Just like I know there are always a few folks who think they ought to."

"I can't believe that anybody on Mishkwa would dabble in this sort of thing."

"Somebody's gone to a lot of trouble to practice alone, Lila. You've got to wonder why."

She shook her head again. "I have no idea."

"I think I do." Rush turned to Goose and said, "I think your counterfeiter is hedging his bets."

Goose stared at Rush. "You think my counterfeiter is covering his tracks via *black magic*?"

Lila stared at her. "Your *counterfeiter*?"

He said to Lila, "Goose was sent here to investigate the possibility that somebody is smuggling high-grade counterfeit money into the U.S. from Canada via Mishkwa. That means somebody on this tiny island thinks they're special. Faster, smarter, more talented than normal people, and therefore exempt from the rules binding normal people."

"Both activities *would* take a certain personality type," Goose murmured, struck. "A drive for power paired with a disdain for the rule of law. The sort of person who'd—"

"—buck generations of religious tradition to dabble in black magic." Lila sighed. "For money. I see your point."

Goose frowned. "Okay, so let's assume for now that Mishkwa really is our point of entry, because I do think at least that much of our original theory holds up. It's a very convenient location with a surprising amount of international travel going on." She looked back and forth between them. "Can we rule out Yarrow's involvement?"

"Yarrow?" Rush stared at her while Lila pressed her lips together in disapproval.

"I gather she's had a troubled adolescence," Goose said carefully, "including a brush with the law of which no record exists." She held up a hand to forestall Lila's no-doubt-pithy comment. "She let it slip herself, Lila. I had to check it out. It's my job. Now, I have no interest in digging out painful details I have no business knowing, so just give me the broad strokes, okay? Is there any way she could be connected to people who might use her exile on Mishkwa to turn a profit?"

Lila sent her a scorching glare that actually comforted Goose a great deal. No matter how troubled or angry, a kid couldn't be completely lost when somebody believed in her the way Lila clearly believed in Yarrow.

"She was arrested," Lila said stiffly, "never charged, and for reasons that are, as you mentioned, none of your business. It's her heart that was broken, not the law. But if it sets your mind at ease, you should know that her parents have strictly forbidden her access to the outside world while she's here."

"No cell phone, no Internet access?"

"None. Which means that even if she were somehow mixed up with a bad element, she's had no way of communicating with them, let alone arranging to meet them. Not that she's been off-island even once since she's been here. Not without supervision." Lila shook her head. "And to answer what will surely be your next question, her parents have also asked me to keep her strictly separated from our religious tradition as well. The chances of her having any interest in the Stone Altar, let alone the motivation to explore it, are extremely remote."

"Fair enough," Goose said. Yarrow had never felt right as a suspect to her, anyway. But somebody had, and since she was already way deep into Lila's red zone, she went ahead and pitched. "Tell me again why we're not looking at Einar?"

Lila waved that off with a weary shrug. "Einar may be impulsive but he isn't stupid. I'm sixty-nine years old, Agent di Guzman, and when I retire, he stands to inherit everything he wants. Why would he risk his freedom to buy something he's going to get for free in a few years anyway?"

Goose absorbed that. It was a fair point. Einar struck her as showy, not self-destructive. His regard for his own comfort seemed extremely healthy, and likely far outweighed his impatience.

"You'll ask around, then?" Rush said to Lila. "Discreetly?"

"Of course. But again I doubt any of my people—*our* people—have been involved in anything so unsavory as blood sacrifice."

"You think it's gone that far?" Rush asked, his eyes sharp on his aunt. "Actual sacrifice, not just ritualistic bloodletting?"

"Like pricking fingers or cutting palms," Lila told Goose before she could open her mouth to ask. Her utter stupefaction must've shown. "Blood is life, and as such is a powerful and sacred offering. You don't have to kill to make it." She pursed her lips and said to Rush, "Though

I think the person in question must have killed. Or will soon. He—or she—may not have taken human life yet but perhaps animal life. If you're hungry enough to spill blood for power, you're hungry enough to kill for it." She came to her feet. "I'll ask."

"Thanks, Lila." Rush rose and Goose followed suit.

"Blessed be, nephew. Blessed be, Agent di Guzman."

"You, too," Goose said, and accepted the woman's cheek kisses with less surprise this time, and a bit more grace. A quick, dark movement beyond Lila's shoulder caught her attention. To her surprise, she saw Yarrow kneeling by the fireplace, a piece of kindling in her hand, her dark eyes fixed on the leaping flame.

"Hey, Yarrow," Goose said, with a guilty heart. How much had the kid overheard? "I didn't see you there."

Lila turned and said, "Yarrow! Goodness, child, how long have you been there?"

Yarrow didn't turn. She poked at the shimmering blue-yellow embers and a shower of sparks danced up the chimney.

Lila sighed and rolled her eyes at Goose. "She's got her earbuds in. I swear it's like living with a deaf person. When I want her attention, I have to flick the lights."

Rush walked over and tugged on the thin wire that disappeared into the harsh black of the girl's dyed hair. An earbud popped out and she looked up. "What?"

"We have preseason conditioning tomorrow at three."

Yarrow rolled her eyes. "Great."

"You coming?"

"Do I look like an idiot to you?"

"That's a trick question, isn't it?" Rush gave his cousin a good, hard stare. "Let's try that again. The ski team, to which you belong and of which I am the coach, is holding preseason conditioning tomorrow. Will I see you there, Yarrow? Yes or no."

She heaved a sigh. "Yes, Ranger Rush. I'll be there."

"Good. Ferry's at two. I'll pick you up."

"What, you don't trust me?"

He handed her earbud back. "Do I look like an idiot to you?"

She rolled her eyes so hard Goose feared she might overbalance and tumble into the fire. Rush just shook his head.

Suddenly a high whine filled the air, a vibration that buzzed inside Goose's chest, her ears. It rattled the books on the shelves and Lila's teacup in its saucer. Goose grabbed Lila's arm.

She'd never heard that northern Minnesota was particularly prone to earthquakes or anything, but logic dictated that little bitty rocks poking up in the middle of large bodies of water couldn't be the most stable things in the world.

"What the hell is that?" she asked.

Lila shook her head and peered out the window.

"That boy," she sighed.

Goose looked, too, and saw a little black-and-yellow prop plane zip over the harbor. It tipped its wings in a jaunty salute and roared off over the house in a full-bodied wash of noise that even Yarrow heard. She popped out the earbuds herself this time, and scanned the sky with an intensity that drove impending natural disasters straight out of Goose's head.

She didn't smile—of course not—but Goose's heart wrenched at the eager joy in the girl's dark eyes when she said, "Einar's back."

Chapter

12

YARROW HAD learned a few things during her exile on the Rock at the End of the Fucking Earth.

First, Sunday evenings were Lila's favored time frame for cleaning the tea shop. Extensively. What she was cleaning for, Yarrow couldn't actually say. Like there was going to be some huge rush on tea come Monday morning. Like commuters would be rolling through demanding their scones and lattes.

Only wait, there wouldn't be any commuters because there weren't any fucking *cars*. Or, Jesus, any *people*.

The sheer lunacy of expecting customers appeared not to factor into Lila's decision to prepare for them, however. Thus Sunday nights were spent diligently filling sugar bowls and making up tea bags and topping off the honey pots.

At least they were until Yarrow learned to disappear.

Lucky for her, she'd had plenty of practice disappearing. It had been a little easier back home, of course. There were crowds, for one thing. For another, she was invisible at home. Had been since the day of her brother's diagnosis. Getting lost was a snap. She could hop the light rail to the Mall of America, a bus to Southdale. She could be at a mall, a movie theater, a library or any one of a dozen coffee shops on the university campus in minutes. She and Jilly had passed for freshman, easy, and—

Pain slid in, vicious and greasy, and she stopped. Backtracked. Then carefully, deliberately, she ripped the thought out of her head. She couldn't go back to that place. Never again. Even if it existed—the past as she remembered it—she wasn't the same girl she'd been. She couldn't go back there, and what was worse, she didn't deserve to. If the past was gone, it was because she'd destroyed it. What was done was done.

The point was, disappearing wasn't so easy on Mishkwa. Lila had a decent library, though, full of big fascinating books. Books about herbs and spells and potions and power. Books that spoke to something inside her that twisted and yearned. Books that would make her parents—if they knew she was reading them—completely stroke out.

Or they would have once upon a time. They didn't care so much about her reading material anymore.

Regardless, Yarrow liked to grab the thickest book she could carry and tuck herself into some unexpected corner until Sunday-night prep was finished.

But Yarrow had learned something else during her exile on Mishkwa. She'd learned that Einar always came by the tea shop after he'd been away. Always. And if Yarrow wanted to see him—which, *God*, she did—she'd get her ass to the kitchen.

She was stuffing spoonfuls of decaf green tea into little square packets of handwoven linen when the sleigh bells at the door jingled. Her heart rocketed into her throat.

"Hey, ladies." Einar strolled through the door, hands tucked into jeans pockets, jacket open over a flannel shirt the color of autumn leaves. She felt his gaze touch on her then move to Lila. Heat bloomed in her cheeks, and she kept her head down until it faded.

"Hey, Einar," she said.

Lila said, "Well, the world traveler returns!"

"I don't know if Mackinac Island qualifies as world travel, Grandma," Yarrow said. "It's, like, around the block."

"You kidding?" Einar draped himself over a stool and propped an elbow on the counter. "It's three Great Lakes away. I'm exhausted."

"Poor baby," Yarrow crooned. He threw her a sharp look, and she hastily dropped her eyes to the tea bags.

"Exhausted and hungry, I assume?" Lila asked, a laugh in her voice. Yarrow nearly sagged with relief. The last thing she needed was Lila catching a clue.

Einar gave his aunt a charming grin. "Am I so transparent?"

"Like glass, darling. Like glass."

He snatched up her hand across the counter, pressed a lavish kiss to her knuckles. "A grilled ham-and-cheese? With that fancy mustard? I swear, nobody makes it like you do, Lila."

"Sweet talker." She swatted at him, but headed for the kitchen. She peered over Yarrow's shoulder on her way by. "Don't pack them so full, honey. The leaves need room to breathe."

Yarrow scowled at the pile of plump tea bags in front of her. Like she didn't know that already. She just hated seeing the bags all limp and half empty. Like there wasn't enough inside them. "Whatever."

Lila pushed through the kitchen doors, then poked her head back into the shop. "Why don't you come into the kitchen a minute, Einar? Keep me company while I cook?"

"Of course." He unfolded himself from the stool with a lazy grace that had Yarrow's heart hammering in her chest. He caught her eye as he cleared the pass-through, tossed her a questioning glance.

She gave him a shrug. She'd heard some of what Rush and Goose had talked to Lila about, sure. The weirder she looked, the less people noticed her. Throw in some earbuds that were only occasionally plugged into actual music and she was as invisible here as she had been at home. At least she had been before di Guzman turned up. Agent Smiley Face was the only reason she'd even turned on some actual music halfway through their conversation instead of listening to the whole, fascinating thing. Left to their own devices, Lila and Rush would never have noticed her there in front of the fire.

Einar disappeared into the kitchen, and she crept over to put an ear by the door. Lila turned on the water in the sink full blast and the murmur of their voices disappeared into it. *Shit*. She tossed the tea bags she'd prepped into the pretty silver canister Lila had set out for them, then took her time hauling out the box of stir sticks from under the counter next to the kitchen door. The water turned off as she slipped the sticks one by one into the blue-glazed vases Lila liked, but then Lila switched on the exhaust fan over the range.

Yarrow gave up. She grabbed a tray and moved into the dining room, where she gathered napkin dispensers and sugar bowls from all the tables. By the time Einar bumped through the kitchen door again—grilled cheese in hand—she was at the counter, slopping sugar into bowls.

"Thanks, Lila," he said. Hair flopped into one eye as he hit her with a lopsided smile. "You're a queen among women."

"And don't you forget it," Lila said, flicking him with a dish towel. "You'll think about what I said?"

"Of course. But I seriously can't imagine who would—"

Lila cut him off with a pointed look at Yarrow. *Jesus*, Yarrow thought, *like I'm deaf* and *blind*.

"Just . . . come to me," she said. "With anything, all right?"

"*Ain't no mountain high enough*," he sang. "*Ain't no valley low enough*."

"Oh, for heaven's sake." Lila shook her head, though Yarrow could see the smile tugging at her lips. "Yarrow, I'm going upstairs. Yule is coming up and I'm already dreadfully behind. Will you top off the sugar bowls?"

Her stomach went light and jumpy at the idea of being alone with Einar, but she covered it with a pointed look at the sugar sack in her hands and the heaping bowls in front of her. "Gosh. I'll try to remember."

Lila sighed. "Lock up when Einar leaves, will you?"

"Okay."

"Good night, dears."

Lila disappeared, and Yarrow listened to the receding tap of her steps. Her eyes were fixed on the tray in front of her but every nerve in her body was fixed on Einar. He set aside the sandwich he'd wheedled out of Lila, crossed to the outside of the counter and sat down directly in front of her. The breath in Yarrow's lungs went hot and useless.

"*Ain't no river wide enough.*" He sang the old song softly, his voice a rich, low throb she could feel in her own chest. "*To keep me from gettin' to you, girl.*"

"Diana Ross? Really?"

"Please. That was the Marvin Gaye version."

"Like I care."

"Oh, you care, pretty girl." Einar reached out and took her chin in long, warm fingers. A fluttery shimmer exploded in her belly and shot all the way up to her throat.

She jerked her chin away. A cold spark glittered in his blue eyes, but amusement curved his lips.

"Why the pout, little cousin?"

"I'm not pouting."

"Looks like a pout to me." He leaned forward, those icy hot eyes on her mouth. Her stomach lifted on a jet of pleased terror. Or terrified pleasure. She wasn't exactly sure, but it was a killer rush. More than she'd felt—or allowed herself to feel—since she'd landed on this god-forsaken island. "And I consider myself something of an expert on women's lips."

She tossed her head and gave him a cool stare. "So I'm a woman now? Here I thought I was a little girl."

"You're in the mood to play with fire, aren't you?" he said softly. "Take care you don't get burned."

"Right," she muttered, and reached for the sugar sack. "Because you're completely Mr. Dangerous."

His hand shot out, snatched her around the wrist and slapped her palm down on the counter. He jerked her forward, his fingers rough and strong around her wrist, his face hard and near—so very near—her own. He'd come half out of his seat to fix her with those wild blue eyes. Eyes burning with anger, yes, but something more. Something hot, immediate, demanding.

She'd pushed him, pushed on purpose. She'd wanted a response. She'd been invisible so long, and for the most part she didn't care. But he mattered. She wanted this man to see her.

"Einar?"

Instantly, his grip on her wrist gentled, and relief eased through her like fog.

"I'm sorry," he said, a rueful smile in those lightning eyes. "I'm such a beast. But something about you just gets me, Yarrow."

"It does?" She went still, breathless with delight.

He lifted a vaguely helpless shoulder then touched the back of her hand with one finger. "Did I hurt you?"

"I'm not a baby, Einar." She gave him what she hoped was a sultry look from under her lashes. It felt a little weird— God, her entire body felt weird—but his smile grew, so she must be doing all right. "I'm not that breakable."

He traced his finger up the faint ridge of tendon in the back of her hand, circled the knob of her wrist. A flush crawled into her cheeks and her breath hitched. Heat burned down her chest and into her stomach like she'd gulped boiling tea and she swayed toward him.

"So," he said. "Sounds like Agent di Guzman and our cousin Rush have been busy little beavers while I was away."

Her happy glow died and she snatched back her hand. He wanted information. He was softening her up to spill everything she knew. Fuck that. She might be young but she wasn't stupid.

"Oh, yeah," she said. "She and Ranger Rush have been joined at the hip since she got here." She gave him a significant look. "They're shacked up out at the Ranger Station, you know."

Einar gave her an indulgent smile. "I'm sure my high-minded cousin is taking good care of her."

She made an irritated noise. Damn, what had she been thinking? Of course Einar wasn't going to be jealous of Rush. The guy lived like some kind of monk, to the point that people had started to wonder if maybe he'd gotten his dick shot off in one of those tragic, sandy countries he'd spent so much time in. Yarrow had half believed it, too. Then she'd gotten a load of the way her oh-so-serious cousin looked at Agent di Guzman, and changed her mind.

She hoped, nastily, Einar would get his changed, too. The hard way.

"They've got Lila all worked up about something, Yarrow. What's going on?" he asked softly.

She jerked her shoulders. "I didn't hear that much."

"But what you did hear?"

The urge to please him trickled back in around the anger, the hurt. She looked away. "Something about the mines," she said. "They said they hiked to the mines a few days ago. Somebody's been messing around with the Stone Altar or something."

"Yeah, Lila said that." He leaned back, farther out of her sphere, and she felt the loss. Jesus, she was an idiot. "Somebody's playing at black magic?"

"That's what they said."

"Do they know who?"

Yarrow tipped her head. "I didn't hear."

"I hope they're not looking at you."

"Me?"

"Yarrow, don't be a child." Einar shook his head, folded his arms on the counter. "You think they don't know what's in you? You think they can't sense it?"

Fire licked up from her belly all the way out to her fingers. "Sense what?"

"Power." His eyes were bright and hot on her, though his voice was cool as rain. "Any idiot can see it. The goddess gifted you with something amazing. It's why you have such a hard time keeping friends. You're different. Special. There's something in you that's not in them, and they're jealous. And Lila's a fool not to allow you into the coven."

"My parents made her promise she wouldn't—"

"Your parents don't care about you."

Pain bloomed, surprising and ugly. She'd thought it couldn't hurt her anymore, thought she'd gotten used to it. This being tossed aside like so much garbage. She sucked in a sharp breath and he slid his hand over hers.

"I don't mean to hurt you, Yarrow. Remember, though, I've been where you are. Forgotten, overlooked, thrown away. My mother dumped me here, too." His lips twisted in self-mockery. "Or haven't you heard the stories?"

"I've heard," she said softly.

"You need to be trained, Yarrow. What you have is too rare, too special to go undeveloped."

Something gaped inside her, raw and dizzying and fierce, and she *wanted*. She wanted recognition, she wanted belonging, she wanted revenge. She wanted to stop fucking hurting all the time. What if he was right? What if it wasn't her fault, the stinking mess she'd made of her life? What if this thing inside her, this slow boil of rage and desire and impulse, wasn't a sin? Wasn't a flaw? Wasn't the root of all evil?

What if it *was* a gift? A gift she simply didn't understand but could learn to use? And if she learned to use it, maybe she would stop hurting people. Maybe she could be normal again.

He leaned in, dropped his chin until he could look straight into her eyes. Into her soul. Into her mind. It was as if he could see the words she was thinking and they made him smile.

"Normal's overrated," he said softly, and the shock of it ripped into the very center of her. It wasn't her imagination. It wasn't wishful thinking. He saw her. This man, this beautiful, golden man, he *saw* her. He saw what was inside her; he recognized it and it didn't scare him. Didn't disgust him. He valued it. Valued *her*.

"Think about it, okay?" he said, then rose.

"Wait!"

He stopped but she didn't know what to say next. She only knew she didn't want him to go. He smiled and feathered his fingers along the line of her jaw and into the warm hair at the nape of her neck. An involuntary shiver rocked her as he pressed the ritual kiss to each cheek.

"Blessed be, sister."

Chapter

13

GOOSE STOOD shivering in her running clothes by the rail of the ferry the next afternoon as it eased in to dock. Hornby Harbor was a tiny mining town literally dynamited out of a granite cliff. To the south, ore docks arched out into Lake Superior like a rusty cathedral, while to the north Highway 61 barely eased off the accelerator on its way to Canada. Perched on the rocky patch in between was the North Shore's answer to civilization—a cluster of gas stations, bars, pie shops and churches clinging to the highway like ticks on a Labrador.

Gas spread its oily rainbow on the water and Einar breathed in the fumes like the sommelier had offered him a cork. "Ah, civilization," he said. "There's nothing quite like a combustion engine."

Yarrow snorted. "Tell me about it."

"I could do without 'em," Rush said, leaning on the rail beside Goose. "But then I have to bust anybody dumb enough to poach moose on Park Service land from a snowmobile."

"Are there a lot of people that dumb?" Goose asked, smiling.

"You'd be surprised."

Einar said, "To be fair, that bull moose *has* been kind of a nuisance lately."

"Good ol' Sir Humpalot," Yarrow said. She'd gone with her usual basic black, from the two lifeless pigtails hanging out of her knit cap all the way to her baggy socks. White running shoes stood out like an electric shock on her feet. "I think he and Lila's Dumpster are going steady."

"If the Park Service wants him taken out, they'll let me know." Rush's jaw tightened. "Until then, the law stands."

"Which law?" Yarrow asked. "The one against hunting, or the one against motor vehicles?"

"Both," Rush told her. "All. The legal system isn't cafeteria style. You don't get to pick and choose."

"What if Sir Humpalot gets tired of Dumpsters, though?" Yarrow asked. "What if he moves on to, I don't know, horses or canoes or, shit, what else is really big? What about Ronnie Samuelsson? She's frickin' enormous."

Einar sucked his teeth, clearly trying not to laugh. Goose shook her head.

"I'm just saying. Would she be allowed to defend herself? Or would you arrest her for putting down a horny moose?"

"Yarrow," Goose said softly. "Unkind."

Yarrow shrugged and yanked her cap down over her ears. She fiddled with the touch screen of her iPod then closed her eyes, lost to them.

Rush shot a look at Einar. "Why do you encourage her?"

"I didn't say a word."

"You say lots of words. Just never the right ones."

"At least I speak."

"Oh, look," Goose said. "The crew has the gangway secured." Rush gave his cousin one last glare and headed for the dock. She half expected him to cuff Einar up the back of the head on his way by, but he didn't. Good thing, too. Einar would return the favor, and then it would be World Wrestling Entertainment *SmackDown!* right here on the ferry. These two might be cousins but they behaved more like brothers. Which, given the way they'd been raised, made perfect sense.

Given that, however, she would have expected a certain amount of gruff affection between them as well. All she picked up was a bedrock loyalty, though. Duty, not warmth. At least on Rush's part. On Einar's, she felt nothing at all.

Something to consider, she thought as the three of them fell in behind Rush without a word, Einar and Yarrow exchanging eye rolls they weren't particularly careful to conceal. They found the Park Service vehicle in the lot, and Rush climbed in. He cranked over the ignition and the old Jimmy's engine roared to life while Goose urged Einar into the passenger seat.

"You're as tall as I am," he said, dropping a lingering glance over her legs, encased in slick running tights. "Why should you cram into the back?"

"We might be close to the same height but there's more of you than there is of me," Goose countered, putting a deliberate note of appreciation in her voice. She gave him a once-over of her own for good measure. "Considerably more."

His brows lifted in smug pleasure. "Well," he said, squaring his jaw. "If you're sure?"

"I'll be fine." She gave him a little nudge toward the passenger seat. A token bit of body contact to seal the deal. God. Yarrow had been right the other day. Boys *were* simple. "Yarrow and I will cozy up together in the back, just us girls."

"I do love it when girls get cozy," Einar murmured, so low she barely caught it. She swallowed the disgust that rose in her throat and turned a friendly look on Yarrow. The hate and jealous rage in Yarrow's eyes hit Goose like a sucker punch. She pulled in a quick breath and dropped back a step.

Not that the kid's fury surprised her. Given how openly
Einar had been flirting with Goose since the minute he'd
declared his intention to join them for preseason conditioning this afternoon, she'd have been shocked if Yarrow
didn't hate her.

No, reading the girl so powerfully wasn't what disturbed her. What really shook her was the sharp snap of
recognition. She didn't just know what Yarrow was feeling.
She *recognized* it. She'd experienced it herself, years ago,
but that didn't dim the toxic, punishing clarity with which
Yarrow's hate-filled gaze brought it back. Only she hadn't
hated some stranger for stealing a man's attention. She'd
hated her sister.

"Get in, Yarrow," she said, but couldn't keep a note
of sympathy out of her voice. Yarrow's face twisted like
Goose had sprinkled her with holy water and commanded
out the demons. But she got in. Goose got in beside her,
careful not to crowd her. And she wondered.

RUSH LEFT Einar leading the kids through a few warm-
up laps around the high school's track while he and Goose
marked out the longer-mileage run through town they'd
tackle next. Weather was unpredictable this time of year.
They'd run while it stayed warm, switch to skis when they
could. They'd likely be back to jogging midseason sometime. That was just the nature of the North Shore.

"Is it always like that?" Goose asked, wrestling the
truck into first gear while Rush consulted the map.

"Like what?" he asked, distracted. The spicy, green
scent spilling off her hair distracted him from the map on
his knees and he found himself studying her instead.

She wasn't conventionally beautiful, his Goose. Not
with the aggressive jut of those cheekbones, the stubborn
thrust of that jaw. Her nose was straight and fine, yes, but it
was a bit too long for true beauty.

But her mouth. Lord, that mouth. If her face was a

puzzle, her mouth was the bastard piece that looked like it had migrated over from an entirely different box. It was a wide, lush slash of emotion, and with the upper lip just slightly fuller than the lower. Something about that top-heavy mouth made him think of fruit on the vine—full and sweet and begging to be plucked. It made him want to bite. Taste. Suck. Gently, then maybe a little harder, depending on what kind of noise she made when he gave it a shot.

He shifted uncomfortably on the old, butt-sprung bench seat of the Jimmy. Jesus, look at him. Dreaming himself half hard just looking at her profile. As if he needed a reminder of how low he was running on polite patience.

She'd made her move that first day, and he'd countered. Asked for more than she'd wanted to give. That had surprised her, but he'd given her plenty of time to get used to the idea. Now it was his turn to make a move, whether she was ready or not. He glanced out the window at the pale round of moon that hung against the day-lit sky, and half smiled to himself.

Soon, he thought. He'd move soon.

"Like *that*," Goose said, pointing her chin toward the rearview mirror.

"Hmm?" Rush scrambled to pick up the thread of whatever she'd been asking him.

"Yarrow," Goose said. "With the other girls. Is it always that bad?"

"Pull over here," Rush said. He hopped out when she did and plunked an orange pylon down on the corner. "Six blocks straight ahead, then left."

She wrestled the truck into first again, checked her mirror for nonexistent traffic and pulled out. "Did you even see what was going on at the track?" she asked. "It's a warm day out, but things were subzero back there."

Rush frowned. "What, you mean the way Yarrow doesn't really talk to the other kids?"

Goose pulled her eyes from the road long enough to

give him a disbelieving look. "Are you kidding me? She might not talk much but she was saying a hell of a lot."

"Like?"

"Like 'I'm not one of you losers.' Like 'Screw you.' Like—"

"Life's been rough on her this past year," Rush said. "Cut her some slack. It's not like she wanted to join the team, you know. Lila made her—"

Goose snorted out a sound that was all female derision. "Oh, please. Since when can you make a teenager do anything? She's here because she wants to be." She pulled over and nodded at the sidewalk. "There's your next spot."

Rush got out, planted his pylon and got back in frowning.

"A mile south next," he said. "And why would she do that?"

"What, purposely alienate the only peers she has contact with?" Goose shot him a sidelong look as she headed south. "I gather Lila homeschools?"

"In her own way. Which, yes, means limited contact with other girls. So why would she turn up her nose at the chance to make friends?"

"Punishment."

"She doesn't even know them. Why would she punish them?"

Another of those exasperated looks. "She's not punishing them, Rush. She's punishing herself."

"Herself?"

"You think it's easy for a girl with Yarrow's bones to ugly herself up the way she has? That takes some serious effort. I've got to think the same principle applies to her behavior. For some reason—you'd probably know what it is better than I would—Yarrow's decided she doesn't deserve nice things. Doesn't deserve a pretty face. Healthy hair of a color found in nature. The friendship of other girls." She shrugged. "Love in general."

Rush considered her, this woman he'd initially taken for shallow. How had he missed the razor-sharp brain operating just behind those dark, sad eyes? How had he missed the fact that she didn't miss anything? Probably because he was an idiot.

But even now he couldn't quite connect all the dots the way she was obviously expecting him to.

"Which is why she drags her ass all the way into town?" he asked. "To shun friendship?" He nodded, as if pondering it. "Yes, I see. It's convoluted, inconvenient, vaguely insulting. Totally Yarrow. Brilliant."

She snorked out a laugh, something so different from her usual bell-like chuckle that he broke off to stare at her. Goose was a snort-laugher? How . . . fascinating. Everything about her was so polished and sophisticated, from the smooth fall of her hair to the calculating way she wielded that powerful smile. But every now and then the façade cracked and an oddball slice of daffy humor sparkled through. A humor Rush found thoroughly and unexpectedly . . . adorable. No other word for it.

Damn, he was in deep. Double damn if he wasn't feeling unaccountably cheerful about it, too. Figure that.

"Very Yarrow," she agreed, then her grin died. "But it does make sense. Think about it this way. It's one thing to put yourself in the middle of everything you crave—community, gossip, cute boys, other girls—and reject it. But it's another thing entirely to put yourself in the middle of everything you want most, and allow it—no, *force* it—to reject you."

"You think she's—" He broke off. She hadn't said it outright, but she'd clearly circled back around to Yarrow as a suspect. A girl who would reject friendship in such a painful manner would reject love even more violently. And who loved her more gently, more persistently than Lila?

Which meant that his troubled young cousin was, in all likelihood, dabbling in black magic in an effort to do the one thing Lila might find unforgivable. And calling black magic for money? That just doubled the slap, which was likely the point. If Goose was right about the kid, she wasn't in it for the money so much as the self-flagellation.

He'd have to make an uncomfortable phone call to Yarrow's parents, ask some unpleasant questions. They'd clearly done a thorough job expunging the kid's record if Goose couldn't rustle up any information through official channels. Beyond that, though, he didn't have the first clue what to do. Yarrow was a mystery to him, but she was family and therefore his responsibility. A precious responsibility, though he knew she wouldn't believe that.

Goose would, though. Look at her there, practically holding her breath as she refused to put too fine a point on what she'd just said. She'd nudged him toward it, then backed off so he could draw his own conclusions. Perhaps even take some action toward protecting the girl before Goose and her badge were obligated to step in.

She glanced his way, caught him staring and hitched a self-conscious shoulder. "It hurts more if you let them do the rejecting," she said, then pulled over. "She'd want that. The hurt." She nodded out the window. "There's your last corner."

Rush didn't open the door. Goose frowned past him at the street sign. "You did say a mile south?"

He slipped a hand under the glossy black hair that spilled out of her hat and over her shoulders like night, cupped her warm nape in his hand. Then he pulled her forward and simply put his mouth on hers. The peppery scent of her hair, the shimmer of her surprise, the quick melt of that surprise into pleasure—it swirled around him in a dizzying updraft. And something inside him that had been silent for years, something he feared would never wake again, spoke.

Mine.

He pulled back, despite the sharp grind of hunger, the breathless surge of desire. He knew he should smile at her, reassure her. Probably apologize. Definitely laugh off the moment as impulse. But he wasn't a smiler, he damn well wasn't impulsive and this was nothing to laugh about anyway.

"What—" She broke off, blinked slowly and rubbed

her lips together as if tasting him all over again. Rush ached to dive back into that barely begun kiss. "What was that?"

"Fair warning," he said.

"Of . . . what?"

He caught her eyes with his, held them and took them deep. "I want you, Goose." He said it baldly. Roughly. Honestly. Exactly as it was inside him. "All of you. Not just the pretty smile and shiny hair, either. No, I want the girl who snorts when she laughs and says 'fuck' when she's angry." He leaned in until he could almost taste the shocked desire in the air around and between them. "I want the girl who can look at an ugly, tumbledown cabin and see a snow globe. Who can look at an angry, unlikable kid and find her heart with both hands. I want *you*, Goose, and I'm about out of patience with waiting."

He got out, planted his cone on the corner and slammed back into the truck. She was still gaping at him like he'd knocked her over the head with a brick. He reached over and gently nudged her drooping jaw into place.

"But what I have to do," she said finally. "To you. To your family—"

He gave his head an impatient shake. "We've covered that already. I know exactly what you're doing here and how it'll affect my family. Just like you already know I'm okay with it." He held up a hand to forestall her protest. "I'm not happy about it, but I'm okay with it. The law is the law, no matter who's breaking it. I get that. But it doesn't have shit to do with what I feel for you."

"Rush." She stared out the windshield, her hands on the wheel. "I don't want to hurt you."

"Then don't try to make this about your job. You're not scared of investigating my family. But you *are* scared of something, and sooner or later you're going to have to tell me what the hell it is. Because I'm not going away and I'm not giving up."

She closed her eyes for a long moment, and Rush entertained the terrifying notion that she might be fighting tears. When she finally met his gaze, though, her eyes were dry and steady.

"Fair enough," she said. "But not today."

He considered the tense angle of her jaw, the fiercely rigid line of her spine. "Not today," he agreed slowly.

But soon.

Chapter

14

"SO, YARROW." Agent Smiley Face jogged alongside her down the streets of Hornby Harbor, pacing her easily. Yarrow hated her and the endless legs Einar had so openly admired earlier. "You have a minute to chat?"

A greasy wave of pain crested in Yarrow's gut. *Einar was right*, she thought bitterly. *Lila thinks I was the one fucking around with the Stone Altar.* Her own grandmother had sent a slick, smiling cop to do some kind of autopsy on her blackened soul. To figure out where everybody had gone so wrong. The pain receded and a swift clench of anger took its place. Fuck that. Lila wanted to figure out what inherent evil made her tick? She wanted to know exactly how upper-class, white-bread suburbia had spawned such a dangerous freak? She could ask for herself.

Right. Like that was going to happen. Her own parents refused to get within shouting distance of her. Keeping their *good* child alive was a full-time job, and they didn't have any energy left over to trouble themselves about redeeming the bad one. Why would her grandmother—her step-grandmother, at that—go to more trouble than her actual blood relatives?

Not that she deserved redemption. She was bad news. Ask anybody. Ask Jilly.

Only Jilly wasn't talking. Not to her, anyway. Not after what she'd done.

She picked up the pace one more punishing degree, but Agent Smiley Face wasn't even breathing hard. "Jesus," Yarrow said finally. "Talk if you're going to talk. I don't have all damn day."

"How long have you been in love with Einar?"

Shock surged through her body at the sound of his name, same as it did every time he touched her. The electricity between them had all but knocked her on her ass the other night. And when he'd gazed down at her with all that gentle compassion in his warm, blue eyes, like he already knew her—freaky brain, damaged soul and all—she was a goner.

But she was also jailbait. She knew it, he knew it, and worse, Agent Smiley Face here knew it. There was only one person on this entire planet who understood her. Who accepted her. Who might even love her, if she worked hard enough at it. Problem was, loving her anytime in the next two years would get him arrested. Whoops.

She'd be damned if she'd let her love bring Einar harm, though. She'd be double damned if she'd let this woman with her slick charm, her scary badge and her nosy questions snuff out the one bright spot Yarrow could see in the endless fucking night that was her future.

"You think I'm in love with *Einar*?" She snorted out an ironic little chuckle. No easy thing with her heart in her mouth. "Oh my God. He's so . . . old. Plus he's, like, my cousin."

"Stepcousin. No blood relation."

"Still. Aren't there laws about things like that, even up here in the wilderness?"

Goose sighed. "I'm not going to arrest you for crushing on your cousin, Yarrow. I'm just trying to help you."

"Really."

"I know it's hard to believe, but I've been where you are. I know what it's like to be invisible, or to wish you were. I know what it's like when you think somebody finally sees you in spite of that. I know how that feels, and how you'd do nearly anything for the person who performs that particular miracle. But, honey, that kind of gratitude, that kind of love? It's real and God knows it's intense. But it's really, really dangerous, too. You need to be careful."

Her words sprayed Yarrow like buckshot, a thousand stinging insults at once. They popped tiny holes in the blackness inside her where she'd buried the pain, the rage, the need. That awful, shameful need.

"You don't know shit," Yarrow said coldly as the old hurt bubbled up fresh and hateful inside her. "You know less than shit."

"I know enough," Goose said. She stopped running, grabbed Yarrow's forearm, dragged her to a halt. Yarrow seized the woman's hand—she meant to throw it off, to tell this woman where she could stuff her self-righteous bullshit, but she lost control.

The instant Goose's skin hit hers, the freak that lived inside her took over. The freak who fed on the vicious swirl of dark emotion churning in her gut. The freak who not only fed on it but got off on inflicting it on others. She dug her nails into Goose's palm, stared into those big, ridiculously sincere eyes and didn't hide a thing.

She let it all loose on her face, everything she usually kept such a careful lid on—the hostility, the jealousy, the rage. The dark, keening love for Einar. The glittery shards of self-hatred and the lies from which that hatred had grown.

Goose snatched her hand back, her face pale, her mouth set with bleak knowledge. Yarrow's stomach clenched with a mixture of disappointment and satisfaction. She was just as toxic as she'd always been. Toxic enough to nauseate a hardened officer of the law, anyway. No surprises there. The only person ever to look inside her head without disgust was Einar.

"Well, this has been just swell. Let's not do it ever again, 'kay?" Yarrow wiped her hand down her sweats with deliberate disdain. "Gotta run."

And she sprinted down the street as if the hounds of hell were at her heels. Goose didn't follow her, and she didn't look back.

GOOSE WATCHED Yarrow race away, leaving her to gather up the shards of her composure. *She thinks I'm disgusted*, Goose thought, her throat aching. *She thinks she's disgusting.*

She sensed more than saw the rest of the team jogging up the street toward her at a more dogged pace. Einar led the pack, while Rush brought up the rear, encouraging the stragglers. They streamed around her, all heaving lungs and the occasional wheezed curse. Rush pulled up beside her.

"Goose?" he asked, a thrum of concern in his deep voice. "You all right?"

"Yes," she said. But she wasn't. Far from it. Yarrow had meant to slap at her, and she'd landed a good one. That harrowing, fast-forward spin through the girl's bleak emotional landscape had sucker-punched her but good. It had been wretched and familiar all at once, a confusing stew of high passions, self-hatred and fatalism. At a certain point she hadn't been able to tell, entirely, where Yarrow's feelings left off and the memories of her own ill-fated sixteenth year began. She knew only that the overlap was huge and painful.

She had to give the girl credit. Maybe it had been a wild punch, but she'd landed it pretty solid. Her little tromp through Goose's psyche had tripped more land mines than she could have possibly imagined. But the girl had also revealed more than she'd intended. Way more.

Because now Goose didn't just suspect Yarrow was in love with Einar. Now she knew. And because a love that intense didn't bloom without at least a little hope, she also knew Einar must have encouraged it on some level. She just didn't know how. Or why. Or what, if anything, Yarrow had to do with the supernotes she suspected Einar was smuggling into the country in his cute little bumblebee plane.

Which meant Goose was about to take a good, hard run at Einar. No matter what Rush and Lila thought.

THE FOLLOWING night, Yarrow loaded up her tray with a couple bowls of soup and a few hunks of bread. She considered spitting in Agent Smiley Face's barley bean. God knew the bitch deserved it after the crap she'd pulled yesterday. Poking around in her personal life like it was the Secret Service's business who she was fucking. Jesus.

She debated the idea for a minute then decided against it. Lila would kill her. Yarrow didn't know if she had hidden cameras or ESP or what, but the old lady was sharp. Way sharper than either of Yarrow's parents. Or maybe she just paid attention. Which would've put her way out ahead of the folks, too, Yarrow thought bitterly.

But if Lila found out she'd defiled the sacred covenant of providing nourishment for a traveler—or whatever bullshit language she used—there would be hell to pay. So no spitting in the soup.

But she wanted to. Damn, she wanted to. If only because she'd happily sell her soul—whatever was left of it anyway—to be the one sitting across from Einar right now, basking in the glow of his eager attention. But she wasn't, was she? She was the one wearing the apron and schlepping the lovebirds their dinner. Typical.

She wadded up her anger and her hurt like a used napkin and stuffed it down into the dank, black place inside her where she kept the rest of the pain and rage she didn't know what to do with. She wiped her face clean of anything but cynical detachment, shouldered her tray and headed into the dining room to serve her beloved and her enemy.

* * *

GOOSE DIPPED her spoon into the rich, tomatoey broth and smiled up at Yarrow. "It's delicious," she said. "Do you and Lila make it?"

Yarrow snorted. "In the microwave."

Einar shared a look with Goose that said *kids*. "Lila's more a baker than a cook. She handles the pastries and breads in-house but has a contract with a fantastic little café in Grand Marais for the soups," he told her. "I fly in a fresh supply for her every week."

Yarrow made a noise that might've been confirmation, might've been scorn as she stomped off. Goose watched her go, her concern carefully concealed. She knew how Yarrow felt about Einar, but Einar's feelings for—and uses for—Yarrow were as yet undetermined.

She considered him carefully, from the sunny tousle of his hair to the assured curve of his smile. Flattery, she decided. She'd start there and see where it took her.

"So, Einar," she said, lifting a spoonful of soup to her mouth. "What's kept you on Mishkwa all these years?"

He shot her that weapons-grade smile and said simply, "It's home."

"Well, sure. But with your brains, energy, ambition? Not to mention that pretty face?" She blasted him with a smile of her own. "You could go anywhere, do anything. Why limit yourself to—" She broke off, seeking a word that could sum up the jagged, claustrophobic beauty of Mishkwa. ". . . this?"

His smile died and he eyed her as if weighing something. "Can I show you something?" he finally asked.

She set her spoon aside and said, "Absolutely."

"Back in a few, Yarrow," he called toward the kitchen.

He held the door for her and in moments they were standing on the wooden pier that shot out from South Harbor into the sluggish, gunmetal waters of Lake Superior.

Like the water, the air was heavy and thick. A full moon

curved ripe and fertile as a pregnant belly in the unseason-
ably warm sky, painting a hazy halo in the night around
it. If the damp air didn't steal her breath, Goose thought,
surely the sight of that moon would have.

"That's why I'm here," Einar said. He tucked his fingers
into the pockets of his jeans and nodded toward the sky. "Her."

"Her?"

"Our Lady."

"Our Lady? You mean the moon?" Goose blinked at
him in honest surprise. When Rush had said Einar didn't
believe in magic, she'd just assumed . . . "You're a witch?
Or, what, a wizard?"

"Pagan," he said, laughing. "Or Wiccan, if you like.
I don't think they have actual wizards outside of Oz or
Harry Potter movies."

"Huh," she said.

"Uh-oh." His eyes twinkled. "You didn't know about
the coven here?"

"Not till a few days ago," she said.

"A pity but not a surprise." He sighed. "Mishkwa Coven
is one of the oldest blood-bonded covens in this part of the
world, you know."

"Blood-bonded?"

"It means the leadership is handed down along family
lines. No actual bloodletting involved, though I understand
why you'd be edgy about that sort of thing after what you
and Rush stumbled onto at the Stone Altar." He met her
sharp look with an easy smile. "Lila mentioned it to me.
Asked me to, you know, keep an eye out."

Goose nodded.

"Point is, we're an ancient coven with a rich tradition,
a breathtaking location and a potential tourist attraction in
the Stone Altar that rivals Ireland's Newgrange." He shook
his head at the waste of it. "It's a shame Lila keeps it so
low profile."

"Her call," Goose said carefully. "Her being high priestess and all."

"Her call," he agreed. "At least until she retires."

"And when she does? You'd run things differently?"

"I *will* run things differently." He grinned, boyish and handsome in the moonlight. "We're blood-bonded, remember? I'm next in line."

"What about Rush?"

He shrugged. "Rush doesn't do religion. Even if Lila begged him to take over the coven, even if it was her dying wish, he wouldn't do it."

"So it'll be you, then." Goose gave him a look she hoped was both speculative and flattering. "What'll you do first?"

"Renovate the Stone Altar, of course. It'll require significant structural enhancement before it's ready for Paganpalooza."

"Paganpalooza?"

He grinned at her. "Hey, the lunar standstill only happens five times a century. You think I'd let another one squeak by without a party? It's a damn good thing I've got fourteen years to wait, though. It'll probably take that long to get that old mine shaft up to code."

He went on in that vein for a few more minutes, with Goose throwing in the occasional encouraging noise to keep him rolling. Lila had been right, she thought as she studied the avarice lighting up his pretty face. He'd turn Mishkwa into a theme park. Probably had plans drawn up and stashed in his desk drawer, just waiting for his aunt to kick the bucket.

Theme parks didn't come cheap, though. Neither did power. And it might take significantly more power than Einar anticipated to ensure his inheritance. She thought about Rush, who, at that very moment, was tending to that list of complaints she'd accidentally gathered. Stopping at one house for a quick chat about the proper storage of trash barrels, probably sprinkling salt on the unshoveled walks himself. Maybe taking out a few unwelcome garden pests along the way. Einar could be in for some stiff competition if Rush felt like giving it to him.

Goose didn't like the ugly, complicated picture starting

to develop in her mind. So far she had Einar aiming to destroy the pristine, harsh beauty of this island, and financing the effort with money he'd earned funneling supernotes into the United States. And if that weren't enough to keep her up nights, she still had to figure out where, if anywhere, Yarrow fit into this whole mess.

Because she did. Goose could feel that in her gut, knew it with an absolute certainty she couldn't explain but believed with every cell in her body. Einar was doing something with— or to—Yarrow, but Goose hadn't the faintest idea what.

It was going to eat at her, too, the Yarrow question. She'd need to resolve it, one way or the other, before she left Mishkwa. It was outside the scope of her duties, but she couldn't even think about leaving until she knew the girl was safe.

Then she'd have to think about it. About leaving.

A tiny spark of pain danced through her at the prospect, but she put it away. Focused. Called on the self-control and single-mindedness she'd honed with years of unstinting sweat to dredge up a doubtful nose-wrinkle for the man beside her.

"So you're gambling your entire future—and I assume your life savings—on an event that happens once every twenty-ish years?"

"Yep." He tucked his hands into his pockets and turned his face to the night sky.

"I don't know, Einar. Building your life plan around moonlight seems a little risky."

"Around your moon, sure. The one you can see from your window back in Minneapolis. But this isn't that moon."

Goose squinted upward. "I'm pretty sure it is, actually."

He shook his head. "Does your moon look like this? Feel like this?" he asked as moonlight bathed his perfect face. "Can't you sense it, Goose? How close She is here? How full, how ripe? How powerful?"

"And you want that?" Goose asked slowly, blinking at the naked hunger in his eyes as he gazed up at the moon. "Power?"

He shook his head ruefully, the hunger in his face taking on an unwelcome earthiness as he brought his attention back to her. "I want lots of things," he said, his eyes dropping to her lips. Uh-oh. "Who doesn't?"

Crap. She'd known it was dicey, letting him get her alone under a romantic moon. Even puppies had teeth, and she'd just gotten a look at the sort of bite Einar had to offer. It was decidedly more carnal than she'd anticipated. Most men who toyed with teenage girls didn't have the balls to approach a woman their own age, but Einar didn't appear to have any problem on that front. So did this mean he *wasn't* preying on Yarrow's feelings for him? Or that he just wasn't your ordinary child molester? She stared at him, frozen by the debate raging in her head.

"Goose," he said softly, and reached for her.

Then the night air was rent by the bellow of an enraged moose and the bright twinkle of breaking glass.

Chapter

15

GOOSE RACED down the street with Einar trailing behind at a leisurely amble. She'd never seen him move faster than a reluctant trot, now that she thought of it. Which was fine with her, considering the wicked intent she'd recognized in those Caribbean-blue eyes back on the dock. Lord knew she didn't want the guy moving any faster than absolutely necessary.

She spotted a knot of people standing in the street between Lila's place and Ben Barnes's. Rush was there already, his shorn head and closed face looming over his aunt, and Goose jogged over to him. She slipped a hand into his elbow and tugged.

"Rush, hey." She threw a wayward hank of hair away from her mouth while Rush angled himself to shield her from the wet slap of the wind. "What happened?"

"Sounds like our rogue moose was looking for love in all the wrong places again," Rush said.

"It's that damn garbage pile in your backyard," Ben Barnes said to Lila. "How many times do I have to tell you? Compost only works if you maintain the pile. You can't just throw your trash out the back door and expect not to attract wildlife."

Lila tossed her head. "The wildlife was here first, Mr. Barnes. I don't think my compost has anything to do with a rogue moose who's confused about when mating season ended."

"It seems," Rush interrupted when it looked like Ben was about to go for Lila's throat, "the moose was stomping around by Lila's compost pile and caught his own reflection in Ben's bay window across the yard. Pretty bright moon tonight, I guess. Took offense and charged himself."

"Yeah, and I've got the shattered window to prove it," Ben said bitterly. "You know what it costs to replace a window that size?" He stuffed his hands into his pockets and glared at Lila. "My insurance premiums are going to go through the roof."

"Not necessarily," Goose said. "Not if somebody else's insurance processes the claim."

Lila frowned at her. "You want *my* insurance to pay for *his* window?"

"Of course not." Goose gave her arm a reassuring pat. "I was thinking more of the Park Service's insurance."

Rush frowned down at her. "The Park Service's?"

"Sure. Isn't it their job to manage the moose population on Mishkwa?"

Lila and Ben both bent a stern look on Rush.

"Yeah," he said slowly. "It is. That could actually work. I'll make some calls."

"In the morning, though, please," Lila said. She checked her watch. "We have esbat in a few minutes, and we'll want to get started right on time. There's a spell casting tonight. Libby Lane's fibromyalgia is acting up." She glanced at Rush, hope in her eyes. "You *are* coming?"

Rush looked up from the notepad where he was scribbling something. "Ah . . ."

"Rush. You promised."

"Okay, all right. I'll just see Goose back to the Ranger Station," he said. "Be back in half an hour. Forty-five, tops."

Einar appeared at Goose's side and she jumped. She'd forgotten he was even there. Whoops. "May I see you home, Goose?" he asked.

"But then you'd miss esbat." She blinked innocently at him and hoped the subtext would sink in without further effort on her part. *I'd rather you go to church than try to kiss me again, 'kay?*

"They come once a month." He smiled deep into her eyes. Seductively. Crap. "There'll be another one."

"Still." Goose turned to Lila in near desperation. "I'm about to be unforgivably forward," she said, "but do you think I could come? To esbat?"

Lila clapped her hands in delight and Ben heaved a disgusted sigh. "You seem like a decent enough girl," he said to her. "Why would you want to get mixed up with a bunch of naked, aging hippies?"

"Why, Ben!" Lila laughed. "Have you been spying?"

He flushed. "Hard to miss a conga line of idiots cha-chaing through my backyard in the altogether, Lila."

"And you all alone in that big house," she said softly. "You must be dreadfully lonely."

"Oh, for God's sake." Ben shook his head and fixed an eye on Goose. "There's a nice Catholic church in Hornby Harbor if you're feeling the need for services. Wednesday and Saturday nights, Sunday mornings."

Goose put a hand on his arm, gave him a warm smile. "Thanks, Ben," she said. "I'm more curious than faithful, though. I've never been to a pagan service." She turned to Lila. "Do you mind if I sit in?"

"What a wonderful idea!" Lila gifted her with a warm smile and turned to Rush. "Rush, isn't that a wonderful idea?"

"Yep." He sounded distinctly less than thrilled. "Wonderful."

Goose peered through the darkness at Rush while Lila disappeared into the house, presumably to gather equipment or robes or incense or, cripes, for all Goose knew, broomsticks and pointy hats. Einar followed her and Goose nearly sagged in relief. The reprieve was temporary, of course. She knew that. He'd try again. A guy like Einar always had a second act. But for tonight, anyway, she was in the clear.

"Come on, then," Rush said. He grabbed her hand and pulled her toward the footpath running between Ben's and Lila's front porches.

"Where are we going?"

"Esbat."

She blinked as he led her deeper into the darkness between the two houses. "Wait, there's not really a naked cha-cha during this thing, is there?"

Rush threw her an unreadable look over his shoulder. "A cha-cha? No. It's been a while, but I'd remember that."

"I should hope so," Goose murmured. It didn't escape her notice that he hadn't addressed the naked part of her question, and she took a moment to wonder what she'd gotten herself into. It was warm out for December, but not so warm that she was interested in taking off even her mittens, let alone her clothes. Then again, if Rush went first—

She nearly plowed into his back before she realized he'd stopped on the path ahead of her. She peered over his shoulder toward the people milling around Lila's backyard.

"Aren't we supposed to be out there?" she asked, nodding toward the minglers.

"In a minute." He dropped his chin, leveled her a shrewd look. "Just as soon as you tell me what you're up to."

"Up to?" She gave him very big eyes. "I just want to observe the esbat."

"Mmm-hmm." He folded his arms, planted himself. "Why?"

"I like a good show?"

"It's church. Not theater."

"Oh, please. What church isn't theater? I'll bet Lila knows her way around a dramatic moment, too."

He maintained a skeptical silence.

"And, all right, I've also got my eyes open for a power-mad counterfeiter with bloody fingers. Don't pretend you aren't looking, too."

The silence grew. Goose rolled a shoulder.

"And it's possible, I suppose, that I wanted out of Einar's chivalrous offer to see me home."

"I see. And why is that?"

"Sir Humpalot threw him off his moves earlier but he was ramping up for another pass, okay? I didn't feel like making excuses."

His brows came together. "Einar moved on you?"

"Not like it was a big surprise. I think he moves on every woman in a five-mile radius. It's like a reflex or something." She frowned. "Which isn't very flattering, now that I think about it."

"So you took evasive action? Why bother? He doesn't hear 'no' very often, but he understands the basic concept."

She hesitated. "It's not that simple."

His eyes went flat, cool. "No?" He stepped back. "I thought it was."

She stepped forward. "Rush, it's not what you're thinking."

"Isn't it?"

"God, of course not! It's just—" She broke off, looked around him to the crowd gathering in Lila's backyard. Candlelight danced on the air, laughing voices rose and fell. This wasn't the time or the place to get into what exactly she was doing with Einar. What she suspected him of.

"Just what?"

"It's time for esbat," she said. "Can we please talk about this later?"

She didn't wait for an answer, but sidestepped him and moved into the yard. It was full of brown-robed people in many of whose living rooms she'd sat and sipped tea and nibbled cookies a few days ago. Rush followed like her own personal storm cloud, though only she seemed aware of the dark menace in his frown. Hands reached out from all directions to pat his shoulder, touch his elbow. People greeted him with surprise, with smiles but above all with welcome.

They've missed him, she thought as she joined the line of women waiting to enter the candlelit circle. Rush joined the line of men. *This is his family, and they've missed him*.

Lila stood just inside the circle, greeting the men. Einar stood beside her, greeting the women. When Rush reached the front of the line, Lila dipped her fingers into a small bowl, smeared something oily on his forehead and said, "In the name of the goddess, in the name of the god, I bid you welcome to this sacred place." Her voice dropped, went husky with emotion, and she placed ritual kisses on both cheeks, a step she'd skipped with everybody else. "Merry meet, nephew."

A sniffle sounded from inside the circle and Goose saw Ronnie Samuelsson blink back a tear. She wasn't the only covener watching aunt and nephew with suspiciously bright eyes, either. *He's home*, Goose thought again, her heart squeezing unbearably. He was finally back home and everybody knew how much it meant except him. Even Einar.

Maybe especially Einar, she thought. He stood in front of Goose, his fingers stiff on the bowl of oil or whatever it was he and Lila were anointing people with, his eyes fixed on the little scene between his aunt and cousin. And he wasn't crying happy tears, either.

Goose cleared her throat and Einar turned back to her with a smooth smile. He touched wet fingers to her forehead and said, "In the name of the goddess, in the name of the god, I bid you welcome to this sacred place." He laid a hand on her shoulder. "Merry meet, sister."

She gave him an automatic smile and moved into the circle described by the candles. After a few moments of distracted milling about, three bells sounded and Lila raised her voice above the crowd.

"Welcome, peace and love to each soul in this place."

"Welcome, peace and love," the coven murmured.

"We've got a full schedule tonight," Lila said, smiling out over the crowd. "We'll have the Rite of the Full Moon, plus a spell for healing for Libby's fibromyalgia. Are there any announcements before we begin?" She let a long beat of silence pass, then lifted her arms and turned to face the yellow candle at the circle's entrance. "Hail to the East . . ."

TWO HOURS later, Rush hiked back to the Ranger Station with the moon riding high and ripe in the night sky overhead, and temper rumbling low and ominous inside him.

"You didn't tell me Einar was a pagan," Goose said from behind him. "Let alone a pagan *priest*."

"Was I supposed to?" He kept his tone carefully even. He didn't want to talk about Einar. Einar with his Greek-god face and his affable charm, who'd just tonight tried to put his sticky, greedy hands all over the only thing Rush had wanted in years.

Mine.

It had chimed inside him, this inconvenient *mine*, the instant he'd kissed her in that ugly old truck. It was like his moral compass had just woken up and declared Goose true north. She *drew* him now in some fundamental way he couldn't even explain, let alone argue with. Then along came Einar—pretty, amusing Einar—and threw his ante into the pot. Shit.

"Does the Secret Service care what religion he is?" Rush asked now, perhaps a trifle sharply. "Do you?"

"No," she said slowly. "It's just interesting. I mean, his religion is none of my business, obviously. But paganism seems to be an integral aspect of the island community. An integral aspect of his—and your—family history."

"And you care about the family history?"

"Of course."

He stopped, turned on her. "Why?"

She blinked, those dark eyes going wide with surprise. "Why?"

"Yes, Goose. Why are you interested? So there's a pseudo-hippie population here that likes to strip down and perform ceremonies under the full moon. So what? It's a national park. If there weren't naked hippies, I think we could lose funding or something. What is it about it—or him—that you find so fascinating?"

"I just wondered if it was new," she said. "Einar's devotion to the family religion."

He stepped closer, and his belly hollowed at the sight of her guarded, bottomless eyes in the pale wash of the moonlight. She was keeping something back, he thought with a dull thud of dismay. Hiding something. Not the investigation. He already knew about that. Feelings for Einar, then? Feelings that would hurt poor, pathetic Rush? She wouldn't want that, would she? Of course not. God.

"New? How could it be new? It's like you said—it's been going on as long as my family's been tangled up with this place."

"But for him," she persisted. "Is it something he's always believed in?"

Was she really going to pump him for information on her new crush? He laughed, even as anger rose inside him. Even as it twisted together with the hunger and grew to an aching want. A sharp, compelling need. "You want to know what Einar believes? He believes in getting what he wants."

"Which is?"

He jerked his shoulders in a rough shrug. "Everything. He's like a fucking seagull, okay? If it's bright, he wants it. If it's shiny, he wants it. If other people have it, God, does he want it. Gets it, too. He's good that way."

He loosed an ugly chuckle. "You're not his usual, but I can see why he wants you." He yanked off his glove and reached for her. Her eyes were huge in her angular face, but she didn't flinch away from him, and the thumb he ran over the sharp blade of her cheekbone was, thank God, gentle. Because what burned inside him was anything but. "You're so very, very shiny, aren't you? Polished bright as a new penny."

"Rush, I—"

He cut her off before she could ask even one more question. "I don't know what Einar believes in terms of religion," he said impatiently. "All I know is that people have been getting naked here and howling for the moon since there was a moon to howl for. Some places strip away the civilization better than others, and Mishkwa is one of the best. We're all just animals here. Not so different from that damn moose, all heat and anger and drive and want." He slipped his hand into the glorious warmth of her hair, felt it slide like living water over his fingers to pool in his palm. "Einar, though, he's a greedy bastard. He wants everything."

She stared up at him, her eyes impossibly wide and deep.

"Me, though?" He shook his head. "I only want you."

And he kissed her.

Chapter

16

IT WAS like crashing through the ice, Goose thought as the black waters of Rush's kiss closed over her head. A devastating, disorienting, full-body shock. Not cold, though. Jesus, no. His mouth was hot on hers, aggressive and assured and uncompromising, and she understood that diplomatic relations had just been terminated. This was no warning, fair or otherwise. This was taking.

Taking. Satisfaction sang through her even as sharp-edged hunger began to churn. The clean, male scent of him filled her, enveloped her, sang to her, and desire rolled up hot and thick from that dark place in her soul where appetite lurked, dangerous and relentless.

But she didn't check it. Not this time. No, this time she rode the surge of it, gloried in the whippy, consuming thrill of *wanting*. He'd only whetted her appetite with that sneaky, sucker punch of a kiss back in town. He hadn't satisfied, only fed that dangerous, smoky little fire she'd been stamping at ever since landing on this island.

And now he breathed that fire into flames. Flames that roared. Crackled. *Craved.*

His big hand tipped her chin to a different angle, and she lost herself. Lost the self she'd cultivated so carefully over the years. The self with the strength to resist, control, moderate. She rose up on her toes and met him, matched him, opened to him, not in eager invitation but in fierce demand.

His tongue slid hot and wild into her mouth, sending a liquid pulse of *yes* through her entire body. Her hands fisted in his coat collar, wound themselves into the fabric there. She anchored herself into the heat and strength of his body, rocking and sliding and pleasing herself against the hard length of him. She tipped her face up, let the moonlight spill over her skin, and kissed him back.

She kissed him with everything inside her. With all the heady, driving desire, yes. But also with the loneliness, the pain and the weariness she hadn't even been aware of until he'd shoved aside her charm and her smile and demanded to see somebody else. The woman she used to be.

The woman she sometimes—despite of every ounce of her strength and courage—still was.

A shock of shame and guilt, more powerful for its familiarity, rolled over her and she snapped back to herself with a gasp. Rush had already released her. Had sensed, knowing him, the split second in which she'd withdrawn her real self, the self he'd been tugging on since that first kiss. He didn't want this other woman she'd cultivated. He didn't want Goose. He wanted the girl she'd been. The woman that girl would have grown into. The one who wanted without thought and took without limit. He wanted Maria. She knew that. He'd told her so, hadn't he? Walked away from her offer of some sweaty, no-strings sex in the hopes that he could have something more? Somebody more?

But he couldn't have that woman. Neither could Goose. Fire was glorious but it was nothing to play with.

"Rush," she began, regret an aching tightness in her throat. "I'm sorry. I—"

"Don't apologize." He reached down to retrieve the glove he'd let fall to the snow. "Just . . . don't."

"It's this *place*," she said anyway. She had to say *something*. A hot knot of tears lodged in her chest as she waved an arm at the whole ridiculous scene. The perfect bowl of evergreens skirting the quaint little cabin, the homey invitation of wood smoke hanging in the air, the full, fertile moon plastered round and lush in the night sky above them. "It's so—" Frustration had her fisting her hands on either side of her head, like she could threaten her brain into providing some magic words to fix this situation. Neutralize it. God, *erase* it.

"Einar's no fool," she finally said with a bitter laugh. "This island *is* a gold mine. It's a drug. And the guy who figures out how to bottle and sell whatever this place does to people is going to end up richer than hell."

"Fuck that." Rush shoved one hand into his snowy glove and glared at her. "And fuck lying, too, Goose. To yourself *and* to me."

She stared at him, openmouthed. "Lying?"

"Honesty, Agent di Guzman." He shook his head. "You promised."

"I *am* being—"

"The fuck you are," he said, and the banked fury in his silver eyes knocked her back a step. "Blaming your shit on an *island*? Please." His hard mouth curled in disgust. "Mishkwa doesn't do anything to people except cut them off from all the noise. It doesn't put anything in you, Goose. It strips things away. Forces you to look yourself right in the eye." He gave a ragged laugh. "Jesus, what do you think I'm here for?"

"The view?" She tried for a flip smile but her lips were numb with shock.

"I came back to face myself. I needed to look at what was in me. To figure out if I could live with it. Turned out I could. I *can*." His eyes locked on hers, and compassion swirled into the burning anger there. "Can you?"

Anger slapped at her, sudden and nasty. "Of course I

can live with myself," she snapped. She'd spent the last twelve years proving it, hadn't she? To herself? To her family? To the world? "Hell, I'll go you one better. I not only live with myself, I *improve* myself. Daily."

"Well, there's your problem."

"My *what*?"

"You're not living *with* yourself, Goose. You're living in spite of yourself." He touched her cheek, his fingers gentle despite that stony gaze. "You don't need improvement. You just need to be yourself. And until you figure out how to do that, you're no good to anybody. No matter how pretty you are."

She stared at him in stunned dismay, her head ringing like he'd smashed her upside it with a Mallet of Truth or something.

Because he was right, damn him. She wasn't living *with* herself. She was living *around* herself. Around what was inside her. She'd built a life based on avoidance, where every choice she made—from her career down to her hairstyle—allowed her to pretend she was making herself *better* rather than different. Making the most of what God had given her rather than simply creating a pretty shell in which she could lock away her dangerous and disappointing— and truest—self.

And up until this very moment, it had worked. Hell, it had rocked. Because twelve years ago she'd been awkward and passionate and angry and hungry. But now? Now she was shiny and successful and well dressed and . . .

And still hungry. Still passionate. Still angry. But now she could throw in tired, scared and lonely, too.

And just when the hell had *that* happened? The plan had worked, and worked well, for years. How had things come apart with such spectacular suddenness?

It was Rush. Of course it was. The problem, she realized, was that the plan only worked when she wanted to be in control more than she wanted anything else.

And now she found herself wanting something— some*one*—as much if not more than her precious control.

"Rush," she said, reaching for him in spite of herself.

He stepped back, and her stupid body mourned. "Figure it out, Goose. Figure out who you are and what you want." His eyes dropped to her mouth. "Soon."

Tears prickled in her eyes, swift and shaming, but he didn't see them as he'd already turned his back on her. Small mercies, she thought. He headed down the trail toward the Ranger Station, and after a single, wretched moment, Goose fell in behind him. She didn't weep as she followed, though. Didn't allow herself even one single, self-indulgent tear.

Chapter

17

"TEA, DEAR?" Lila asked the next morning, and Goose smiled. Tea seemed to be Lila's all-purpose antidote for whatever ailed a person. No wonder she had a pot in every room.

"No, thanks. I don't want to put you to any trouble, especially not so early." She glanced toward the window, where the winter sun struggled to achieve liftoff from the horizon. "You're going to start locking the doors before business hours if I keep dropping by at dawn."

Lila gave her a smile as she settled into the curvy wire café chair across from her. "Dawn works just fine for me, Agent di Guzman. You get to be my age and sleep is rarer than rubies."

Goose shook her head. "You're not exactly elderly, Lila."

Lila gave her hand a brisk pat. "Sweet. But what about you? I know for a fact Rush's been snowshoeing you all over the island. Why aren't you sleeping the sleep of the righteous this morning?"

"I have one of those brains," she said easily, though

she was anything but easy over the sleepless night she'd passed. "The kind that won't turn off if there's a good question to chew on, no matter how tired I am."

"I see."

Goose feared she did, actually. Lila didn't miss much. But she didn't press, so Goose didn't offer. She just pasted on a smile and said, "Do you mind if I ask you some questions about the coven here on Mishkwa?"

"Of course not, dear. Ask away. I'll confess I'm surprised, though. I thought you'd have asked Einar anything you wanted to know last night."

"Sir Humpalot cut our conversation short." Thank God.

"Mmm," Lila said, as if she'd heard the mental aside. Goose shifted uncomfortably. She hadn't considered until just this moment how Lila might feel about her rejecting Einar's romantic attentions. And if Lila didn't like that, she really wasn't going to like the rest of this conversation.

"So," Goose said with a determined briskness. "Einar tells me he's in line to inherit the coven."

"He and Rush," Lila said. "We're the last of our line, the boys and me. When I'm gone, it'll just be them."

"Which one will inherit leadership? Have you decided?"

"My hope is that they'll lead together."

Goose let the skepticism show on her face. "Does Einar know that?"

Lila tipped her head. "You think he'd feel slighted?"

"You think he wouldn't? He's the dutiful son, after all. Staying, working, tending, while Rush disappears for years at a time. He's earned his half of the birthright, easy, and Rush's, too. Probably even has plans for it already."

"Plans?"

"It was my impression," Goose said carefully, "that Einar would like Mishkwa Coven to be a bit more high profile."

"Oh," Lila said. "The Paganpalooza thing." She waved a dismissive hand. "Einar can't help himself. He's an entrepreneur to his bones. The boy loves people, parties, crowds."

"Money."

Lila's eyes went shrewd and sharp, but she inclined her head in acknowledgment of that truth. "Money, too. Things for which Rush cares not at all. They'd balance each other."

"Why don't you trust him?"

"Who, Rush?"

"No, Einar."

Lila drew back. "Of course I trust Einar. Why wouldn't I?"

"I don't know, Lila. You tell me. You made him a priest, you gave him the title, the responsibility, the show. But when push comes to shove, you don't want to let him fly solo."

"What are you saying, Agent di Guzman?"

"I'm not saying, I'm asking." Goose leaned in, her voice as soft as her words were harsh. "Why don't you trust him, Lila? What is it you see in Einar that you don't like?"

Lila shook her head slowly. "You're asking me if it's Einar, aren't you? You're asking if my nephew is your money runner."

"Or your bloodletter," Goose said.

Lila flinched at that but didn't break. "If a hunger drove him, for either money or power," she said slowly, "surely he wouldn't have stayed on Mishkwa all these years. Surely he'd have sought out something larger, something brighter—"

"You're giving me logic now." Goose shook her head. "Logic, I have. What I want from you isn't what you know or what you've concluded. I want to know what you feel." She caught Lila's eyes with own, refused to look away. "Is it in him, Lila? That hunger? That need? That appetite for more, always more, that might drive a person beyond caution?"

"It's inside you." The words drove Goose back against her chair. As slaps went, it was a good one. Clean and cold, exactly on target and breathtakingly unexpected.

"In me?"

"You," Lila snapped, her lips tight in her stern face. Then she softened, relented. "In everybody, dear. It's universal.

It's just closer to the surface in some than in others. I see it in Einar, yes. But I see it in you, too. You're just better at reining it in. You've likely had a great deal of practice."

"I have, yes." She could admit that much. Why not? Rush had all but bashed her over the head with it last night. It took daily, unstinting effort to be better, always better, than she actually was. An effort she was committed to, no matter how seductive Rush could make freedom sound.

"Einar has a bit of growing up to do yet. Then again, Rush has some road to walk himself. That's why I'm hoping they can find a way to get along. Those boys need each other."

Light and dark, Goose thought. Words and silence. Style and substance.

"I'm just trying to make them see it while I still can," Lila said. She rose, and Goose took the hint.

"Thanks so much for sitting down with me, Lila," she said, coming to her feet. "This has really clarified a few things for me."

"I'm glad."

Goose headed for the door. Then, hand on the knob, she turned. "Can I ask you one more thing?"

"Of course."

"Does Yarrow ever talk about Einar?"

Lila cocked her head. "You mean does she talk to me about her feelings for him?"

Goose lifted her brows. Lila might play at New Age earth mother, but not much got past her. "Yeah, that's what I mean."

"No. She doesn't talk about it and I don't pry. Our Lady didn't lay out an easy path for that child. It's not my story to tell, but she's healing up here. I hope she'll come to me when she's ready."

"And if she doesn't?" Goose swallowed back a sudden lump of remembered anguish and pressed forward. "Do you trust Einar to keep her safe on your behalf? Do you trust him that much?"

Lila held her gaze for a long tense moment. "He's my blood."

A nonanswer, Goose thought, and it fed the embers of concern glowing inside her.

"Talk to her about him," Goose urged. "If you haven't yet, please do. If there's nothing to worry about, you won't have hurt anybody. But if there is—"

Lila crossed the space between them and deliberately took Goose's cold hand between her two warm ones. She stood frozen while Lila studied her, their palms clasped loosely together. It was an oddly intimate sensation, and yet not invasive. A touch. A tender, almost motherly connection. When was the last time somebody had touched her like this? The last time anybody had tried? Certainly her own mother hadn't.

Finally Lila said, "There's so much darkness trapped inside you, dear. Sorrow and rage and hurt. Love and desire are twisted up in there, too, but even they have dark, sharp edges." She released Goose's hand and said gently, "Perhaps if you let some of it go, you'd have an easier time telling the difference between what's inside you and what's outside."

"I—" Goose broke off, swallowed. Was that true? Was she projecting what was inside her, her own pain, her own past, onto Yarrow and Einar? She shook her head. She couldn't worry about that. Couldn't yank out everything inside her to examine it every time her gut raised a red flag. "If I'm wrong, I'll be embarrassed and sincerely apologetic," she told Lila. "But what if I'm right? Could you live with yourself if you didn't take every opportunity to protect a child under your care?"

"That's why I'm saying this," Lila said serenely. "You're not a child and you're not mine, but somebody needs to care for you. You're carrying a terrible burden, dear. An old burden. Don't you think it's time to put it down?"

"How?" The word escaped her, almost involuntarily. How could she possibly put down everything she'd carried all these years?

"Both my nephews were looking at you with a very masculine appreciation last night," Lila said. "Take your pick. That might help. Or don't pick. Take them both. Whatever works."

At Goose's openmouthed stare, Lila gave a light laugh. "We're a very sex-positive religion, dear. The who, how many or how many at a time is completely up to you. But sex and love are a gift from Our Lady. Your body, your passions, should be a source of pleasure. It's not natural for a woman as young and beautiful as you are to feel so old and tired inside."

Goose thought about Rush's kiss and everything in her flashed hot. "I don't feel old or tired right now," she said slowly.

"No, I picked up on that, and it's a nice start. But you're still blocked." Lila's smile spread. "Finish the job, dear. You'll feel better. And more to the point, you'll see so much more clearly. Both yourself, and those around you."

YARROW SCRUBBED at her eyes as she stumbled into the kitchen. Lila had a hot pot of something black as midnight on the table and Yarrow poured herself a generous cup. It might taste like boiled weeds but it was hot and strong and caffeinated. Which was ideal because she hadn't slept for shit last night. Not with the electricity of her little chat with Einar still kicking around her system.

She smiled into her cup. Maybe she was reading into things. Maybe she was an idiot for imagining Einar thought of her as anything other than his perennially fucked-up little cousin. It hardly mattered. Last night was the first decent thing that had happened to her in months. The only ray of light in the endless night of future. And until Einar himself disabused her of the notion, she was going to enjoy the hell out of it.

She hummed as she tied on her apron. Lila had already churned out a day's worth of baked goods and breads, filling a bakery rack by the kitchen door. Yarrow pulled in a greedy lungful of butter and sugar fumes. This island might be at the ass end of the earth, but there were a few perks. Lila could *bake*.

She slid the tray from the rack and backed through the swinging door from the kitchen into the dining room. She headed for the counter, ready to load the pastries into the glass-fronted display case, but stopped short when she heard the one voice that could cut through a happiness this pure.

Agent Smiley Face said, "Lila, I'm not here to—"

"Of course you're not," Lila said.

"But you just said I should—"

"My opinion only." Lila folded Goose's hands into hers with a benevolent smile. "Do whatever feels right to you. Blessed be, child."

Lila gave Goose's cheeks the ritual pecks that always went with the "blessed be" then swirled toward the kitchen. Yarrow sidestepped to make way, only to receive her own cheek pecks.

"Up already?" Lila said. "And at work, too? Good girl."

Then Lila was gone, leaving Yarrow and her deflated mood alone with Agent di Guzman. She turned to the bakery case and started filling it as if she were completely alone. Then there was a gentle throat clearing at the counter.

Crap. Could nobody on this island take a hint?

"Yarrow?"

"What?"

"Any chance I could get a loaf of that sourdough?"

Yarrow snatched up a tissue paper from the dispenser box on the counter, grabbed out a round little boule of sourdough and shoved it into a brown bag. She tossed it onto the counter with a swing that might've done an Olympic discus thrower proud. Goose caught it before it could bounce away.

"Five-fifty," Yarrow said.

Goose held out the money instead of putting it on the counter. Yarrow eyed her silently for just long enough to be insulting, then sighed dramatically and reached for the money. If Agent Smiley Face wanted another little taste of Yarrow's brand of crazy, she was welcome to it. She focused the blackness inside her to a crude shiv of anger and hate and put it all in her eyes, in the palm of the hand she reached toward the happy, shiny agent.

Goose put the money into her hand, but she didn't flinch at the contact like she had yesterday. Like most people did. This time she only smiled, though it was a little bent around the edges.

"Why so sad, Yarrow?" she asked softly.

"I'm not sad," Yarrow said as a quick pulse of shock chased itself through her system. Was she? She fought the urge to pull back, to cover herself as if Goose had walked in on her naked. Being seen was being seen, though. That was something. Still, she glared at Goose over their joined hands. "I just hate you."

"For what?" Goose asked. She didn't back away from Yarrow's touch.

"For wanting what's mine."

"I don't want what's yours. I just want to help you—"

"Then go the fuck away."

Chapter

18

IT WAS only ten A.M. but Rush had been on trail for five-plus hours already. He hadn't slept much after his little throw-down with Goose last night, and as soon as it wasn't technically the middle of night anymore, he'd strapped on the snowshoes and gotten hiking.

He did his best thinking while his body was busy, one of his primary reasons for taking this job in the first place. He'd given the matter some serious thought as his breath sawed in and out, his brain moving in time to the shuss of his feet, and he'd concluded that while his timing maybe sucked—and what else was new—his content was right on.

There was a war raging inside Goose. Rush knew that. He'd sensed it in that first desperate kiss, and he'd sensed it again last night. Instinct and passion and *yes* wrecked themselves against reason and control and *no*, like waves crashing onto the rocky shore. And all Rush could do was sit on the sidelines and cheer like hell for *yes*. Because while there was nothing he wanted more than to wade into the battle himself, Rush knew a thing or two about facing down personal demons. This was a fight Goose had to tackle alone.

Which was exactly what he'd told her last night. So while his delivery was probably regrettable, he stood by everything he'd said. He squinted through the trees at the smoke twirling cheerfully from the Ranger Station chimney. That was no banked fire. That was a nice, warm-your-hands blaze, which meant Goose was home, feeding the fire and waiting to yell at him. Which meant he'd be getting the chance to repeat himself sooner rather than later.

He broke into an eager jog—damn, he had it bad—but stopped the instant he broke the tree line. Anticipation shifted abruptly to foreboding. Goose's snowshoes weren't in the snowbank. She wasn't here. But judging from that thick curl of smoke coming from the chimney, somebody was.

His hand was curled around the butt of the SIG in his pocket before he was even conscious of stripping off his glove. He melted back into the trees and circled around until he could approach the cabin from behind. He edged along the outer wall, careful to keep a silent inch between his jacket and the rough wood. He wrapped his off hand around the doorknob and slipped into his own house on silent feet, his finger utterly steady where it lay beside the trigger.

"Einar." Rush shoved his gun back into his pocket and glared at his cousin, squatting in front of the woodstove with a sly grin. Adrenaline crashed uselessly through his system. "One of these days I really am going to shoot you."

Einar laughed.

"Seriously. You need to start knocking." Rush gave the fire Einar was poking a dark look. "You might consider waiting for an invitation before coming in, too."

Einar ignored that. He tossed the stick into the flames and closed the stove door.

"You still make a nice fire," he said as Rush slapped the door shut behind him. "The coals were banked exactly right. Took me like three seconds and a handful of kindling to bring 'er back." He grinned. "Grandpa would be proud of you."

"I didn't bank it." Rush peeled out of his jacket and hung it on a peg by the door. "Goose did."

Einar laughed. "Some woman you got there, Rush."

Rush ignored that and hung up his backpack. He didn't have Goose. Not yet. He would eventually. He didn't doubt that. But there was some rough ground to cover between here and there. He chucked his damp hat and gloves on the floor in front of the stove to dry, then moved into the kitchen and rattled around in the cupboards.

"What are you doing here, Einar?" he asked, peeling a coffee filter off the stack and sticking it into the machine. He kept his eyes carefully away from the spare bedroom. Goose's room.

"She's not here," Einar said, a thread of amusement into his voice. "I already looked."

Rush scowled, shoved the pot under the drip and punched the brew button. He wasn't sure what pissed him off more—that Einar was looking for Goose, or that he himself couldn't walk through a doorway without looking for her, too. Even when he knew full well she wasn't there. "Who?"

Einar helped himself to a bar stool. Front-row seats, Rush thought. "Goose," he said. "The woman whose very name is apparently enough to have you pacing around your own house like a bear in the zoo."

Rush slammed a drawer shut, then caught himself.

Einar laughed. "It's that good, huh?"

"What is?"

"The sex."

Rush went very still. "What makes you think I'm having sex with her?"

"Rush, please. I was like four feet from the two of you last night and I swear the heat nearly singed my eyebrows off."

Rush treated him to a stoic silence and Einar sighed. Theatrically. "I know she doesn't think you're really gunning for the governor. And I'm pretty sure that while the Secret Service has its fingers in a lot of pies, they don't actually care if a couple of rogue pagans off a few house cats by the light of the full moon. And yet, she remains on-island, and shows not one sign of departing anytime soon. So I'm forced to conclude that either she's conducting a super-double-secret investigation or she's a slave to your mind-blowing sexual prowess."

It wasn't a question, and Rush didn't treat it like one. He wasn't great with words but knew better than to answer a question nobody had actually asked.

Einar sighed again. "So? What's the story?"

"No story." Rush carefully blanked his face and met Einar's eyes with nothing in his own. "She'll stay till she gets what she needs, I guess."

"I thought you were giving it to her," Einar said, a wicked twinkle in his eye. Rush spent the ensuing beat of silence debating the merits of putting his fist through his cousin's pretty, gleaming teeth. Einar's brows rose slowly. "Oh my God. You're not getting any? Seriously?"

"Any what?" Rush growled. He knew perfectly well *what*, but he'd be damned if he'd do any of Einar's talking for him.

"Sex."

"From who?"

"You really want me to say her name again? You almost tore the cupboard off the hinges last time."

Rush poured himself a cup of coffee with tightly controlled motions.

"Listen, Rush, I know you don't like to talk about the woo-woo stuff of our childhood, but your balances are all out of whack here. Light, dark. Good, bad. Positive, negative." He shook his head, as if filled with pity. "You need to get laid, buddy."

Rush let the comment pass in silence. He would love—truly love—to get laid, but he wasn't discussing it with Einar.

"But I'd like to get laid, too," Einar went on. "And if you're really not going to take a cut at that truly fine piece of federal ass?" He paused significantly, likely waiting for Rush to jump in with something—clarification, denial, contradiction. Rush clamped his teeth down around all of the above and remained silent. Einar's smile spread. "Then, damn, boy. I will."

Rush had been working on it, but his trigger finger was still a hair touchier than would be considered acceptable by the general populace.

Okay, a lot touchier.

Sneaking into Rush's house unannounced was a damn good way to get your ass blown to kingdom come. Announcing your intention to seduce the woman Rush had singularly failed to seduce the night before? The woman who still had desire whispering hot through his veins this morning? That was a pretty good way to get shot, too.

It took every ounce of self-control Rush had to take a leisurely sip of coffee and say, "Best of luck, son."

Einar peered at him, head cocked. "Seriously? You're not going to rip out my throat or anything?"

Rush shook his head. He had a feeling Goose could take care of that all by herself if it became necessary, and the accompanying visual had the tight smile on his face morphing into something more genuine. "Girl's got a mind of her own," he said simply. "Guess she knows how to make it up for herself."

Einar gave a delighted laugh and pushed to his feet. "You keep on believing that, cuz," he said as he pulled on his coat. "You just keep on believing that."

He was still chuckling as he strode out the door into the drip of melting snow. Rush sipped his coffee and watched him go. He wasn't really surprised to see that Einar was gearing up for an official move on Goose. It made him want to punch something—specifically Einar—but he was actually sort of surprised the guy hadn't announced himself sooner.

But while taking his ladykiller cousin out of commission would be vastly satisfying on a personal level, Rush also knew it wouldn't help his cause with Goose at all if she discovered him and Einar trading punches to determine ownership of her hand. It would only be a distraction, a side fight, and she was busy enough already battling her way from no to yes. Rush didn't need to give her even one reason to suspect he didn't trust her judgment enough to pick the right answer, let alone the right guy.

But he was still landing extremely gratifying mental punches on Einar's smug, lantern jaw when Goose breezed through the door.

"Hey, Rush," she said, hanging her coat on the hook next to his. She lifted her face to the air, closed her eyes and drew in a breath. A beatific smile spread over her sharp face and she said, "Ah, coffee. You're a prince among men. Anybody ever tell you that?"

"Not lately."

"Then I'll do it." She came into the kitchen and patted his arm with that brisk, platonic touch she used so effectively. It was deliberately impersonal—a not-too-subtle reminder of last night's "no thanks"—but it sent a surge of awareness skittering over his entire body anyway. "You're a prince among men," she said, and reached past him into the cupboard for a coffee cup.

"You might not think so after the next few days."

"Why's that?" she asked, her eyes dancing over the rim of her cup.

"Weather's coming."

She glanced out the window, where fingers of trailing mist slid through the trees, and melting snow dripped slowly from the roof. "Aw. It's going to get cold again?"

"Yeah." Rush cleared his throat. "It may snow and blow a little, too."

She frowned at him. "Okay, so translating from Rush into Human, that's roughly, what? Negative sixty, winds up to eighty knots, and twelve, fourteen feet of snow?"

"Roughly," he agreed.

"So what does that mean?"

"It means we're eating anything that can't be stuck in a snowbank until the power comes back on, and recharging all our batteries and cell phones before it goes out. We should bring in enough firewood for the weekend at least, and if you're interested in one last hot shower, you might want to do it sooner rather than later. That precious hair dryer of yours will be collecting dust by tomorrow morning."

He took in her stricken expression and decided to drop the final bomb. Better to deal with it all at once. "We'll lose Internet access first, so if there's any pressing e-mailing you need to do, you should get on it."

She set down her coffee cup and stared at him. "You don't have, like, a backup generator or anything?"

"Nope. People come to Mishkwa for a pristine, wilderness experience." He stretched his lips in what he hoped was a comforting smile. "We aim to please."

She reached a concerned hand up to the smooth fall of her hair. "How long does the power outage usually last?"

"Twenty-four, forty-eight hours after the storm, sometimes," he said. She sighed with relief, and honesty compelled him to add, "It can be up to a week, though."

She actually paled. "So we're going to be stuck together in this little cabin, without electricity, showers or—my God—the Internet, for an unspecified amount of time that could possibly be measured in *weeks*?"

Rush's stomach sank a little at the prospect stated so baldly. He hoped to God his good intentions didn't go out with the power, or he'd be busting out every move Einar thought he had, up to and including the old let's-conserve-body-heat line.

He paused. That was a good one, actually, because it was so true. Fucking like minks kept folks nice and toasty.

He snatched back his wayward thoughts before they generated an image of Goose wearing nothing but all that golden skin of hers and a whole bunch of firelight. This was her battle, he told himself sternly. No fair planting land mines. He'd thrown down the gauntlet last night—he wanted her to come to him of her own free will, with *yes* on her lips and in her heart. What good was *yes* if he stole it from her?

The fucking-like-minks thing came to mind again and he shoved it resolutely away.

"I'll just get started on that firewood," he said, and hustled toward the door. He snatched his jacket off the hook and shoved himself into it. Or tried to anyway. It took his preoccupied brain a few baffled beats to register that his sleeve was extraordinarily tight. And short.

And purple.

"That's my jacket," Goose said mildly from the kitchen.

"I see that." He tried to peel it off, but it was stuck like a burr on a golden retriever.

"You're welcome to it, but I don't think it fits very well."

He glared at her and gave up yanking on the cuff in exchange for just whipping his arm around. Violence and velocity often succeeded where reason and patience failed, and this was no exception to that handy rule. The jacket sailed across the room and landed on the sagging couch.

Goose snorted out one of those half-swallowed belly laughs of hers. As usual, it transformed her face from interesting to incandescent, and everything inside him went abruptly still.

Mine.

"Is that a 'no thanks'?" she asked, grinning.

Rush didn't answer. He knew if he opened his mouth, *no* wasn't the word that would come out. He stomped out into the damp yard to wrestle with the woodpile, her unabashed laughter chasing him out the door.

Chapter

19

THREE HOURS later the sky dropped onto the island, exactly as Rush had predicted. Snow rose and fell in strange, howling twists outside the frosted windows, driving the evergreens to moan and rock and weep. Icy air leaked into the Ranger Station straight through the walls, or so it seemed to Goose. It reached deep into the core of her and leached away something vital and warm.

"Good Lord," she said, rubbing her arms and moving closer to the stove. Unease perched lightly in her belly. "Was that thunder?"

"Yeah." Rush opened the stove door to feed the fire and Goose all but crawled up his back in an effort to get at the heat. She spread her hands in the blast of hot air.

"You can have snow and thunder at the same time?"

"Sure." He threw her a glance over his shoulder, blinked at how near she was. "Chilly?"

"Aren't you?" She looked out the window—the part that wasn't yet buried in snow anyway—and shuddered.

"You might want to put on a sweater or something," he

said. "I don't think this old stove will pump out much more
heat. It's pretty much running at capacity. Plus we'll want
to be relatively conservative with the wood. We don't know
how long this little squall will last yet."

"Little squall?" The wind battered the door like a wild
beast that had scented its prey. "You call this little?"

"Sure." He fed the fire a log and closed the stove door.
"We've still got power, don't we? Until the power goes out,
it's hardly—"

The lights flickered, dimmed, then died.

"—a storm." Rush sighed. "Okay, now it's a storm."

"Wonderful."

"Come on. Help me light the lamps. Then we can get set
up in here for the night."

He groped through the storm-induced twilight and
came up with her arm. His hand was so warm and solid
and reassuring that she leaned into him. She was so damn
cold. After a single startled moment, he gave her arm a
brisk scrub, a quick up-and-down with his hand. The sort
fathers give chilly daughters. If she hadn't been so freaked
out at finding the passionate battle raging inside herself
suddenly reflected in the out-of-doors, she might've been
offended. Or at least amused.

As it was she simply leaned closer.

"Wait, get *what* set up in here?" she asked as he led her
into the kitchen, where he'd arranged a series of antique
hurricane lamps earlier. He handed her a disposable lighter
and she lifted the glass globes and began filling the cabin
with an oily yellow light.

"Our beds."

Goose fumbled the lighter.

"Excuse me?"

"Power's out," he said, slipping a glass globe over the
wick she'd finally managed to light. "Which means the fans
that move hot air through the cabin are also out. Unless
you're looking forward to waking up tomorrow morning
with icicles on your eyebrows, we're bunking down in here
for the night."

"Oh."

"We'll close off the doors to the bedrooms, too. Mini-mize the space the stove needs to heat. I filled a few five-gallon buckets before the water pump went out. We can use a few for drinking and cooking; the other we can use to flush the toilet. We can back that up with melted snow, push comes to shove."

Goose stared blindly at a tiny flame licking at a cold, oily wick. What, she wondered, was more terrifying? The prospect of manually flushing a toilet? Or the prospect of spending a night—two nights? three?—sleeping close enough to Rush to take advantage of the heat from his body?

The memory of his kiss, hot and avid, blazed through her and she sighed.

At least she wouldn't be cold.

BY BEDTIME—or what the clock said should have been bedtime, as it had been dark for hours—Rush was only too happy to get outside. The screaming wind sliced cleaner than his old combat knife, but what was cutting at him inside that warm little cabin—the smell of her, the sound of her, the quick skate of those dark, liquid eyes that wouldn't quite meet his—was worse. He was almost grate-ful for the wind that snatched and shoved at him as he trot-ted out back for another armload of logs, freezing one eye and both nostrils shut within seconds. It cleared his mind and reset his body quicker than a cold shower, and wasn't quite as obvious, which was a nice bonus.

He banged back into the cabin and lost any headway he'd made against lust the instant he saw her.

He didn't know why it should surprise him that she'd dragged the cot mattresses from their respective rooms and arranged them in front of the stove. That she'd taken the care to lay out his sleeping bag and place his pillow at the head. That she'd brought out her own and done the same. He'd live in eternal regret that she'd laid them out carefully head to toe rather than zipping them together, but he couldn't say it surprised him.

No, what surprised him was that while he'd been out doing the manly thing, wrestling what they needed from nature to survive the storm, she'd taken the traditional female role and built their nest. He didn't know many women—many people in general, actually—who'd just do what needed doing without squawking about who did which job and what getting stuck with a certain job declared other people believed about them. Goose was about the most competent cop he'd ever run across—and he'd run across plenty in his former life—but she didn't balk at making beds. Didn't balk at tending somebody else in a small, mundane way.

She sat cross-legged in the middle of her sleeping bag, the earflap hat Ben Barnes had hooked her up with plastering her hair to her cheeks so hard the ends were starting to bend outward and upward a little. Cute.

Or it should have been cute. But lust uncurled slow and warm in his belly at the sight of her there, her huge eyes nearly purple in the lantern light, her lip gloss worn off hours ago, the polished veneer cracking good and solid as the real woman underneath gazed at him with concern and trepidation.

"Rush," she said. "We have to talk."

He dumped his armload of logs into the wood box next to the stove. "That sounds ominous."

She didn't smile. "It's not good."

"Does it have anything to do with the fact that I've been making this mental list of Ways to While Away a Stormy Night with Goose, and *talk* doesn't feature in the top ten?"

She did smile at that. "Not exactly, no." Her smile died and she met his eyes. "But by the time I'm done talking, you'll probably be making a different list. Top Ten Ways to Get This Woman off My Island, Pronto."

He pulled off his hat and gloves and tossed them onto the floor beside the stove to dry. "Doubt it."

She twisted her fingers together in her lap and slid her eyes away from his. "You shouldn't."

He stripped out of his jacket, hung it on the peg by the door. "Should I brace myself?"

"Will you sit down, please?"

And that was a big fat *yes* if he'd ever heard one. He came to the couch, sat facing her. She didn't stand up, or even join him on the couch. Anxiety stirred in his stomach. A woman like Goose would have mastered all the unspoken ways to use body language to assert authority, and the fact that she stayed on the floor below him spoke to her intense desire to keep him off the defensive. His heart pinched.

Either she was about to rock his world with some really, *really* bad news—maybe she *was* into Einar after all?—or she was making one more last-ditch effort to play the tired old we-can't-be-together-because-I'm-after-your-family card.

Not that he could blame her for trying Door Number Two one last time. Hauling all your shit into the bright light of day for an unforgiving inventory was no picnic. Rush knew this firsthand, and he sympathized. But was she really so desperate to avoid it that she'd encourage him to crucify her on the cross of his family loyalty instead?

Only one way to find out.

"Okay," he said. "I'm ready. Hit me."

GOOSE SWALLOWED hard and gazed up at Rush. He sat leaning forward on the couch, elbows on knees, his long, tough fingers linked loosely between them. He gazed at her with a steady patience that put a sharp strain on the controls under which she generally locked her more dangerous appetites. She damned Lila for even putting the idea in her head that sex would set her free. She damned *him* for suggesting the same thing.

Because ever since he'd walked away from her in the moonlight, she couldn't even look at him without remembering the feel of his mouth on hers. Without reliving the way his big hands raced hot and demanding on her skin.

Without considering his quiet assertion that she was some kind of fraud. That her dedication to stamping out her worst impulses was born of cowardice rather than altruism.

And she certainly couldn't look at him now, sitting right there on the couch above her. Not when it was so completely clear that he'd consider it his pleasure—no, his *honor*—to help her toss some of that emotional baggage overboard. That he'd be more than happy to reacquaint her with her body and everything it knew how to want. And maybe even introduce her to a few things she had never even thought to want.

She drew in a deep breath and snatched at the shreds of her self-control. If she was going to take him up on that offer—and that was a huge *if* she was still deeply conflicted about—she wouldn't do it while lost in lust. If she said yes, she would say it from a place of cool, reasoned decision. It was one thing to embrace your more carnal nature. It was another thing entirely to turn off your brain and let your body—markedly unreliable in certain situations—call the shots.

So if she was going to get through this night without taking a bite—just one little bite—out of that gorgeously solid shoulder of his, Rush was going to have to help. Which meant she was going to have to remind him why spending their evening doing anything more than talking was a really, really bad idea.

It was time to come clean. At least partially.

"So I've been thinking," she said. "About this situation of ours."

"Which situation?" he asked. "The counterfeiting? The black magic? Or the fact that I kissed you last night, and somewhere between 'oh my God' and 'no thanks,' you kissed me back?"

Heat spiraled out of her core, settled heavy between her legs, in her breasts. Okay, this wasn't a good start. "Um, the first one. And the second." Though God knew she'd been thinking about the third, too.

He made a vaguely disapproving noise, like he could sense the basic cowardice that kept option number three off the agenda. But all he said was, "You have a suspect?"

"Yes, but I need your help before I can move forward." Her hands wanted to fidget, so she clasped them neatly in her lap. "And please, I need you to understand that I wish like hell I didn't have to ask you this."

He leaned forward, his eyes warming with . . . sympathy? "Goose. You're doing your job, and you're doing it with honor. I appreciate that, and I'll do whatever I can to make this easier on all of us."

She blew out a breath. "Say that again in five minutes," she muttered.

He cocked a brow. "You think I won't?"

"Why would you?"

He reached out and tugged on a lock of hair her hat couldn't contain. Hair that was already starting—God help her—to wig out. "Yarrow's a very troubled young girl, Goose. You think I can't appreciate that what you're doing will ultimately benefit her?"

Her heart stopped for three solid seconds, then thudded back to life. Jesus, she hadn't planned to go quite as far as the Yarrow situation tonight. She stared at him in open-mouthed shock. "You know about Yarrow?"

"It doesn't take a genius to connect the dots you've been drawing me, Goose. You think she's the one making herself at home at the Stone Altar, don't you?"

She frowned at him. "Why would I think that?"

He stared at her this time. "Because of what you said the other day. About her needing to reject love?"

She closed her eyes. "Oh God. Lila. Black magic would be a big slap at Lila. An ugly one, too. I hadn't thought of that."

"But you'd clearly thought of something." She opened her eyes to find him giving her a sharp appraisal. "What was it?"

She shook her head. "No, let's follow yours through for a minute. What about your theory that the two are connected—the altar and the smuggling? How on earth would Yarrow be connected to importing supernotes?"

"I made a few phone calls after our conversation in Hornby Harbor the other day. It's Yarrow's story to tell, and I won't get into all of it, but I will say that part of the reason her parents moved her up here was to separate her from a bad influence. Some college dope dealer. Apparently he was in pretty deep with a Minneapolis-based gang."

Goose's agile brain made a few quick leaps. "The Fire Eaters?"

"Yeah. I figured you'd have heard of them. Korean, mostly first generation. Based out of Minneapolis's Jordan neighborhood."

She gave him a speculative look and he hunched his shoulders. "What, you think you're the only one who knows how to use the Internet?"

"I'd clearly be wrong if I did." She cocked a brow. "Go on, Mr. Font of Information."

"I don't have much else. Just that most of them speak Korean in the home and have relatives—close ones—still in Korea." He spread his hands. "It seemed to fit with what you told me about supernotes."

She nodded slowly. "Yeah, I can see it. Most of the supernotes in circulation today *have* come out of North Korea. And getting them from there to here in any significant quantity certainly requires people with the language skills and the connections to wheel and deal in both countries."

"And who have a certain disregard for the rule of law, I imagine."

"You'd imagine right. Gangs do bang-up business in supernotes."

"So if Yarrow really is still in contact with this kid moving drugs for the Fire Eaters?"

"Then, yeah, it's possible the gang is also aware of her

exile to a geographically advantageous location for their business. Airport security has gotten too rigorous since 9/11 to allow the importation of supernotes in any real quantity through mules flying directly into the country. Mostly the money enters the U.S. via Canada or Mexico, in our experience. Which means the smugglers are always looking for porous places on the borders."

"Places like Mishkwa."

"Exactly."

"And yet that's not the news you were gearing up to break to me."

"No." She hesitated. "Not that your theory isn't a good one."

"But it's not the one you arrived at." He passed a hand over his scalp, looked at her from under concerned brows.

"No." She caught her hands trying to fly away again, and tucked them under her thighs.

"Your theory required my cooperation. A favor?"

"Yeah." She fought back the urge to smile reassuringly. Fake smiles would only make him angry and she was already dangling by a thread here. So no smiling, but it left her feeling naked. She didn't know what else to do with her face, how else to prevent it from showing him all the anguish and reluctance inside her. Better to just blurt it out before he could spend too much time trying to read it from her expression. "You have a key to Einar's place, don't you?"

"Yeah."

"And a standing invitation to use it?"

"Sure. He's a pilot, runs his own charter flight company. His schedule changes at the drop of a hat."

"I need to search his cabin without his knowledge," Goose said. "Preferably the next time he's away from Mishkwa overnight. Will you invite me to do it?"

"To search Einar's cabin? Why?"

"I don't need a search warrant if somebody with routine access invites me in."

He shook his head. "I didn't mean why do you want me to invite you to do it. I meant why do you want to do it in the first place?"

"Because I think he's importing supernotes into the country in his cute little plane, and if I could find evidence of that without a search warrant, I could wrap this whole thing up in a neat little package without creating a big ugly scene."

Chapter

20

SILENCE SPUN out, thin and fragile as glass threads. He didn't move, didn't shift. He hardly breathed. A quick blink was the only sign that she'd surprised him. "You're looking at *Einar*? For smuggling supernotes into the country? *And* for the Stone Altar?"

"Yes."

"Why?"

"Because he has opportunity and motive for both."

Rush leaned forward, pinched the bridge of his nose. "Explain."

"Does the term *Paganpalooza* mean anything to you?"

"Paganpalooza?"

"Yes. As in a giant, multiday festival aimed at pagans."

"This is about *that*?"

"No, I think it's about more than that. Because I think Einar *wants* more than that. You know what you said about Mishkwa the other night, how it strips away all the artifice and pretense? How it seems to force people into getting in touch with what they really are?"

His eyes went the color of smoke. "Yeah."

"I think *that's* what he wants to sell. That, along with his credentials as the crown prince of it all. Jesus, can you imagine? Take Joel Osteen—or any of those toothy televangelists—give him a dark, sexy, edgy twist and you've got about what Einar's envisioning. Himself at the helm of a multinational corporation that makes a killing off people's desperate need to find their own truth. To pursue the dream that getting back in touch with nature in its rawest, purest form will cure what ails them."

"It sounds like Pagan Disney."

"It is. And that's no low-rent dream, either. Not the kind of thing you can finance flying a puddle jumper and selling chickens."

"He sells fish, too." He said it absently, though. His focus had gone inward.

"There aren't enough fish in Lake Superior to bankroll what he's dreaming of."

"No." He shot her a troubled look. "And the black magic? Where does that fit in?"

"He doesn't just want money, Rush. He wants power, too."

"Power over what?"

"Over the coven. Over the island. Over the people who populate both. Over the hundreds, thousands more who'll *want* to populate both."

"He has it already. He's a priest, Lila's second in command. When she retires, the whole enchilada is his. He doesn't need power; all he needs is patience."

"I'd have agreed with you last week. Then I went to esbat."

"Esbat." He frowned. "What happened at esbat?"

"The prodigal son came home," she said softly. "Didn't you notice?"

"Notice what?" But he'd sat up, folded his arms over his chest.

"The way they welcomed you." She touched his knee, ignored the way sparks of awareness shot up her arm and landed in all her most interesting—and interested—places. "I don't know why you haven't taken up your hereditary role within the coven since you've been home, but they've been waiting for you. Aching for you, if the reception they gave you the other night is any indication."

He drew back. "That's overstating it a little, don't you think?"

"Rush." She tipped her head, gave him a stern look. "Your aunt teared up when she welcomed you into the circle. Everybody wanted to touch you, greet you, physically pull you into their midst and circle around you. They *embraced* you, Rush. You didn't just drop in on esbat; you came home." She studied his closed face. "And you're not the only one who isn't exactly over the moon about it, either."

"Over the moon." He glared at her. "Aren't you the funny one?"

"Aren't you even going to ask who?"

"I'm not an idiot, Goose."

"You see it, then? What a threat you are to Einar's master plan?"

He remained stubbornly silent.

"Rush, come on. How's he going to transform a sleepy little island coven into a personal fortune if he has to get your stamp of approval to do it?"

"I'm not running for high priest, Goose."

"You might want to tell that to Lila. She's hoping you and Einar will dredge up enough brotherly love to share and share alike when inheritance time rolls around."

"Oh, crap."

"Crap, indeed. Lila told me herself that she intends to bequeath the coven to you and Einar jointly. In the hopes that, rather than murdering each other, you'll find a way to co-chair the coven into the foreseeable future. Apparently pagans place particular value on duality. Balance. The power of two." She cocked a brow. "Anything sound familiar so far?"

Rush rubbed a palm over his face. "Well, shit."

Goose nodded. "That was pretty much my reaction as well." She got up and plunked herself onto the couch, though she was careful to leave plenty of space between them.

Rush blew out a breath and shot her a sideways look. "Okay, fine. Einar's ambitious, but that doesn't mean he's the one playing around with the Stone Altar. He doesn't believe in black magic any more than I do."

"But he believes in money, right? In the power of appearances? Think about it, Rush. If he's going to sell something, especially something as sexy as dark magic, wouldn't he make sure it looked damn good first? And that he looked damn good selling it?"

Rush stared, struck. "That's what you think he's doing down there at the Stone Altar? Dress rehearsals?"

"Makes sense to me." She tipped her head. "You?"

He was silent for a long moment, then blew out a breath through tight lips. "Yeah," he said finally. "It makes sense." He dropped his head into his hands, elbows braced on knees. "Fuck me, though, I don't want it to."

Her heart broke a little at the weary distress in his voice, the defeated slump of those strong shoulders, and she abandoned common sense for compassion. How could she *not* touch him? She scooted closer, until her thigh snuggled up against the hard length of his. The heat of him burned through the flannel of her pajama bottoms, but she ignored it. Or tried to. She put her palm between his shoulder blades, on the muscle and bone that spread tense and vital beneath her hand.

"I'm sorry, Rush. I hate it that I have to ask this of you. For you to betray your own cousin's trust."

He speared his fingers through the hair he didn't have and shook his head. "Fucking Einar." His tone was more weary than upset. "Hey, though. It's not your fault, Goose. Don't take it on, okay?"

"Fault." She made a rude noise. "Like fault counts for shit when something blows this hard."

He gave her a wry almost-smile. "I love it when you talk dirty."

She grinned back, too relieved to do otherwise. "Hey, I'm not above crude language if merited. And this situation definitely merits it. If you want, if it'd cheer you up, I could probably drop you an F-bomb or two."

"A well-placed 'fuck' is a joy forever."

"Um . . ." She grappled with that one for a moment.

He did smile at her this time. Smirked, actually. "I didn't mean literally."

"Oh." Her cheeks went bright. "I didn't think—"

"Sure you did. Your mind's in the gutter, di Guzman." He shook his head in mock dismay. "How utterly sophomoric." Then he leaned in, effectively paralyzing her lungs. She should move back, she knew, but he'd somehow paralyzed her fight-or-flight mechanism, too. Damn him and those snake-charmer eyes.

"My mind," she said indignantly, as trumped-up outrage was about all she could manage in terms of self-defense, "is nowhere near the gutter."

"My mind," he said, "is on about number four of that list I mentioned earlier. Top Ten Ways to While Away a Stormy Night with Goose?"

She blinked at him, all innocence. "You want to play Stratego?"

"I want to play something."

THOSE BIG sad eyes went wide, then darted toward the stove, the door, the window. She edged toward the arm of the couch.

"That's, um, probably not a good idea," she said.

Of its own volition, Rush's mouth curved in a half-amused, half-predatory smile, and his heart gave a hard thud of something like joy. Because for the first time in ages, he didn't wonder if he was smiling at the right time or the right place. He didn't worry or wonder or second-guess himself. He just let the smile well up from the darkest, most primitive corner of his soul—*mine*—and slide right onto his face.

He inched forward until she'd scooted her butt right to the arm of the couch. "No? Because I think it's a great idea." He reached across her to lay a hand on the worn armrest, effectively caging her between his arms. He didn't touch her, though. He simply allowed the air between them to go heavy and electric with the weight of what snapped between them so relentlessly.

"Didn't you hear any of what I just said?" She glared at him, but he noticed she didn't touch him. Didn't put so much as a finger on his chest to nudge him aside. Desire rose up within him, slid hot and dense through his veins to settle, hard, between his legs.

"About you wanting me to ask you into Einar's house for a sneaky-peeky?" He leaned in, dipped his face into the warm, scented air beside her throat until he could feel as much as hear her swiftly indrawn breath. See as much as sense the mad flutter of her heartbeat. And still she didn't touch him. Damn, he wanted her to touch him. "Yeah, I heard you."

"And you still want to . . ."

He cocked his head to meet her baffled, embattled eyes. "Yeah."

"Why?" It burst from her, reluctant and tortured, like she didn't want to ask, didn't even want to broach the subject, but was powerless to resist her desire to know the answer. "Why would you want to—"

"Kiss you? Touch you?" He nuzzled the fine, slippery strands of hair away from the side of her neck and allowed himself to place one chaste kiss there. The urge to gorge himself on the sweet silk of her skin savaged his self-control, but he locked it down. Barely. "Take you?"

"Yes." It was a bare, ragged whisper. "I'm gunning for your family, you know. Your blood. You shouldn't want anything to do with me."

"And while I'm not thrilled with the idea, I'm okay

with it. Which I've already told you. Multiple times. If you don't do it, somebody else surely will. And frankly?" He flicked the tip of his tongue against the sweet warmth of her skin and her strangled gasp nearly undid him. "I like our chances better with you running the show."

He felt it then. The first tentative pressure of her hands against his chest. Not pushing him away, not yet. But not allowing him any closer, either. He grabbed desperately at the desire raging within him, driving him closer, harder, throbbing mercilessly through his body, his soul. He gathered it all up, held it in a precarious, fragile balance and waited.

"Don't look for me to play favorites on this, Rush," she said quietly. "If it comes down to choosing between business and pleasure, business wins. Every time."

"Goose. Honey." He leaned in to inhale the sweet warmth at the base of her throat. "Don't be an idiot."

"Excuse me?"

"Am I asking you to pull any punches? To play extra nice with any criminals I may or may not be related to?" He leaned back far enough to meet her wary eyes. "I'm not, okay? That's a totally separate thing. Right now all I'm asking is whether or not you want me."

"Do I—" She broke off on a sharp exhale. "No, Rush. Of course I don't. I might throw you a pity bang in a few minutes here but only because I feel sorry for you." She shoved at his chest and snapped, "Do I *want* you. God."

He laughed as triumph flashed through him. "A pity bang, huh?"

She closed her eyes, as if realizing upon mental review that her last few comments had been less than prudent. "Okay, I didn't mean— It's not like I'm really going to—" She broke off, wary. Good for her. Rush suddenly felt very dangerous. "I just—"

"You just what?" he asked softly, and what he saw in her eyes had fear leaping sharp and ugly into the lust already churning inside him, creating something hotter and earthier than either of them alone. Something danger-ously unstable. Combustible. He'd promised himself he'd back off, let her come to him with her decision, whatever it was.

But that was before. Before he'd looked into her eyes and saw her teetering perilously close to *no*. Before he'd realized that while wanting her, waiting for her, was ago-nizing, losing her might actually kill him. And he was afraid—okay, he was *terrified*, damn it—that he was about to find out for sure if being rejected by her was a surviv-able event.

So. New plan.

He'd never been one for waiting around anyway.

He moved forward, crowding her until she'd scooted herself right into the corner of the couch. Her eyes were huge and wary on his face, but still those warm hands on his chest didn't move. Didn't pull him in but didn't push him away, either. He came up and over her, slipped a knee into the gap between her hip and the armrest until he'd caged her neatly between his thighs. Until every inch of his skin begged him to close the gap, to press his desper-ate body into the welcoming heat of hers, but still he didn't touch her. Didn't dare.

He shook his head slowly. "I'm having a hard time fig-uring you out, Goose."

"What do you mean?"

"I mean you smile like Miss America but your eyes are sad enough to make me ache. Sometimes you laugh and it's like bells ringing. But every now and again, you snort instead. So who are you really? Who did I kiss last night?"

Her mouth opened—those lush and curvy lips—but no words came out. But that wasn't a problem because for once words just wouldn't stop pouring out of his own mouth. And he was powerless to stop them. "Are you Goose? Or are you Maria?"

She flinched. "Don't call me that," she said.

"What? *Maria?*" He tugged at the braid of yarn hanging

off one of her earflaps and gave her a grin that was all teeth. "That *is* your name, isn't it?"

She didn't meet his eyes. "I prefer Goose."

"I think I prefer Maria. That's who I kissed the other night, isn't it?"

She shoved against him and he obligingly backed up. She shot to her feet and something inside him rejoiced at the idea that he could do this. He could break through that plastic veneer and make whatever was inside her come out into the light. "I don't know what you're talking about," she said, her mouth pinched tight.

He rose, too. Even with her in stocking feet, he was still only three or four inches taller than she was. He liked that, too. She wasn't some fragile little thing he had to worry about intimidating. She was tough, strong, and under all that charm just as stubborn as he was.

"Sure you do," he said. He took another deliberate step toward her. Until he was so far inside her personal space he could feel her body heat, could hear the quiver of her breath. "Come on, Maria. Come out to play."

Then he went ahead and threw the Hail Mary.

He yanked her in and planted his mouth on hers. He poured everything into it, too. All the aching want he'd been bottling up, the yearning to push inside her, to connect. To get past all that shiny, slippery charm of hers to the roiling cauldron of emotion underneath.

He expected her to shove an elbow into his midsection—a well-deserved elbow, he would admit. He expected her to slap his face, or worse, laugh in it. He expected her to stomp on his instep, remove herself from his distasteful embrace and retreat with offended dignity to her room.

He did *not* expect her to kiss him back. He'd had his hopes, of course, but nothing as solid as expectation. So when she wound her arms around him, arched into him and exploded in his arms, he couldn't tell if his answering wrench of desire was from the act itself or the shock of it. He didn't much care to reason it out at that moment, however. Not that he had the mental faculties to reason at all.

For the next several moments, all his mind was capable of registering was the pulling and snatching and panting and grabbing. It was some sort of primitive autopilot that had him boosting her up, wrapping her legs around him and lowering them both to the floor. Then space and time sort of disappeared on him, leaving him with nothing but a refractory jumble of heat and want. He was caught in an inferno of pulsing, glowing desire, fueled by the satin sweep of her skin under his fingers, her hair on his face, the sweet hitch of her breath in the crook of his neck.

MINE.

It rang through his soul like a bell, shock waves sailing out and bouncing back until he couldn't think, couldn't speak, couldn't do anything but stake his claim with hands, lips, teeth. God, he wanted to *mark* her. It hammered at him, the primal urge to make her his in absolute terms, until nobody, not even Goose—not even *Maria*—could deny it.

Maria. That rang through him, too. It was her name. Her self. Her vast and hidden truth. How had he not seen it before? And it was in his arms now; *she* was in his arms now. Wrapped around him, seeking his mouth, his kiss, his body with an avid hunger that both humbled him and inflamed him. She was a gift. Unexpected and undeserved. And was he satisfied? Hell, no. He wanted more.

His hands flew over her, plucking at the layers upon layers of clothing between them. He was reluctant to leave the wonder of her mouth, but he was also mad to feel the heat of her skin against his. Skin that was locked away behind this ridiculous maze of buttons, zippers, ties and hooks. He needed to unwrap this package, *now*. And he was going to start with that ugly hat.

He levered up onto one elbow and grabbed a handful of utilitarian gray wool. He pulled it free with a grunt of satisfaction, then stared in shocked delight at the riot of glossy black ringlets that tumbled free. They bounced around the

quirky oval of her face with passionate abandon and something inside him said *yes, of course.*

His cranky, foulmouthed, snort-laughing temptress was
also curly-headed. Beautifully, madly, crazily curly.

He grinned at her. "Hello, Maria."

Chapter

21

HELLO, MARIA.

She went perfectly, utterly still. Not that she had much choice, pinned as she was to the floor by the glorious weight of him. Pinned, hell. Like she was trapped by anything other than the inescapable gravity of her own desire. Look at her. She was twined around him like a climbing vine, twisting and seeking and grasping and gasping. Pushing herself closer and closer, higher and hotter. Rocking herself shamelessly into the hard heat of him, indulging herself and her worst instincts without conscience or restraint.

She braced herself for the shame that was about to roll in. The guilt. The remorse. Separately, they were uncomfortable, but together they formed her own personal holy trinity of emotions, inevitably painful but mercifully familiar. Penance was no walk in the park, but at least she understood it. Whatever this was she felt for Rush, though? She didn't understand the first baffling thing about that.

Because, damn, she should be crying right now. Wailing.

At the very least kneeing him in the nuts and making her grand escape into the teeth of a blizzard. She should *not* be battling back the completely inappropriate urge to laugh. *Laugh*.

Not that anything was funny. God, it wasn't. It was just that there was the strangest, tiniest trickle of joy sneaking around inside her.

Joy. Sparkling, clear and so absolutely, breathtakingly unexpected. She'd spent so many years taking such scrupulous care to ensure that nobody—but *nobody*—really knew her. It was only in her worst nightmares that somebody like Rush came along and peered behind the curtain. She'd built an entire life around the grim task of making sure this day never came.

But here it was. Here *she* was. Flat on her back and completely exposed, and what was she feeling?

Joy. The joy, after all these years, of having somebody call her by her *name*. Of having somebody not only see the crumpled, crippled Maria she'd buried so well, but *want* her. Want her more than the shiny, slick shell she'd hidden herself inside. God. Even her family had been content to let Maria slip away, unmourned, while the infinitely easier Goose took her place. But not Rush. Hell, no. Rush had tugged and pulled and harassed and cajoled until she'd had no choice but to give him exactly what he'd asked for.

Maria. In all her lustful, selfish, curly-haired glory.

And he actually liked what he saw, if the astonishingly sweet smile spreading across his thunderstruck face was any indication. Liked it? Hell, he *wanted* it. Wanted her.

And suddenly Maria had had enough running. She'd had enough hiding. This man—this beautiful, fiercely private man—had declared himself to her. In some bizarre cosmic misunderstanding—and it *had* to be a misunderstanding because she'd done nothing to earn such a miraculous event—he'd offered himself to her, and for once she wasn't going to stop to wonder if she deserved what she wanted.

Because of course she didn't deserve him. She knew

that wholeheartedly. Didn't deserve him at all. But she'd take him. God help her, she'd take him. Even if only for tonight.

The reckless hunger that was part of her nature, that she'd so successfully hemmed in for so long, burst free in a blazing explosion of need and want and gleeful appetite, and she arched up under him. Into him. A glorious satisfaction surged through her as she scraped her splayed fingers into the severe stubble covering his warm scalp and took his astonished mouth with hers.

She squirmed under him until he rolled over onto the rumpled pile of their sleeping bags, and she leaped on him like a starving woman jumped a buffet table, indiscriminate and ravenous. She took his mouth first, the harsh beauty of it opening like sin under hers. She welcomed the dark invasion of his tongue, and answered it with her own. She took his want, his need with a primitive noise deep in her throat, and turned her own loose on him.

Her hands streaked over his lean chest, under his shirt, across his skin. She delighted in the tough, wiry jerk of muscle under her palms, in the constant reminder of his superior strength. Strength he kept as sternly leashed as his darker nature, as the hands he kept under polite, rigid control on her hips.

Hands she wanted in less polite territory. Now.

Desire flowed through her, hot and heavy, settling deep into her belly and pulsing lower. She slid herself against him until the glowing center of her want rocked into the hard evidence of his. The blatant demand of his desire against her melting softness twisted the roaring need inside her higher, hotter, and she arched into him, whispered her need into his mouth.

"Rush," she said. "Touch me. Please. I need—"

She didn't get any further, which was just fine with her, as she found herself suddenly on her back again, Rush's length settled firmly between her thighs, the weight of him a dizzying thrill. His eyes burned in his serious face, a face gone dark with a hunger everything in her rose up to greet.

"Maria," he said, the words halting, reluctant. "You're sure?"

Something inside her cracked, and tenderness poured hot and sticky through the fault lines. Asking permission was *so* not in Rush's nature. He was totally a do-what-needs-to-be-done-with-a-minimum-of-conversation kind of guy. And yet even in the face of extreme provocation, he'd tamed himself far enough to make absolutely certain she was getting what she wanted.

Was it any wonder her stupid heart had run all out of defenses against this guy?

But still. There was out of control and then there was outright self-destructive. She reached deep for the last tiny shreds of her composure and gave him her trademark sideways smile. "I've been trying to get you to talk to me since the day we met," she said. "Are you seriously going to chat me up *now*?"

His hand froze on the ladder of her ribs—oh God, please don't stop *there*—and he glared down at her.

"Don't do that," he said, his face harsh and closed. "Don't you dare *do* that."

"Do what?" she asked, mystified.

"Disappear like that." He sat back on his heels, left her there, splayed on the floor like a half-finished meal. "I told you, Maria. I don't want your plastic smiles and I don't want your snappy comebacks. That was the deal, remember?"

Remorse and shame ran through her like a chilling wind, even as the hunger inside her howled. "What do you want, then?" she asked baldly.

He planted one hand just above her shoulder and slowly leaned in until his body was six shimmering inches above hers, his mouth a wicked brush against her ear. He threaded a finger through an errant curl and said, "You."

His mouth closed on the lobe of her ear with a suddenness

that sent a towering wave of desire crashing over her head. "Just"—he moved the hot magic of his mouth to the side of her neck—"like"—then lower, to the vulnerable hollow of her collarbone—"this." His hand came up and took swift, breath-stealing possession of her breast.

She arched into him with a mindless moan. She'd give him anything he asked, be anything he liked, so long as he never stopped whatever crazy game he was playing with her, teasing her aching nipple with a touch that was *this close* to being exactly what she needed.

She shifted under him, restless, seeking, a discontented little noise mewling out of her. He chuckled, dark and wicked.

"Better," he said, and lowered his lips to that desperate nipple. Satisfaction shot through her like fire at the wet pull of his mouth through the thin fabric of her long johns, and when he tugged at the hem of her shirt she lifted her arms obediently. She had no recollection, later, of whether or not she helped very much. She knew only that suddenly her clothes were gone, his clothes were gone, the condom was dealt with—thank *God* for Rush's military preparedness— and then there was the sizzling satisfaction of his skin—oh God, all that beautiful *skin*—on hers. Hot and wild and real and *him*. All of him, pressed into her like glory.

She bowed up under him, not to throw him off—Jesus, no—but so she could sink her teeth into the muscle of his shoulder, exactly where it curved up toward his throat. He made some kind of noise, a growl of pleasure and surprise, and she jerked his mouth down to hers. Feasted on him, reveled in his feasting on her.

Because they *were* feasting—biting, snatching, gobbling each other up in huge, greedy mouthfuls. They'd both have marks in the morning, and a dark, primitive satisfaction edged into the hunger. She'd wear the proof of his want when the sun came up again. He'd wear hers. She smiled then, a fierce baring of teeth, as she wrapped her legs around him, fell into the madness.

Fell? Hell, she leaped into it, surrendered herself to the swirling vortex of heat and want unleashed. It pulsed through her, this naked, ancient imperative, and she squirmed under his glorious weight, slippery and needful and hungry.

And then he was there, just *there*, the hard length of him against the most secret center of her. Demanding, not asking. Warning. Preparing. Taking.

"Maria," he said, and she opened her eyes to the wild blaze of his. Possession gleamed starkly on his face.

"Now," she said. "God, please. *Now*."

Her words seemed to snap that last bit of control and he lunged forward. She cried out at the shock of it, the incredible, vast, world-altering blitz it dealt to her, body and soul. He was inside her now—in *her*, Maria—driving into her, driving out the loneliness, the terrible stark aloneness she'd lived with so very long.

He froze at her cry. "Did I—" he asked, his voice strangled and strange. "Oh God, did I hurt you?"

"*No*." She wrapped herself around him, stabbed her fingers into what little hair he'd left on his head and jerked his mouth down to hers. Kissed him with all the raging desire and fierce possessiveness boiling inside her. "You didn't hurt me. You never could. It was just"—she bit his ear and reveled in the answering jerk of his body inside her—"so"—she drew her tongue down his throat, glorying in the taste of his sweat and his need—"*good*."

He shuddered and pushed forward. Slowly. She clamped her teeth into the meat of his shoulder and moaned. He pulled back and her fingernails raked little crescents into his back. He surged forward again and she twisted under him, brought him deeper, closer.

He shoved his hand into her hair and tugged until her head fell back, leaving him her throat. He fell on it, the stubble on his jaw burning her skin like a brand.

"Mine," he said against the pulse beating wildly in the hollow between her collarbones. "You're mine."

"Yes." She twisted mindlessly beneath him, her desire a wild whip inside her, a driving tyrant. "Yes."

His hand went to her bottom then, urgent, rough, and flatly commanding. Everything in her said *God, yes.*

He jerked her up to meet him and took what was his.

IT DIDN'T take long for Maria's Holy Trinity of Penance to catch up with her.

As long as Rush was inside her, she was good. Even afterward, with him sprawled over her like an accident victim, with her legs still wrapped tight around him, with both of them wheezing like steam engines, she'd been okay. But then he'd brushed aside a handful of ringlets to drop a tender kiss on the side of her throat. Then he'd flopped over on his back and brought her with him, his eyes closed, his hands slow and sweet on her back. Then she'd cracked open one lazy eye and had gotten her first good look at what she'd done to him.

Oh God. Were those bite marks on his shoulder? She eased back, her heart hammering inside her chest. A hickey bloomed just under his left nipple. She slid off him, knelt to the side and nudged him with shaking fingers until he obliged her and rolled over. He probably thought she wanted to spoon or something. She didn't. Not when she saw two matching sets of long red welts scoring his beautiful back, shoulders to waist, courtesy of her nails.

Nausea trembled in her stomach, and she had to close her eyes against a punishing wave of shame. When was she going to learn? Whatever this was inside her, this beast that hungered and wanted and demanded? It *hurt* people. *She* hurt people. She knew that, yet she'd indulged herself anyway. Nobody had died this time—yay, her—but still. That was cold comfort while she was looking at what she'd done to Rush's back.

Her stomach cramped even as tears, stupid and useless, stung her eyes. And of course, Rush chose that particular moment to realize she wasn't, in fact, spooning him.

He rolled onto his back again and looked up at her with a crooked smile that pierced her heart.

"So. That was Maria, huh?"

She scrambled to her feet. "Don't call me that."

She found her hat and snatched it up. She yanked it back onto the treacherous mass of her hair. Kind of shutting the barn door once the horses were out, but what the fuck else was she supposed to do?

"What? Maria?" He stayed on the floor, one arm tossed over his eyes, completely at ease. "Screw that. It's your name. I'm going to use it."

She swallowed, hard. Averted her eyes from the glory of that long, lean body. From the ugly marks her desire had left on it.

"It's not who I am," she said finally. Desperately.

He tossed her a skeptical glance from under his elbow. "Screw that," he said again. "We don't get to pick who we are, *Maria*. Trust me on that one."

She opened her mouth to argue then thought better of it. There was a gravity in his words, a fatalism that made her think he wasn't necessarily talking about—or even to— her. At least not only to her.

"This was *not* the way you were supposed to take the news about Einar," she told him. She snatched up the first T-shirt she found on the floor—his—and jerked it over her head. It smelled like him, and desire pulsed once—hard— inside her.

"No?"

"No." She forced herself to turn away from him, to pace the length of the cabin. "You were supposed to be furious with me. You were supposed to hate me." She shot him a bad-tempered scowl as he sat up and eyed her speculatively. "You were supposed to keep your damn distance for the rest of this damn storm."

"I'm sorry." He didn't look particularly sorry. "I'm clearly doing it wrong."

She glared at him, then snorted. "You're not sorry."

He shrugged. "Not really, no." He lifted himself up

just enough to jerk their sleeping bags—the evidence of her self-control run amok—back into some semblance of order. Then he stretched out on them, supremely unconcerned with his nudity. "This isn't going to go away, Maria. This thing between us. It's too big. And tonight didn't do much more than take the edge off." He paused. "And that's the wrong response, too, isn't it?"

"*Yes*," she said feelingly.

He stacked his hands behind his head and contemplated the ceiling. "You have curly hair."

One fat ringlet dangled in front of her eye—mocking her—and she stuffed it under the hat. "Shrewdly observed, Ranger Guthrie."

"Really curly," he said, and shot her an unexpected grin. "I like it."

"I'm so glad." Her tone indicated quite the opposite.

"Me, too," he said serenely. "It's wild. Just like you. Next time I'm inside you, I'm going to tangle myself up in it and take us both to fucking paradise."

"Next time you're—" The breath left her lungs in one hot, mindless rush. Oh God, *inside her.*

"Yep." He grinned, at ease now, all supple, dangerous jungle cat. He patted the mattress beside him. "Why don't you come to bed now, Maria?"

"*Goose.*"

"I won't touch you, promise. Not unless you touch me first." He lifted a hand, scout's honor. "Come on. You're safe. From me, at least. Come to bed. It's late."

She stared at him in narrow-eyed suspicion.

"Unless you're afraid?"

She didn't deign to reply, only stomped over to her mattress. She jerked her sleeping bag away from his, flipped it so her head was at his toes and crawled inside. She zipped it to her chin, turned her back on him and yanked the drawstring, retreating into a polypropylene cocoon. The low rumble of his laughter drifted through the lightweight material, and she heard him get up to kill the lanterns. Then his mattress rustled and squeaked as he arranged himself behind her, his feet at her head, his body curved in a loose *C* a few aching inches behind hers.

"Good night, Maria."

She ignored him and his breathing went deep and even in a matter of moments. Then she was alone in the darkness, her body still shamefully alive and hungry.

God, she was in trouble.

Chapter

22

SHE HADN'T thought sleep was possible. How could she sleep, after all, while there was still this crushing gut load of guilt and fear to digest? It was true what they said—no rest for the wicked, and she'd been very, very wicked tonight. Plus, a girl had to have standards, and Maria's included not dropping unconscious while there was penance to be done.

But as her priorities were clearly and rather profoundly fucked up this evening, she slept anyway. She must have. Because when she jolted out of the nightmare she was on her hands and knees on the rough wooden floor, a half-strangled scream still stuck in her throat.

After several panicked heartbeats, she slowly lowered her head to the cold wooden planks. She locked both clammy hands over her mouth and fought to break free from terror's sweaty choke hold. She swallowed hard against that last scream in her throat, but it leaked out anyway, a small pitiful noise of pure fear.

"Maria?"

And oh God, now she'd woken Rush. Of course she had. He was an ex-SEAL. What he considered sleep hardly passed for woolgathering in normal circles. She shivered convulsively and pressed her hands harder to her mouth.

"Maria?" Curiosity became concern, and she could hear him patting around in the blackness trying to locate her. She rocked, tried to let go of the terror, willed it to drop away from her like the sleep. Or at least go sit in the corner while she found an even tone of voice in which to reassure him that she was fine. Just fine.

A big, warm hand landed on her ankle, then moved up the curve of her behind, which was situated conveniently on top of the ankle he'd found. He didn't linger, though. Just smoothed that hand up the trembling line of her back to the hideous mess of her hair. "Jesus, Maria, what's wrong?"

He lifted her by the shoulders, turned her to face him and set her back down, all with a disconcerting ease, as if she weighed nothing. Which she did not. And, Jesus, was she really going to entertain lustful thoughts about Rush's upper-body strength right now?

She dropped her head, and it landed—startlingly—on Rush's bare shoulder. She jerked back, only to find the hard cup of his hand on the base of her skull, holding her firmly against the living warmth of his skin.

"The lantern?" she managed. "Please?"

He left her shivering in the cold damp of his stolen T-shirt. The lighter scraped to life seconds later and there he was, filling the little kitchen with light and staring at her with startled concern.

"Jesus, Maria. What the hell?"

She tried a tentative smile. "I'm sorry," she said. "It was nothing. I'm overreacting."

"Overreact—" He broke off, closed his eyes. "Shit. This is about the mice, isn't it?"

"Mice?" She blinked at him, then shot an involuntary look at the floor. "We have mice?"

"What? No. Of course not." He rubbed a palm down the outer seam of his boxers and cleared his throat. "Bad dream?"

She stared at him, less concerned about a possible rodent infestation than grateful for something—anything—to talk about other than the raw fear still clinging to her. "We have *mice*?"

He sighed. "This is a log cabin in the woods. Of course we have mice. But unless they're chewing off your hair in the night, don't worry about them."

"That happened in one of the *Little House* books," she said, perfectly willing to engage in a conversational side trip. "The mice ate a bald spot into Pa's hair. Ma had to give him a bad haircut to cover it up." She frowned at Rush's shorn scalp, then stared. "Oh my God. That's why you keep your hair so short?"

He scrubbed a hand over his head. "No."

She tipped her head and squinted. "Receding hairline?"

He pinched the bridge of his nose. "You're changing the subject."

She frowned, suddenly struck. "It's quiet," she said slowly.

"What?"

"Listen." She cocked an ear. "The storm. It's over."

He gazed at her, uncomprehending. "And that freaks you out? That the storm is over? Isn't it usually the other way around?"

She lifted her shoulders. How could she explain to him how that sudden silence had crept into her sleep and terrified her? How her subconscious had translated it into the deadly, tense stillness that precedes death falling unannounced from the heavens? Or worse, from somewhere infinitely more familiar?

Unease clung to her even now, chased away only by the weak light of the lantern and his solid, steady presence.

"What can I say?" She gave him a shaky shrug. "I'm a head case."

It was probably the truest thing she'd ever said to him.

"You're not a head case. You're afraid."

"No, I'm okay." She smiled at him to demonstrate how very okay she was. He made an extremely rude noise and marched over to their makeshift bedrolls. He kicked his mattress up against the couch and dropped to it cross-legged. Then he pulled her into his lap, sleeping bag and all.

"You're still shivering," he said against her hair. Her curls. She'd lost her hat somewhere in her epic battle with the sleeping bag—super—and he nestled his chin into the tangled mess of her hair.

And, shit, he was right. She *was* a mess, and she didn't have the strength to pry herself away from the rock-solid comfort of his arms right this very second. She would, though. In a minute or two, she'd be fine. Until then, where was the harm in just sitting here?

She leaned into his chest, where his heart beat steady and reassuring under her cheek and his solid warmth chased the chill from her bones.

"Talk to me, will you?" She kept her eyes closed. It was easier, somehow, to endure this wretched vulnerability from the safety of darkness. "I don't want to go back to sleep. Not yet."

"Okay." He juggled her into a more comfortable position and settled his back against the couch. "I don't know any fairy tales, though."

"I don't care. Just talk."

"Talk's not exactly my thing. You may have noticed."

"I noticed." She gave in to temptation and rubbed her cheek against the sleek heat of his chest. "Why don't you tell me why you came back to Mishkwa after you got out of the service?"

"I told you already. I needed to figure my shit out."

"And did you?"

"Yeah. I did."

"So was this shit of a classified nature?" She snuggled deeper into the warm circle of his arms. "Or was it shit you can tell me about?"

* * *

RUSH HESITATED. It was a simple question, a simple answer. He'd been dangerous when he'd left the military. He'd needed space. He'd needed distance. He'd needed time. Mishkwa had given him all three in spades.

But he'd been alone for a long time now. Long enough for time to have done its magic. He hadn't been lonely, though. Never lonely. Just . . . alone. At least he would've said so before Maria showed up and started loading up his carefully empty world with all her stuff. Her laughter, her thoughts, her ideas, her *words*.

Most people talked and it was just noise. When Maria talked, though, it was like she'd cracked open a window into the screwy inner workings of her head. She might not speak the God's honest truth, but it was *her* truth and she handed it out over breakfast like it wasn't anything. Like it was free.

And now she wanted words from him. Words that would cost him. He rested his chin on that riot of spice-scented curls, and thought, *What the hell*. He'd tossed her own truth square in her face a few hours ago. What kind of man would he be if he refused to look his own truth in the eye now? If he refused to offer it up to her?

"You know the difference between a solider and a killer?" he asked, but it was a rhetorical question. He didn't expect her to answer, and she didn't. "Soldiers kill other soldiers while killers just kill." He hesitated, then took his courage in both hands and gave her the truth she'd asked for. The truth she deserved. "I came back to Mishkwa because I'd crossed that line and I needed to know if I could cross back."

She stiffened in his arms. He didn't blame her. It had taken him nearly two years to find a measure of peace with what he'd done. What he'd become.

"What does that mean, 'crossed that line'?"

"It means I killed a lot of people while I was playing in that bloody little sandbox on the other side of the world.

Most of them deserved it. But one day I murdered a woman and her baby."

"You did not."

"I did."

She pulled back to gaze up into his face, a serene disbelief in her eyes that warmed him. "No. You didn't. You were a sniper, Rush. I read your file. If you shot a woman or a child, it was on orders."

"Orders." He made a dismissive noise. "Orders don't make people any less dead, Maria. They don't make me any less of a killer."

She nestled her cheek back into his chest, and the trust, the comfort implied in that small concession, brought the unfamiliar sting of tears to his eyes. "Okay, you've killed a lot of people. I get that. I'm not saying your soul is pure as the driven snow. But whatever you did, you did on orders from a superior officer. Which means it *wasn't* murder, Rush. It was war."

She made it sound so final, he thought. She believed it, therefore it was true. End of story. If anybody could make something real simply through the power of belief, he had a feeling it was Maria.

A long beat of oddly peaceful silence passed, then she said, "So? Tell me the rest."

"What makes you think there's more?"

She pushed a warning finger against his chest. "There is. Tell me."

Rush remembered with a hard, hot flash how sharp those nails of hers were and how willing she was to use them if properly motivated. He wondered if he could motivate her again a little later. He pushed that aside to focus on the task at hand.

"As it turned out," he told her, "it wasn't actually a woman and a baby I shot."

Maria gave a disdainful sniff. "Ha. I knew it. Didn't I say so?"

"You're very wise." She dug at him with that fingernail

again and he caught her hand in his, twined their fingers together and let it rest on her knee. "It was actually a fourteen-year-old boy with a really girlie face. And the baby in his arms? That was a bomb."

"So you left the military because you shot a suicide bomber?" She shook her head. "No wonder you needed to straighten your shit out. That makes no sense whatsoever."

"Do you want to hear this story or don't you?"

She shut up.

"See the thing is, I wasn't there to shoot a cross-dressing teenager and his fake baby. I was there to take out a fat, male, middle-aged double agent. Dutch guy, worked for the CIA then decided to switch teams. Dangerous business, switching teams. I don't advise it."

"I'll take it under consideration," she murmured.

"The guy figured out we were onto him, and instead of meeting his handler as usual, so we could blow him away, he decided to send us a little message instead."

"A boy with a bomb. Dressed up as a woman with her baby."

"Yep. So there I was," Rush went on. He couldn't stop now to save his life. He'd uncorked this beast and by God it was coming out. The whole thing. "Rifle snug into my shoulder, eye to the scope, kill zone established. This thing was precision-engineered down to the second. Watches synchronized, the whole deal. I get the word that the target's in the building, about to cross the crowded square I'm covering. About to sit down for a coffee with the handler at this outdoor café. So my finger's on the trigger, taking up the slack, counting heartbeats now, and you know who walks into my kill zone instead?"

"The boy with the bomb." Her voice was gentle, filled with the beautiful, boundless compassion she extended to everybody but herself.

"But I didn't know that. As far as I could see, it was a woman. With her baby."

"But it wasn't, Rush." She wrapped both hands around

his biceps, warm and confiding. "It was a boy with a bomb. Not that that's any comfort to you, I know. A child is a child, and I can't imagine what it cost you to shoot. But your pulling the trigger had to have saved countless lives."

"You're missing the point," Rush said. "Because it doesn't matter what really happened. What I really did. What matters is what I *thought* I did. Because I didn't *know* it wasn't a woman in my sights. I didn't even *suspect*. You want the truth? You really want to know what was going on in my head when I pulled the trigger? *Nothing*. It didn't occur to me to even *wonder* if this person was or wasn't the right target. I didn't fucking *care*. I had clearance to shoot, she crossed my kill zone and I took her—and what I believed to be her baby, Christ forgive me—out."

He didn't dare look down at her. If he'd finally reached the limits of her compassion, her forgiveness, he didn't want to know. Not right now. Not yet.

"That's what's inside me," he said softly. "That's what I'm capable of, and I needed to figure out if I could live with it. That's why I came home."

"And can you?" Her voice floated soft and small from the cradle of his arms. "Live with it?"

He sucked in a steadying breath, planted himself firmly in the here and now and said, "Yeah. Yeah, I can. Turns out my moral compass wasn't dead, it was just frozen. Took me the better part of two years to thaw it out again, and it's rusty as hell, but I'm starting to think it still works." He cleared his throat of a suspiciously wet lump. "Touch and go for a while there, though."

She slipped her arms around him, pressed her cheek to his heart and said, "I know what that's like."

Wonder blew sharp and wild through him, and he tightened his arms around her. "You do?"

"Yes." She nestled closer, as if trying to get inside his chest and take his pain, his guilt, onto herself. "I know what it is to find something dangerous inside yourself. Something dark and unstable and unworthy. I know exactly what it is to do something unforgivable. And I know what it costs to tear down what you were and build someone better on the wreckage."

So that was it. She'd scared herself somewhere along the line, just like he had. He'd suspected as much.

She laid a hand against his heart, gentle and merciful. "I don't know who you were then, but I know who you are now. And the man I know earned forgiveness a long time ago."

"Forgiveness," he said slowly. A strange lightness filled his chest, new and yet somehow familiar. Gratitude? Peace? Love?

"Forgiveness," she said firmly. "For all your sins, real and imagined. You've earned it. Now you just have to believe it."

His throat simply closed and he gathered her to him, his lips in her hair, his heart a raw ache within him.

"Thank you," he said finally. "That helps."

And it was true, he realized. She *had* helped. He could still pull the trigger easier than most people flicked a light switch. No escaping that, not that he'd tried. His was an awful but necessary talent, and nobody who'd seen evil at work in the world could argue otherwise.

But he'd forced himself to face the living, breathing cost of exercising that talent. To realize that putting his particular skill set in the hands of anybody but himself—even the good guys—was abdicating responsibility. Because separating the act from the reason for the act—killing on orders—only separated Rush from his soul. Finding his way to wholeness again had been a long, bloody battle. One, God willing, he'd never have to fight again.

So he'd accepted himself, but he'd never thought to forgive himself. But she had. This sad, valiant woman in his arms had not only seen him but forgiven him.

Now if only she could forgive herself as easily as she'd forgiven him.

Chapter

23

RUSH WOKE the next morning to the muffled buzz of a blow-dryer. Damn, he'd slept hard. He flexed his empty arms and blinked gritty eyes at the ceiling. Power must be back. Which meant Goose was probably back, too. Sleek, polished, slippery Goose.

The hair dryer cut out and, yep, sure enough. She stepped out of the bathroom, her cheeks flushed from the blast of hot air, her hair ruler straight, her eyes perfectly made up with some kind of smoky bronze stuff. She gave him that friendly, keep-your-distance smile and he smiled back, slow and hungry.

Her smile faltered, and she veered toward the kitchenette.

Good, he thought. She ought to be nervous. What, did she think he was going to roll over and play dead? Did she think he could be defeated by a *blow-dryer*? Fuck that. He didn't want this perfectly manicured, exquisitely groomed doll. He wanted *Maria*. Funny, sharp, wounded Maria. The woman she kept as hidden as her curls and her shocking ability to kiss a man into near insanity.

And he meant to have her.

"Power's back," she said with determined cheer.

"So I see." He studied her for two long beats, then pointed his chin at her. "You really think that's going to work?"

She touched the smooth spill of her inky hair. "What's going to work?"

He sat up to run a squint over her face, her hair. "All . . . that. It seems like a lot of effort for nothing."

She didn't pretend to misunderstand. "It's not nothing."

He gave her a skeptical look. "No, I can see that. But why bother? I mean, I've already seen what you really look like. Who you really are." He rose to his feet and she averted her eyes, as if she weren't already intimately familiar with what he looked like, too. Even without the boxers he currently wore. "Plus I like you better curly. Way better." He let his smile spread as he moved toward the kitchen. Toward her. "So why don't we just head straight back into the bathroom and start again? Come on. I'll scrub your back."

She shot out a hand, palm first, the universal sign for *Stop right there, buster.*

"As it happens, I didn't do this"—she waved a hand toward her exquisitely groomed person—"for you, okay?" She glared at him. "I did it for me."

Rush stopped. "For you?"

"For *me.*" She threw him a bitter glance. "I'm not stupid, Rush. I'm well aware of what you saw last night. Who you saw." She made a noise that was half disgust, half regret. "It's hard to miss when I left the evidence all over your body."

He glanced down at himself, then back up at her. "You're upset because you gave me a hickey? So what? I'm pretty sure I gave you one, too." He took a moment to consider that. "More than one, actually." He smiled. "Want me to find them for you?"

She pressed those perfectly glossed lips together, hard. "Check out your back, Rush." She turned away to fiddle with the coffeemaker. "You look like somebody zipped half a dozen feral cats into your sleeping bag last night."

Rush followed her into the tiny kitchen. "So you scratched me. Big deal. Did you hear me complaining?" She didn't turn to face him, stayed stubbornly focused on the coffee, so he grabbed the counter on either side of her hips and leaned in. He left a few inches of space between their bodies, between his mouth and her ear. He treated himself to the clean, green smell of her hair as he murmured, "Did you hear me say anything to you that wasn't 'harder,' 'more,' or 'God, just like that'?"

Even the shell of her ear went pink but she stayed silent. Still. Unhappy. God, that broke his heart. How unhappy she was.

"Will it make you feel better if you go back into the shower—alone—to have a look at all the marks I left on *your* body? Because you weren't alone last night, Maria. I was there, too. And—I have to be honest here—the fact that you could drive me far enough around the bend to forget to be gentle with you? The fact that I can do the same to you? It turned me on. A lot. I'm turned on right now just remembering it. So if you want to talk about it much longer, you're going to have to deal with the consequences."

He closed the gap then, erased those few electric inches of space between their bodies. A hiss of agonized pleasure escaped her when the ache of his desire nestled into the soft curve of her behind, and he said, "I know, right? It's crazy, what you do to me. But it's so"—he rolled himself against her, slow and hot—". . . *so* good."

She spun around suddenly but not—to his everlasting regret—to hop onto the counter and wrap her legs around him.

"Rush." She met his gaze head-on, made no attempt to hide the heat leaping in her eyes. The heat that was so at odds with her straight-arming him back to a civilized distance. Rush decided he fucking *hated* civilization. "I'm going to be honest here, too. That's what you want, right? Honesty?"

"No, Maria. I like it when you lie to me. Because I'm *so* into subterfuge." They both glanced at the massive erection tenting the front of his shorts. He sighed. "Yes. Please be honest."

"What happened here last night. What I . . . did to you?" Her eyes dropped to the faint teeth marks on his shoulder. "It scared the hell out of me. It's been a long time since I lost control like that and I'm feeling kind of fragile, okay?" She swallowed visibly. "I realize this is something we're going to have to talk about eventually. But if it's all the same to you, can we please just table it this morning? At least until I get my balance back?"

"Not if by 'balance' you mean painting your face and terrifying your hair."

"Terrifying my hair?"

"Honey, you're scared straight." He frowned at her head. "I don't know what you do with that blow-dryer of yours but it's clearly hard-core. And I'm starting to have a real soft spot for those curls. I won't have them bullied."

A smile ghosted across her lips, faint but real. "No more straightening. Fine."

"But as for the rest of it?" He tipped his head, considered. "Fine. I'll give you today. But I'm not going to wait forever. What happened last night? What you did to me? What I did to you? I'm planning to do it again as soon as possible." He leaned into the eye contact. "As *soon* as possible, Maria. Count on it. And when we do? You're going to talk to me the whole time."

She closed her eyes as if praying for strength. She kept them closed for a solid ten count. Then her cell phone did a little dance on the counter and sang its you-have-mail song.

"We have a deal?" he asked.

She nodded slowly, her pupils huge, her lips parted. He backed away from her open palm before he could talk himself off the high road. She'd come to him next time, he swore it. With that *yes* not only on her lips but in her heart. Even if it killed him.

"Go ahead," he said, nodding toward her phone. "Go to work."

She blinked, a flutter of blinks really, then focused and scooped up her phone. His own cell phone chirped like a demented cricket a little farther down the counter, indicating he ought to download his messages, too. Well, crap. He dialed his voice mail and scrolled through to the most recent messages.

Einar's voice drifted small and tinny into his ear.

"Hey, Rush. Some storm, huh? Listen, Sir Humpalot demolished half my chicken coop this morning. Are you ever going to shoot that damn thing? Because I'm about ready to put a cap in his ass myself. Poor chickens, all crowded and traumatized and shit. I'm not going to bother rebuilding, either. Not until you've figured out the fucking wildlife around here, Mr. Park Ranger." He paused. "I guess I could move up the slaughter a month or two. I might borrow your ski team for slave labor. Team building, you know?" He laughed. "Hey, speaking of chickens, I'm scheduled to fly out tomorrow morning, Tuesday. I won't be back till Wednesday afternoon, earliest. Feed the girls while I'm away, will you?"

The sun pasted a watery yellow square on the old wooden floor and Rush realized that his cousin had just provided the perfect opportunity for Rush to invite Maria into Einar's cabin for that search she was so anxious to perform.

He glanced down the counter at her as he dialed his boss at the Park Service and explained the moose situation. The glare off Maria's hair was blinding, but he could still see the frown pinching her brows together as she scribbled on the pad in front of her. She flipped her phone shut, and he did the same.

"Lab results are back on that sample I sent in," she said.

"Sample?"

"Blood sample. From the Stone Altar."

"Yeah?" His chest tightened.

"It was chicken blood."

"I . . . don't know how to feel about that."

"I know. I mean, thank God it wasn't human, right? But still, chicken blood points pretty strongly in the direction I was already looking."

"Einar." He tapped his phone against his thigh. "Speaking of whom."

She lifted her brows.

"I just got a voice mail. He's leaving town tomorrow morning. Overnight. Chickens'll need feeding."

She studied him. "You up for company on that?"

He jerked a shoulder.

"Rush." She reached across the counter as if she were going to touch his elbow, but then encountered all the bare skin of his chest and drew back before she made contact. "It's better to find out than to wonder."

"Yeah." He shook himself, shook off the idea that his own cousin, his blood, could have possibly tangled himself up this badly. "Not going to find out today, though." He pointed his chin at the snowdrift blocking most of the window. "Today, we dig out." He gave her a speculative look. "Unless you'd rather stay snowbound for a few days?"

"Start shoveling, Rush."

He sighed. "I was afraid you'd say that."

BY LATE morning, Rush had cleared a path from the door to the woodpile and reacquainted the windows with daylight. In spite of a bright sun and still sky, though, the mercury hovered stubbornly around fifteen below. And conditions inside the cabin weren't much better, with Maria just as stubbornly ensconced inside the slick, impenetrable Goose. He was losing patience with that, promises be damned.

It was—in Rush's personal opinion—high time to shoot the shit out of something.

He banged into the cabin on a blast of frigid air, clapped his gloved hands together as if he were a cruise director or a camp counselor and said, "On your feet, di Guzman. It's time to earn your keep."

She blinked up at him from behind the glowing screen of her laptop. "Excuse me?"

He grabbed her jacket from its hook near the door and said, "I just got a message from my boss. He gave us the go-ahead to take down the moose."

"Sir Humpalot?"

"The very one."

"You're going to *shoot* him?"

"That's the plan." He tossed her jacket toward her. It floated through the air and landed on her head like a purple parachute. "And you're coming with me."

She lifted the hem of her jacket and peered at him. "I'm not sure that's such a good idea."

"No?" He gave her a smile that dared her to explain why exactly several hours alone in the woods together wasn't a good idea.

"I don't really . . . hunt."

"I bet you'll pick it up quick enough, seeing as you're an expert marksman." She stared at him and he shrugged. "Again, you're not the only one who knows how to use the Internet."

"You read my file?"

"Enough to know that you're perfectly capable of taking down a bull moose at two hundred yards with the proper equipment." He gave her a significant smile. "And since *you've* read *my* file, I'm pretty sure you won't be surprised to know I do have the proper equipment."

"Of course you do." She sighed and set aside her computer. "You seriously want me to go moose hunting?"

"Yes."

"There's nothing I can say that'll change your mind?"

"Depends on who you are when you say it, *Maria.*"

She gave him a polite smile. "Give me a minute to get geared up."

Chapter

24

MARIA STUMBLED along in Rush's snowshoe prints for several frozen, silent hours, a high-powered hunting rifle in her icy hands, a perverse gratitude in her heart.

Not that she was enjoying tracking Sir Humpalot. God, no. Traipsing around the frozen tundra after a moose that had, for all practical purposes, vanished into an alternate dimension was about as entertaining as it sounded. But after last night she was hanging on to her composure by a thin, fragile thread, and the enforced silence of the hunt was nothing short of a blessing as far as she was concerned.

Last night. Pleasure and fear spurted through her in equal, baffling amounts. It had been so many years since she'd come face-to-face with her truest self, but Rush—*hello, Maria*—had set that woman free simply by refusing to accept that she didn't exist. Most people saw what you showed them and nothing else, but Rush? Rush didn't look away until he had the whole picture. And since he knew as well as she did that he didn't have the whole picture yet, he wasn't planning to look away anytime soon. Which was precisely why enduring an endless hike in the moose-less wonderland of Mishkwa—minus conversation and eye contact—wasn't exactly torture.

Rush stopped short and Maria nearly plowed into his back. She jerked the barrel of her rifle to the side and said, "Jesus, Rush, you could *say* something—"

The words died in her throat when he reached out one big hand and, for the first time since he'd all but set her on fire next to the coffeemaker, touched her. But there was nothing loverlike in this touch. He simply spread his big hand on top of her head and stuffed her down onto her knees into a clump of sticks that had probably been a berry bush in friendlier seasons. He cut off her muffled exclamation with a gloved hand and jerked his chin toward the clearing beyond the brush in which she was now crouched.

The moose was there, maybe twenty yards away, his big nose to the ground, huffing and snuffling in a churned-up patch of snow. His rack arched wide and impressive away from his giant head, and his waggly beard dangled in the snow, white with the frost of his own breath. Awe broke open inside her at the sight of something so huge and wild, so close she could hear it breathing.

Rush's mouth came down to her ear, his warm exhale sending a completely inappropriate tingle through parts she thought had gone numb hours ago.

"We're upwind," he said, his words more breath than voice. "He can't smell us, but you don't want to waste time. You have a round in the chamber, so—"

She stared at him, shocked. "You want *me* to shoot him?"

"I didn't chamber a round," he said. "He'll hear if I do it now. But I chambered a round for you when I showed you how to do it back at the cabin." He nodded at the moose. "It's your shot."

A screaming panic filled her brain. Oh God, oh God, oh God. She didn't want to shoot this moose. She didn't want to shoot anything. She didn't care what her file said—she was a computer geek, not a sharpshooter. She'd pointed a loaded gun at a living creature exactly once before in her entire life and she still wasn't out from under the cosmic debt she'd incurred that day.

But what else could she do? After last night's debacle, she was holding together Goose's cultivated composure with duct tape and bravado. Did she really think it would survive one more blow? Did she really think she could refuse to pull the trigger without explaining why?

She slowly shouldered the heavy gun and sighted down the barrel. She breathed, willed her trembling hands to steady, her thundering heart to slow. And she prayed. Prayed to whoever was in charge of desperate wishes that the strength, the courage and the composure she'd perfected the appearance of could be hers in reality. Just this once.

The moose raised its head. He glared at her, as if he'd sensed her intention, and didn't care one bit for the impudence. *You think you can take me?* it seemed to ask. *You think you have anything that would wound the majesty of* me?

Her blood thudded in her ears and her body went through the motions without her volition, the action bred into her through years of rigorous practice. She pulled in a shaky breath then squeezed the trigger with her exhale. Squeezed it slowly, deliberately, though her heart beat crazily and her vision started to dapple. She sent up one last prayer, tried valiantly to control her breathing then absorbed the big rifle's kick with a sense of submission. Her pain—even this small one—was well deserved.

The shot skewed high, cracking a tine off the moose's rack but otherwise leaving him unmolested. He snorted out a great, derisive raspberry, wheeled and bolted into the brush. Rush patted her shoulder.

"Okay," he said. "Not bad for a first try."

"Thanks," she said, handing him the gun. He sounded like he was talking to her from the other end of a train tunnel. "Hold on to this, will you?"

"Why?"

"I'm going to pass out now."

"What?"

The dancing black spots closed in on her and she gave herself up to them.

RUSH SHOVED a cup of coffee into Maria's hand as she sat, pale and unhappy, at the tiny kitchen counter of the Ranger Station.

"So," he said conversationally. "Do you pass out every time you fire a gun?"

"No." Her lips barely moved. Nothing did. Not her hair, her hands or even the brows that normally animated her face. She looked taut, as if even an attempt to smile might shatter her. "Only when I aim it at a beating heart before pulling the trigger."

"And how often have you done that?"

"Just the once." She shook her head, as if rattling things back into place. "No, twice. If you count today."

Rush fixed himself a cup of coffee. He didn't want one but he needed something to do with his hands. He still didn't know why she was wrapped up so tightly in this slippery shell of hers, but he'd bet the farm it had its roots right here in whatever had her going lights-out every time she fired a gun in earnest.

"How old were you?" he asked softly. "The first time this happened?"

"Sixteen."

"Were you shot?" His mouth went desperately dry at the very idea.

"No."

Relief flooded him and he said, "Somebody you loved, then."

"My sister," she said, her beautiful face wooden. "She died."

He squashed down the surge of sympathy he somehow knew she wouldn't welcome. "You saw it happen?"

Her mouth twisted bitterly. "Front-row seats."

Rush tried to wrap his mind around that, around watching a sibling die and being helpless to prevent it. Around being introduced in that way to the black power of a gun to give and to take away. Around an immensity of pain he knew he himself had caused countless times.

"Okay, so you were really, really young," he said, trying to feel around, to go gently. "Impressionable. And that's a pretty huge thing to try to understand when your worldview is still pretty small and self-centered."

She winced and he hurried on. "Not you personally," he said. "Just teenagers in general, you know? They tend to think they understand everything when they've really only seen a little slice of the world. It would screw up any kid's head, witnessing a violent death that young—"

"I didn't witness her death." Her eyes snapped to his, dark and bottomless and filled with an endless sorrow that stole his breath. "I caused it."

MARIA WAS oddly serene, given that she was having some kind of breakdown. She couldn't say when she'd first noticed the hairline cracks in her control. Last week, last month, last year? All she knew was that Rush had noticed them, too. And, being Rush, he'd relentlessly wriggled himself into those cracks, pulling them inexorably wider, calling to the hungry, dangerous woman inside her.

And now he'd done it. He'd wrestled from her a single, bald-faced admission—*I killed my sister*—and it had shattered the façade. Shattered *her*. Or what she'd led the world to believe was her for nearly half her life.

The experience was not, she mused with a strange detachment, what she'd expected.

She'd braced herself for a muddy gush of guilt and rage and pain and regret. For a howling maelstrom of destructive energy. For anything but this profound, quiet sorrow. It rolled through her, crushing the air from her lungs and extinguishing whatever small, foolish sparks of hope she'd allowed Rush's desire to nurture inside her.

Then Rush seized her hands, his touch hot, vibrant and

so alive. It burned her, and she closed her eyes against the pull of it. Of him.

"Tell me," he said, his voice low and steady and full of a compassionate understanding that made her throat ache. "You have to tell somebody. Whatever it is, it's got you all tangled up inside. It's got you hiding behind somebody else's face and laughing somebody else's laugh." She felt his thumb brush her cheek, and that harsh voice went impossibly soft. "Maria," he said. "You can tell me. I need to know."

Tears threatened at the sound of her true name, and for a long awful moment she didn't know if she'd be able to swallow them down. But she did. He'd asked for the truth, *her* truth. He'd earned that much from her, so she'd give it to him. She didn't have anywhere else to hide anyway.

"I killed my sister," she said.

"No, you didn't." He said it with a certainty, an immediacy that sent pain lancing through her. God. She didn't want to do this. Really, *really* didn't want to. She wished she could just stay right here, safe in the beautiful cocoon of his trust. But she was out of options. It was time to lay her cards on the table and let herself be judged.

"I didn't pull the trigger or anything, no. But it was my fault anyway. My own stupid fault."

He smoothed away a tear she hadn't been aware of shedding with the pad of his thumb and said again, "Tell me."

"Marisol was my twin," she said. "Beautiful, smart, ambitious, with this sense of justice that even high school couldn't dent."

"And you?"

"Me?" She forced a chuckle. "I wasn't. I was geeky, awkward, mathematically inclined. I laughed too loud, I had all these insane curls. And I was *tall*."

"Totally your fault."

"Like that matters in high school." She gave a jerky shrug. "But Marisol didn't let anybody torture me. She was the type to use her power for good, not evil. Which is why being jealous of her was so wrong. But I was. Jealous. Of her straight perfect hair. Of her curvy little body. Of her giant smile and her gorgeous boyfriend." Maria sighed. "*All* her gorgeous boyfriends, actually. But especially Ridge."

"Ridge?"

"Ridge Calloway. She met him when he was fresh out of the police academy and she was doing a summer internship at the station house. Prepping herself for a brilliant career in law enforcement. Marisol was always planning ahead." She smiled at him, and it was small and wretched but genuine. It was the only kind she had left. "So he was a few fabulous years older, and he had one of those faces that belonged on a recruiting poster for the Marines. They made an astoundingly good-looking couple. The kind who actually stun people with their beauty. To this day I don't know if I wanted him for myself, or if I just wanted to be Marisol, but when she broke things off with him—she said he was getting too possessive, if you can believe it. Who would complain about a guy like Ridge Calloway wanting you all to himself, Jesus!" She shook her head. "So when he started calling me? Well. It was a dream come true, right? He'd been blinded by Marisol's physical perfection and her surface charm, but that wasn't enough to sustain a man of Ridge's depth. He'd want something more. Some*body* more. Somebody deeper. Somebody more like . . . well, *me*."

She laughed but she wasn't amused. She didn't sound amused either, judging from the wince in Rush's eyes. "So when he asked me out, of course I went. Because I wanted him. Wanted him in the worst way. It was like a physical hunger, this want. This love. I craved him, you know? It was like I'd die if I couldn't have him. Which made it relatively easy to overlook a few troubling facts."

"Like?"

"Oh, like his insistence on keeping our love a secret. We wouldn't want to hurt Marisol's feelings, would we? Like the fact that, when we talked, it was all about Marisol. But hey, he had to heal, didn't he? He needed closure, and my hard-hearted sister wouldn't even speak to him. So I talked to him instead. About her. Her schedule, her friends.

Her dates. Was she seeing anybody? Was it serious? I told him everything he wanted to know, right down to the minute. And when he turned up in the school parking lot the morning before our prom with his service revolver and an ultimatum for Marisol, I told myself I was as stunned as anybody."

Nausea quivered in her stomach as that day came back to her in the vivid Technicolor of her dreams. "Was I really stunned? I don't remember anymore. You want to know what I do remember, though? I remember the way the heat radiated up off the parking lot. I remember the way Marisol rolled her eyes and told him to get lost. I remember the way she looked at me, with pity and compassion and understanding. *Understanding*, Rush. Can you imagine? She should have been angry at me. Furious. Here she'd given an unbalanced stalker the old heave-ho and I, in my infinite selfishness, had brought him right back into our lives. But she wasn't pissed. No, she *understood*. She understood that I was just that desperate, just that pitiful, that I'd not only want my sister's leftovers, but I'd yearn for them. I'd crave them. Sell my soul for them."

She huffed out a disgusted laugh. "I was in love. In deep. Beyond reason, for sure. But it was pretty obvious by then that the feeling wasn't mutual. Marisol was the Garden of Eden, and Ridge wasn't about to let himself get kicked out. He swore up and down he just wanted to talk, but Marisol, she was a smart cookie. She didn't chat with angry, armed men. So of course Ridge handed over the gun."

"To Marisol?"

"To me." She stretched her lips in a grotesque parody of a smile. "The neutral third party."

"Shit."

"Tell me about it. Because then it was in my hands, his service revolver. I'd never held a gun before. It was heavier than I'd imagined."

"They always are." Rush brushed a lock of hair away from her sticky cheek.

"After that it was the usual." She waved an airy hand.

"It was all 'I love you, Marisol. You're mine. I won't let you leave me. We belong together. Forever. And if this is the only way, then fine.'"

"He had a clutch piece," Rush said. "Ankle holster?"

"It's a classic for a reason." She shook her head. "But I had a gun, too. I should have shot him. It should have been automatic. And I tried to, Rush. I really tried. At least I think I did." Nausea crawled up her throat, thick and suffocating as memory. "But the gun was so heavy, and I didn't know how the safety worked, and he was so fast. He'd shot her before I could even point it at him."

"Maria," he said, his voice rich with pain and pity. "God, you can't—"

She cut him off. She didn't want his pain or his pity. She just wanted him to know.

"Then he asked me to shoot him."

Rush didn't say anything, only held her cold hands in his warm ones, his eyes steady and patient as he waited for the rest. So she gave it to him.

Chapter

25

"HE CRIED and asked me to kill him. And I'm standing there," she said, "with my ears ringing and my vision doing that broken filmstrip thing. My sister's crumpled on the pavement like an old doll and I was trying—Christ, I was trying to pull the trigger. But I was too slow."

"He shot himself." It wasn't a question.

"That's what they tell me. I didn't see that part myself because I'd passed out. That's what I do when I try to pull the trigger on another living being." She laughed, a jagged, bloody noise. "Even, apparently, a living being who's just murdered my own twin sister. My mother's never forgiven me for not blowing his ass to kingdom come when he asked me to. It was the least I could do, in her opinion."

"She would have put that on your conscience?" he asked quietly. "Taking a human life?"

"People do a lot of horrible stuff in the grip of passion." Maria shrugged. "My passion just happens to be aroused by exactly the wrong things."

Understanding flooded those cool gray eyes. "A flaw you've spent your life trying to erase."

She spread her hands. "It's a goal."

"You were a child, Maria. A teenage girl. You made a mistake, a horrible one, but—"

"But nothing. Marisol's dead."

"Yeah, she is. And that's a shame. I'm so sorry for your loss." His quiet words thudded into her, both painful and beautiful. Her loss. Nobody ever talked about *her* loss. Her guilt, sure. That had been covered, ad nauseam. But her loss? No. It had always been her mother's loss, her family's loss, the world's loss. But suddenly it was her loss, too. Her tremendous, profound, world-altering loss, and she ached for her twin the way she'd ache for her right arm if it suddenly went missing.

"But, Maria?" Rush leaned forward, pinned her with those sharp, uncompromising eyes. "It's not—"

"—my fault?" She squeezed his hands, so strong and warm around hers, and smiled, though it was a little shaky. "Please don't forgive me, Rush. This isn't confession, and I'm not telling you any of this in the hopes that you'll grant me absolution. I'm telling you this so you'll understand why I can't love you." She shook her head hard. "No. Honesty. This has to be honest." She forced herself to meet his eyes. "I could totally love you. I want to love you. God, in the worst way. But I won't do it."

"Why not?"

"Because I'm dangerous when I love, Rush." She said it softly, which didn't do a damn thing to diminish the slicing pain of having to say it. "Don't you see? I don't have any checks, any controls. I love too much, too hard and too unwisely. It already cost me my twin. I can't let it cost me anything—anybody—else. Particularly not you."

"I wasn't going to say it wasn't your fault."

She blinked at him. "What?"

"Earlier. When I said 'it wasn't'—and you cut me off to

refuse my forgiveness? I wasn't going to offer it. I wasn't going to let you off the hook."

He still had her hand between his, and she left it there while she stared at him, dumbfounded.

"After last night, after what I told you about myself, did you really think I wouldn't understand? Of course you didn't *actually* kill your sister, but there's fault and there's fault. It's not what you did but what you found inside yourself. There's some deep, scary, uncontrollable passion in there. And you're right to be wary of that. Believe me, I know what it is to live with some dangerous shit inside you. Taking responsibility for that isn't easy and you had to learn way too young about the consequences of being thoughtless and impulsive. I can't tell you how sorry I am about that. But you have to *live* with those consequences, Maria. There's no undoing the mistake."

It took a few tries to find her voice. "I'm not trying to undo—"

"Of course you are. You're not mourning Marisol; you're trying to *be* her. As if straightening your hair, dressing to the nines and earning that badge she wanted so bad is going to ease your mother's pain or your guilt." He smoothed his hand over the smooth fall of her hair. "This is pretty, Maria, but it doesn't help. You're not looking at your problem. You're trying to pretend it doesn't exist. And you're not going to solve it if you won't look at it."

She gaped at him, her ears ringing from the brutal truth of his words. Finally she cleared her throat. "You seriously weren't going to forgive me?"

"Nope. I'm the honesty police." He gave her a crooked smile. "Forgiveness is your department."

RUSH STOOD against Einar's counter the next morning and watched as Maria searched, with meticulous care, every drawer and cupboard in his cousin's kitchen. She applied the same professional thoroughness to the tiny bedrooms, then the minuscule bathroom and finally the sitting room. She even inspected the chicken coop—what was left of it—and the slaughter shed. Then she came back to the kitchen, her lips tight, her brows pinched.

"No luck?"

"No." She squinted out the window toward a patch of frigid blue sky. "I was hoping to stay low profile on this, but I'm going to need a warrant to search the plane. I'll make some calls this afternoon." Her eyes snapped back to his, dark and troubled. "But first I want to go back to the Stone Altar."

"Why?"

"I'm thinking about installing motion-sensitive surveillance equipment."

"You have that kind of stuff handy?"

"Of course not. But I could have some sent up."

"I commend the outside-the-box thinking, Maria, but I'm not sure it'd be worth the effort. Even if you managed to drill a hole in the frozen wall big enough to stash a camera, this kind of cold is hell on batteries. They wouldn't last six hours."

"I know." She sighed. "But I need to search the mine more thoroughly anyway. I might as well check out surveillance possibilities while I'm there."

"What are you searching for?"

"Cash. If there's a stash there, I want to take it into custody before Einar's back on-island."

"How will you connect supernotes in the mine to Einar, though? They could belong to anybody."

"Yarrow, for example?" She blew out a frustrated breath and the curls on her forehead danced. Rush grinned at them in spite of himself. Maybe Einar was in some deep shit, but Maria had kept her promise. She was flying her curly-headed freak flag this morning, and he loved it.

"I stand by my logic," he said now. "Yarrow's the one with the connections to move supernotes. And you yourself explained how exactly she's motivated to hurt Lila by screwing around with black magic. So why aren't you looking at her?"

"I am," Maria said. "As a victim, though, not a criminal."

"A victim?" Rush stared. Yarrow was a tough kid, all hard eyes and scathing words. He couldn't imagine her being taken at any game she chose to play. "A victim of what?"

She hesitated. "Of who."

"What?"

"A victim of *who*, not what."

Rush's brain did a few confused circles, then his mouth dropped open. Oh God. First smuggling counterfeits, then black magic, now she wanted to accuse Einar of— He broke off, unwilling to follow the logic through even inside his own head. That would make it too ugly. Too real.

"Sexual abuse." Maria supplied the conclusion grimly but without hesitation. "Yeah, that's what I'm thinking."

"*Why?* Why on earth would you think that?"

"I can't explain it. I just know it when I see it."

"See what? Okay, Yarrow has a crush on him, but so do half the girls on the ski team. So what?"

"A crush? You think she has a crush? Jesus, Rush, she's in love. Completely, irrationally, worshipfully in love. And I think Einar is taking advantage of that. Of her." Her eyes were dark, direct and full of pained regret. "I don't take any joy in pursuing this," she said quietly. "But Yarrow's an innocent, if troubled, child. We protect her safety before we protect Einar's feelings."

Rush shook his head, though not in denial as much as to impose order on the crazy, disjointed thoughts tumbling around in there. "Maria, come on. I know Einar. I've known him his whole life. He couldn't—"

"Of course he could," she said. "Even if he's not sleeping with her, he could be using her feelings to manipulate her into any number of illegal acts, up to and including moving supernotes. It happens all the time." He opened his mouth to refute this blanket condemnation of humanity, but she cut him off. "*All the time*, Rush."

He shut his mouth and looked at her. At the pain in her face, the fierce determination to protect an innocent, a keening drive to punish the guilty. And suddenly he understood.

"Maria," he said, his stomach churning with echoes of her experience with misguided love. "It doesn't happen to everybody just because it happened to you."

Hurt moved through her eyes, then they went shuttered and blank. "I'm not talking about me."

"I am." He wanted to move toward her, take her into his arms and ease away the stiff unhappiness in those long, pretty limbs, but he knew she wouldn't allow him that pleasure. Wouldn't allow herself the comfort. "Calloway was a weak, cowardly bastard who did the world a favor when he blew his own head off. I can't even tell you how sorry I am that he was able to damage you and your family so much." He did reach out then, took one of her wooden hands. "But you have to admit that an experience like the one you had is formative."

"Formative?"

"It's the lens through which you see the world." He spoke reluctantly but honesty compelled him, the way instinct compelled her. "I'm not saying you're necessarily wrong about Einar and Yarrow, but I do think you need to be aware of your bias before you take action here."

"My bias." A vast ocean of pain uncurled in her eyes, pulling him into the cold, swirling depths. "You think I don't recognize my *bias*?" She shook her head, but slowly. As if it were unthinkably heavy and caused her unbearable pain. "My bias is my gift, Rush. I earned it; I may as well use it. Isn't that what you said yesterday?"

"I—" He snapped his mouth shut. "Did I?"

"I only recognize the trouble Yarrow's in because I survived it myself. And what she feels, what radiates off her whenever she's anywhere near Einar? It's no crush. It may have started that way, but the innocence has been perverted into something dark and greedy and ugly. And that doesn't happen by itself. That kind of twisting takes guidance. Encouragement. Help."

"Help you think Einar provided."

"Yes."

"Why?"

"I don't know yet. But I'll find out. I need to find out."

"Have you tried talking to Yarrow about this?"

"Of course."

"And?"

She shrugged into her shell, zipped it with a jerk. "She was . . . uncooperative. It's not unusual for victims to protect their abusers, you know. I'm hoping to have better luck with Lila. But right now I'm heading out to the mines." She met his eyes. "Are you coming?"

"You need to do this?" Rush asked her. "To be satisfied that you've done everything in your power to help a child, you need to do *this*?" He wasn't talking about hiking to the mines.

"I do."

He didn't hesitate. "Let's go, then."

BY THE time they trudged into Mother Lila's Tea Shop that afternoon, Maria felt like somebody had tied cinder blocks to her heels. They'd skied rather than snowshoed this time, and had exactly nothing to show for the miles they'd logged. Not one shred of evidence tying Einar to any of the crimes her gut insisted he was guilty of. Exhaustion covered her like a sodden blanket. Piled on top of the confusion she was already staggering under, it was enough to drive a girl to her knees.

Lila took one look at the two of them and slid warm cinnamon scones under their noses with a sympathetic cluck. "Hard day?"

Maria sighed. "You have no idea."

Lila lifted her omnipresent teacup to her lips and sipped. The afternoon sun slanted through the plate-glass front of the tea shop and painted sterling streaks into her gray hair. "You might be surprised."

Maria broke off a corner of her scone and chewed thoughtfully while Rush said, "We went back to the Stone Altar today."

"Did you?"

"Maria was hoping to find evidence that would tie the two crimes together—the black magic and the smuggling—but we came up empty."

Maria frowned at her scone. "I know something's there, Lila. I can feel it in my gut. Something's there and I'm missing it. Something important. Something that's going to point the way out of this mess."

Lila shot a questioning glance at Rush and received a what-the-hell shrug in response. She reached across the table and took Maria's hand. "I can help you, dear. If you'll let me."

Maria blinked at the older woman's hand on her own. She thought about the vicious slap of emotion in Yarrow's touch, about the warm comfort of Lila's. She thought about Rush's conviction that Mishkwa stripped something away, something essential to artifice. Something that kept people in ignorance of their own truths. She looked up to find Rush's eyes on hers, warm and encouraging.

"If you can help me see more clearly," she said slowly to Lila, "I'm game."

"Brave girl." Lila gave her hand a quick squeeze. "This way. Both of you."

Chapter
26

THEY FOLLOWED her through the doors that separated the tea shop from her living quarters, through the kitchen and up the spiral staircase in the back corner. They entered the sun-filled sitting room and waited as Lila gathered up an odd assortment of knickknacks from a nook in the built-in bookshelves. She bent and shoved a low, round coffee table into the center of the room, and Maria noticed for the first time the pattern of constellations woven into the midnight-blue rug, and the compass points marked into edges. How had she missed that?

Lila moved around the compass, casting the now-familiar circle with candles, then held out a hand to Maria and said, "Come."

Maria shot a questioning look at Rush and Lila said, "Just you, dear. For now."

Maria moved around the outside of the circle described by the candles and joined Lila at the easternmost point. Lila moved into the circle and knelt beside the round table in the center. Maria followed, but hesitated. Was she supposed to kneel? Or just hang back and watch?

"Lila?" she whispered. "Um, what should I—"

Lila smiled up at her and said, in a perfectly normal tone of voice, "Kneel here beside me, dear."

"Right." Maria folded herself into a kneeling position and tucked her hands between her thighs. She felt ridiculous. "Lila?"

"Yes, dear?"

"What are we doing?"

Lila grinned at her. "Nervous?"

"Oh, of course not," Maria said airily. "I do this kind of thing all the time. I was just curious."

Lila laughed. "Don't worry, dear. I won't hurt you." Her grin went sly. "Or convert you." She patted her knee. "I just need to see more clearly."

Maria glanced around the sun-flooded room. "See what more clearly?"

Lila produced a pretty ceramic dish, its blue bowl so deeply glossed it could've been used as a mirror, and placed it in the center of the coffee table. She tipped a flask of water into the dish until a glassy pool covered the bottom. Then she moved around the bowl, as if looking for a better vantage point. She settled onto the floor across from Maria and laid out her hands, palms up, one on either side of the bowl. Maria hesitated, then put her hands into Lila's.

Lila stared hard into the little dish for a few seconds then shook her head. "Yarrow!" she shouted. "Come here!"

Yarrow's black head poked into the room, earbuds hanging around her neck. "What?"

"I need you, dear," Lila said. "In the circle."

Yarrow rolled black-rimmed eyes. "I'm not allowed, remember?"

"Your parents will understand."

"So, what, it's okay for me to be a pagan when you need something but not when I do?"

"I'm making a judgment call," Lila said, her tone gentle but absolutely commanding. "A call that, given my age and experience, I'm infinitely more qualified to make than you are. Now, in the circle, please."

Yarrow shrugged and moved to the easternmost point of the circle before she stepped in. She glanced at Maria and her lip curled. "A sacred threesome, huh? I'm honored."

"Smart girl," Lila said. Maria blinked, then turned beseeching eyes on Rush.

"Don't look at me." He shook his head. "She needs another female."

"It's true," Yarrow told her. "Pagans dig girl-on-girl action."

Lila ignored her and said to Maria, "You grew up Christian, I assume?"

"Catholic."

"Then you're familiar with the Holy Trinity."

"The Father, the Son and the Holy Ghost? Sure."

"Three different forms of the same divine, yes? A sacred trinity?"

"Yeah."

"Pagans have their own version of this, only our divinity is female. We revere the feminine power, in each of its three incarnations—the maiden, the mother and the crone."

"I'm the maiden," Yarrow said, going heavy on the irony. She jerked her chin at Lila. "There's your crone."

"In all my infinite wisdom," Lila said aridly.

"Which makes me the mother?" Maria laughed. "I don't think I'm qualified."

"It's ceremonial," Yarrow told her. "I haven't been a maiden since—"

"Join hands, please," Lila said. Maria expected Yarrow to kick up a stink about touching her, but she obediently placed one hand into Lila's and held out the other for Maria's. After a moment, Maria took it. An immediate sense of peace stole into her, a calm completeness she hadn't felt in years, if ever. It flowed into her through her palms, drifted lazily up her arms and into her center, where it smoothed out the static that had lived in her head and heart so long she'd forgotten to be aware of it. A stillness rushed into the space it left behind, a patient quiet.

"Concentrate, Maria, on the Stone Altar," Lila said, bending over the little bowl on the table. "How it smelled, how it looked. What you felt as you looked into that rough clay bowl. What you thought as you descended into the earth."

Maria concentrated as directed, and suddenly she was there again. Her mitten was tight in Rush's elbow, the smell of his warmth reassuring in her nose. She lost herself in the memory until the scent of frozen dirt was as strong as the scent of Lila's tea cooling on the window seat.

For long moments, Lila peered into her pretty little bowl as if the fate of nations hung in the balance. When she looked up, concern darkened her eyes.

"What?" Maria asked, snatching her hands back. The quiet snapped and broke, the pieces drifting away like smoke. "Did you actually see something in there?"

"Nothing I could identify," Lila said.

"What does that mean?"

"It's a scrying dish," Yarrow said. "Not a crystal ball."

"Yarrow." Lila's tone made the name a gentle reproof and Yarrow rolled her eyes again.

"Are we done here?" she asked.

"Yes. Thank you."

"I'm going to be late for practice," Yarrow said as she stalked out of the circle. "Write a note to the coach for me, will you? He's a real hard-ass."

"Have a nice time, dear," Lila said absently as Yarrow disappeared. She fixed her attention on Maria. "Yarrow's tone was a bit harsh, but the information was accurate," she said. "It's not a crystal ball. I don't read the future or anything. A scrying bowl shows emotions more than pictures. Suggestions rather than certainties."

"What did it suggest, then?"

"There was a darkness," Lila said softly, and her gaze shifted to encompass Rush now, too. "A rage. A hopeless sorrow that took my breath. And a hunger, a driving, insatiable appetite."

"For what?" Rush asked, elbows on knees, eyes intent.

Lila shrugged. "It wasn't entirely clear. Power? Fame? Money? Worship? I'm not sure. But it was an appetite I fear blood won't sate."

"It was chicken blood, by the way," Rush said suddenly.

Lila blinked, startled. "What?"

"The blood we found at the Stone Altar. Maria got word yesterday. It was chicken blood."

"Oh. Well, thank heavens it wasn't . . . something else." She leaned forward, touched the back of Maria's hand. "I know I'm probably a nervous old woman, but I'd feel so much better if you'd let me protect you."

"Protect me? How?"

"The moon is past full but it's still above half. Enough for a protection spell. I'd like to cast one for you."

"Oh, wow, I don't—"

"You don't have to do anything at all," she said. "Just be here at eight Friday night. Both of you."

"We'll be here," Rush said before Maria could open her mouth. He checked his watch and winced. "Damn, Yarrow was right. I'm going to be late for practice."

BACK IN the front room of the tea shop, Maria drew on her mittens slowly while she turned Lila's offer over in her head. She wasn't really eager to put herself through a pagan ceremony that took place at a moonlit minus twenty, but allowing Lila to perform it might be a wise move. It would go a ways toward laying a foundation of trust and mutual respect, a foundation she'd need to draw on if it turned out she was right about the kind of mess Yarrow was in.

The girl clomped into the tea shop's front room as if Maria's thoughts had conjured her, a pair of skis over her shoulder, her jacket unzipped.

"Where's Ranger Rush?" Yarrow asked.

"He went ahead to meet the rest of the team."

Yarrow accepted this in silence and headed for the door.

"You seem to know a lot about the pagan tradition," Maria said to her, falling in beside her.

Yarrow curled her lip. "Anybody who lives here more than, like, two minutes does," she said.

Maria pulled on her hat against the bitter blast of arctic air that assaulted them the moment they stepped outside.

"Nice curls," Yarrow said.

"Thanks." Maria tucked a few into her hat. They sprang out again. She sighed. She hadn't wrangled with her real hair in a long time. It was a handful. "So, you know anything about blood sacrifice?"

Yarrow barked out laugh. "You're fingering me for the chicken-murdering bandit?"

Maria lifted a brow. "Eavesdrop much?"

"Sure. All the time. Nothing better to do." Yarrow yanked her zipper up to her chin and shook her head. "I'm not bored enough to off chickens by the light of the full moon, though."

"You know anybody who is?"

"No." She moved past Maria toward the harbor. "I have to go ski the bridge now," she said.

"The bridge?"

"The ice bridge. You know, between here and the mainland? The lake froze during the storm. Enough to ski to town, anyway. The team does the round-trip—four miles each way—every afternoon while the ice is stable."

"You know, I think I'll go with you," Maria said pleasantly. "I skied in today from the Ranger Station, so I'm all equipped and everything."

"Great," Yarrow muttered.

"They seemed like nice girls. Your friends from the team."

"I don't have any friends on the team."

"I know."

"Of course you do." Yarrow stalked down the street, and Maria followed.

Chapter

27

MARIA CLICKED her boots into her skis. She flexed her feet a couple times to make sure the bindings were secure before putting her skis into Yarrow's tracks and taking off.

Back home she'd spent a lot of time in the gym, logging grueling hours on the treadmill, the elliptical machine, in the weight room in an effort to turn her body from a terrifying liability into a professional asset. But skiing and snowshoeing, she'd discovered, was a whole other thing.

It was soothing somehow—the quiet shush of her skis kissing the snow, the rhythmic pumping of her arms, the solid push of her legs against the earth. It put her higher-order brain into some sort of a trance, leaving her primitive, reptilian brain to enjoy the feeling of her muscles doing what they'd been designed for. It was only while skiing that she could contemplate with any kind of calm the idea that her body might really be a blessing instead of a burden.

She caught up to Yarrow as the rest of the team skied toward them from the mainland, all colorful winter wear and puffing breath.

"Are you going to turn around to ski with the team?" she asked.

"No," Yarrow said. She didn't slow down.

Maria squinted at the approaching team, Rush encouraging them from behind like a big, implacable sheepdog. Yarrow blew past the oncoming team without even a nod.

"If you don't ski with the team, why come out now?" Maria asked. "I mean, if you don't want the company, why not ski earlier? Or later?"

"Lila likes me to interact with my peers."

"Ah."

Yarrow poured on a burst of speed and Maria let her pull ahead. She skied in the girl's tracks for several thoughtful minutes. She looked up a while later, startled to find Yarrow already kicking off her skis in front of a little shack on the bank of the mainland. It was a warming hut or an old fish house or something, Maria saw as she moved closer. Yarrow disappeared inside and Maria picked up the pace, her long legs eating up the distance to the shore. There were, she mused, some marked benefits to unseemly height.

She reached the banks, kicked off her own skis and joined Yarrow inside the little hut. "What is this place?" she asked, following the girl's lead and propping a boot on the bench to stretch out.

"It's Einar's fish house. He leaves it here at the turn-around so I can cool down out of the wind."

Maria peered out the tiny slit cut at eye level into the wall. The trees were thick enough to conceal whatever lay behind them. "Where are we?"

"Just north of Thunder Bay."

"Canada?"

"No, France."

Maria stuck out her tongue at Yarrow's back.

"So," she said, switching legs along with the subject. "You don't ever ski with the team?"

"No." Yarrow went to work on her hamstrings.

"You don't get lonely? Don't miss having friends?"

A bitter laugh shot into the air. "No."

"How about your family?" she asked. "You miss them?"

Yarrow said nothing and Maria pressed a little harder. "You're what—a junior now? You'll be making college decisions pretty soon. I'll bet your folks are all over you about SAT scores."

"They don't care about my SAT scores."

Maria made her voice skeptical. "No?"

"Bigger fish to fry and all that."

"Bigger than their daughter's future?"

"Oh, yeah."

"Like what?" Maria didn't figure she'd get an answer, but that had never stopped her from asking a question. That plus the judicious application of some friendly silence sometimes yielded fascinating results.

"They have their hands full keeping my sainted brother alive," Yarrow said, going after her quads like they had personally offended her. "It doesn't leave them much time to worry about their perennially fucked-up firstborn."

Maria chewed on that for a moment. "You have a brother?" she asked.

"Stevie," Yarrow said. "He has cystic fibrosis. Been drowning in his own lung crap from the moment of conception. Pale, perpetually suffering and saintlike in his endurance. In other words, my complete opposite."

"You're pretty darn pale," Maria observed.

Yarrow rolled her eyes. "And oh so saintly."

"I didn't say that."

"Of course you didn't." Yarrow yanked her arm across her chest and worked viciously at her triceps. "Who would? I'm the devil, didn't you know?"

"I thought you were more a slut." Maria gave her an innocent look. "Isn't that the whole idea behind the maiden thing? The goddess of sulky, sexy energy?"

"You *have* been paying attention." Yarrow surprised her with a laugh. "Good for you."

"Are you?"

"What, a slut or the devil?"

"Either." Maria paused. "Both. You pick."

For a long time, Maria didn't think Yarrow would answer. The silence stretched out between them, broken only by the quiet in and out of their breathing. Maria bent her forehead to her knee and sighed at the blessed release of her hamstrings.

"I got arrested last spring," Yarrow said abruptly. A fierce thread of self-hatred ran under a surface calm like an underground lava flow. Maria froze for an instant, then resumed her leisurely stretch.

"That's what Einar meant last week? About your folks getting some charges dropped?"

"Yeah. We got picked up for possession, me and my friend Jilly and this guy we were both into." She snorted. "Or maybe we were just into the shit he sold us. Hard to tell now. But we were all pretty high when we got pulled over. And wouldn't you know, the glove box was full of pot?"

"It happens when you ride around with drug dealers."

"It wasn't his car. It was Jilly's." She shrugged. "And *that's* what happens when you fuck drug dealers then lend them your car."

"I see."

"And when the police put us in separate rooms and asked us who the pot belonged to, Jilly said it was his. He said it was Jilly's."

"And you?"

"I lied," Yarrow said baldly, as if daring Maria to judge her. To condemn her. "I knew he had a record and would go to jail if I told the truth. I also knew Jilly wouldn't. Her rich parents would get her a slap on the wrist." She looked Maria straight in the eye and said, "But mostly? Mostly, I wanted Jilly out of the way so I could have him myself."

"What happened?"

"Jilly got probation from the state. She got Catholic boarding school from her parents." There was a burning brightness in her black eyes a less sympathetic person might have mistaken for evil or, at the very least, heartlessness. Maria knew better. "I told you her parents were rich."

"Did she forgive you?"

"Not exactly." Yarrow threw her a wretched smile from the snow-packed floor, where she'd dropped to work on her gluts. "Every guy in the greater metro area now thinks I'll suck his dick for a dollar's worth of meth."

"Ouch." Maria drew her arm across her chest to stretch her triceps. "Was he worth it? The guy?"

"He threw me a gratitude fuck and moved on. Fast."

"Ouch again. What did you do?"

"Oh, I went *high* drama. Swallowed a bunch of pills, a fifth of Jack and put myself in the hospital." Yarrow didn't look up, just shook her head as she bent over her knee. "As it turns out, my parents only sympathize with kids whose health problems are involuntary. So here"—she waved an expansive hand—"I am."

Maria didn't say anything. She didn't figure Yarrow expected her to. She let the silence play out while she tried to decide where to step next. Yarrow had revealed more than Maria had dared hope and she didn't want to break whatever unexpected magic had prompted the confidences.

Apparently, she waited a beat too long, because the girl suddenly leaped to her feet.

"You know what? Whatever." She snatched up her backpack and headed for the door. "Like it matters."

Maria jumped up and said, "Yarrow, wait! Let me—"

Yarrow shoved her arms into the pack and turned on Maria with a hard smirk. "Jesus, settle down. I'm just going to pee, not kill myself. I'm not stupid enough to try that shit twice."

"See that you don't," Maria said, with deliberate coolness. Everything in her said it would put Yarrow more at ease than some heartfelt speech. "I'm counting on drafting off you on the way back to the island. I'm not as young as I once was, you know."

"Yeah, I know," Yarrow said, her smirk losing a degree or two of ice as she pushed through the door. "Granny."

"Bite your tongue," Maria said mildly.

Yarrow laughed as the door swung shut behind her, but

Maria watched with worried eyes as the woods behind the hut swallowed the girl up with alarming ease.

ON FRIDAY night, Maria let Rush lead her into the circle Lila had cast in her snowy backyard. Flaming torchères on long bamboo stakes marked the compass points, their tongues of fire spearing straight up into the still night air. Not a breath of wind stirred the flames, while beyond them, through the trees, the lake was a serene white stretch glittering under a gibbous moon.

Maria wore nothing but the thin white shift Lila had provided, and her hair bounced crazily on the crystalline air, but she didn't feel the cold. Maybe it was the adrenaline, or maybe it was the sauna Lila had insisted she take beforehand, but even her bare feet radiated heat.

She saw Lila waiting for them by her backyard altar, and Rush threaded his fingers through hers.

"Are you sure you want to do this?" he asked softly. He didn't seem to feel the cold either, and he wasn't wearing much more than she was—a boy-cut version of the same thin tunic thing, his in black.

"Sure." The strength and calm that were his essence flowed into her through their joined hands and steadied her. "It's a protection ceremony. How could it hurt?"

"You look nervous."

"I was." She lifted her shoulders as if to say, *Go figure*. "But I trust you." She smiled. "Let's do this thing."

They joined Lila in front of her altar, where three slim candles—black, white and purple—burned.

"Merry meet, children," Lila said. She glanced at their tunics with disapproval. "You're sure you wouldn't prefer to do this sky-clad?"

"Sky-clad?" Maria looked to Rush for translation.

"Naked."

"Hell, no." Maria looked back at Lila, her free arm over her chest, where she knew her nipples were beaded and plainly visible against the thin white material. "This is bad enough."

Lila sighed. "All right, then. Let's get started." She laid her hands over Maria's and Rush's joined ones. "I come before the goddess this night, in the fullness of the moon, to seek Her blessing on Maria. To anoint Rush Her champion and to request for him Our Lord and Lady's strength that he may turn aside any wickedness that seeks Maria, and defeat any who wish her harm." She lifted her arms to the nearly full moon hanging bright and low in the sky, tossed back her head and proclaimed, "An' the goddess will it."

"So mote it be," Rush said.

Lila folded her arms over her chest in what looked like some sort of ritual cross. "Begin," she said to Rush.

A wave of awareness washed over Maria, along with something prickly and powerful and unknown. She kept her eyes pinned to Rush, somehow sensing it emanated from him.

She stood silent and waiting, her arms loose, her hands relaxed in spite of her exquisite vulnerability. She was all but naked, yet she burned. Burned with heat, yes, but with hunger, too. For what she didn't know. All she knew was that relief could come only from the man standing before her with an answering hunger in his eyes.

Rush turned to the altar and picked up the white candle burning there. With his left hand he reached across his body to hold the candle above Maria's left shoulder. His eyes hot on hers, he tipped it, allowing a single drop of melted white wax to fall onto her skin. Skin that was already too hot even to register the sting.

With the candle, he drew a line in the air from her shoulder to her opposite hip. A tingling need sprang up in its wake, as if he'd stroked her with his hand. He stepped closer, brought the candle behind her back and the heat pumping off his body slid into hers. The half inch left between them went heavy and hot, and Maria forgot how to breathe.

He reached behind her with his other hand, the loop of his arms encircling but not touching her. Certainly close enough to touch, though, Maria thought wildly. Close enough to taste. To smell. She closed her eyes and dragged in a greedy lungful of him. Even with her eyes closed, she knew the taut swell of his shoulder was *right there* next to her cheek. All she had to do was lean forward a scant inch and put her mouth on it.

The hot splash of a second drop of wax joining the first on her shoulder startled her out of her lustful little daydream. God. She could see what Lila meant about paganism being very sex positive. She shook herself lightly and almost chuckled. She opened her eyes, ready to share the joke with Rush, but he wasn't laughing. His eyes were on hers, direct, patient, serious.

He said, "My shield be thy shelter."

Any urge to laugh died a swift and unsettling death with those old-fashioned words, spoken in that economical voice of his. Rush might not be a pagan anymore, and he might not believe in the ceremony Lila was performing, but this promise to protect her? To put her firmly under his aegis and take all comers until anybody who wished her harm was in bloody shreds at his feet? That was serious, and he was in deadly earnest.

Something shifted inside her, something huge and heavy and vital. She gazed at him in wonder while her internal landscape heaved and cracked like all her tectonic plates had come unexpectedly unmoored.

And suddenly Maria knew. Her body wasn't responding to smoke and moonlight. Her head wasn't turned by magic and goddesses. This wasn't paganism. This wasn't even that dangerous, heated hunger that lived inside her. This wasn't sex at all. This was love.

She'd fallen in love with Rush.

Chapter
28

MARIA'S CAREFULLY constructed world had already sustained some heavy shelling over the past few days, but now it collapsed into rubble around her bare feet and she could only stare at the man responsible. She was in love? With Rush?

Her face must've shown her utter dismay because he gave her a reassuring look as he replaced the white candle. Then he took up the black candle, this time with his right hand.

Okay, Maria thought. She tried to breathe while he drew another tip-tilted circle in the air around her with the candle, only in the opposite direction this time, right shoulder to left hip. *Okay, this is bad. It's bad but it's manageable. I can figure this out. I can—*

A line of fiery want followed the candle across her skin and she knew she was lying to herself. She couldn't figure this out. She couldn't fix this. She was in love. With Rush, who refused to tolerate even polite social fictions, let alone all the willful dishonesty that made her little world go round. What the hell was she going to do?

He sealed the circle with a second stinging drop of wax and she forced herself to meet his gaze.

"My sword, thy guarantee," he said, and his voice washed over her skin like a rough caress. The need inside her spiraled higher and tighter and suddenly she didn't care how dangerous this was. How inconvenient or unscheduled. This was love and it was inside her. She couldn't change it. Wasn't that what he'd said? She was what she was. Now all that was left was to look it in the eye and decide if she could live with it.

He set aside the black candle and lifted the purple one. He brought it into the charged and vibrating space between their bodies. She gazed past the flame into his steady silver eyes, eyes that held humor and heat and that terrible, beautiful honesty that made him what he was.

And she thought to herself, *Okay, yeah. I can live with this.*

Then he hooked one finger into the loose neckline of her robe and she realized it was less a question of living with it, and more a question of dying without it. Her nipples beaded, begging shamelessly as he allowed a single drop of purple wax to slip from the candle into the valley between her breasts. She lifted her arms as he passed the candle around her rib cage, completing a third circle. A final drop of wax joined the first drying on her damp, unsteady chest.

"My courage be thy safeguard," he said, and the words ran into her bloodstream like warm honey.

"Our Lady will it," Lila sang out. Maria jumped. She'd forgotten Lila was even standing there. A flush rose in her already overheated cheeks as she imagined the sharp-eyed Lila watching the whole byplay between her and Rush from six inches out. No wonder there were no secrets on Mishkwa.

"So mote it be," Rush murmured.

He set aside the purple candle and held out his hands. Maria laid hers into them with a sigh of near relief. She ached for him with a dizzying need, a physical hunger that unstrung her. She had the rest of her life to worry about what loving him meant. Right now she needed his touch. His skin. His palms against hers.

She needed *him*.

He bent his head and, without warning, laid his lips against the white drops of wax on her left shoulder. Her heart nearly exploded in her chest and a desire geysered up inside her that made what she'd experienced during the circling part of the ceremony look tepid.

"My shield is thine," he said, then kissed the black wax on her other shoulder. "My sword is thine." He dropped to his knees and pressed his lips to the purple droplets between her breasts. She nearly went to her own knees. "My courage I pledge to thee. Circles to keep thee, charms times three."

"An' the goddess will it," Lila said.

"So mote it be," Rush murmured against her skin.

"Blessed be this woman," Lila said, authority ringing in her tone as she turned her face up to the flowing moonlight. "May the goddess protect and strengthen her against all forces that would impose their will on her, whose appetites would sate themselves at her expense, who value their ambitions more highly than her life."

Lila knelt to the earth and scooped up a handful of snow. "Blessed be this man, who dedicates himself to that most sacred duty—protecting the source of all life, all love, all compassion and forgiveness."

She lifted the snow up to the moonlight, and droplets of meltwater fell from her fingers as she said, "Blessed be this pair, this man and this woman together. Invest in them the strength to turn aside attack, the vision to see themselves and their enemies clearly, and the wisdom to lay down crippling burdens. Grant them compassion enough for mercy, strength enough for might and the insight to know which is which."

She dropped her arms. "An' the goddess will it."

Rush said, "So mote it be." And this time Maria joined him.

Chapter
29

IT WAS well after midnight by the time Maria and Rush made it back to the Ranger Station. Maria hung up her jacket on its wooden peg while Rush brought the embers in the stove back to a blazing crackle. The little stove pumped off heat like a blast furnace, but Maria's fingers ached with the cold as she combed them through the wild thicket of her hair.

Nerves, she told herself. She tucked her frozen fingers into her elbows, then thought, *Oh, shit. Honesty.* She couldn't lie anymore, not even in her internal monologue. Rush could sense a lie at twenty paces. Her big confession of love wasn't the time to test him.

So, fine. She wasn't nervous. She was terrified. The kind of terrified that came in one color (flat black), one size (extra large) and sucked the light and hope out of everything it touched like a Harry Potter Dementor. Because what she felt for Rush made her crush on Ridge Calloway look like a kiddie ride, and if those feelings had cost her a sister, what might loving Rush cost her?

Not that it mattered. Not loving Rush would cost more. Infinitely more. The prettily painted, perfectly composed Goose was nothing but a shell. Safe, attractive but ultimately empty. And Maria wasn't content with emptiness anymore. Rush had shown her more and she was addicted. Now she not only wanted more, she needed it. Required it.

But asking for it—for him—would take courage. A lot more than she had, unfortunately. Still, she scraped up what she could find, hid her trembling fists in her elbows and said, "Hey, Rush?"

"Yeah?" He closed the stove door and threw her a look over his shoulder. She started to smile at him, big and reassuring, but caught herself and killed it. No smiling unless she was actually happy, and since she thought she might die any minute from pure fear, she probably shouldn't smile.

He blinked. "Yikes. That bad, huh?"

She swallowed. "What's that bad?"

"Whatever has you doing *that*"—he circled a finger in the air—"with your face."

"I'm trying to be honest here." The trembling in her hands threatened to escalate into full-body shivers, so she banded her arms tighter across her chest. "Isn't that the deal? Honesty?"

"Well, sure." He rose, slapped at the sawdust on his jeans and studied her carefully. "But that looked more like nausea than honesty."

She wasn't nauseated, she was nervous. *Liar.* Okay, fine. Terrified. She was trying to confess her damn love and doing such a good job he was worried she might boot her lunch. Wonderful.

Temper swooped to the rescue and she said, "Okay, let me make sure I understand. According to the Honesty Only policy, I can smile if and when I feel happy, but in all other situations smiling is prohibited and you get to mock me?" She glared at him. "Because if that's the case, I think honesty sucks. I think *you* suck. Because I'm trying here. I'm trying really hard and you're sitting over there taking potshots at my face."

"It wasn't a potshot. And I like your face. But it was all—" He broke off, clearly aware he maybe shouldn't take that conversational ball any farther down the field. Good for him. "So your stomach is okay?"

She closed her eyes. "My stomach is fine."

"Are you sure? Because you look a little pale." He came across the room to her, concern in his eyes. "A lot pale, actually." He took her chin in one hand, turned her face up to the light and inspected her pupils. "Nausea is one of the first symptoms of advanced dehydration. I wonder if Lila's little sweat fest didn't—"

"Rush. Stop."

She wrapped one hand around his wrist and forced herself to look straight into his eyes. Eyes that held concern, yes, but also . . . nerves? And not over her health, either. Hope sparked to life inside her, feeble but undeniable, and propped up her faltering courage.

"I do *not* have indigestion," she told him firmly. "My gastrointestinal system is fine. My bowels are in good working order, too, if it matters. I suppose I could be a little dehydrated after the sauna earlier, but it's nothing a bottle of water won't cure. Otherwise I'm in perfect health."

He frowned down at her, clearly unconvinced. "Then why do you look like you want to throw up?"

"Because I'm in love with you."

His hand fell away from her chin. "You're *what*?"

"In love," she said grimly. "With you."

"Which makes you want to throw up." He shook his head. "Wow. That's . . . not flattering."

"I know, right?" She laughed, though she didn't really find the situation very funny. "I was surprised, too. I mean, never having experienced the real deal, I kind of expected hearts and flowers, you know? But love sort of sucks. It's inconvenient and painful and I'm not really enjoying it, if you want the truth, which, of course, being Rush, you do. But I'm definitely in love." She patted his shoulder, stonelike under the soft flannel of his shirt, and tried desperately to stem the torrent of horrifying words pouring out of her. "With, um, you." She closed her eyes against a wave of intense embarrassment. "So, that's it." Oh God, it wouldn't stop. It was like a hiccup, involuntary and spasmodic. "I'm in love with you." Jesus, another one? "Sorry."

She pressed bloodless fingers to numb lips and prayed. *Please let it be over now. Please let that have been the last one.*

"Maria?"

She forced herself to meet his eyes. "Yeah?"

"Are you done?"

"I think so."

"Good. Because I have something to say now."

"Oh, goody. Will it be as fun as mine was?"

"I don't know," he said seriously. "Yours was pretty fun. Especially the part about your bowels being in good working order."

She closed her eyes again.

"Hey, don't do that. Don't check out." He reached out, drew one gentle finger down the edge of her face. Her heart shuddered inside her chest and she opened her eyes cautiously. "Not when I'm about to pledge my troth."

She stared at him in openmouthed astonishment. "Pledge your *what*?"

"My troth. My fidelity. My loyalty." He hooked a hand around the back of his neck and squinted down at her. "My undying love? I was planning to break it to you later, but after you said . . . what you said—"

"That I'm stupid in love with you?" *Hic.*

"Yeah, that." He smiled. Beautifully. "It seemed like I should say something. Sooner rather than, you know, later."

"You should. Definitely." The first tiny bubbles of joy started rising, sliding up through her panic and fear. "I'm listening."

"Okay." He paused. "I'm crap at this kind of thing."

She gave him a narrow stare. "Yeah, well, after what I just did, you owe me this, so start talking."

"Right. Okay. I'll try."

"You could maybe start with 'I love you,'" she said helpfully. "See where it goes from there."

"I love you," he said obediently. Baldly. Uncomfortably. And utterly, completely sincerely. She'd never heard three more beautiful words in her entire life. "It happened during the ceremony tonight—"

A bolt of dismay shot through her. "Wait, you're in love with me because of a pagan ceremony?"

He lifted a brow. "Do you want to hear this or not?"

She shut her mouth. "Go on."

"Give me a little credit, will you? I know better than to think there's some deity up there with a master plan and puppet strings. I haven't believed in anything like that for a long time, if ever. But Lila needed reassuring and you needed Lila's trust, so I figured I'd just do the ceremony. What the hell, right? Everybody gets what they need in one quick, if chilly, half hour. It wasn't until I was actually saying the words, until they were tumbling from my memory to my mouth, that I realized I meant every one of them. By the time I understood that I wasn't reciting an old prayer so much as making some deadly-serious promises, it was too late. I'd already given my word." He lifted his shoulders, a curiously helpless gesture from such a strong man. "I'd already pledged my damn troth."

"And a troth is what, exactly?"

"Hell if I know. But whatever it was, it totally moved us beyond let's-just-jump-each-other-and-see-where-this-goes territory. I'm yours now. You're mine. No matter who you are." He gave her a hard look. "Or who you choose to be. I'm in love with you. With all of you, including the odd pocket of crazy here or there."

"Hey."

He held up a hand. "Not that I'm complaining. I have a few pockets of crazy on board myself."

"Amen."

"Look, I don't know why or how this happened, Maria,

so I can't give you that. I'm sorry. I only know that I *feel* it. I feel *you*. And that's a fucking miracle because the days when I just *knew* things, just *felt* what was right and true and good? I buried those days in the sand with all the bodies. But then you came along and lit me up like the Fourth of July. One look at you and everything inside me sat right up and said *mine.*" He gave her a crooked smile. "You're beautiful and smart and terrifying and so damn complicated, but I waited a long time for the voices in my head to start talking again. Now that they have, I'm not about to argue with them."

He took her hand, threaded his fingers through hers. "So that's it. There's my troth, pledged to you." He looked gravely down at her. "So . . . are you supposed to accept it? Or thank me? Or, shit, am I supposed to wrap this up with flowers or something?"

"I have no idea. Nobody's ever pledged their troth to me before." She touched the sharp edge of his cheekbone with her thumb as joy and fear tumbled around inside her like a couple of puppies. "I never wanted anybody to. I didn't let myself want anything. Then you came along."

"And you wanted." A grin spread across his face, smug and self-satisfied. He dropped onto the couch and tugged her down beside him. "Yeah, I get that sometimes. Sorry."

She sighed theatrically. "So I tried sex. I thought maybe one wild night of hoopty and you'd be out of my system."

"Not my hoopty, babe." He tipped his head back, spread his arms across the back of the couch and closed his eyes. "Women get hooked on my hoopty."

"Tell me." She grinned and laid her head next to his on the couch cushion. "And your hoopty wasn't even free. Hell, no. You had demands."

"Well, yeah. You give away the milk, who's going to buy the cow?"

"Can I just say how refreshing it is to hear that old piece of crap and have the guy be the cow for a change?"

He rolled his head to the side to meet her eyes, and she

saw laughter in them. But there was more, too. A gravity. A beautiful, uncompromising honesty. "I wanted, too, Maria."

"I know. And not that pretty, polished robot I'd become, either. You wanted *me*. And I was such a fool, such a complete *idiot*, that I honestly debated. Do I scrape up the courage to actually participate in my own life? Or do I keep punishing myself by living somebody else's?"

He found a single ringlet in the bramble of her hair, tugged the end and watched it bounce. "Do I get a vote?"

"Yours is the only one that counts."

"I love you, Maria."

She had to swallow hard to find her voice. "And that's a miracle," she said softly. "A gift. I don't understand it and I certainly don't deserve it, but I'll take it."

"You'd better." He threaded his fingers through her curls to cup her skull in his big, hard palm and bring her mouth to his. "Don't argue. Just marry me and be done with it."

MARRY ME.

The words fell out of him without forethought or consideration. They just jetted straight up out of his heart and leaped into the air between them. No parachute, no net. They hung there, suspended in time and space, while she stared at him with a wild-eyed terror that almost made him long for one of her old fake smiles.

"Okay," he said, "I hadn't planned to go quite this far tonight, but I have that terminal honesty thing going for me and, well—" He lifted his shoulders and plunged forward even as he cursed himself for a fool. "Screw it. I have no patience. I love you, Maria. I always will. You don't have to marry me right this minute, but fair warning? I'll want that eventually. I'll push for it, too, so brace yourself. For now, though, I'd be happy if you just stayed. Here. With me." He cleared his throat. "Or somewhere else. It doesn't have to be here. On Mishkwa. Because I could go to—" He broke off. "Where do you live?"

"Minneapolis."

"Minneapolis. I could go there. Or we could—"

"Rush?"

"Yeah?"

"I hate Minneapolis."

"You do?" He searched her eyes and found the sorrow he knew would always be there to some degree. He found barely checked fear hunkered down next to some serious doubt. But he also saw hope. He saw love. And he saw his future.

"Yes," she said. "I want to be here. With you." She smiled at him and it was shaky but genuine. Growing. "I won't lie to you, though. The whole let's-get-married thing? It scares the crap out of me. I only just hopped off the Penance Express. I don't even know what my life *is*, and the idea of promising it to somebody—anybody, Rush, not just you—is really—" She broke off. "I just don't know if I can."

"You can. You absolutely can. But for now?" He pressed his mouth to hers with an aching tenderness, and everything inside his chest shifted. Settled. Bloomed. "For now, this is enough."

Then her mouth opened under his and all that lovely tenderness went hot and needy. An ache filled him. A desire. A fierce imperative to take and hold and claim, but he battled it back. Just for tonight, just this once, he wanted to be gentle. He wanted to give her the moonlight and roses she deserved and he was so bad at. He wanted to give her poetry.

He tore his mouth from hers and buried his face in her hair. His heart tried to stop, then go, then settled for knocking against his sternum like it was trying to get out. He breathed in the green, earthy smell that clung to her hair, which was spectacularly unhelpful in terms of maintaining his self-control, but he bore up under the temptation. He held. Right up until she licked his throat.

"Oh Jesus." His fingers twisted into her hair, and he dragged her onto his lap.

"Hallelujah," she mumbled as she straddled him and

gave him her sweet mouth. His hands found the neat angle of her hips and he jerked up underneath her, ground his want shamelessly into her heat. And she purred. Actually *purred*.

"Maria," he said, but then her tongue slid up to his ear.

"Hmm?" She bit his lobe with exquisite tenderness. His blood leaped into a rolling boil.

"I wanted—" He desperately tried to think.

"Yes?" She circled her hips against his in a knowing, lazy swirl that incinerated a good half of his meager vocabulary.

"I wanted—"

She trailed her tongue along the rim of his ear. And there went the other half of his vocabulary. He was starting not to care. He managed, with a great deal of focus, to say, "I wanted to go slow this time. To be gentle. Last time I was so—"

Her hands—those clever, quick, blessed hands—slid under his thermal. Every inch of his skin sang as she jerked it up to smile fondly down at a series of love bites she'd left on his chest a few nights before. "Yeah. You were. Me, too."

He blinked at her, dazzled and more than a little confused.

"Rush," she said, leaning in until their foreheads touched. "Listen to me, okay? I've spent a lot of years hating the way I wanted. Fearing the strength of my desire. But I'm finally in a place where I can look it in the eye and it doesn't scare me. Not when I'm with you." Her eyes went hot and she nipped at his shoulder with a sharpness just this side of pain. A vicious pleasure sliced into him. "What's in me isn't gentle. It's not soft and it's not sweet. And, Rush?" She soothed the sting with her tongue. "It's asking for you. All of you. I want you to come into me with everything you've got. And if you even think about holding back . . . well. I might have to punish you."

A wondering joy settled into his stomach alongside the relentless churning want. "Punish me? Really?"

"Oh, Rush." She sighed but her eyes sparkled with molten mischief. "Do you need me to prove it?"

A smile broke across his face then, slow and considering. "Would you?"

She shoved him down on the ancient couch and did exactly that while moonlight spilled over them like a benediction.

Chapter

30

IT HAD been, Maria mused as she sat between Einar and Yarrow in the deserted front room of Mother Lila's Tea Shop the next morning, a very disorienting twenty-four hours. First there was her headlong tumble into unexpected love. Then there was Rush's mind-boggling confession of a matching tumble. Then there was a terrifying proposal of marriage she still didn't have the first clue what to do with, followed by several hours celebrating their matching declarations, the memory of which pinked her cheeks.

She buried her nose in her teacup and forced herself to focus on Yarrow, who was inexplicably lying her ass off. She set down her cup and gave the girl a skeptical look.

"That's quite a confession, Yarrow."

"I'm quite a girl."

"I thought you said you had better things to do than behead chickens by the light of the full moon."

Yarrow lifted sharp shoulders. "I lied." Her mouth, painted just this side of black, quirked into something between a sneer and a grimace. "I'm good at it, you know."

"What, lying?"

Again with the grimace-sneer. "Listen, I was really angry, okay? The backstory's boring, so I won't get into it, but let's just say I was on the wrong side of a bad breakup. I was hurt, I was angry, I got into some bad stuff. Oldest story there is, right?"

"What, boy meets girl, boy dumps girl, girl steals a chicken, snowshoes five miles to an abandoned mine shaft— which is *dangerous*, by the way—and whips up a little love potion number nine for paybacks?" Maria tipped her head, considered. "I don't think I'm familiar with that one."

Einar leaned forward to insert himself into the conversation. "To be fair, Goose, it's not all that far afield. There's a certain culture up here on Mishkwa that lends itself to that sort of thing. Maybe on the mainland it would be a hard sell, but up here? People cast spells all the time, for everything from healing to protection. Why *wouldn't* a bright kid take a page from her elders' book?"

She gave him a tight smile. "True." She turned back to Yarrow. "You're claiming responsibility for the counterfeit money, too?"

She picked at her nail polish, refused to meet Maria's eyes. "That guy I told you about? Back home? Sells pot on the university campus? He asked if I'd meet a guy for him in Thunder Bay, pick up a backpack and bring it back to Mishkwa. No drugs or guns or anything, just money. He sent a guy to pick it up at the end of tourist season before the ferry stopped running."

"You knew the money was counterfeit?"

She shrugged. "I didn't care what it was. I only cared about what he was paying me." She gave Maria a burning glare. "No college fund in my future, you know?"

Maria accepted that in silence. Einar was right, actually. It wasn't a bad story. It was pretty believable, all things considered. Teenagers were unpredictable, emotional and volatile. They did stupid things.

But Yarrow was no ordinary teenager. She wasn't impulsive, and she was the farthest thing from stupid Maria had ever seen. Oh, maybe she'd been more normal once, but walking through the fiery hell that her stupid, selfish, impulsive behavior had landed her in had likely burned all that foolishness out of her. That was something Maria could attest to from personal experience. She'd been through her own reckoning with the evil that came standard with her soul. And, worse, with the consequences it held for the innocents around her.

That sort of reckoning knocked *all* the nonsense out of a girl. Exactly the sort of nonsense that prompted kids to off chickens by the light of the full moon for revenge. Or risk juvie for a few bucks and a bad mood.

And that was only the intellectual evidence. Her gut smelled something off, too. The girl was lying to her. Hiding something. So what was it, and why was she hiding it? And more importantly, why was Einar facilitating it?

Yarrow flaked off a big chunk of black polish from her thumbnail and glanced at Maria from under heavily mascaraed lashes. She flicked her gaze to Einar, then back to Maria. "Are we done here?" she asked. "Is confession time over?"

Maria purposely didn't follow her glance to Einar, just kept her eyes steady and cool on Yarrow's. "You tell me," she said softly.

"I don't have any other crimes to barf up, if that's what you're asking." She picked at her cuticles until Maria was afraid she'd draw blood. "So? You planning to arrest me or what?"

"Not today." She reached toward the girl's forearm to deliver a comforting pat, and Yarrow jerked back as if Maria had threatened her with a dirty hypodermic needle. "I'll discuss this with my superiors, have them fact-check your story with a few key people, and we'll figure out what to do next. In the meantime, just stick close, hmm?"

Yarrow cast a pointed glance toward the frozen lake out the window. "Where the fuck would I go?"

"Good point," Maria said evenly. "Well. You know

where to find me if you think of anything else. Or if you just want to, you know, talk."

"Yeah, because this has been *so* much fun."

Then Yarrow was on her feet and through the swinging kitchen doors without a backward glance. Maria turned to Einar, who sat watching the doorway that had swallowed up all that anger and tightly wrapped pain.

"She just, what, turned up at your door and laid all this at your feet?" she asked.

"Who else could she talk to?"

"What about Lila? I mean, if you're going to cop to an unauthorized jaunt into black magic, surely the island's high priestess would be the logical choice for a confessor?"

Einar shook his head. "Lila's pretty stern when it comes to the darker side of our religion."

"And you're not?"

He pursed his lips and made a so-so motion with his hand. "Paganism is an old religion, Maria. One of the oldest. It way predates this idea that a deity has to be purely good."

"It's about balance," Maria said impatiently. "I know. Good and bad, dark and light, male and female. Lila explained."

"It's about more than neat little pairs of attributes marching up the plank to Noah's ark, though," Einar said. "It's about embracing all the aspects of the human experience, light *and* dark."

Maria sat back and studied him. "You think Lila's a fair-weather pagan? Only practicing the parts she likes?"

"That's not a bad way to put it, actually." Einar leaned forward, warming to his subject. "It's not as simple as good and bad, light and dark. There are multiple faces to Our Lady. Faces Lila doesn't want to acknowledge, or if she does, only in the most cursory way. Lila wants to focus on the gentle, forgiving mother goddess. The wise, all-knowing crone goddess. She glosses right over the angry, sexy maiden goddess that runs roughshod over—and through—so many teenage girls."

"And that's the goddess Yarrow was calling on? Sacrificing to? The goddess of hot sex who might help her bring a bad boyfriend to heel?"

"Why not?" Einar gave her a rueful smile and spread his hands. "It's a very primal female weapon, an old and essential one. Lila doesn't like to talk about that incarnation of the goddess, though. She's too messy." He leaned back, shook his head. "But, damn, she packs a punch."

"The kind of punch that's been short-circuiting men's higher-order thinking since time immemorial," Maria observed.

"Yep." He grinned. "Our circuitry holds up better as we get older, though."

She gave him an if-you-say-so face.

He leaned in, suddenly intense. "That face of the goddess? That petulant, moody sexuality? It's the least interesting and least powerful aspect of Our Lady."

"Is it?"

"Of course. Men—real men—know how to look beyond the face and body, and into the heart. Into the mind. Into the true power." He reached out with one finger, touched her hair, her cheek. She held her breath, willing him to forget himself in the moment, to say something—anything—that would clue her in to what the hell was going on here.

"You're incredibly powerful, Goose," he said, his eyes dancing over her face, over the bounce and sway of her unstraightened hair. "I see all of Her in you."

"All of who?"

"Our Lady. The maiden, the mother and the crone. Sex, love and knowledge, all wrapped up in one compelling package. You're really quite extraordinary. You deserve somebody with a bit more depth than Rush."

Rush. Maria's heart galloped into triple time. "What does this have to do with your cousin?" She let a mild interest and a hint of guilt color her eyes. Enough to let him think he'd nailed it, nailed *her*. Let him think he had her all figured out.

"Not that Rush isn't a perfectly nice guy," he said,

keeping up the soulful eye contact. "He is. But you? You're not ordinary. You need somebody who'll talk to you, Maria. Who'll care enough about what's inside you to go after it. Somebody strong enough to hold the burden of your secrets when they get too heavy, somebody who can understand what it means to love a woman of your depth and strength and power. Somebody who can engage your mind, your body and your heart, all at once."

"That sounds . . . impossible," she said. But it wasn't. Rush was all those things. Deep without being weighty, smart without being intellectual, strong enough not to feel the need to prove anything to anybody. Strong enough to carry his own burdens, and understand that she'd have some, too. Strong enough to make her look at them before she decided to carry them any further.

He was everything she'd ever wanted. And everything Einar would never be. She thought about pointing that out, then shrugged it off. What was the point of explaining something to somebody who wasn't equipped to understand?

"You raise some excellent issues," she said to Einar. "I'm going to have to give that some serious thought."

He smiled, leaned back in his chair.

"Take your time," he said. "No pressure."

"Thank you." She stood.

"What will you do?" he asked, bobbing to his feet as she did. He held up his hands in surrender at her sharp look, laughing. "About Yarrow."

She chewed the corner of her mouth. "I don't know yet," she said. "Talk to her, I suppose."

"In terms of legal action, I mean. If she's going to need a lawyer, I ought to make some phone calls."

"I'll have to talk to my boss, but I don't think we'll arrest her." Maria sighed. "That's the last thing she needs. More legal action."

"Thank you. A lot of people in your position wouldn't understand a girl like Yarrow."

"I doubt she'll thank me."

"But I will. I do."

But something in his eyes, something under that layer of concern, made her wonder.

"Yeah," she said slowly. "No problem."

MARIA COULDN'T claim a great deal of experience with parenting, but it seemed to her that the best parents seldom blamed their kids when something went wrong. They blamed themselves, and Lila was no exception.

"Yule is tomorrow," she said when she'd stemmed the tears. "I've been so busy with it." She crushed a Kleenex in her hand. "But how could I not have *seen*? How could I have failed the child so badly?"

"I'll take care of her," Maria said, leaning forward to grip the woman's hand. "Trust me to do that much. If everything is as she's said, I'll do everything in my power to make sure she's treated gently. But, Lila, Yarrow's a complicated kid."

Lila managed a weak smile. "Tell me about it."

"And I strongly suspect that what she's told us isn't the whole story. Or even a true story."

"You think she's lying?"

"I don't know what she's doing. All I know is that there are holes in her story I could drive a truck through."

"What do you mean?"

"I mean she's only been on-island since August, and the supernotes I'm tracking started trickling into the Federal Reserve midsummer. Which means they were passed earlier yet."

"Which means Yarrow couldn't have been involved in getting them there." Hope brightened Lila's face. "Or at least not all of them."

"Exactly."

"And the Stone Altar? The black magic?"

"I don't know, Lila. All I can tell you is that my gut says Yarrow's lying. Now, I'll protect her as much as I can, but I spoke to my boss a few hours ago. He wants to interview her himself." Lila blanched. "He'll do it here, with you present if you want. But if I'm going to help her, I need to get the truth out of her—or more of the truth anyway—before he gets here."

"When will he arrive?"

"Day after tomorrow, most likely. Which doesn't leave us much time to get through to Yarrow."

"She doesn't talk to me," Lila said helplessly. "I don't know how to make her talk to me. But maybe she'll talk to you."

"I'm hoping she will." She paused. "I may have to be harsh with her, Lila. Scare her."

"Do what you need to. I trust you."

"Can I talk to her now?"

Lila stood. "She's gone to ski the ice bridge. Left not five minutes before you arrived. You'll likely find her there."

Maria stood. "Thanks, Lila."

"Bring her home to me."

"I'll do my best."

She kissed Maria's cheeks. "Blessed be, child."

Chapter

31

HALF AN hour later, Maria finally caught sight of Yarrow. She didn't care what the kid said about hating the ski team—she skied like she'd been born on the snow. It had taken three miles of flat-out sprinting before Maria had even glimpsed the girl's parka—black, of course.

By the time the warming hut came into view, the sun was already heading for the mainland's granite cliffs. Trees packed the shore like crooked gray teeth, and she had to squint to find the little hut among them. The weekend's storm had scoured away any landmarks Maria might have used to orient herself. If she hadn't been skiing in Yarrow's fresh tracks, she might not have found it at all. She'd heard that the islanders hauled their old Christmas trees out onto the frozen lake come January to use as guideposts, an oddball fact that hadn't made much sense until now. A girl could lose her bearings out here.

A motion at the shoreline caught her eye. A figure came out of the warming hut, head down, backpack on, and slipped into the trees. Yarrow, she knew. The girl disappeared disconcertingly fast into the woods, and there was something furtive in the dip of her head, the clipped movement of her body, that had Maria lengthening her stride. She didn't know what she was hurrying to, only that she needed to hurry.

Two minutes of hard skiing later, she glided up to the warming hut, still carefully inside the tracks Yarrow left there. She kicked off her skis and slid them through the loops on her backpack. The weekend's storm had dumped a good amount of new snow and Yarrow's boot prints were plainly visible. She stepped silently into the prints, and followed them into the woods.

The forest's half-light engulfed her as she moved slowly forward, praying fervently to stumble across Yarrow peeing behind some tree any second. It would be a mortifying moment, yes, but better than the alternative.

Which would be, she wondered, what exactly? What did she think she might be walking into here that had her subconscious on red alert and her nervous system pumping out the adrenaline? She didn't know, but whatever it was, it made intruding on a bathroom break look like a best-case scenario.

A sharp hiss broke the silence of the forest. A zipper, Maria realized. A backpack being ripped open. She froze. Stopped moving, stopped even breathing, as if the white puff of her exhale might give her away. She edged closer to the sizable tree in front of her and tipped her head the barest inch or two that allowed her to see past it.

Yarrow was kneeling in the snow at the base of a dead tree maybe twenty yards away. At least it looked dead to Maria. Hard to tell in the winter. There was something sinister about the naked branches, black and bony against the gray sky. Or maybe it was just what she was seeing that gave the whole scene an evil vibe.

Because while in one hand Yarrow held a perfectly benign gray backpack, in the other she held a plastic-wrapped bundle. A bundle that looked really, really familiar to Maria. She stuffed it into her pack, reached into the husk of the tree and pulled out another. And another. And another.

Maria didn't wait around to see how many it took to fill up that innocuous-looking pack. She retraced her steps, careful to stay inside Yarrow's original prints, and headed for the frozen lake.

By the time Yarrow emerged from the woods, Maria was kicking off her skis as if she'd just arrived.

"Hey," she said, and bent at the waist, breathing hard.

"Hey," Yarrow said with her usual lack of enthusiasm.

"Damn, you're fast," Maria said. "Lila said you'd left to ski the bridge like five minutes ahead of me. I've been skiing like hell and never even saw your jacket."

"Yeah, well." Yarrow clicked into her skis. "You're old."

Maria huffed out a laugh. "Aren't you a charmer?"

"That's me," Yarrow said, adjusting the straps on her pack. "Little Miss Sunshine." She gave her skis a testing wiggle. "So, what do you want?"

"Want?"

"You chased me four miles across a frozen lake for something."

"I spoke to my boss this afternoon."

"Yeah?"

"And Lila."

Something ghosted across Yarrow's hard little face. Sorrow? Guilt? Regret? Then it was gone, stuffed behind that brittle shell of hers. "Bet that was fun."

"My boss says he'll be here as soon as he can arrange a flight. Day after tomorrow, probably."

Her eyes went wide. "He's arresting me?"

"No. Not yet, anyway. But Peter Harris is nobody to screw with, Yarrow. He's a powerful guy and he's not exactly famous for his mercy or his sense of humor. If you need to amend, extend or in any way clarify the story you told me this morning? Now's the time. It's one thing to screw with me, but you do not want to play this man for a fool."

Yarrow shifted her pack into a more comfortable position. "I know what I'm doing, Agent di Guzman."

"Do you?"

She gave Maria a long, cool look. "See you back on the island." Then she put her skis in the tracks and kicked off.

Maria waited until Yarrow was nothing but a vague shape on the horizon. Then she put her feet back into Yarrow's original prints—just to be on the safe side—and headed into the woods again. The light was moving from gray to purple as Maria arrived at the dead tree where Yarrow had knelt, but there was still enough sun for her to confirm with her eyes what her instincts had already told her.

Yarrow's dead tree was stuffed with bricks of cash.

Maria hefted one in her gloved hand, the weight and shape of it as familiar to her as an infant's face to its mother. She'd spent nearly a decade chasing down counterfeit cash for the U.S. government; she knew exactly what stacks of money felt like. What they smelled like. She pulled off her glove and carefully peeled back the plastic wrapping to liberate a single bill.

She rubbed the hundred-dollar note between two cold, shaking fingers. She prayed that she was wrong but knew she wasn't.

This was no genuine American hundred. It was a Korean supernote. She was positive of it. Oh, she could be wrong. That was the beauty of a supernote. Only Federal Reserve banks had the tools to tell for certain, and even they were sometimes fooled. But Maria knew, *knew* in her gut, that she was holding a fake of the highest quality. A fake the likes of which was created only when a true artist, backed up by enormous resources—usually those of an entire government—lost sight of his moral compass long enough to perfect his trade.

A fake that made Yarrow's lies look one hell of a lot

like the truth. A fake that made the truth screaming inside
Maria that much more implausible.

What the hell was she supposed to do now?

"YOU ACTUALLY saw her with the counterfeits?" Rush
asked. He sat at the counter in the Ranger Station, his eyes
pale and steady, his hands calm and still. Must be nice,
Maria thought, eyeing him. She herself had eaten off her
lipstick hours ago, and her hair had abandoned all dignity
back on the ice bridge somewhere. But she didn't want her
blow-dryer or fresh lipstick. None of her old tricks brought
her order or calm anymore. Only Rush did. So she'd gone
to him, thrown herself on his mercy and barfed out the
whole baffling story.

"I saw her all right." She slumped onto the stool across
from him. "I backtracked after she'd left and found the
rest of the stash, too. The details didn't exactly match up
with her original story—she didn't meet anybody, and who
knows what she's planning for a pickup—but she definitely
skied a shitload of supernotes from Canada to the U.S."

She dropped her head into her hands, and curls spurted
through her fingers. "Rush, what am I going to do? My
boss is coming here tomorrow—*tomorrow*, I just got the
voice mail—to grill the kid, and I caught her red-handed
doing exactly what she said she'd been doing."

"But you still don't believe she's doing it."

"No." She rocked her head back and forth. His hand
came to rest on her curls, warm and solid and reassuring. "I don't. I just . . . I don't know, Rush. She gave me
this look, and it was almost apologetic. 'I know what I'm
doing, Agent di Guzman.' " She tipped her head to meet his
eyes. "She knows what she's doing? Not 'Get off my back,'
not 'Fuck you and your white hat.' Just 'I know what I'm
doing.' There's more to this, Rush. She's not a dumb kid.
But what's the goal here? What's the endgame? What does
she think she can possibly gain by playing chicken with the
Secret Service?"

"Have you talked to Einar?"

"Einar." She snorted. "Yarrow made her big confession this morning, gazing at him the whole time with these huge, adoring eyes. She's not out of the room thirty seconds before he's explaining why you're a poor choice for me in terms of lovers, and making a case to sub in."

His eyes went dangerously flat. "He offered to sub in?"

"In so many words." She reached across the counter, took his hand. "I didn't tell him to go fuck himself, but it was a near miss."

He twined his fingers through hers. "You're not going to let me punch him, are you?"

"Not today. Maybe after I sort Yarrow out."

"After *we* sort Yarrow out." He shook his head. "You're not alone anymore, Maria. Get it through your curly head, will you?"

She hesitated. "Rush, why are you behind me on this? I have no proof. It makes no sense for you to believe me."

"I don't believe you. I have faith in you. There's a difference."

"Which is?"

"Belief requires proof. Faith just accepts." He stood, dropped a kiss on top of her head. "You know yourself better than anybody I've ever met, Maria. You've spent years dissecting your soul, mapping it down to the finest detail, holding yourself to an impossibly high standard. You know precisely what's in you, how it makes you strong and how it makes you weak. If, knowing that, you're still willing to go to bat for Yarrow, then I am, too."

Love for him poured through her, hot and reckless and intense to the point of pain. She breathed through that first wave of beautiful agony then shook her head. "I still don't get it."

"You don't have to. You just have to believe it."

"It's not that easy."

"Of course it is." He pulled her to her feet and she leaned into the solid strength of his body. Of his faith. "Now let's go to bed."

* * *

"HEY, LILA," Maria said as she let herself into the tea shop the next morning. Lila looked up from the bakery case she was filling, her eyes tired and puffy.

"Maria." She shot a look at Yarrow, who sat silent and sullen behind the register. "Good morning."

"Good morning." She shrugged out of her jacket and hung it on the coat tree.

"What can we do for you?"

"I wanted to give you an update." Maria sat at the counter and Lila automatically slid a steaming cup under her nose. "My boss sweet-talked a chopper out of the Coast Guard. He should be here by midafternoon. I told him he could be here sooner if he was willing to ski the bridge, but he felt the chopper suited his dignity better."

Lila tried gamely for a smile. Yarrow didn't bother. "He'll want to talk to you, Lila." She shifted her glance to include Yarrow. "And you, too, of course. He'll make the decision about what to do next based on what he hears." She looked sharply at the girl. "So what's he going to hear, Yarrow?"

"Same as you heard yesterday."

Maria glanced at Lila, who gave her a tiny shrug. "She won't talk to me," she said. "I tried."

"There are problems with your story, Yarrow." She leaned in. "It doesn't add up."

The girl remained stubbornly silent.

Maria looked at Lila. "Do you mind if Yarrow and I speak privately?"

"Of course not." Lila put a hand on Yarrow's shoulder and had it promptly shrugged off again. "I'll just be upstairs, dear."

"Whatever."

Maria watched Lila disappear through the doors, her shoulders stiff and unhappy, then turned her attention back to Yarrow. She was going to have to step very carefully these next few minutes. Teenage girls were delicate and

combustible. It was going to take every ounce of her attention and skill to guide this conversation to a place that
would allow Yarrow to be honest with her. With herself.

Maria sighed. Grown women had trouble accepting
that a man was manipulating them. Was a sixteen-year-
old really going to do better? She could only hope Yarrow
would let her help. She summoned up the last reserves of
her strength, and dove in.

"Okay, Yarrow, listen. I'm not going to ask you any
more questions."

"Hallelujah."

"But I would like to tell you a story."

The eyebrow with the ring lifted. "Will there be a quiz
later?"

"Zip it, smart-ass. It's time to listen to somebody else
for a change."

"Since you put it so nicely."

"It's a true story, as it happens. And I know it's true
because it happened to me. And to Marisol."

"Who's Marisol?"

"My sister. My twin, actually."

"You have a twin?"

"Had. She died."

"Bummer."

"Yeah. It was my fault."

Yarrow's eyes flicked to hers, suspicious. "You killed
your own twin sister?"

"I didn't pull the trigger, but she died. And it was my
fault."

"How?"

So Maria told her. Told her the whole story in precise,
merciless detail. When she was finished, Yarrow swallowed audibly. "Why are you telling me this?"

"Two reasons. First, you need to know that people fuck
up. People make mistakes, terrible ones, but it's possible to
recover. It's not free and it's not easy, but I'm here to tell
you it can be done."

"And second?"

"I want you to think. Think, Yarrow, not just feel."

Yarrow opened her mouth, a hot objection at the ready, but Maria cut her off with an impatient hand.

"I know you love him. And you think he loves you." She leaned in, stared hard into those angry, pain-filled eyes. "But nothing's free, sweetie. Particularly not the good things in life—love, money, success. Honor, trust, fulfillment. They all cost. It's just a question of what you're willing to pay. And then making sure you don't get taken."

"Like you did?"

"This is the voice of experience, honey. Think about what he's asked of you, what you're risking for him. Then ask yourself what he's risking for you. What's his goal? What does he want? How does he envision this ending? Because I see you taking the fall and him skating. I see you in juvie and him shaking his head over the decline of America's youth. That's what I see." She leaned forward, touched the back of Yarrow's cold hand. "What do you see?"

A long pulse of silence stretched between them.

Finally Yarrow said, "I don't know what you're talking about."

Maria gave her lifeless hand a strong squeeze. "Think it over," she said. "If you figure it out, I'll do everything I can for you." She fished out her cell phone and checked the display. "I have to pick up my boss in a few hours. I'll have my phone if you need me."

Please, she thought. *Need me.*

Chapter

32

"YOUR SIR Humpalot's a wily beast," Einar said. He was crouched beside Rush in the snow, completely ignoring the fresh moose track Rush was examining. "With a strategy clearly superior to ours. What do you say we surrender?"

"What? And forgo the manly and rewarding art of the hunt?" Rush rose to his feet and Einar followed suit with a grudging sigh.

"If by 'hunt' you mean dragging your beloved cousin over every single godforsaken square foot of rock-infested snow on this frozen island, then yes. That's what I mean."

"That, Einar, was a fresh moose track." Rush moved with automatic stealth along the ambling path laid out by the moose. "We're close. We're going to win. Why would we give up now?"

Einar fell in behind Rush with another long-suffering sigh. "Because it's *cold*, Rush. People aren't designed for this crap. And unless we're utter morons—which I propose we're not—there are better things we could be doing."

Rush shot a look at his cousin. "Like?"

"Well, I don't know what nonsense you get up to in your spare time, but I have to prep for the Yule Eve sabbat tonight. Lila's about out of her mind over this thing with Yarrow, and somebody's got to take the wheel while she's freaking out."

"The kid just confessed to some serious stuff, Einar. I think Lila's entitled to a little freak-out."

"Exactly. Which means I ought to be covering for her instead of stomping all over the island after a sexually confused bull moose."

Rush stopped. "What do you make of it?" he asked. "This thing with Yarrow?"

"Kid's fucked up, cuz. Drove her parents around the bend with her self-destructive shit, and now she's spewing it all over Lila. The only surprise is that Lila's so damn surprised."

"You saw it coming?"

"Dude, that girl had trouble written all over her." He shook his head. "*Fatal Attraction* just waiting to happen."

Rush cocked a brow. "That's putting it a little strong, isn't it?"

Einar laughed. "Let your little cousin school you on this one, Rush. Never be nice to jailbait. Not unless you want to get your ass sued for sexual misconduct."

"She came on to you?"

"Fuck, no. Never gave her the chance. I was *never* alone with that kid if I could help it."

"She ever talk to you about the money? Or the mine?"

Einar frowned at him. "Why are you asking me this, Rush?"

"Maria's not buying it. Yarrow's story."

"What's not to buy?"

"Beats me. Something about the timing being all wrong. The money trail starting before Yarrow got here? I don't know." He lifted his shoulders and started following the tracks again. "Her boss'll be here this afternoon, though."

"This afternoon?"

"Yeah. Got a Coast Guard chopper to drop him." He checked his watch. "Probably here already. I'm guessing that'll wrap things up."

"Fuck. Just in time for Yule. Lila'll be a mess tonight."

Rush shook his head. "You can take the wheel, can't you?"

"Been waiting my whole life to do it, cuz."

"Yeah. You have."

IT OFFENDED every principle by which he'd lived his adult life, but Rush left his rifle on the porch before entering Lila's tea shop. It was one thing to carry concealed. Lila didn't like that but she tolerated it. It was quite another to walk into his aunt's home with a bolt-action Winchester M70 slung over his shoulder capable of putting down anything from a moose to a bear.

He propped the rifle in the corner of the porch and let Einar precede him into the tea shop. He found Maria sitting beside Lila at the table in the bay window. A man sat across from the women, medium height, medium build, medium brown hair, medium brown eyes, medium brown everything.

Maria and the man—presumably her boss—came to their feet. Lila stayed seated, a tissue pressed to her lips.

Einar stuck his hand out. "Einar Olsen," he said in hearty tones. "Lila's nephew."

"Peter Harris," Medium Man said, shaking Einar's hand. Rush glanced at Maria, who gave him an invisible shrug.

Lila said, "Rush, for heaven's sake. Where are your manners?"

Rush nodded at Harris. "Rush Guthrie," he said.

"Also my nephew," Lila said. "He serves as Mishkwa Island's park ranger."

Maria said, "We were just talking about Yarrow."

"Yarrow." Einar gave Harris some soulful eye contact. "I can't tell you how shocked we all are about this situation."

"She's not a situation," Lila snapped. "She's a child. A confused, wounded, angry child."

"Of course." Einar spoke to Harris even as he made soothing noises for Lila. "We can only hope that this will force her to get the help she needs. I trust the Secret Service will deal as gently with her as possible?"

Harris said, "We'll do everything we can for her." He turned to Lila. "If it's possible, we'd like to speak with Yarrow now."

"Of course." Lila stood up. "I'll just fetch her. She's upstairs."

Einar slipped a hand into Lila's elbow. "I'll go with you."

She leaned into him gratefully. "Thank you, dear."

Rush said, "Can I see you for a moment, Agent di Guzman?"

"Of course." She rose. "Excuse me, sir."

Rush drew her toward the front door. "He stuck to his story," he said.

"Crap."

"Given Yarrow's history, it's a pretty solid story."

"On the surface, anyway. Did you feel him out on the timing issues?"

"Yeah. He seemed more concerned about the fact that your boss was already here than he was about inconsistencies in Yarrow's story."

"Interesting. I might put *him* in a room with Harris just to see what happens."

"Ouch." Rush had been a SEAL long enough to recognize the sharp efficacy under Harris's bland exterior. "And if that doesn't get you what you're looking for?"

Her smile died. "Then I let it go. I admit I'm wrong and I apologize profusely. Then I take Yarrow down to the Cities myself and hand-deliver her to the best lawyer—and the best psychologist—her parents can afford."

Rush nodded. "Okay," he said. "Okay. Let's just—"

He broke off when Lila appeared in the door to the kitchen, her hands twisted together, her face ashen.

"She's gone."

Harris came to his feet and Maria flew forward. "What?" She took Lila's hands in both her own. "Yarrow? She's gone?"

She nodded. "Yes. Einar and I went upstairs to fetch her and she wasn't there." She turned frightened eyes to Rush, then the agent on the other side of the counter. "She's not here. She's gone."

* * *

Thr cmng 4 u. Rn. Mt u l8r 2nite @ stn altr.

Einar's text message had arrived while the dead-eyed Secret Service agent was sitting down in the tea shop with Lila and Maria, and Yarrow hadn't taken even a moment to wonder what she should do. She simply threw a change of clothes, some granola bars and a water bottle into her backpack.

Then she'd crept down the back stairs and run. Run straight into Einar and Rush, almost. She'd hunkered down in the shadows between Lila's and Ben Barnes's front porches as they passed within three feet of her head. Then she'd flown into the falling darkness. Away from danger. Toward true love.

Or at least what she hoped like hell was true love. It was markedly less amazing and more fucking frightening than she'd always imagined.

"WHERE WOULD she go?" Lila's eyes were wide and wet as she stared out the window. "It's getting dark, and it's so cold." A tear slid down her sharp cheekbone. "She doesn't know the island. She's only been here a few months. She could get lost, or hurt. Or she could fall through the ice—"

"We'll find her," Maria said, putting a hand on Lila's tense shoulder.

"She's a damn strong skier," Rush said softly. "If she wanted off-island, she could be on the mainland in forty-five minutes."

Lila sobbed softly and Einar said, "I don't think her leaving the island is our biggest worry."

Lila lifted her head, her mouth a perfect, trembling O. "Einar, no. She wouldn't—"

"She's tried before," Einar said. He shifted his gaze to Harris. "She's a suicide risk."

Harris absorbed that, then turned to Rush. "You're the park ranger here. How much territory are we talking about?"

"Twenty-six square miles, give or take," Rush said.

"Can we use the chopper to search any of it?"

"Not likely. There are only three trails running end to end, and all of them are densely wooded. One on the mine side of the island, one on the mainland side and one running down the center. There's also the ice bridge to consider."

"The ice bridge?"

"It's a trail of ice, four miles, connecting the island to the mainland. The ski team laps it every afternoon as soon as it gets cold enough to freeze solid."

"And it's solid now?"

"Hasn't been above minus ten for a week." Rush tucked his hands into his pockets. "It's good."

"How do you propose covering the territory?"

"Lila stays here in case Yarrow comes home. That leaves four of us and four trails."

"Fine." Harris looked down at his polished brown loafers. "Any chance the Park Service can lend me some weather-appropriate gear?"

Lila swiped her fingers over her cheeks and drew in a shuddering breath. "I'll call Ben. My next-door neighbor," she told the agent. "He runs an outfitter. I'll let him know you're coming."

"Get him set up," Einar told Rush. "I'm already geared up. I'll start on the mine trail."

He was out the door before Maria could disentangle her hands from Lila's. She caught Rush's eye. "Let's get this party started," she said.

RUSH WATCHED Maria point Harris toward the ice bridge as a half-moon breached the horizon.

"He'll be fine," he told her. "Trail's well established and the ice is dead solid."

She nodded, then turned big, determined eyes on him. "I want the mine trail. I'm going after Einar."

"Fine." He didn't waste time arguing. "Let's go, then."

"Rush, no." She frowned. "You should take the ridge trail. I already feel bad enough that we're leaving the lake trail uncovered on nothing but a hunch. You need to—"

"And if that hunch is right, you'll be facing down an uncooperative teenager, and a potentially dangerous man who has you by a good fifty pounds."

"I'm an armed federal officer," she said. "I'm trained for that kind of thing."

"Not as well as I am."

There was a long beat of stubborn silence, then she sighed. "Plus you don't pass out when you shoot at people."

"There's that."

"Rush?" Lila appeared in the yellow rectangle of light pouring from the tea-shop door. "Maria?"

Rush's heart gave a hard thud and he followed Maria into the tea shop at a dead run. The heat was stifling after the bitter outdoor air, and Rush pulled off his hat.

"Did you find her?" he asked.

Lila's eyes went wide with chagrin. "Oh, no. I'm sorry. Of course you'd think, with me shouting out the door like that . . . no. I just thought you should know that day I had Maria and Yarrow together in the circle? The day I asked to perform the protection ceremony?"

He nodded his encouragement when she stopped, but she had turned to Maria. "I thought it was you in danger, but it wasn't. It was Yarrow." She pressed her lips together until they were a thin white line. "I can't believe I was so blind. You begged me to protect her and I still refused to *see*. I could have helped her. I could have—"

"Lila, stop," Maria said. She snatched up Lila's hands and squeezed them strongly. "That's done and gone. Forget it. Help her *now*. Tell us what you saw."

"Danger," she said. "She's out of the light of Our Lady. She's been drawn into darkness. Such great and terrible darkness. Wicked. Malevolent." She shook her head. "Dark."

"Dark?" Maria asked. "What does that mean? Like literal darkness? Is she—"

"I don't know," Lila snapped. "Do you think I'd be talking in riddles if I did?"

Maria shut up.

"All I know," Lila said, her teeth clenched over what looked like the mother of all headaches, "is that the danger is now. It's *present*. Immediate." She pulled a hand from Maria's grip, offered it to Rush. Her skin was cold against his palm, but her eyes were hot. Hot and urgent. "She needs a soldier, Rush. A warrior." She shifted her eyes to Maria, blasted her with that gaze as well. "She needs forgiveness. She needs hope. She needs you both. Find her."

"We will." Maria took Rush's free hand with hers, made them a circle and power flowed into him, through him. "We'll bring her home to you, Lila."

Lila bowed her head. "An' the goddess will it."

"So mote it be," Rush said. He pulled on his cap with one hand while Lila pressed something into the other.

"Take this," she said, and Rush looked down at an old carved knife in his hand. The ritual knife Lila had used at every esbat and sabbat Rush could remember.

"Your athame?"

"It's moose horn," she said, and turned to Maria. "The warrior god is often symbolized by a stag. A horned beast." She turned back to Rush. "It's Yule Eve. The god is close and the veil is thin. Reach out for him, Rush. You're a soldier, a warrior. You're his child. He'll help you."

Rush had a little more confidence in the rifle waiting for him on the porch but didn't argue. He took the sharpened antler and stuffed it in his belt. He and Maria hit the mine trail at a sprint as the Yule moon began its ascent.

Chapter
33

YARROW WAS cold. Not a biting, burning cold, but something sluggish and weighty that dragged at her. Without Einar, the altar in the mine was barren and stark. Not just uninviting, but actively hostile. She wished she could light a candle, chase some of that dark malevolence away. Provide a little heat, if nothing else. But she didn't dare. She knew they'd be looking for her, and if they caught up to her before Einar did, it would all be over.

Einar. He'd come for her. He'd come and they'd fly away in his plane just like he'd promised. With all the cash she'd helped him bring on-island, they could afford to go anywhere they wanted. Somewhere warm, she hoped, but far enough away that nobody would know them or ask questions. Somewhere they could be happy together. In love. Just like he'd promised.

She curled her hand around the phone inside her mitten, around the text message that had saved her. She wanted to see it, to let the proof of his love warm her the way a candle never could, but she didn't want to wear down her battery. God only knew when she'd see an electrical outlet again.

Then she heard it. The shush-shush of snowshoes whispering over squeaky-cold snow. Her heart thudded painfully in her ears, and she shuffled on numb, clumsy feet around the altar where she squatted in the shadows.

A flashlight beam played over the rocky walls and she stopped breathing.

"Yarrow?"

Relief blasted through her so hard that tears came to her eyes and she knew she must have doubted. Some part of her must not have believed he'd really come. The uncertain, vulnerable part of her that had actually listened while Agent di Guzman talked. *Fuck you, Agent Smiley Face*, she thought, and stood up.

"Yarrow!" Einar rushed across the room and swept her up in his arms. "Oh, thank Christ. I was half worried you'd run away."

"From you?" She laughed. "Not likely. I'm totally frozen to death, though."

He set her back on her feet, a small smile playing over his beautiful lips. "Well, we can't have you freezing to death, can we? That would hardly do the trick."

She blinked up at him. "What trick?"

He rubbed his gloved hands up and down her arms. "No trick, honey. It was just a figure of speech." He hugged her. She made a noise and burrowed into the solid heat of him. She was so cold. She reached up for his kiss, his warmth, but he pulled back, his eyes feverish and bright. "It's time, Yarrow."

She nodded. "Yes. All right."

She was still smiling up at him when his fist clipped her chin and she fell into a starry, pain-washed blackness.

CONSCIOUSNESS DRIFTED back on cold, gasoline-scented air. Yarrow shivered and tried to turn away from the bitter scent, but pain shot hot and brilliant from her jaw all the way to her hairline. Jesus, her head ached like a motherfucker. She couldn't remember exactly why. Couldn't see any point in trying to figure it out, either. Pain was pain.

Blackness beckoned, heavy and warm. She'd had enough of the merciless cold anyway. She turned toward oblivion, then a voice drew her back.

"Yarrow."

She knew that voice. A thin thread of anxiety unspooled inside her. Einar. Beautiful, terrifying, beloved Einar.

"Yarrow, darling. Wake up."

She forced her gritty lids to open and saw him looming over her. His face was shockingly handsome in the flickering light. Candlelight? Her eyes wheeled about and she suddenly understood a number of realities, none of them particularly encouraging.

First, she was naked. Which explained the cold. Especially since she was outdoors. Well, not outdoors exactly. Underground. That was it. Earthen floor, rocky walls, thick timber beams. Cold stone under her skin. The Stone Altar.

Memory came rushing back and she bolted upright. Or tried to. Pain—shattering and immediate—bloomed behind her eyes and she lay back.

"Oh, darling, your head?" Then his hand was on her forehead, his touch cool and obscenely gentle.

"Einar," she managed. "What the fuck?"

"I'm sorry, Yarrow. It couldn't be helped."

She glared at him through slitted eyes. "You couldn't help punching me?"

"There's been a change of plans." He gave her a flat-eyed smile and her stomach clenched. *Nothing's free, sweetie. It's just a question of what you're willing to pay. And then making sure you don't get taken.*

Betrayal sank sharp claws into her chest as Agent di Guzman's words echoed in her head. Which was stupid. Absolutely fucking *retarded*. Because what right did she have to feel betrayed? You couldn't be betrayed unless you had expectations. Unless you believed the world owed you good things.

And Yarrow knew better. She knew what the world owed her. Shit. Trouble. Pain. Everything she'd been dealing out her whole life.

Knowing that, she reflected bitterly, wasn't quite the same as experiencing it, though.

"What . . ." She curled onto her side and drew up her knees, hiding her nakedness, her pain. "What do you mean?"

"You're a very special girl." Einar gave her a soulful look and an ocean of agony welled up inside her. "I wish I could keep you. I do."

"But?"

"But everything costs. And what I want? What I'm destined to have? It doesn't come cheap." He smoothed the hair back from her forehead with fingers that smelled of gas. "Our Lady requires sacrifice, Yarrow. Always."

"Sacrifice?" Fear jolted through her and she struggled to sit up. To stand up. To run. Einar twisted his fingers into her hair and cracked her head back against the stone table with a careless strength that sent hot shards of nausea dancing in her stomach. She cried out, partly from the pain but mostly from despair.

"Shhh." He leaned forward, placed something cold against her lips. She blinked away the film of desperate tears and focused on the wickedly sharp blade that was laid flat against her mouth. Panic struck like lightning at the sight of the knife Einar had used when he taught her how to offer blood to the goddess. She whimpered.

"Don't be afraid," he said, his voice somehow both gentle and stern. "I'll take care of you. It won't hurt."

"I thought—" She swallowed past a hard lump of horror and shame. "I thought you loved me."

"Loved you?" He chuckled. "Yarrow, please. Nobody loves you."

The words rang inside her with the purity of truth. *He's right*, she thought. *How strange that I knew that but didn't really understand it until somebody said it out loud.*

"You've been a disease to anybody who's ever tried," he went on. "Look at your parents. At Lila. At your friend, what was her name? Jilly? Are any of those people happy, healthy or whole?"

"No," she whispered. Candles burned by the dozens all over the mine floor, their light thin, their heat stingy. She trembled uncontrollably against the unforgiving stone beneath her.

"And what do they all have in common, those poor, plagued people?"

"Me." She gazed past the merciless blade into eyes that burned with fervor but also with honesty. She forced herself not to blink, not to shrink from this ugly truth.

"Your life was a waste, Yarrow. But your death will be priceless."

Her death. The words spurted into her with the inevitability of a drowning victim's first lungful of water.

"Think about it." He crouched beside her, slid the flat of the knife across her cheek to the line of her jaw. Her heart pounded with fear, with anticipation, with resignation as the blade scraped against her skin. "Alive you're nothing but sorrow and heartbreak. A disappointment at best, a legal nightmare at worst. But dead? Think of the gift your death would be. Your parents could finally let go of their guilt and shame over walking away from you. Lila could enjoy her twilight years in peace. Jilly could have the satisfaction of seeing you punished."

"And you get my blood."

"And I," he said, smiling slightly, "get your blood. But you—you get absolution, Yarrow. You get to pay for your sins and finally, finally be free."

Yarrow considered this, the gift of her death. Einar had scrupulously avoided mentioning the obvious bonus for him—dead girls seldom recanted confessions—but whatever. Compared with everybody else she owed, everybody to whom her death truly would be a blessing, one man's selfishness faded into insignificance.

Everything inside her already felt dead anyway.

She wet dry lips and asked, "What do I do?"

IN THE dark of the mine shaft leading to the Stone Altar, Maria made a noise of suppressed fury and Rush threw out an arm to keep her behind him. "Wait," he mouthed, though an answering fury welled up inside him. At Einar, yes, but also at himself. At Lila. At everybody who'd failed to see this desperate, endangered child now at the mercy of a psychopath.

At everybody except Maria, who'd seen just fine.

He reached into the pocket of his jacket, pulled out his SIG Sauer and offered it to her. She took it, her hands quick and competent on the weapon. He put his mouth beside her ear and said, "It's loaded. Concentrate on Yarrow. I'll take Einar."

Then he stepped out of the shadows into the maze of candles. Einar crouched behind the altar, his lips next to Yarrow's ear. The girl sat before him, naked as an abandoned doll, her eyes dull inside black rings of tear-streaked makeup.

"Hey, Einar." He leveled the rifle at his cousin with perfectly steady hands, and circled slowly to the left as he sought a line of fire that wouldn't endanger Yarrow. Maria followed him into the altar room, but moved in the opposite direction, the SIG firm in a two-handed grip and trained on Einar's chest. "I see you found our little cousin."

"And you found me. Hello, Rush. Maria." Einar, unsurprised, rose to his full height, the candlelight dancing on the polished bone blade in his hand. "Aren't you two clever?"

"Nah. Just disgusted." Rush edged forward, instinct demanding caution in spite of the fact that he held a moose-hunting rifle on a man armed with nothing but an antique knife. "What the fuck are you doing, Einar?"

"Only what's necessary."

"Necessary." Maria breathed the word with a sharp-edged scorn. "How the hell is talking a fragile young girl into suicide *necessary*?"

"Christians," Einar said in amusement. "Your Jesus redeemed an entire people by allowing Himself to be nailed to a cross and still you question the power of blood willingly spilled?"

"Spare me the religious bullshit," Maria snapped. "Nobody believes it, least of all you. We all know the only thing about her blood that interests you is its ability to buy you a pass on a nice long prison term."

His lips quirked. "There's that, of course. Her suicide—though tragic—won't exactly be unexpected. A troubled young girl seduced by black magic? It's an old, sad story, but not an unusual one. I doubt anybody will want to put her family through the pain of investigating her story too closely."

"Oh, but I will." Maria gave him a smile that was all teeth. "I'm kind of a bitch that way. It won't take me long to prove there's no way she was the one smuggling supernotes into the country. Not alone, anyway."

"Mmm." Einar considered her with a sharp amusement that had Rush taking the slack out of the trigger.

"And what about you?" he asked, unexpectedly turning to Rush. "Looks like it's coming down to brass tacks here, cousin. Choices to be made and all that. Your little girl-friend's obviously made hers. Now it's your turn."

Rush shook his head. "You haven't left me a choice here, E."

"Of course I have. There's always a choice, and in this case it's a pretty simple one. Family versus the dick." He grinned, the usual devil-may-care charmer. Rush felt sick. "No denying your Maria has a certain appeal, but she's not blood. She's not ours."

"You can talk to me about honoring blood when you're ready to spill our cousin's?"

"Stepcousin's." Another smooth smile. "She's not really

ours. Plus I'm not the one doing the spilling. She's doing that all on her own, and it's powerful stuff. Can't you feel it?"

"All I feel's a bunch of crazy and I'm pretty sure it's coming from you. Now put down the knife."

"If you like."

Einar flipped the knife in his hand and offered it, hilt first, to Yarrow. She looked up at him with huge lifeless eyes. Then she took the knife and brought the wickedly sharp blade to her wrist. She pulled it across her skin with the delicate motion of a violinist playing something sad and sweet. Just hard enough to break the skin but not hard enough to do real damage. A thin line of blood bloomed on her waxy skin and she looked up at Einar. He smiled down at her like a fond parent, a proud lover.

"Good girl," he said. "Now for real."

Rush's heart knocked hard against his ribs, but his hands were steady as he sighted down the barrel of his rifle at Einar's chest.

He flicked a glance at Maria. *Now.*

Chapter
34

MARIA SHOVED the SIG into the back of her waistband and launched herself at Yarrow. She took the girl in a flying tackle that rattled her teeth and jarred her bones but knocked them both out of Rush's line of fire and onto the dirt floor of the mine shaft. The knife leaped from Yarrow's hand when they hit the ground, and she and the girl tumbled willy-nilly through a minefield of lit candles.

Maria braced for the blast of Rush's rifle but heard nothing. Then she was too occupied with Yarrow to wonder why not. The girl fought like a cat, all claws and teeth and fury. Maria tasted blood, bright and metallic, on her lip when the kid landed a lucky elbow.

"For God's sake, stop *fighting*!" Maria straddled the writhing girl, pinning her wrists to the floor. "You're going to get us killed!"

Yarrow bucked and twisted under her, her breath coming in ragged sobs. "That's the whole idea, bitch."

Maria stared down at her. "You don't want to die, Yarrow."

"The fuck I don't."

* * *

TIME SLOWED to a crawl for Rush as Maria knocked Yarrow to the ground. Rush kept the rifle steady on Einar's chest, instinct and skill allowing him to anticipate and adjust for the man's startled step back and to his right as Maria tackled Yarrow out from under his nose. He let the breath flow out of his body as the women cleared his line of fire, and for the first time in two long years, he prepared to pull the trigger on a fellow human being.

This man wasn't his cousin, he told himself. Not anymore. This man had forfeited family—hell, humanity—for pure selfish madness. But he dropped the barrel anyway. Not far, just an inch. Half an inch. Just enough to ensure that his bullet would put Einar on the ground rather than six feet under it.

The hammer clicked home into an empty chamber.

Einar's laughter rang through the small room even as Maria rolled with a wildly clawing Yarrow into the far wall.

"You'd have done it." He chuckled delightedly. "You really would have shot me. For shame, Rush. Where's your sense of loyalty? It's a damn good thing I thought to unload your gun back on Lila's porch."

Einar was still smiling when he bent and scooped up the knife Yarrow had dropped when Maria hit her. Rush threw down the gun and gripped the carved handle of the moose-bone knife at own waist. The instant the hilt hit his hand, a certainty blew through him. It was right, he knew suddenly, that he should face Einar with nothing but this ancient knife, an almost exact replica of the one in Einar's hand.

"You want blood, Einar? Leave the kid out of it, you fucking coward. Come get something the goddess can really sink her teeth into."

"Rush, please. Your blood is useless to me."

"But I'd get a real kick out of spilling yours." Rush flipped the knife in his hand, tested the heft and balance of it. He moved into the candles until he stood at the center of the room. He held the knife loosely in his hand, spread his arms. "Come on, Einar. I'll even give you the first shot."

"Oh, Rush," Einar said with a small smile. "You tempt me. You do."

Candlelight flickered over Einar's handsome face as he balanced his weight on the balls of his feet like a boxer. He was a big man. Big enough that he ought to lack speed, but he didn't. Einar was quick and vicious and lawless. Rush would have to be quicker, meaner and beyond lawless if he was going to get out of this cave with both women alive. He'd have to be inhumane.

Lucky for Rush, inhumanity was something of a strong suit.

"Come on, Einar." Rush smiled at his cousin. "Let's dance."

"YARROW, PLEASE." Maria gazed down at the girl with a mixture of horror and pity. "You don't want to die."

"You don't know what I want." She spit the words, a savage burst of pain. "Like I'd listen to you even if you did. Jesus. You think I want to end up like you? You spend all your time making yourself look like somebody you're not, trying to act like somebody you're not, trying to be something you're not. You're a fucking cop and you can't even fire a gun." Her laughter dripped rage. "You talk all kinds of shit about bouncing back from mistakes, like you can make up with the universe or something. But look at you. There's no forgiveness. There's no paybacks. You fucking hate yourself, just like me. You want to kill yourself, too, only you're doing it one tiny sliver at a time. I want to just get it the fuck over with."

EINAR STRUCK, as fast as a snake and twice as silently. The knife was a lethal flash in the pale light, then a burning bright pain on Rush's shoulder. He'd spun with the blow and managed to avoid the full thrust, but blood eased down his biceps and began soaking into the sleeve of his long johns.

Adrenaline rushed through him with a wild, whippy

thrill as he danced away from the reach of Einar's blade. The pain was minor. A flesh wound, nothing more. But his adversary had engaged him in battle, and had proven himself worthy by drawing first blood.

"There'll be a fire later," Einar said, smiling at blood blooming on Rush's arm.

"Will there?"

"Here in the mine. All those candles, the old timber beams? In the trauma—completely understandable—of you and Maria discovering Yarrow's body—suicide, so sad—one or the other of you will knock over a candle."

"That's too bad."

"It is." Einar flashed out with a vicious thrust and Rush twisted, measured, assessed. "This place'll go up like a tinderbox. Neither of you will survive."

"Unfortunate."

"Lila will take it hard, I imagine, losing all three of you. But I'll be there for her. I'll shoulder full responsibility for the coven in her twilight years."

"That's nice."

Einar, Rush realized, fought exactly like he lived. Sharp bursts of a raw, explosive genius tempered by a shocking lack of discipline. He was quick and unpredictable, but Rush countered him with a patience and endurance honed by years of grueling training. Einar's attacks grew sloppier, then edged into desperate, and still Rush waited.

Then Einar dropped his right hand. Just a bit. But Rush had noticed that he always dropped his right just before striking with his left, leaving his midsection completely unguarded for the space of two deadly heartbeats.

The right hand drooped, and Rush danced into the deadly circle of his reach, his blood singing for the kill. Einar's eyes went hot and vicious and he slashed out with his blade.

And met nothing but air, because Rush was already under his arm. He slid behind his cousin's back, twisted the guy's off hand up into the socket-popping range between his shoulder blades and kicked away the knife as it clattered to the stone floor at his feet.

* * *

YOU WANT to kill yourself, too, only you're doing it one tiny sliver at a time. I just want to get it the fuck over with.

Maria reeled under the truth of Yarrow's accusation like it had been an open-handed slap to her face. Then a calmness flooded her, a serenity that welled up from utter certainty. Because suddenly she knew exactly what she was doing here. She knew exactly why she'd walked the path she had, knew exactly why life had taken her to just this place.

Everything she'd lived through, all the mistakes she'd made, the sins she'd committed, the years and years of penance she'd performed for those sins. Falling in love, rediscovering the woman she might have been, struggling to accept even the possibility of a happy ending. All of it had led her to this. To being present at—no, being absolutely crucial to—a life-altering decision faced by one very troubled young girl.

She raked her heart for the words, any words, magic words. Words that would break the lock under which this child had imprisoned her will to live. She'd already tried telling her own story and had had about as much success as she should have expected. How many people had tried to comfort her when she was Yarrow's age by talking about themselves? It didn't work then and it wouldn't work now. The only thing that had ever worked for her was Rush.

Rush, dropping his love like a rope into the black well of her self-hatred but refusing to climb it for her. Rush, forcing her to face herself, to own her desire to live, to love. Rush, calmly informing her to stop feeling sorry for herself. To figure out what she wanted and choose it. Rush, reminding her of a dream she'd suppressed for so long she'd forgotten it was even there. A happily-ever-after.

Yarrow would have to choose, too. She'd had so many choices taken from her by so many people, well meaning and otherwise. The only way Maria could possibly prove to Yarrow that she had worth was to treat her as if her worth were a foregone conclusion. To act like she had a brain in her head, a soul in her body. Like Maria trusted her to make good decisions and take care of herself.

It was a dangerous thing, giving a kid with Yarrow's track record a free hand with her future, but it was that or not have a future to be free with.

Maria's heart jumped into her throat, but she deliberately opened her hands and released Yarrow's wrists. The knife Rush had kicked away from Einar moments before lay on the ground near her knee. She picked it up and handed it hilt first to Yarrow.

Yarrow snatched it from her and stared up at Maria with suspicious eyes. Maria eased off the girl's body and sat back on her heels. "You want the gloves off? Fine." She threw a layer of stoic briskness over her breaking heart. "Your life is fucked up. Bad. Some of it was rotten luck, but most of it you did all by your stupid, selfish self."

"Nice pep talk. Is this what they teach you in Secret Service school?"

"That's the bad news," she went on. "The good news is you can totally get things back on track and achieve a happy ending all your own." She put a finger in Yarrow's face to forestall commentary. "If I can, anybody can."

Yarrow put her mouth in a sulky line.

"So let me bottom-line it for you, okay? You want to die? Fine. Do it." She waved a casual hand at the knife in Yarrow's fist. "But know this—it's a choice, and a cowardly one at that. Happiness is out there. Forgiveness, second chances, redemption, the whole deal. They're expensive but they're out there. All you have to do is pony up the courage to ask for it. To believe in it."

"Happiness." Yarrow tried to sneer it, but the word came out with a plaintive edge that nearly snapped Maria's control. "I wouldn't know where to start."

"Open your ears, kiddo. I'm telling you where to start. With a choice." Maria caught Yarrow's eyes with her own. The pain and rage shining there thudded into her soul like a flaming arrow, but she managed to keep her voice deliberate and steady. "Dark or light. Love or hate. Will your life mean something, or will you throw it away like so much trash? Nobody gets the final word on that but you, hon, and we're out of time here. What's it going to be?"

EINAR GAVE a cry and dropped to his knees.

Rush tried very, very hard not to give in to instinct and dislocate his cousin's shoulder. It would be a nice way to ensure the guy would go down and stay down, yes, but he knew that wasn't why he wanted to do it. What he really wanted—wanted quite desperately—was to hear him weep with pain.

But he didn't want Maria to see that in him. Didn't want her to see him glorying in the physical destruction of a fellow human being, no matter how well that fellow human had earned the pain.

"It's over, Einar."

"Is it?" Einar didn't fight the ruthless hold Rush had on his arm, only swept out with a foot. He sent a handful of candles on the floor tumbling, and they rolled flickering into a pile of rags against the far wall.

For a moment, there was silence, like an indrawn breath before a scream. Then fire roared up from the rags, and flames licked hot and hungry at the ancient wooden beams that kept the earth from burying them all.

Einar laughed and lashed out with his other foot. He sent a few more candles tumbling toward what Rush now recognized as piles of gas-soaked rags against the other wall. The wall where Maria crouched, silent and still, her fingers knotted between her knees, her eyes tight on Yarrow and the knife the girl had pressed against her own wrist. Shit.

In one tense motion, Rush threw Einar toward the altar and whipped off his jacket. He threw it on the rags closest to the women and stomped on it, killing whatever flames he could. He didn't know what the hell Maria was doing, but whatever it was, she'd just run out of time to get it done.

"Maria!" The smoke was already thick and suffocating. "Get Yarrow out of here!"

MARIA IGNORED Rush. She ignored the flames licking up the wall behind her, too. She ignored everything but Yarrow. The girl's eyes were squeezed shut, her lips peeled back with the effort to make her bleak choice. Maria's own heart crumbled under the weight of the girl's pain, her own remembered pain, the struggle not to snatch the knife away and pull Yarrow out of that smoky cave by her hair and shake some sense into her.

But this wasn't Maria's choice to make. It was Yarrow's. If she was going to get better, if she was going to have any chance at all, she needed to commit to life. And Maria couldn't do that for her. Nobody could. It was now or never.

The muscles bunched and shook in Yarrow's thin arms as she hunched over her own wrist, the blade trembling against her skin. Maria rocked in silent despair, but still she sat.

Please, she thought. *Please. Let it have been enough.*

With a broken cry Yarrow flung the knife aside and Maria scooped the girl into her arms like a rag doll. "Oh, sweetheart," she said, tucking the girl's head under her chin, wrapping her arms around her bare shoulders. Their tears ran together and soaked Maria's jacket. "Oh, my brave, good girl."

"I couldn't do it," Yarrow wept. "I couldn't. Not if there's even a chance I could be—" She broke off into a wretched sob.

"Happy." Maria's throat ached. "You will be," she said. "I promise."

Then suddenly there was fire. Everywhere. The little tongues she'd been vaguely aware of during Yarrow's life-and-death struggle had multiplied into roaring rivers that devoured the ancient beams holding the mountain off their heads. Einar was on his knees in front of the altar, his face contorted with rage and pain as he cradled his shoulder.

Rush stamped at snakes of fire that slithered across the floor and up the walls while smoke gathered heavy and dark on the ceiling.

Maria scrambled to her feet and reached down for Yarrow. Then pain exploded on her scalp as Einar twisted his hand into her hair and yanked her aside. She skidded across the dirt floor like a skipped stone and watched in horror as Einar lifted a booted foot and drove his heel into Yarrow's temple. The girl crumpled to the floor without a sound, blood a thin trickle down her pale cheek.

Einar turned to Maria then, one arm folded across his chest, the other holding it in place, pain etching deep ugly lines into his handsome face. *Score one for Rush*, she thought. *I hope he fucking broke it.*

"Lights-out for you next, pretty Maria." He smiled as he advanced on her, a chilling baring of perfect white teeth. "Nothing personal. Just something to keep Rush occupied while I get out of here."

She scrambled to her knees and yanked the SIG out of the waistband of her jeans, where it had miraculously remained.

Einar froze, though his smile didn't slip. "Oh, dear," he said. "So prepared. Such a Boy Scout, my cousin."

"Yeah. I love that about him." She leveled the barrel at his chest. "I believe this one's loaded."

"For all the good it'll do you." He smiled. "Yarrow told me about your little phobia, Maria. You can't pull the trigger. Don't pretend you can."

She gave him a tight half smile. "Who says I'm pretending?"

Smoke filled the air with a choking heat, and flames licked greedily up the walls to the ceiling beams, but Maria didn't shift her gaze from Einar. She saw Rush in her peripheral vision give up on the flames and scoop up his rifle from the ground. He took it by the barrel, Louisville Slugger style, and every tense line of his body announced his intention to knock Einar's skull out of the park.

Then his eyes met hers and she saw the grief in them.

The sorrow and the regret that crouched down beside the cold determination to take out whoever and whatever threatened her and Yarrow. Up to and including this man who'd been a brother to him.

Since the moment she'd met Rush, she realized with a vicious pang of regret, she'd been concerned with one thing and one thing only—protecting herself. It hadn't occurred to her that *she* could protect *him*. That he might need her to. She wondered if he'd let her. She certainly hadn't earned his trust. She'd been too busy accepting his. Regardless, it was time to find out.

She caught his eye and gave her head a single, short shake. He went suddenly and perfectly still, then took two steps back. Just like that, he gave her the shot. With full knowledge of her weakness, with his life, her life and Yarrow's life all on the line, he could still believe that she'd be able to aim, fire and hit the correct person before it was too late.

He *trusted* her.

He'd said it so many times but she hadn't believed it. It wasn't that she hadn't believed him capable or sincere. She simply hadn't believed herself worthy. Like Yarrow, she'd needed the proof. And now she had it.

Einar smiled at her hesitation. "Good girl," he said, and stepped toward her.

Gratitude bloomed in Maria's chest like a rising sun, like spring after a hundred-year winter.

And then, her hands perfectly steady, she pulled the trigger.

Chapter
35

AFTER MARIA calmly drilled a textbook flesh wound through the meaty part of Einar's upper thigh, Rush helped her wrap Yarrow in whatever they could find in the mine that hadn't caught fire yet. Rush carried the girl outside and placed her in Maria's lap to sleep off her concussion.

Then he carried Einar out, too. Less gently. Einar cursed bitterly, of course, but Rush wasn't overly concerned about him. Between the dislocation—whoops—of one shoulder, the bullet in one thigh and Rush's absolute willingness to put another one in his ass if necessary, Einar had run out of options. He sat sullenly in the snow while flames leaped greedily for the moon and a pillar of smoke climbed into the sky like their own personal bat signal.

It didn't take long for reinforcements to arrive.

Harris, whom Rush had rightly pegged as the handy sort, commandeered the urgent care's emergency snowmobile to transport a stable but foulmouthed Einar to the island's airstrip. A Coast Guard chopper medevaced him to the nearest medical facility, where—considering the

quantity of supernotes Harris and his search warrant had
discovered in Einar's plane—he was very likely hand-
cuffed to the bed.

Yarrow had begged to stay with Lila instead of going
to the mainland hospital herself. Rush and Maria saw her
safely into her grandmother's waiting arms before they
returned, by silent and mutual consent, to the Ranger
Station.

MOONLIGHT FLOWED through the windowpanes with
a creamy clarity as Rush sank onto the couch, spread his
arms along the back and closed his eyes.

"Well," he said. "Some night."

"Yeah." Maria stood in front of the woodstove and
watched him, her heart a clenched fist inside her chest.
"Are you going to be all right?"

"Yeah. Sure." He didn't open his eyes. "You were right,
though. About Einar."

"I know." Regret welled up inside her. "I'm so sorry,
Rush. I wish I hadn't been."

"Yeah. Me, too. Harris said they turned up a couple mil-
lion in supernotes in his plane."

"I heard."

"Anybody claiming rightful ownership?"

"Not willingly. But we cross-referenced Einar's flight
plans with our list of suspected supernote movers and
ended up looking at one of those Canadian businessmen
Einar flies to all corners of the earth. We've long suspected
this guy had his fingers in a few less-than-legitimate pies. I
guess he offered to share the wealth."

"Not an offer my cousin was wired to pass up."

"Harris says he's been ferrying cash across the border
gym bag by gym bag for a couple years now. You were
right about the Fire Eaters, by the way. They were Einar's
U.S. contacts."

Rush squinted at her. "Is that supposed to make me feel
better or worse?"

Maria shrugged miserably. "I don't know. Better in the sense that using Yarrow as a mule was a recent development?"

"But worse in the sense that he was doing this under my nose for years." Rush put his knuckles to his eyebrows. "And worse yet in the sense that somebody I claim as family could abuse a vulnerable kid so badly. I mean, my God, Maria. He was talking her into suicide so he could skate on this."

She didn't say anything. She couldn't. He leaned forward then, propped his elbows on his knees and stared at his linked fingers. "Thanks, by the way."

She goggled at him. "For what?"

"For shooting him. For taking that off my plate." He looked up, an unhappy gratitude in his pale eyes. "Because I wouldn't have just wounded him the way you did. I might have killed him." He dropped his head again and snorted. "*Might have*. Fuck me, I would have. I wanted to. When I saw him standing over you like that, I—"

Love for him exploded inside her, and the fist around her heart disintegrated. She fell to her knees in front of him, threw her arms around those bent shoulders and pressed her cheek to his.

"But you didn't," she said, and drew back to cradle that hard jaw in her palm. "You didn't have to. Because I finally got my shit together."

"It was . . . not together at some point?"

"Rush, come on. You've been giving to me nonstop since we met. It's about damn time I thought to do something for you." She took his hands and forced herself to meet his eyes. To strip herself naked, banish the static and just give him the words. The truth. "I'm a mess, Rush. I barely know who I am most days, and you not only want me, you want me forever. You asked me to *marry* you. But did I accept? Did I go down on my knees and thank God for the miracle of you? No. I was so worried about what it would cost me to accept your love that I never stopped to wonder what it cost you to offer it." She shook her head in disgust. "You *love* me, Rush. And that's a gift. It's forgiveness and peace and absolution."

"Your specialty."

"What?"

"You love people, Maria. Tangibly. I confessed my deepest secret to you, and you told me how the killer that lived in me lived in you, too. Yarrow showed you all the blackness in her soul and you dove in there so you could show her the way to hope again. You loved us in the most concrete sense of the word. How can you be so surprised when we love you back?"

She dropped her forehead to his knee. "Yarrow called me a hypocrite tonight, and she was right. I tried to tell her I was all better, all forgiven, all secure in my happy ending, but she knew I was lying. Because I was too scared to reach for it. To trust it. To trust you. But I'm not anymore." She stopped, winced. "Oh, fuck it, honesty." She sucked in a fortifying breath. "Okay, I'm still scared. I'm terrified. But I love you. I love you so much I ache with it, and I'm so happy and afraid and mixed up. But I'm ready to do whatever it takes, risk everything I have, to make this work."

She shook away the tears she hadn't exactly planned on shedding and looked up at him with a smile that felt fierce and sharp and brilliant. "You loved me," she said. "Forgave me. *Saw* me. I was lost and you showed me the way back to myself. I don't know how, but it hardly matters." She searched those pale, honest eyes, and found love there. She found faith, forgiveness and hope. She found her future. "Will you marry me?"

And suddenly she was off the floor and onto his lap, being kissed with a slow, greedy thoroughness. She kissed him back while astonished wonder slipped into aching joy.

It was several long, interesting moments before he pulled back and rested his forehead against hers.

"So." She paused. "That's a yes?"

"What? No." Another clinging, endless kiss. "That was clearly an I-need-time-to-consider-my-options kiss. When

I give you a yes-I'll-marry-you kiss, you won't have to ask. You'll know."

Laughter bubbled up alongside the peace and awe and desire pulsing within her. "Honesty, Rush." She put a grave disapproval into her voice even as she rocked herself into the blatant *yes* in his lap. His breath hitched and she smiled. "This won't work without your total, complete honesty."

"Mmm. You're right." Then she was underneath him on the old, lumpy couch, his *yes* snugged right up against her glowing heat. His silver eyes laughed down at her. "Okay, I'm going to be honest with you now. Ready?"

She smiled up at him, brilliantly. "I'm ready."

"Then yes." His kiss was a miracle of dazzled heat. "Yes."

She wrapped herself around him and leaped fiercely into her happily-ever-after.

FROM *USA TODAY* BESTSELLING AUTHOR
CHRISTIE RIDGWAY

Crush on You

First in a contemporary romance trilogy about the bonds of family and friends—and weddings—in the heart of Napa Valley.

The Baci sisters are on a mission to save the winery that's been in their family for generations by transforming it into the perfect wedding destination. If only Alessandra Baci—affectionately known as the "Nun of Napa"—didn't need the help of tempting new neighbor Penn Bennett.

> "Christie Ridgway captures the true magic
> of falling in love."
> —Robyn Carr,
> *New York Times* bestselling author

penguin.com

It's a...

Total Rush

Free spirit Gemma Dante wishes her love life were going as well as her New Age business. So she casts a spell to catch her Mr. Right. But when the cosmic wires get crossed, into her life walks a clean-cut fireman who's anything but her type.

Sean Kennealy doesn't know what to make of his pretty neighbor who burns incense. He only knows that being near her sparks a fire in him that even the guys at Ladder 29, Engine 31 can't put out.

From
New York Times Bestselling Author

Deirdre Martin

M205T0209